WASHED BY A WAVE

OF WIND

WASHED BY A WAVE OF WIND

Science Fiction from the Corridor

Edited by

M. SHAYNE BELL

Signature Books Salt Lake City 1993

For Marion K. Smith,
Professor of English, Brigham Young University.
He continues to influence so many of us.

ACKNOWLEDGEMENTS

"Dealer," by Michaelene Pendleton, was first published in *Amazing Stories* 65 (Sept. 1991): 31-37.

"Pageant Wagon," by Orson Scott Card, was first published in *The Folk of the Fringe* (West Bloomfield, MI: Phantasia Press, 1989), 110-90.

"The Shining Dream Road Out," by M. Shayne Bell, was first published in *Tomorrow: Speculative Fiction* 1 (July 1993): 38-45.

Cover design by Clarkson Creative

∞ *Washed by a Wave of Wind* was printed on acid-free paper meeting the permanence of paper requirements of the American National Standard for Information Sciences. This book was composed, printed and bound in the United States.

97   96   95   94   93   6   5   4   3   2   1

Library Of Congress Cataloging-in-Publication Data

Washed by a wave wind : science fiction from the corridor / edited
   by M. Shayne Bell.
     p. cm.
     ISBN 1-56085-038-8
     1. Science fiction. American—Utah. 2. Science fiction, Amercian—
Idaho.   I. Bell, M. Shayne, 1957-
PS648.S3W38   1993
813'.08762089792—dc20   93-13567
                                               CIP

Contents

EDITOR'S INTRODUCTION: TOWARD A SCIENCE FICTION FROM THE WEST

*T*he history and geography of the Corridor—the area of original Mormon settlement in the West stretching in a narrow band from Alberta to Sonora (but limited in this book to Utah and southeastern Idaho)—would have inevitably produced writers of science fiction. Any man or woman with imagination, growing up or moving here, would thrive on the possibilities of the story of this place: the Corridor was settled by people who traveled across vast stretches of dangerous, largely unexplored land to seek religious freedom—and in the process transplanted a civilization. What they accomplished more than 150 years ago parallels what women and men will do as we move off Earth into space; the skills they developed are the skills we need to face the future, whether on this planet or off it.

The settlers of the Corridor had to bring with them everything necessary for their survival, but very quickly they were forced to learn to live off their new land, to make do with what they had, and to adapt. They had to learn the languages and customs of the indigenous populations, to discover ways of trading with them, of living with them, of settling their differences, sometimes violently. They adopted the values of the frontier, necessary for the survival of any large group of people transplanted from the centers of European civilization: hard work, courage, the ability to adapt with good humor, confidence in one's ability and imagination, an appreciation for the unique worth of individuals, hospitality and kindness to strangers, personal freedom and human dignity, concern for the future, fascination with technological innovation that make up for the lack of adequate human resources, and appreciation of beauty in making a new home and finding peace in it. This history and these values, still transmitted to writers generations later, influence the fiction written here, certainly the science fiction.

The land, furthermore, holds its own power over the imagination of science fiction writers in the Corridor. No one can escape the land's austere and serene presence, even in the cities: look up and you will see mountains. In Utah the mountains circle you. On the plains of Idaho, they are farther away, but the skyscapes still make you look up at the endless banks of clouds by day and stars from one point of the horizon to the other by night. A thousand abandoned cities of the Anasazi civilization lie in the deserts of southern Utah, and the modern cities in the north are built in an ancient lake bed—you can see the beaches on the slopes of the mountains above you. In places, where the wind has not blown it away, these beaches are still sandy. Wind and water have weathered the land into almost alien landscapes of canyons and mesas and arches and 300 mile-long cliffs, exposing everywhere, in sedimentary layers, clear evidence of the passage of time.

The simplest experiences with the land can be deeply moving. I remember when we were in college, my writer friends and I would walk each November up Rock Canyon northeast of Brigham Young University in Provo, Utah. The land was hard and still then, ready for winter. A mile up the canyon, we'd go down into the dry creek bed, below rocks that during the spring thaw formed waterfalls, and gather leaves and driftwood from the banks and build a fire. We'd sit close to it for warmth and look at the ancient, layered rock. Eventually, as darkness fell, we could see nothing beyond the firelight. It was as if time itself and condensed around us and concentrated on us and our point in it. We've since climbed mountains together and heard the quiet of the land and once saw the rain make a hundred waterfalls over the canyon walls above us. Ultimately, none of this diminishes you. It gives you a perspective on the shortness of life and the relative unimportance of daily problems and the joy we should have in our time.

And these Western values and impressions inform the stories in this book.

The stories show that the authors in this collection share some beliefs about what constitutes a good life and how to live it. They are about acts of kindness, about courage and adapting to difficult circumstances, about valuing individuals and working together to survive, about freedom and the lack of it, about living life with imagination and good humor, about faith, love, the need for beauty, and about the land.

What makes these stories science fiction is that with these underlying Western frontier values, the characters in the stories face future ecological disasters, adapt to technological advances, fight possible threats to individual and artistic freedom, and bring in the twenty-first century with hope, which is a hallmark of science fiction.

But these stories are about one more thing. They are about the people we live with, the land where we live, and our hopes and love and respect for it all. Ultimately, these stories are about home.

This book is the first to draw together stories by professional science fiction writers from the Corridor, and it makes the most complete—and representative—collection of the work being done here. Nearly every member of the Science Fiction and Fantasy Writers of America who is from Utah or has lived here is represented in this anthology—together with several newcomers who make their first professional mark in this collection. I'd like to thank them all for their enthusiasm and support for this project.

I am pleased with the demographics of this book. Historically, science fiction has been written and read largely by men, but in the last two decades that has begun to change dramatically as more and more women write and read science fiction—bringing with them their unique contributions and view of the world and its future. Over half of the writers in this anthology are women. But of course we should expect that in *this* book: women of the frontier had to be strong, had to work side by side with men, and were expected to take part in every meaningful way in society.

I want to thank Julie Helm for the telephone call in July 1992 that got me to try one more time to sell an anthology: too often we limit ourselves by thinking we already know the answers. She helped me see past what I thought I knew.

I realized a week before my deadline that I would have room to print a history of science fiction in the Corridor. I called Barbara R. Hume, a friend and a fine scholarly writer, and asked her to write the history—which she agreed to do and which she finished on time. It took an enormous effort to conduct the interviews necessary to write the history in just one week. Thank you.

Pat Bezzant helped me pull together the bibliography of publications for most of the writers living in Utah County and parts south. David Doering helped me with Orson Scott Card's bibliography.

Dr. Richard Cummings and Donna Boam are father and mother of James Cummings, and I'd like to thank them for letting me print James's story, "Space People," and Dr. Cummings for finding it on the disks James left behind. I knew the story existed, because a few months before James died in February 1992 of complications related to AIDS, he invited me to his apartment and read me this story. James was afraid to read it to me, but there was no need for him to be nervous. I thought it a fine story then, and still do. James was in a creative writing master's program at the University of Utah—a program renowned for being unsympathetic to science fiction—but even so James wrote this story: because he was stubborn, because he had read and loved science fiction all his life and recognized in it the same qualities that make any work of literature worthwhile, and because he was a man who would fight wrong ideas and prejudice. When he finished reading me the story, I told him how finely crafted I thought it was, and how moving. We talked for some time about the writing careers we'd dreamed about, and he started to cry. At the time we both knew he was dying, and he told me that more than any other thing he had wanted to have a writing career and now he never would.

I knew James for only one year, but he influenced me in big and little ways. I think, at times, we don't realize all the ways our friends change our lives for good, all the ways they enrich us. James, I'm sure, didn't realize everything he did for me. Among other things, he encouraged me to investigate the quiet and tender philosophies of the East, which he had been doing for years, and which had given him hope that there is something, after all, beyond this life. He introduced me to the *Crimson Collection*, a series of Sikh prayers for healing and peace that had been set to music and which are so beautiful. He even convinced me to change the dish soap I use—to a better brand that might cost more, but lasts longer and costs less in the long run. Good things come with a price. James made me learn that lesson again: so I remember him every time I wash the dishes. I miss him. When you read his story, I think you will agree that, in James, we lost a fine writer who would have blessed all our lives with many good stories had he lived.

The title for this book, "Washed by a Wave of Wind," is taken from a line in Virginia Baker's poem, "Sinai" (originally printed in *Sunstone* magazine, June 1990, page 58). I thank her for letting me use it.

I would like to thank the staff at Signature Books for their support and patience.

Barbara Bova, my agent, provided, as always, important suggestions and support throughout this project. Her energy and enthusiasm are infectious. I am fortunate to be able to work with her.

The stories in this book will move you, and entertain you, and make you think. I hope you enjoy them as much as I have.

Salt Lake City
November 1993

PROLOGUE: STRANGE BEDFELLOWS—A HISTORY OF SCIENCE FICTION IN THE CORRIDOR

BARBARA R. HUME

$\mathcal{OS}$cience fiction in Utah? Can something so unconventional flourish in such a seemingly conservative state?

According to Elizabeth Pope, a long-time science fiction devotee who for many years served as science fiction librarian at Brigham Young University, the genre has not always been popular here. "Back in the 1950s, I think there were about two of us who really cared about it," she says. Nor has the growth of interest pleased everyone, including those mainstream writers and academics who scorn science fiction as a sub-genre inferior to "real literature."

But for many Utahns, science fiction enriches our lives in a variety of ways. It expands our intellectual and emotional capacities. It enables us to form satisfying friendships with fascinating, worthwhile people who share our interests. And it gives rise to much of the joy that we as humans are entitled to experience during our sojourn on this planet.

ROOTS

Science fiction fans have a proclivity for finding each other. In Salt

Lake City, for example, the past few decades have seen various manifestations of this tendency. Unfortunately, many of the dates and specifics have slipped from our memories, but the kinds of activities engendered among the city's science fiction aficionados show that they genuinely have cared about the genre.

For example, a science fiction writing organization that includes Julie and Brook West, Deann Larson, John Forbes, and others, meets on Tuesdays for one group and Saturdays for another to exchange manuscripts and offer critiques. An early science fiction reading group, based at the Hansen Planetarium, involved such people as Reuben Fox and Michael Goodwin. A writer named Jerry Loomis gathered a group of like-minded people, apparently by the clever device of culling names from library check-out slips. Another group used to meet at the Salt Lake City library. Linda Taylor heads up a group called SWEET (Screen Writers Editing and Encouragement Team). Kathleen Dalton-Woodbury directs the computer-network Science Fiction and Fantasy Workshop which connects writers from all over the United States. David Zindell published his first novel while living here. One highlight for Salt Lake City science fiction fans was the 1974 visit of Robert Heinlein. His visit motivated many people to become involved in science fiction.

There has always been an active "Star Trek" fandom here as well, including people willing to go to the incredible headache of putting on a convention. InterCon, the first science fiction convention held in Salt Lake City, took place in the mid-1970s. The director pulled out from the project and left things in a shambles, but the efforts of Bjo Trimble helped save the convention from total disaster.

A series of conventions known as SaltCon took place for several years; there was also another series of cons called InterVention and a follow-up con called OuterVention. Currently, an annual science fiction convention known as CONduit has taken place in Salt Lake City each spring since 1989. A fanzine called *Clavius*, edited by Brook West, appeared in the area for some time.

The science fiction movement at BYU goes back to local science fiction clubs in the late 1960s and "Star Trek" clubs in the early 1970s. These clubs eventually evolved into two: Quark, which emphasized a literary focus, and The Association of Fantasy and Science Fiction, which focused on media science fiction (movies and television). About seven years ago these two combined into Quark: The BYU Fantasy and Science Fiction Club.

When enrollment in the English department curriculum declined in the early 1970s, BYU became more receptive to the concept of offering science fiction. At first it was permitted only within an umbrella-course environment. A student named Jim Tucker started a group that met at the Provo City Library. The group eventually was granted a faculty sponsor and became an official class. BYU faculty members such as Marge Wight, Sue Ream, Marion Smith, and Elizabeth Pope have since served as sponsors for such courses.

When enrollment skyrocketed, other science fiction courses became available. Some of these examined science fiction as literature. But in 1980 BYU offered a creative writing course with a science fiction slant. That course—a seminal event in the history of Utah science fiction—became known as "the class that wouldn't die."

THE CLASS THAT WOULDN'T DIE

In 1980 the BYU course catalog for fall semester listed a course in science fiction writing, with Orson Scott Card as the teacher. Although this was early in Scott's career—he had just won the John W. Campbell Award for best new writer in 1978—his name was enough to create excitement among the fledgling science fiction writing community in Provo. Eagerly, we signed up.

As it turned out, Card didn't conduct the course. He went instead to Notre Dame to work on a degree of his own. The instructor who took the class was Marion K. Smith—a regular BYU faculty member.

At first we looked at each other in disappointment. Then we decided, with great tolerance, to give the guy a chance. After all, it *was* science fiction, wasn't it? Surely the class would prove reasonably interesting.

That class was a turning point in the lives of many people. Marion Smith became a favorite among the Utah contingent of science fiction writers. For one thing, he'd read just about everything in the field and actually remembered where all those great stories had first appeared. For another, he helped us sharpen our critical and writing skills within the genre.

And of course he was (and still is) a genuinely nice man. We took to calling him "Doc" Smith, and we loved every minute of the class. Even the final exam was fun, with questions like, "Suppose you're Harlan Ellison. A neophyte writer sends you a manuscript and asks you to critique it. Answer the letter—in Ellison's style."

Some of the people who attended that class turned out to be the movers and shakers of Utah science fiction. For example, these individuals went on to begin *The Leading Edge*, a local publication that has given many science fiction writers the opportunity to publish. Class members also went on to help found an annual BYU science fiction symposium.

Shayne Bell was in that class; so were Mike Reed and Rayda Reed, a husband-and-wife team who worked hard on early issues of *The Leading Edge*. As was Dave Doering, whose let's-not-just-talk-about-it-let's-do-it approach spurred the creation of *The Leading Edge* and the symposium. So was Melva Gifford, who has edited four genre fanzines and written for more than 150 of them. And I credit my experiences there with giving me the courage to leave the ivory tower of academia and make my living as a professional writer.

Every now and then Doc Smith still attends one of our functions. Once during a Xenobia party marking our 400th meeting, a man from outer space appeared at the front door, complete with space suit and helmet. We were totally astounded—until we realized it was Doc Smith in his firefighting gear.

"You gave me the wrong apartment number," he told our hostess, grinning. "You owe your next-door neighbors an apology."

The final assignment Doc Smith gave the class was to write a story *for publication* and turn it in, SASE and all, so he could mail them all after reading them. It was his way to get us to stop talking about being writers and actually do something about it. That assignment led indirectly to the founding of Xenobia, the premier (in my opinion) Utah science fiction writers group and one of the longest-lived such groups in the country.

MARCHING TO XENOBIA

Here's how it happened: Several weeks after Doc Smith's science fiction writing course was over, Shayne Bell called me to see whether I'd yet gotten my rejection letter from the assignment. In the course of our conversation, he mentioned that the class had been so much fun he hated to see it end.

"We should try to get the group together sometime," he said.

"'Sometime' never happens," I told him. "Let's set a date."

So we did.

Shayne, an imaginative young writer named Cassandra Johns, and I got together. Dave Doering joined us before the evening was over.

Dave Bastian, at that time a teenager but already so talented he made the rest of us grind our teeth, joined us at a second meeting.

As time went on, others with the same desire to write and publish science fiction joined the group, which we eventually named "Xenobia," imagining that the word meant, loosely, "love of aliens." Two strong additions were Glenn Anderson, with two Mormon science fiction novels already to his credit, and Diann Thornley, a novelist who researches her work so thoroughly that she spends years on projects. And Shayne gained two colleagues in the small field of science fiction poetry when Cara Bullinger and Virginia Ellen Baker came into the fold.

Like other writing groups, Xenobians tend to make references to each other in their work. The planet Baker in Dave Wolverton's *On My Way to Paradise*, for example, is named after Virginia Baker. And the infamous Doering clamps get their name from the so-named Xenobian.

Not every member of Xenobia has become a nationally known science fiction writer. Many earn their livings as top writers and editors in the computer industry. But everyone in the group has proven him- or herself capable of writing excellent science fiction, and everyone works hard at getting better and better.

Thirteen years later we're still meeting every week to critique manuscripts, exchange market information, and enjoy the company of kindred spirits. We're no longer neophytes. Several members are published novelists, and most have published short stories or science fiction poetry in genre magazines. From this group such fine writers as M. Shayne Bell, Dave Wolverton, Virginia Ellen Baker, and D. William Shunn have emerged to brighten the national scene. Such talent would have emerged with or without Xenobia, but the group has provided an ongoing source of support and camaraderie for everyone involved.

"Xenobia gives its members just the sort of encouragement that writers need," says Thom Duncan, Xenobia member and author of the Mormon science fiction adventure novel *Moroni Smith and the Land of Zarahemla*. "It's easy to lose your focus if you're trying to work in a vacuum."

THE LEADING EDGE OF SCIENCE FICTION

One of the best memories we have of the early 1980s is the creation of *The Leading Edge*. We were miffed that we were finding it difficult, if not impossible, to get our stories accepted in BYU's official literary magazine. "Wouldn't it be great if there was a magazine *we* could be published in?" we moaned.

"Let's start our own magazine!" was Doering's response.

So we did.

Just about everyone in Xenobia at the time wrote a story for it, and we even got a few other people to contribute. We typed up the text, made sixty copies, came up with the name *The Leading Edge* and a cover, and stapled the magazines together by hand. After fifty copies the copy center ran out of green card stock, so we had the last ten covers printed on red card stock.

The BYU Bookstore agreed to sell our publication, so we set up a display on the main floor and then stood around watching to see if anyone would actually buy a copy. "Look!" we'd whisper to each other from behind a pillar or display case. "She actually picked one up! See? She's actually looking at it!" Occasionally, someone even carried one to the cashier and *paid for it.* The issue actually sold out. Copies became collectors' items—especially the rare red-cover issues.

Encouraged by our success, we made plans for a second issue. It still wasn't particularly aesthetic, but it contained more and better stories and poetry.

The third issue was a turning point in the quality of the publication; we had a printed cover and perfect binding. In the fourth issue we stopped duplicating typewritten pages and started typesetting the text on a wheezy old CompuGraphic machine we called Darth Vader. We had to do this work at night; the university gave the convenient hours to its "official" literary magazines (which we consistently outsold, by the way).

By issue 10, Karl Batdorff and Shayne Bell moved production to a Macintosh, greatly improving quality. By issue 16, the magazine went permanently to full-color covers.

As time went on, the magazine passed into other hands. I stopped writing for *The Leading Edge* after the sixth issue (right before they started paying the writers). But I had a novel serialized in *The Leading Edge* which brought me my fan letters and requests for autographs. Although the novel itself is perhaps best forgotten, I treasure the experience.

The Leading Edge is currently in its eleventh year of publication and up to Issue 26. Issue 24, at the tenth anniversary, was a "best of" issue, reprinting stories by Shayne Bell and Dave Wolverton. The magazine is beautifully produced and continues to provide publishing opportunities for science fiction writers. And it isn't only for neophytes; *TLE* has carried stories, essays, and interviews by some major writers in the field—Orson Scott Card, Fritz Lieber, and Jane Yolen, among others.

BYU not only provides funding but also grants co-op education credit for work on the magazine. (One success story is that of Ed Liebing, a Xenobian whose tour of duty as managing editor of *The Leading Edge* helped prepare him for a position as editor-in-chief of a leading computer industry trade publication.) Unlike most magazines that publish fiction, *TLE* still offers comments to the writers who submit manuscripts. The whole thing is, in my opinion, a great success story.

BRINGING IT ALL HOME: THE SYMPOSIUM

Everyone knows that science fiction enthusiasts are so fervent that they hold conventions to share the experience with others and to meet and learn from professionals in the field. Most of these conventions, of course, take place outside of Utah.

"Wouldn't it be great if we had something like that here in Provo?" we sighed.

"Let's do it!" said Doering.

So we did.

From the beginning, the symposium attracted the local science fiction community, eventually drawing people from other parts of the country. In some years the publicity was poor and attendance down, but the offerings have almost always been solid. And many excellent writers have attended: C. J. Cherryh, Ed Bryant, Frederik Pohl, Poul Anderson, Jack Williamson, Algis Budrys, Tim Powers, Orson Scott Card, Octavia Butler, and David Brin, to name a few.

The annual BYU Science Fiction Symposium is now in its eleventh year, offering a three-day track of panels, professional sessions, writing seminars, screenings, exhibits, readings, book signings, dealer tables, and the other trappings of science fiction gatherings. When Scott Card comes, attendance skyrockets. His sessions on generating story ideas are motivational, and his professional sessions are delightful.

A highlight of the symposium is the private reception for guests. Some of the guests are always taken to Elizabeth Pope's home, a showcase for science fiction fans. Practically every wall of every room and hallway is lined with bookshelves filled with science fiction books.

Many of these books have been autographed by the authors, often during symposium receptions.

BYU no longer offers the range of science fiction classes it once did. But the university continues to support *The Leading Edge* and the February symposium with funding and facilities, and the creative writing option is still in place. Quark, the campus science fiction and fantasy club, provides support for symposium activities.

LDSF

Three editions of this anthology of Mormon science fiction have appeared, each containing science fiction stories set in a Mormon milieu. Some stories were dreadful, but others melded the two arenas in memorable ways. The editor, Ben Urrutia, performed a service in calling the attention of Utah writers to the possibilities of combining the science fiction genre with the distinct characteristics of the Mormon subculture.

WRITERS OF THE FUTURE

Any discussion of the history of Utah-based science fiction must include mention of the Writers of the Future contest. This international quarterly science fiction writing contest, sponsored by Bridge Publications, has brought many new writers to prominence in the field. The list of winners includes some of the writers in this anthology. M. Shayne Bell, Virginia Ellen Baker, and Dave Wolverton have all been first-place winners.

Two Provo-based artists, Derek Hegstead and Darren Albertson, have won quarterly science fiction art contests also sponsored by Bridge Publications. The rumor is that the Utah contingent has swept so many science fiction contests that it has become known as the "Mormon Mafia."

SCIENCE FICTION WRITERS
FROM THE WESTERN CORRIDOR

The writers included in this anthology offer an interesting variety of insights about science fiction itself and about the unique twist that the culture of this area brings to it. Glenn Anderson wrote "Shannon's Flight" to make sure he could get a legitimate tax deduction for a trip to Moab in southern Utah. He leans toward writing horror because "I have a lot of fears," and enjoys stories about "why people do things."

Virginia Ellen Baker became interested in writing science fiction from reading "Star Trek" tie-in novels and from reading Melva Gifford's stories. Algis Budrys was a major influence because, she says, he wrote some of the first "people science fiction." Baker won the Writers of the Future contest with the first short story she ever wrote. She, too, prefers writing horror; for this anthology, she wrote a "horror science fiction" story imbued with the cultural overtones of Utah.

M. Shayne Bell began writing science fiction to prove it could be written as well as any other kind of literature. In 1991 he was awarded a Creative Writing Fellowship from the National Endowment for the Arts—one of the first ever awarded for science fiction. His story in this anthology, "The Shining Dream Road Out," was printed in *Simulations: Fifteen Tales of Virtual Reality* and in *Tomorrow: Speculative Fiction.*

Pat Bezzant says that "Utah's atmosphere is conducive to science fiction because we live in a time warp thirty years behind the rest of the world." Salt Lake City makes a good locale for "Finale" because of its earthquake faults and "the doomsday stuff in the culture."

Elizabeth H. Boyer, whose story "A Foreigner Comes to Reddyville" is set in Idaho, is a nationally known fantasy writer. She drew a blank at first at the thought of writing science fiction for this anthology. But then she thought about the fact that science fiction writers like to write about the future and fantasy writers about the past. She became intrigued with the concept of science fiction applied to the past and produced the story included here.

Orson Scott Card, one of the most prolific and popular science fiction authors writing today, has a name readily recognized by any serious science fiction reader. But his work has particular appeal for Latter-day Saint fans. His story "Pageant Wagon" is one of a series of stories concerning Mormons in a post-holocaust world.

James Cummings died in April 1992. His story, "Space People," brings science fiction to the real world of the corridor.

David Doering believes life is for doing, not viewing. His appreciation for science fiction began when, as a child, a librarian forbade him to read *20,000 Leagues Under the Sea,* and nature took its course. "Snooze" illustrates his keen interest in decision-making moments.

B. J. Fogg grew up thinking his Trekkie friends were "crazy." As a reader he is "compelled by issues of relationships" and feels that much science fiction is "gee-whiz driven." Primarily an essayist, Fogg often deals with issues of the Mormon culture, which he considers to be "in a watershed period." Therefore, in "Outside the Tabernacle" he uses a near-future science fiction context to explore his themes.

Melva Gifford remembers "getting my hands green putting together the first issue of *The Leading Edge*." She was interested in the magazine as a place to publish science fiction "that didn't rely on the crutches of sex, profanity, and excessive violence." In love with the "rugged, harsh beauty" of southern Utah, she made that landscape an important part of her story "Scrap Pile."

Charlene C. Harmon's idea for "Pueblo de Sión" came from the title of this anthology. She finished her story in record time "since Shayne forgot to ask me to submit until deadline day." Here she combines her interest in pre-Columbian America with her love of Utah canyonlands.

Diana Lofgran Hoffman prefers hard science fiction. "I don't have much patience with fantasy," she says. In her story "Other Time," she uses Utah culture as a basis for the story and for the character because "the Utah value system creates a lot of pressure. It forces a woman to try to be a superwoman." Hoffman, an Isaac Asimov fan, favors science fiction "not laced with hot bedroom stuff" and considers it a perfect vehicle for allegory.

Carolyn Nicita's father, an aeronautical engineer, made a math machine (binary counting machine/binary computer) for her in the 1960s; her mother was into metaphysics, so "I did not grow up doing conventional thinking." Because of her father's interest in "Star Trek," "I grew up thinking science fiction was real." She discovered Xenobia when she went to BYU. "It isn't difficult to find science fiction material in Utah," says Nicita, who based her story "Solitude" around the theme of the need for aloneness versus the need for companionship.

Michaelene Pendleton feels that science fiction offers a writer the most value in terms of imagination. Pendleton, who has traveled widely, learned from life that "no one way is right." She finds Utah's conservative culture "societally restrictive" compared to other parts of the country, but is happy with the writers and writing coming out of Utah. "Utah provides a wonderful emphasis on art," she says.

D. William Shunn, a software engineer, believes his drive to write began in first grade when he won first prize in a class Halloween story contest—and scared the wits out of his classmates in the process. "Rise Up, Ye Women That Are at Ease" combines his love of Salt Lake City's downtown locale with some serious thoughts on relations between the sexes.

Diann Thornley originally wrote medieval fiction but was converted to science fiction after a friend forced her to see *Star Wars*, which she loved. The *Star Wars* universe has strongly affected her writing. Her story "Thunderbird's Egg" contains several autobiographical elements: her family used to vacation in Moab, she had two native American foster brothers, and she is, in fact, an Air Force captain in the reserves. Her protagonist in the story is also a rebel, much as Thornley herself.

Dave Wolverton, who read science texts as a child, liked writing from an early age. Science fiction gave him a means of combining his two interests. Feeling that most LDS fiction was either preaching for or against the religion, he chose to write a "Mormon story about people." The result is "Wheatfields Beyond."

Kathleen Dalton-Woodbury was initially intrigued by the early science fiction movie *Forbidden Planet.* "I've learned about people from science fiction," she says. "It's a way to see people in new situations." Dalton-Woodbury says the Tongans in her story are based on those she has known in the Salt Lake area, and the comet comes from Comet Bennett, which "didn't get much publicity, but was great to look at."

Lyn Worthen got into science fiction when "a friend lent me a book, and it went downhill from there." She resists the notion that science fiction is inferior as literature: "The same things that touch you in a writer like Charles Dickens touch you in Ursula K. LeGuin." Worthen's real interest is in how people deal with unexpected cultural situations.

M. W. Worthen, who has just finished a second master's degree, started reading science fiction because his "cool" older brother did. He started writing as a teenager. His concept for "You Can't Go Back" comes from the fact that he likes living in Utah but knows he'll have to leave it some day to follow his job. "I wanted to be able to take it with me, so I wrote a story about a guy who did," Worthen says.

WHEATFIELDS BEYOND

DAVE WOLVERTON

ana Rosen met Karl William Ungricht three times in her life, twice before the end of the world and once long after.

The first time they met, Tana worked as a criminal psychologist who spent her days judging violent men—in spite of her petite size. She had thin, fawn-like bones and wiry legs that would easily curl up under her butt for hours as she sat on the floor to watch TV.

In the mornings Tana worked as a pretrial consultant for the Utah State Attorney General's Office, sorting men and women the way another person might sort good pea pods into one pile, culls into another: "This juvenile car thief needs drug therapy; the mother up for child abuse is probably scared straight; and the neo-Nazi in the corner is competent to stand trial for capital homicide."

Tana worked afternoons at the Utah State Prison trying to restore men who were emotionally sick, men ravaged by addictions, men whose brains were so miswired from birth that they did not know right from wrong and were therefore morally crippled. She would advise the doctors and program administrators: "This schizophrenic child molester needs Haldone; that cowboy thief should be taught to read."

At age 28 she had her Ph.D. At age 28 she had a job that would have bewildered Solomon.

People had become things to mend or discard, and over and over again she found herself discarding people she wanted to mend. She would sign papers verifying that a criminal was competent to stand trial, and after consigning some miscreant to hell on earth, she would drop her pen, wring her thin hands, stare at the lines of her own signature that wandered across the paper like an ant trail.

It was a cold night in late January 1991, with Joel working late at Novell. The Gulf War played on TV. Tana didn't watch. She was tired of green tracers flaring into the night, of pinpoint explosions, of chubby American generals flaying their opponents with clever jibes.

With the Iraqis bombed and broken in their trenches, she could think only of their children, malleable little Moslems teethed on desolation, groomed in a society that exults in revenge. She believed that any victory would be temporary, a fitful battle, a long uneasy sleep until the next generation matured.

So she worked late at the prison, drove home to Provo, then stopped to grab a hamburger at the Rocky Mountain Drive-In just off I-15. At night this part of town was desolate. The auto shops and pawn shops closed early, dimming their lights, and the big snow-covered park across the street yawned wide. The scruffy houses to the south were the abode of poverty and Tana's future clients.

Tana felt edgy, feared she might spot one of her past rejects out on parole.

The counter clerk turned out one bank of lights as she prepared to close the restaurant, so Tana sat by a post in a dark corner and toyed with her hamburger.

She had grown comfortable being alone. Living with her husband was about the same as being alone. Tana didn't have any real friends.

Few cars drove by. Across the street in the shadows, a man crawled from beneath a half-demolished bandstand. A low fog had frozen into ice crystals which drifted between the barren branches of the alders in the park. In the 20s and getting colder. Too cold to sleep without a fire, Tana mused.

The cook began tearing down ice-cream dispensers, and Tana scrunched closer to the wall as a pimple-faced boy mopped the floor beside her.

A moment later she heard a *pop* outside. The man from the park pulled the lid off the trash can. He was in his twenties, sunken cheeks, straw-blond hair under a stocking cap, a stained army jacket. Just someone's lost boy, nobody Tana recognized. He pawed through papers, found half a Coke which he set on the ground, then scavenged for loose fries, chicken strips covered with mustard sauce. He wrapped the fries and strips in paper, absently shoved them in his pocket.

A car pulled into the lot, washing Tana with lights. She realized she had been staring. She nibbled at her fries. Through the double-paned glass she heard a man say quite distinctly, "Jesus."

Tana looked up and saw a sagging belly of a man who sat behind a desk all day, white shirt and tie under his suit coat. He wrapped his arm protectively around a little girl, perhaps seven years old, as if to save her from ever having to look upon a homeless person. Clean folks. Bathed in softened water. Citizens out for a bite after an evening movie.

Mr. Belly dipped into his wallet and pulled out a $20 bill, shoved it in the derelict's hand, and said, "Excuse me, garblegarblegarble cat?"

The derelict looked at the money as if pondering the relevancy of currency to his life, crumpled it, and just held it, staring vacantly at Mr. Belly, who finally either got tired or embarrassed and brought his daughter inside.

The derelict fished a hamburger from the trash, a big one with a couple of kid bites taken from it, then put the lid back on the can and sat on the curb to feed, shoving hamburger in his mouth in fistfuls, lubricating with Coke.

Revolted, Tana looked away, thought: *Ah, a story with a happy ending.*

She played with her fries, not wanting to head for her car with the derelict so near. The darkened restaurant was safe, anonymous, and she could watch through her window as if viewing the outside world through a television screen. Mr. Belly ordered. Tana spaced out, thinking about a case at the prison, about a necrophile who had killed his own grandmother and kept her in a freezer.

The next thing Tana knew, Mr. Belly was outside again, shouting, "Damn you! Do you think I want you here? Do you think I want my kid watching you eat out here like some animal?"

The derelict sat on the curb, looking up, fries hanging out his mouth, and tried to swallow.

"What in the hell do you plan to do with the money? Buy drugs?" Mr. Belly shouted. The derelict started scrabbling backwards to get away. He fumbled in his pocket, set the $20 in the snow.

But Mr. Belly's eyes glazed over, a dangerous fixed glare, and he kicked the derelict and started screaming incoherently, "Ahyaahahaha-haaaaa!"

The derelict fell forward, a red gash on his brow. Mr. Belly had opened him up with the toe of his dress shoe. Then the whole thing became macabre: Mr. Belly kicked, and the light from the window shone in his dark eyes, and he was intense, focused. His foot lashed out and the little derelict's gray stocking cap flew off as the boot caught him in the temple.

The derelict rolled, eyes closed, away from his attacker, but the big guy kept screaming, kicking for throat, crotch. Tana heard ribs crunch, saw a splash of blood and a flash of white as some of the little man's teeth flew out, heard the chunk of his carcass (she was sure he would die from the beating) as his head hit cement. The restaurant help stopped cleaning, stopped breathing; the compressors for the refrigerators abruptly died as the freezers went to defrost. Even through double-pane windows Tana could hear Mr. Belly wheeze. The beating became nearly soundless—the grunts of the antagonist, the swish of his clothes as he kicked.

Every day, Tana thought, *I work with criminals but never witness the maniac glee in the attacker's face, the whimpers of the victim, blood splashing over frozen snow.* She jumped from her seat, ran to the door. Mr. Belly half turned when he heard her coming, and he slipped on the ice and some of the derelict's greasy fries. Tana was pleased to hear his shoulder crack as he collided with concrete.

Inside the restaurant Mr. Belly's daughter issued a thin scream, a child's version of the wail an older woman might have made.

Tana ran to the derelict. Blood covered the matted straw of his hair, and he lay twisted on his side, face down in the snow. Blood poured from his mouth and eye, and the hot breath from his nose steamed as if he were exhaling tiny puffs of smoke. He stared into the ground as if he were gazing at the heart of the earth. Some splotches of his blood were impossibly red under the glare of neon, but the blood pooling by his mouth was dark and purple. In the cold air it quickly jelled like pudding with a thin skin on it. In his right hand the derelict held the hamburger, as if he'd planned to carry it if he got away. His left hand held a twisted yellow paper and the last few fries.

The cleaning boy stood at the counter phone, pressing 911. All in all Tana figured the attack had lasted less than thirty seconds.

Mr. Belly grunted and shouted, "Call a doctor, I broke something!

I'm hurt!" Tana glanced back. The fat man was struggling to lift himself from the ground with one hand.

Tana whispered to the derelict, "It's all right! You're all right! The ambulance is coming." The hospital was only nine blocks away. Mr. Belly's daughter screamed in the restaurant while the female cook held her. The fat man had managed to raise to a crouch. Tana shouted, "You keep back! Keep back!" She was sure he would attack again.

"Where's the knife?" Mr. Belly asked. "I swear to God this bum pulled a knife on me." Tana looked into his eyes. Guilt, fear. "It has to be here somewhere." He got up, headed back into the restaurant. Tana watched him go, relieved.

The derelict spat a mouthful of blood, spoke through wheezing breath, "My teeth. Where's my teeth? They dropped here somewhere's." It was useless to hunt for them in the dark, in the snow. Tana retrieved his stocking cap, set it under his chin. Mr. Belly came back outside, and Tana saw silver flash in his hand as he stashed a kitchen knife by the garbage can. She pretended not to notice. The big guy nosed around, recovered the $20 the derelict had dropped.

It seemed to Tana that the ambulance should be coming. Joel kept an emergency blanket in the trunk of the car, a thin piece of plastic with a mylar backing. She stumbled to the car, opened the trunk. When she closed it, Mr. Belly was hunkered over the derelict in a strangler's pose. She looked in the restaurant window: None of the employees were watching. Mr. Belly lurched away, and Tana rushed to the derelict.

Nothing had changed. The derelict lay in the same position, a pool of blood by his nose, breathing shallow. His eyes had closed, swollen white ridges growing around them, but in his right hand, instead of a hamburger, he now held a kitchen knife.

Tana looked up at Mr. Belly, and his eyes were wide, frightened. He crouched by the trash can. "You found it!" he said. "You found the knife! He had it all along! He stabbed me!" He held out his hand, showed a tiny puncture wound.

At that moment, the cashier came outside, the others behind. Tana thought, *even if I toss the knife, these are witnesses. They will have seen a weapon. I'm too late, and if the police dust the knife for prints, I'll bet they find only those of the transient.*

Framed. That easy.

Tana wanted to run. She thought wildly of trying to hide the bum under a building or of dragging him home and putting him in the bathtub. Any place seemed safer than here, but she couldn't move him, knew he needed more than a roof over his head or warm water on his wounds, and down the street an ambulance siren blared. Tana looked up at Mr. Belly and said, "Damn you, you animalistic mother!"

Tana didn't wait for the ambulance. She drove home, her mind racing. She knew she could tell everyone that Mr. Belly had framed the derelict, but she had no proof. A solid citizen would swear that a transient had brandished a knife. The jury would jail the derelict even if they knew him to be innocent because down in their hearts they feared he *might* be dangerous. But what would the charges be? Attempted murder? Even plea bargained down to aggravated assault; he'd be hit with a first-degree felony. One-to-fifteen years. They'd lock him up with the vicious boys in the Gladiator School, the dorm for young offenders.

But Tana could fix it if she never admitted witnessing the fight. She could avoid the trial. *I can run a psyche profile on the transient in the morning,* she thought. *No matter how strait and sane he comes out, on paper I'll show him to be a madman. Hell, half the Mormons in the valley can't pass the Minnesota Mental Health Inventory. As soon as they admit belief in gods and devils and revelations, they're down the tube.*

Tana had faith in her abilities. She'd practiced her presentations on videotape. She knew how her wise little mouth hardly opened when she spoke, the words barely pushing beyond her teeth, so that when she was done, her judgments hung in the air by her taut face like breath on an icy morning, and you could look into her little scythe of a smile, the cold blue unblinking eyes, and she always sounded so damned right.

She could get him committed within the week, and in a few months the state hospital would set him free. In fact he'd be better off. For three months he'd get out from under this godawful cold, have a chance for three square meals a day, a bath.

Tana thought to herself, *I'll be doing him a favor.*

His name turned out to be Karl William Ungricht. She sat at the desk in her office four days after the attack, studying his paperwork. Twenty-four, a high-school dropout up on attempted murder. Like many homeless on the streets in the "kinder, gentler America" created by the current Republican administration, Ungricht was certifiably insane, a schizophrenic lost in a perpetual dream. (*Not unlike the current*

Republican administration, Tana mused.) Still she'd ended up with no firm plans for Ungricht. On the night of the attack it had been late; she hadn't been thinking clearly. It would have been so much easier just to claim that she had seen Ungricht's attacker plant the knife and stab himself, even embellish the incident.

But lying under pressure isn't my strong point, Tana told herself, and so she had set on the equally undesirable course of embellishing his psyche profile. She had thought about talking to her husband Joel about her dilemma but knew that he wouldn't give her any worthwhile advice, since he wouldn't want to risk being wrong. Nor would he offer any sympathy. Over the past four days, Tana's life had been hell, and she wanted now to give up her stupid scheme.

After a soft knock on the door, a guard ushered Ungricht into the office. He wore the fluorescent orange coveralls issued to all inmates at the Utah County Jail. He stumbled in, clumsy and out of place, then stood staring at her or through her, some place a million miles away. Ungricht's mouth was open, showing the gap where two upper incisors and a right bicuspid had been. His face was horribly purpled, clumsily stitched in places, but his hair looked cleaner. He just stood.

"Mr. Ungricht, I'm Tana Rosen, and I'll be doing your psychological evaluation. Are you there? Can you hear me?" she asked, not sure from his paperwork just how far gone he might be.

The derelict finally looked at her. "I hear you, just not awake this time in the morn'." He spoke with a central Utah accent, rare in one so young, so that *morn'* rhymed with *barn*. He smiled, then began laughing.

"What's so funny?" Tana asked. She wondered if she should stay in the room alone with this man or if she should push the alarm under her desk so that a guard would come sit with them through the interview.

"That sign on your desk," Ungricht said, nodding down.

It was a long, three-sided piece of wood. Each side had a different message. The one Ungricht read said, "To err is human, to forgive is not state policy." Tana flipped the sign over so that it simply read, "Tana Rosen, Psychologist."

"I'm sorry," she said.

"No need to be sorry." He smiled, and behind his eyes he looked all right. He was scanning the room now, eyes tracking normally.

"I've been reading your paperwork, Mr. Ungricht—"

"My friends call me Willy," he blurted.

"I'm not your friend," Tana said.

"Humph." For a moment he glared, eyes full of pent up anger, and Tana thought he might hit her. "You're playing it mighty cold," he said. "Thing is, you was there when that fellow put me down. I looked up from the ground, saw your face in the window, and I could see the hurt in your eyes. I know you care. And ever since I got here, strings has been pulled. I hardly got my head stitched up before they shoved the psyche papers in front of me. I been jailed before, and that's not natural. You been pulling strings for me. So don't you go telling me that you're not my friend!"

He talked just like any jailhouse con, too aware of her motivations, a professional manipulator. He'd probably learned it while panhandling, the give in a citizen's eye when he planned to drop a quarter into your palm. He knew her pity clouded her judgment, and he planned to take full advantage.

"Your chances for a light sentence look pretty good. Your urine specimen came up clean, no drugs, so that will go in your favor."

"My chances might look good from your side of the table," Willy said, "But not from mine. They found a *knife* in my hand! Got my fingerprints all over it! They say I dug it out of the trash and tried to stab that guy in the chest, and all this just had to happen four hours after some hobo got beat to death down on the railroad tracks." Tana looked in Willy's eyes, saw genuine fear. He was right. The county was rounding up transients as fast as they could. "They're looking at me real close for that one too, Mam!"

"But they won't find anything, will they?" Tana said.

"I've never hit anyone in my life," Willy said, "and that's God's truth. I stole things once in a while when I was a kid." Tana believed him. Willy had a low-violence profile. She doubted he would ever strike except in self-defense.

"Sit down," Tana said. "I got your jail records from Idaho, and your records from the mental hospital in Arizona. The psyche profile looks consistent. So, tell me, how does God speak to you?"

Willy had pulled up his chair, but as soon as she asked how God spoke, it was as if he left the room. His eyes became fixed and he stared through her once again, almost as if she had thumbed a switch in his brain, turning him off.

"It's a curse from God, that's what it is," Willy said distantly, as if the voice rose from deep within. "A curse from God."

"What is?"

"The dreams. Them's the curse."

"Tell me about your dreams."

"Every night, God sends me a dream."

"Did he send one last night?"

Willy nodded vacantly, licked his swollen lips. "I was a woman in the dream, and I was in the mountains. Real icy cold. Mountains like the Rockies, sandy brown and barren. I remember that someone had said food had fallen from the sky, and I was starving. My ass itched, like I had the runs, and I had thin flabby teats that nursed a baby, only nothing came out. I felt like . . . worms was in my stomach, eating me alive, making my brain itch, and my gums ached, and I knew I was going to die soon and that my baby would die. We was high in the mountains, the air clear and icy, and in the valley on the other side of a ridge I heard the tinny sound of an engine driving up windy roads. The campfire's warmth and light were the only things that made the night bearable.

"Someone whispered that the engine was an Iraqi patrol, and we had to douse the fire. I sat in my robes, the baby sucking my empty teat, and as they doused the fire, I refused to help. Better to die from an Iraqi bullet than cold and hunger. Someone said my name, Irena, but I was already dead."

Willy continued staring at the desk, staring into his own dark world beyond the desk, rocking back and forth. Lost.

The dream was consistent with others recorded in Arizona. Six months earlier they'd sent him packing, having determined that he was no danger to himself or others. They surmised that Willy's eating disorder, his "Moral opposition to eating any food that doesn't come out of a trash can," was caused by childhood trauma, but they didn't know. Ten million kids across the country were badgered into eating dinner every night by being told to "think of the poor starving kids in China." Maybe Willy Ungricht was the only one who really ever did feel guilty about the millions who starved. Perhaps that led to his compulsive desire to eat refuse.

"God, Willy, you had twenty dollars in your pocket. Couldn't you have just bought a hamburger?"

"No." Willy kept rocking. His hands trembled; he breathed shallowly, like a woman in labor. Tears came to his eyes. "You don't believe it. You think I'm crazy, but God told me to live like this. He sent his angels in a dream, and they said, 'You got to follow your heart, Willy, and you'll be okay,' and when I woke, my heart wanted me to walk out the door, leave home, and never go back, so that's what I done."

"When you were sixteen?"

"Something like," Willy said.

Tana fumbled with the mess of papers on her desk. Lots of records testifying to the same thing. "Okay, Willy, I'm going to pull your strings. You're right about the attempted murder charges. I know they're bogus," Tana hesitated. "The thing is, if I try to fight this now, I'd have to go in front of a jury and tell my side of the story against four other witnesses. I could say that I saw him plant the knife—but the value of my testimony has been compromised since I've waited so long. The charges might stick, and, Willy, you don't need prison.

"So, if you agree, I want to stack the deck in your favor and fight these charges my way. If you agree, then I'm going to declare you incompetent to stand trial. It will be a sure ticket to the mental hospital. It's clear that your dreams, your illness, is at the heart of this, and you weren't in your right mind when that guy tried to kick your brains out. Still, if you want, I'll take this thing to trial, and I will be a witness for you."

Willy laughed a melancholy laugh. "You plan to send me down to the hospital?"

"Yeah, Willy, I do. Just for a few months—three, maybe six."

"Will they let me eat from the garbage?"

"Maybe. They'll try to break you of it."

Willy sighed, picked up Tana's name tag and flipped it back over: To err is human, to forgive is not state policy. "I expect the food there is about the same as garbage. If this goes to trial, I'd spend six months in the county jail anyway just waiting for a date. I guess, you're doing what you can. You're saving me."

He sighed. "You know, most folks in the world don't eat food any better than what I pull from the trash. I'm not doing anything wrong."

"I know," Tana said. She paused to study his files. "There is something I wonder about. You did poorly in school, and your psychologist in Arizona says you have an attention-deficit disorder. He's also written something here about a poor concept of time. I just wondered, do you see your life as a story, with causes and effects?"

"No," Willy said.

Tana sighed. "Do you see that your dreams, that your feelings of guilt about eating, are related to what happened the other night? This disorder will destroy you."

"Look, I don't believe that," Willy said. "God told me that if I follow my heart, everything will be okay."

"So life doesn't have causes and effects?"

"Not like what you imagine," Willy said. "Life is just a deck of cards, flashing in front of you, all of them just appearing at random. Shit happens."

Tana shrugged. This one needed mending, so she would send him to someone who did it full-time. She pulled a green spiral notebook from her desk, wrote her work address on the cover, put the pen in the spirals of the notebook. "Willy, I want you to write me. I want you to look at your life, from start to finish, and find a pattern. When you do, write that pattern down while it is clear before your eyes and send it to me."

Willy looked at the pen. "I can't take that pen into the jail. It would just get stolen by some tattoo freak."

"I'll put it with your clothes," Tana said. "The guards will give it to you when they take you to the hospital," and Tana sighed in relief, hoping she would never see Willy Ungricht again.

After six weeks in the Utah State Hospital, Willy's evaluation restrictions were removed, but his therapist took a month to sign the recommend that allowed Willy to leave the locked facility for supervised recreational activities. They released Willy for the first time in early March, when the sun had melted the snow and the endless temperature inversions had let the cloud of polluted air begin to rise from Utah Valley.

The recreational therapist in charge, a kitten of a girl named Lisa Snow, took Willy and a dozen other patients to the dollar theater to watch "Green Card." It was a perfect movie for schizophrenics—no decapitations, no devils inhabiting the bodies of small girls, nothing to feed the delusions of the audience. Willy sat on the last seat of the row, next to a patient who was so far gone as to be a zombie.

All through the movie, Willy ate popcorn that others spilled on the floor and wrote furiously in the notebook Tana had given him. He sketched out his life, looking for cause and effect, but nothing made any sense to him, and he finally threw the pen down in disgust.

At the end of *Green Card*, when the French lead and the weird New York chick realized they loved each other, Willy looked down the row and saw Lisa crying into her hand. The male aide two seats down was no better off. Willy whispered to the zombie, "Wish me luck."

Willy slipped from his chair, walked up the aisle, hit the exit door. He sprinted through the parking lot, leapt a fence, and ran north along the Provo River.

When the credits came on screen, Lisa counted her patients. Willy was three-quarters of a mile away. The zombie at the end of the row turned to Willy's seat and said, "Good luck."

In 1989 the ozone hole over the Antarctic had opened permanently, and across Australia millions of frogs began to die, species that had lived for well over a hundred million years. In 1990 scientists studying the combined influence of ozone depletion and the greenhouse effect testified to a Congressional committee that up to 70 percent of the world's plant and animal species could be destroyed within fifty years. In 1991 the average world temperatures broke heat records for the seventh year in a row.

Frogs and salamanders began dying in the northern hemisphere, but computer simulations of ozone depletion provided President Bush with some happy news: The U.S. could continue polluting at current levels for another decade and cause only 5 percent more skin cancer deaths around the world during the following fifty years.

In the summer of 1991 an El Niño formed in both the Atlantic and Pacific. Warm waters ruined much of the world's fishing for the second time in a decade. In February of 1992 NASA released a preliminary report that claimed that chlorine monoxide in the upper atmosphere was found to be at such high levels that, under cold conditions in mid-winter, ozone could be lost at the rate of up to 30 percent per month. President Bush's aides slammed the report, claiming that NASA's chief was seeking to turn ozone depletion into a campaign issue. NASA's chief left his post in disgrace. A week later the European Space Administration announced that northern Europe had lost up to 30 percent of its ozone in the month of January 1992.

In 1993 NASA administrators played down their reports on ozone depletion, saying only that ozone levels over North American hit "an all-time low." In 1994 the oceans heated again at the equator, reaching 13 degrees above normal, and climatologists coined the term *El Padre* to describe the phenomenon. Tropical storms belted coasts from Texas to South Carolina, and all through April and May, armchair tornado watchers were gratified on nightly TV. In Illinois one enterprising man mounted cameras to an armored truck, vowing to shoot footage *inside* a tornado. When the Wheaton Thresher hit, he got sucked up like all the other chaff, but the salvaged footage was spectacular.

Tana and Joel spent the Fourth of July with friends in Vegas during the summer of '94. The day was deadly hot, 117 degrees, and to Tana the summer sky seemed to glow whiter than she remembered from childhood. They gambled at Circus Circus. Joel's friends had kids and wanted to keep them entertained, but somehow Joel's friends got separated and Tana ended up alone, working the dollar video poker games on the main floor, her eyes stinging from a cloud of other peoples' smoke, winning some, losing more, her ears numbed to the ringing of bells, the chink of tokens spattering into aluminum bins.

Suddenly the lights flashed and the bells kept ringing just two screens down. Over the intercom a pit boss announced a $4,000 winner, and Tana glanced at the winner, annoyed. He was a gaunt man with wheat-straw hair, eyes as blue as her own, shabby Levis, and a Terminator 3 T-shirt. He smiled at Tana, a strange vacant smile, his upper teeth missing.

Tana's heart pounded, for she recognized him only as a client, and she couldn't remember what hell-hole she might have consigned him to.

"Remember me, Willy Ungricht? From up to Provo? You watched me get my face kicked in?"

"Yes," Tana answered, relief washing like cold water through her veins. Then she remembered that he had escaped from the mental hospital. "How are you doing?"

"I'm rich, right now," Willy grinned at the money. Only twenty-five dollars had dropped into the bin, but the pit boss was coming with the check. "Got myself married and had a baby girl. Had to leave though. Couldn't stay in the house. Tried for a while. I wanted to write you, but I lost the address on that notebook you gave me, and I figured it wasn't a good idea to go back to Utah. But I did what you asked, I figured my life out, put it down on paper. Do you want to see?"

It came back to her then, the food guilt, her questions. She really had meant to follow up, but Willy had gotten lost in the pile.

"I've decided," Willy said. "That I ain't human. I ain't like you."

Dizziness struck Tana, and she wondered if she should call the police, have Willy picked up. She recalled something about angels. "If you aren't human, what do you think you are?" She expected him to say "the Son of God."

"Oh, just a transient." Willy sounded embarrassed by the admission, but there was something odd in way it came from his lips—*trans'nt*—crushed as if it were a single syllable. Tana realized that like some yogi out of India who tries to make sense of the world by redefining everything around him, Willy had redefined that word to describe himself. *Trans-nt*. Willy. Not human.

"What's a transient?"

"Oh, well, that takes a bit of explaining," he said, "I'll tell you in a minute." Just then a Mexican in a white shirt came up and took Willy's name, address, and social security number. Willy had the check sent to some girl in El Paso. When he was done, he and Tana sat by their video poker screens.

"After I run off from the hospital in Utah," Willy said, "I tried real hard to do what you asked. I tried writing in that book and making sense of my life, but none of it made sense. I headed south down to Zion's Canyon for a while, and one night a big storm blew in. I sat in the dark and watched lightning strike this big stone mountain, all around, going boom, boom, boom, and the lightning was like the thorns in the crown that Jesus wore when he was crucified—bloody and full of light and cruel—and I realized I had seen this all before, the lightning and the crown on Jesus' head. But it was in another life, a long time ago. Still the memory was all written in my bones. That's when I figured I wasn't human, but I didn't know what I was, and it scared me. So I headed to Texas."

"Why Texas? Did you think it would be more safe?"

Willy looked at her as if she were crazy. "Course not. It was just a place. But on the way, I felt like I was on to something. I could feel something inside me, waking up or coming alive, and I started to understand things, and I wrote them in that notebook you gave me. For a while I thought I might be normal, like you folks, and that maybe I'd been a little sick in the head and I was getting better, but no.

"Anyway in Texas I went to sleep in a culvert one night, and I found this girl, a runaway. She'd left home a month before, had no food. I thought I'd teach her the ropes, and she followed me around. One thing led to another, and I accidentally knocked her up. She said she loved me, so we got married, took jobs and settled."

"What do you mean, settled?" Tana asked hopefully. "Were you able to hold down a job, manage your money? You know, basic life skills?"

"Yeah, we rented an apartment. We both took jobs washing beef carcasses at a meat-packing plant. The money was good, and we made out all right." Willy pulled a cigarette from his pocket, stuck it in his mouth without lighting it. "Thing is, it didn't last. At first it was okay, but after little Juanita was born, I had to start getting out of the house, taking long walks at night—ten, twenty miles at a time.

"I was walking through the park one day, and I'd left Teresa at the apartment watching TV with the baby, and my legs just kept saying 'keep moving, keep moving,' and I looked out in the park—" As Willy spoke his voice grew in intensity. "And that's when it hit me: I saw two kids sitting in boxes, looking out, *pretending they were in caves*, and three other kids was also sitting there with blankets pulled over their heads, and they were looking out as if they were watching from *caves*, and that's when I knew I wasn't human!"

Spittle flew from Willy's mouth. He had stopped blinking during the conversation, and his eyes had grown wide and strange. He clutched the rim of the video poker machine.

"How . . . how did you know you weren't human?" Tana asked, scanning the room quickly, searching for Joel.

"Because. I. *Never*. Played like I was in a cave when I was a kid!" Willy answered. "I *never* sat in a box or wrapped a blanket over me when I was a kid! Even now, when I'm sleeping out in the weather, I never find myself a box to sleep in. The idea makes me nervous. The fear of it seems to be written right at the core of me, and when I saw those kids pretending to be in caves, that's when it all made sense!"

Willy grabbed her hand, hunched forward. "See, when I was a kid, I didn't have a daddy. My mom worked as a waitress at a truck stop, and when I asked mamma who daddy was, she used to say, 'Oh, just some drifter.' I figured he was a truck driver, but now I know he wasn't. And that's when I realized I was a drifter, too, that it was written in my bones, and I'm not like you."

Suddenly, Tana understood. "You mean genetic memories?"

"Call them what you will," Willy answered, and he released his breath.

"But there's no such thing as genetic memories," Tana answered. "If there were, we would know."

"They aren't memories," Willy said. "They're feelings. They're the hidden drummer. I kept walking down the street, and it wasn't just the kids who were pretending to be in caves. I saw some old woman sitting in a rocking chair, looking out the window, and I realized that her whole house was just a cave, and the window was just the mouth to the cave, and it made her comfortable to dream she was in a cave.

"And then I walked down the street and watched the trucks and cars go by, and all the people were sitting inside their little movable caves, and watching outside, and the windows were like mouths to a cave.

"Everywhere I looked, people were in caves. And when I got home and Teresa was there, sitting in the dark and watching TV, I realized that she was sitting in a cave, looking into a machine that was like looking out the mouth of a cave, and my mouth went dry and I started sweating.

"So that night while Teresa slept, I went for a walk. I went down to the railroad tracks, and I just took off my clothes and laid on my back, naked, watching a night sky so full of stars and clouds, and for the first time in my life I felt at home.

"You got to understand. I love my wife and daughter, just like any man, but I couldn't go back and live in that cave with them. I'm a *transient*."

At that moment Joel came over and stood beside Tana. He had played tennis all summer, burning his winter fat away, leaving him lean and muscular. He must have wondered why Tana was speaking to this intense, ragged, toothless man. She imagined that he thought he was saving her. "How are you doing, honey?" Joel said, rubbing his right wrist.

"Fine," Tana answered. "Joel, I'd like you to meet a friend, Willy Ungricht."

Willy asked, "You got something wrong with your wrist?"

"Guess I hurt it playing the slots. Carpal-tunnel syndrome, you know. Doctor says I may have to stop beating off with my right hand."

Willy didn't smile at the tasteless joke, and Tana glared at Joel. Their marriage was on the rocks, and here Joel was tacitly telling a grungy stranger that their sex life had become nonexistent. *Is he trying to bully me into sex,* she wondered, *or let Willy know that I'm available?* For six years now she had been judging men for the courts of Utah, yet she told herself that if the personnel department had seen the mistake she made in picking a husband, they never would have hired her.

Willy rose uncomfortably. "Well, I got to go," he said. "I just wanted to thank you for all you done. I owe you. You folks have a good time here in Vegas, okay?" He walked out, his thin hips not even swaying as he left through the murky gambling hall.

"Who was he?" Joel asked.

"A madman I once sent to the mental hospital," she answered. She wondered if she should turn Willy in. She had sworn to uphold the laws of the state of Utah, and if anyone ever learned that she had failed, her boss would definitely put the screws to her.

"Is he dangerous?"

"Probably to himself," she said. "He told me a story, a tale told by an idiot . . ."

"Hunh," Joel said. "Ungricht. Good solid Aryan name. His ancestors probably fed our ancestors to the ovens at Auschwitz. I don't want you talking to people like him again. I'm going to play roulette. See you later, hon." Joel left, shaking his wrist.

Tana tried to put the episode out of mind. She began dropping tokens in the video poker machine and an hour later came up with four of a kind, then used the doubler button and doubled her winnings twice. She was suddenly up $400 for the day, and she thought of going to tell Joel, perhaps even play with him, but the roulette wheels and crap tables made her nervous. She preferred to gamble in the anonymity offered by the darkness around the video poker terminals.

While waiting for the coins to drop, she looked up. Her eyes scanned the cloistered gambling floor. Amid the clouds of smoke, thousands of people huddled and stared into the bright worlds of their video poker and slot machines. She couldn't help but think of Neanderthals staring from the mouths of their caves into the daylight.

In 1995 for the first time in several years, the world didn't break a new heat record, and the U.S. and Russia began a joint test of a plan to close the ozone hole over the North Pole by seeding the stratosphere with ethane to bind to the hydrocarbons. The first test would be small, allowing them to assess environmental fallout. Everyone was full of hope. It would have been a good summer, if not for a carbonaceous asteroid dubbed 1995 BA.

The University of Hawaii's 2.2 meter telescope atop Mauna Kea first picked up the asteroid, which, with a diameter of 214 miles, would pass within 300,000 miles of earth. Many astronomers believed the asteroid would impact the moon, while others argued that its mass was too great and it would simply blow on past.

Quacks, new-agers, and fanatics of every ilk decided it was a sign, that the asteroid would bring the end of the earth or begin the Millennium or raise Atlantis. On August 9th millions of people watched from their rooftops.

For once the fanatics guessed right. The asteroid approached the moon slowly over a period of hours, a small bright disk about one tenth the moon's diameter, and actually passed close behind. Then the asteroid swung around and for eight hours it seemed to grow in size while all over the world the folks on the rooftops suddenly felt intense sympathy for the dinosaurs.

One might argue that the asteroid landed harmlessly in the Atlantic, and it was only when eight million cubic miles of debris erupted from underneath Perth, Australia, that the real damage occurred.

Microscopic diamonds rained from the sky, and the air filled with black dust. Around the world coastal cities succumbed to massive tidal waves, and dead volcanoes boiled into frenzied life.

The Missouri River Valley raised 92 feet. Fires raged across the world's plains.

Through heat and friction free carbon from the asteroid mixed with oxygen in the atmosphere, and when added to the already dangerously elevated levels of carbon dioxide from years of pollution, the greenhouse threat became an instant calamity. A blanket of black smoke and dust absorbed the incoming sunlight, raising atmospheric temperatures even further.

Sulfuric ash from volcanoes and the meteor mixed with water in the ionosphere to form weak acids that eroded the ozone layer by 70 percent during the winter of '95. As global temperatures soared by twenty degrees, rain forests dried and withered into kindling, which quickly caught fire, so that free oxygen became more and more scarce.

With the ozone depleted and the algae at the poles dying under the onslaught of ultraviolet rays, it soon became apparent that earth would not have much oxygen left to breathe for a long time. Some scientists speculated that with reseeding of the planet, oxygen levels might be restored to near normal within three or four years. They pointed out optimistically that most plants thrived when carbon dioxide levels were somewhat elevated. Others predicted that the oxygen would not return for at least 300 years.

September storms frequently raged with winds in excess of 200 mph, eroding the soil, blowing away seeds and sprouts, eroding the hopes and dreams of the disaster's survivors.

Generations later, rumors said that one of the Arab nations was first to decide to go out with a bang instead of a whimper. They may have hoped that dropping their bombs would let them grab some arable land to the north. No one blamed them.

As the nations of earth began trading nuclear blows, the world became hell, but by God the flaming sunrises and bloody sunsets were glorious.

Near dark, thirty years after the fall, Tana thought she'd finally die. The four dirty young animals who'd taken her captive had raped and beat her plenty, then made her walk ten miles through the wilderness in the Rocky Mountains near what had once been Price, Utah. When she dropped from exhaustion near a stand of stunted aspen, they ripped the last shreds of hides off her for good, tied her to a pole, and carried her to camp.

Dangling from the pole, she closed her eyes and breathed shallowly, pretending to be dead. She could fake it good, and sometime in the dim past, she recalled that it had saved her more than once. As the boys brought her into camp, she opened one eye enough to scope it out. A big fire surrounded by forty or fifty grubbers, wild folks like something that crawled out of California. They wore animal hides and had painted their faces with blue clay to keep out the YouVees, just like the boys who had caught her. They were squatting in front of ramshackle huts next to a coal mine. This place had been abandoned for years, until now. Tana closed her eyes. The boys dropped her by a campfire. Naked little savage children pranced around her.

"What you got there?" a deep-voiced man asked.

One teenager who had carried her into camp, a brute named Scott, pushed her closer to the fire for all to see. "Found a scrawny old birdy woman asleep, holed up in a cave about ten mile from here. She's been there a long time—has a good sized garden with fresh corn, lots of old junk. We found this on her." Tana imagined that Scott was showing her AR-17, brandishing the dear sweet old hunk of steel. She heard the rush of in-drawn breath from the crowd.

The big man moseyed close, grunted as he bent over Tana. She could smell the soured bear fat on his body, his uncured deerskins, the scent of excrement. "You alive down there, woman?" he asked.

When Tana didn't answer, the big man put his hand over her mouth, expertly pinched her nostrils closed. Tana held her breath for forty seconds, then shook her head as she gasped for air.

The brute who hunkered over her was enormous—broad, heavily bearded. "You alive? You answer me straight now when I talk to you!" He slapped her hard enough to make her head spin. "Damn it, don't glare at me, woman!"

He glanced at the boys. "What you figure to do with her?"

Scott shrugged. "I don't know, take her slave, I guess."

The big man spat on her. "She ain't worth the food she'd eat. You boys go on back up to her cave and clean it out. We'll leave her behind in the morning."

"Now hold on, Bronson!" Tana heard someone say from across the camp. The hammer of a revolver clicked, and her smelly captor raised himself up. Across the campfire stood a thin man with blue eyes that gleamed crazily in the firelight, a long wispy gray beard and hair that hadn't been cut in twenty years. He wasn't dressed in ragged hides like the others. Instead he wore tanned buckskins decorated with wooden beads, and he had a revolver pointed at Old Man Bronson's head. "Now stealing everything that scrawny old bird has wouldn't hardly be worthwhile for you, would it? But it's as good as killing her!"

"She ain't long for this world anyhow, as I see it," Old Man Bronson said. "Besides, this is *my* camp and *my* business. You and me got a Traders' Truce—no weapons to be drawn!"

Tana held her breath. Old Man Bronson wasn't the kind of man to show her any mercy. She could hear it in his voice. But this stranger in camp, this madman with the revolver, acted more civilized. If he had entered camp under the protection of a Trader's Truce, then he had to be mighty important—a leader from another camp. And he risked a lot just to pull a weapon. By breaking the truce the stranger could start a war.

Tana feared that the fellow would reconsider, feared he might decide Tana wasn't worth the risk, so she yelled in a cracked voice. "I didn't do nothing, Mister! Save me!" The madman didn't look at her, but his eyes widened, got more and more wild.

Behind Tana, young Scott Bronson snarled and reached for the AR-17.

The madman pulled off a shot. Scott grunted, fell backward, and started kicking in the dust.

"The Traders' Truce is off!" the silver-haired man said. "So you just pull out your knife, sidle up to that woman real slow, and cut her loose, or I'll do *you* like I done your boy!"

Old Man Bronson stood, hand poised on his Bowie knife. His muscles knotted, and he made a low growling as he bent and cut Tana's hands free. Her wrists were pained and rope burned; she could hardly feel her fingers.

"You think this is your lucky day," Bronson said to Tana loud enough so everyone could hear, "but you two won't get far from this camp. I swear—I'll wear your hides come winter."

"I wish you wouldn't threaten me like that," the silver-haired stranger said, and he pulled the trigger and blew the back off Old Man Bronson's head.

Tana rolled, grabbed her AR-17 from the ground, and everywhere the young men began diving for the huts. Two pulled guns, and twice more her benefactor fired, put them down. He only had two shots left, and he leapt through the campfire and grabbed Tana, then they dashed around a building.

Some crazy kid no more than ten years old jumped from a window brandishing a knife, and Tana fired a single shot. Bullets were so scarce, she didn't dare shoot more. She figured she missed, but the boy jumped back a respectful distance, and then they were running through the brush, zigzagging through sage. Five shots cracked behind, and the crazy man dropped on top of Tana. Everywhere behind them gunfire began crackling, thirty or forty shots.

"Stay down!" the fellow whispered. "They won't dare come after us, but let's not let them see our backs." They began crawling uphill in the night, and Tana couldn't seem to get her old body moving fast enough. If it had been a race in the daylight, the Bronsons would have slaughtered her easily.

Once they topped the hill, they ran farther than Tana had run in years, nearly six or seven miles as far as she could tell. Her weak ankles hardly held her, and her feet got cut and bruised on the stones. The old man pulled her along until they climbed a ridge and dropped to a crumbling freeway where there was a camp.

Tana had expected the old fellow to be from a clan something like the Bronson outfit in the mountains, but nothing like this: It was a sea of tents and wagons, horses and cattle, maybe two or three thousand people with five hundred campfires. She could see men and women dressed in real cloth tending the fires, and babies crying, and around the fires people played guitars and sang while youngsters fell in love. It seemed a vast, movable city, poised there on the old highway.

Tana stopped running, heart pounding, lungs wheezing. The stranger took off his shirt, draped it over Tana's shoulders, and she sat cross-legged, holding her sore, bloody feet, her mouth open in wonder as she stared at the camp below. And she cried. Civilization.

"That's my caravan," the old fellow said between breaths. "My name's Willy Transent." He offered her his hand as if he shook hands with strangers every day.

"Tana Rosen."

"I sure—I sure didn't want to do that. Kill those folks!" Willy wiped the sweat from his forehead, and said, "Whew!"

"That Bronson tribe is just a herd of pigs," Tana said. "No harm in killing them."

Willy watched Tana as she spoke, and there was infinite sadness in his eyes. "Well, they were real people once, and I figure maybe they could be real again."

Tana jerked her chin at the tents below. "You their leader?" Willy nodded. "Damn fool of you to go trading up to the Bronson camp alone."

"It was my first meet with them," Willy said. "I wanted to earn their trust."

"Hmmm. What do you call yourself in your camp—the King, Lord, or what?"

"I'm the mayor, elect," Willy said, and he smiled. His upper teeth were gone. She looked hard at him. Somehow it seemed significant.

"I haven't seen that many people in one camp," Tana said, "since the Mormon prophet got up in Temple Square and said that Utah was now about as parched as the hottest corner of Hades, so they might as well head back to Missouri where they believed the Garden of Eden once was."

"You were there?"

"Oh yeah, I saw them leave. Must have been two million people with bicycles and wagons, some artillery scrounged from Army and Air Force bases, all of them heading up highway 215 toward Denver. I've always wondered how they fared. When they left it was like they took the law with them. Grubbers came up out of California, looting and killing. That's when I lost my husband."

Willy nodded. "There's law in my camp, too. It's a scarce commodity, but not too scarce nowadays. Our caravan travels up and down I-15 mostly. We winter down in St. George, summer up in Idaho. When we started, it was rough. My kids grew up on lizard meat and cactus and wild turnips, but we've made good. We trade along the way. Everyone on the trail knows us: We get pecans out of St. George, watermelon from Green River, potatoes and sugar out of Idaho. I don't often run into a pack of grubbers like them Bronsons anymore."

Tana savored the words, "Sugar, pecans, watermelon? Oh please, I haven't had any in years."

Willy moved a little closer. "Look, if you were any other old woman, I'd offer to trade you for some fresh corn, maybe even set you up with cloth and ask you to do needlework through the winter so we could have more to trade next year. But I don't think you had better go back to your cave. Them Bronsons are sure to hunt you. So I'll tell you what: I can send a hundred of my boys up to your place and bring your stuff back down, if you have a mind to come with us. Them Bronsons won't want to go to war with a camp our size."

Tana looked over the camp spread below them with fires like stars fallen to the ground. Her feet were a bloody mess. She listened to the guitars, and part of her wanted to run down there, right now, sit next to those fires. But the camp was full of strangers, and she hadn't seen so many people in one place in thirty years. Old Mr. Bronson had been right. She wasn't long for this world, and she didn't want to be a burden to folks who might not like her anyway.

"I figure I already owe you," Tana said, "so you can have some of my fresh corn. It does get tedious in my cave when the snow flies though, and I'd be grateful if you could lend me some needles and cloth so I can do some honest work for you. Next year, save me a watermelon and a couple pounds of pecans and sugar. We'll make a trade."

"What if them Bronson boys come back?"

"They won't find it easy to get near me this time." Tana brandished her AR-17.

Willy nodded. "I respect that. Still, if you ever change your mind . . . " He looked her over, wiped some blood from his side. Tana suddenly noticed that he'd been shot, but it was a small wound. Willy said, "I'll go on down and get you some bandages and moccasins, send some boys to help you get home. We'll give you some cloth and thread, pecans and sugar, maybe some butter and salt to go with that corn of yours. Consider it advance payment. Next year, maybe you'll plant a bigger garden knowing that we'll be back."

Tana thanked him, and then Willy left. An hour later some boys came up. One of them introduced himself as Willy's grandson, a black-haired boy that could have been a Mexican or Navajo. The boys had to carry her home.

Once she'd sent the boys away, Tana went to the back of her cave, lit a poorly made candle. It was a rare treat, but she felt she needed the light. She surveyed her belongings, looking for damage. Tana didn't have much. Four people could haul off everything she owned. But the Bronson boys had smashed the old oxygen compressor that had carried her and Joel through the rough years at this high altitude. They'd opened all her clay pots and food bags, searching for weapons. She looked at the spilled food. *Is this what they want to kill me for?*

She went to the mouth of the cave and watched the valley by moonlight to guard her patch of corn and tomatoes. She doubted the Bronson boys would come raiding tonight, but she couldn't take the chance, so she cradled her AR-17 in her lap as she ate a little raw brown sugar Willy had left. The sugar tasted stronger than she remembered, almost sickening in its sweetness.

A great-horned owl hooted in the distance, breaking the peaceful silence of the night, while locusts whirred in the Russian olive trees. Thirty-four years since the meteor hit. In the past five years, Tana had seen a world on the brink of ruin suddenly begin to thrive, grass and trees shooting up so quickly she could hardly believe it.

Finally the ozone, the world, people—seemed to be coming back. She thought about the campfires of the Mormons as they fled Salt Lake Valley for the Garden of Eden. One of their prophets, Brigham Young, had once said that when the Mormons returned to Missouri, there wouldn't be "one yellow dog there wagging its tail to greet them." She suspected Brigham was right, and Tana wondered if maybe the Mormons were still out there somewhere, tending their golden wheatfields. She'd often envied them. She'd lived with the Mormons for years, feeling like the only Jew in Provo, Utah. She'd never liked them particularly, never made close friends with one, but she envied how they clung together, envied them because they were not alone.

She thought about Joel, who had never been worth a damn as a husband even after the meteor fell. She missed him though. She missed everyone desperately—the whole big, sweaty, cantankerous, rollicking world.

Willy Transent. She fondled the name in her mind, saying it over and over, so that if he came back next year, she'd remember.

Up in the hills along the ridge where the aspens grew thick, Tana heard a twig snap, followed by a cough and the sound of many walking feet. The sounds carried clear and far in these mountains, and the Bronson boys may not have realized how close they had come to her camp. Tana listened to the boys stalking her, then felt the ground beside her knee. She had five full clips for her AR-17, more than enough to handle these grubbers.

Tana sat in her cave, stared out into the starlight, and wondered about the Mormons. On tough days she imagined that there were golden wheatfields beyond the cave where children could dance and play without a care. Missouri might well be an abundant garden, lush and green, where the living was easy. Dreaming about it made her hard life more bearable. So it had to be out there, somewhere, a place with food, shelter, law, and love.

Or more likely these were all just dreams that the Mormons had died for, and even now their skulls, bleached white by the sun, littered the tall bluegrass on the plains of Kansas.

One of the Bronson boys laughed cruelly, and some of the others made shushing noises, trying to quiet him. Death, stalking the cave. Tana looked out at the skies: dawn was hours away. She could hear them grubbing Bronson boys, softly moving down the long slope of the hill, sliding through the grass on their bellies like snakes.

They're coming, Tana realized, and she didn't know how to stop them. *Let them come then*, she thought. *They might kill me, but they can't drive me out. I'll never let them drive me out!*

Tana stepped out of her cave, set the AR-17 to full automatic, and sprayed the hillside. Someone screamed in terror. In the dim starlight, a dozen shadows howled and danced away in fear. Tana hadn't left so much as a rock on that hillside for cover. They ran full tilt in the darkness, taking long strides as they tried to reach the hilltop and the safety of the trees, and Tana just stood in the open where any one of them could have turned and shot her. She let them escape.

She began panting and found her hands shaking. The grubbers would come back, Tana knew. Maybe they'd even kill her, but they couldn't drive her out of her home. She took comfort, realizing she could have shot them boys. No, no one could drive her out. She had proven that now.

Tana stayed on watch, but her eyes grew itchy, tired. Sometime during the night, she fell asleep and dreamed of a younger Willy, a madman with his teeth kicked out who told her about people who lived in caves and people who just couldn't. His pale blue eyes were flashing like the win lights on a slot machine, and he held a three-sided piece of wood that spun magically in his hands, flashing the messages:

To err is human, to forgive is not state policy.
Tana Rosen, Psychologist.
People are more varied and fascinating than you imagine.

When Tana woke she sat for a long time and forced herself to remember. For years after the meteor she had blocked off her past life, found it hard to think about. Tana believed she didn't need to think about the past because it had become so obsolete. But the fact was she had blocked the memories because it pained her to recall what she had lost.

Tana considered. Civilizations had collapsed before: Pizzaro struck down an Incan king and after five hundred years his people remained scattered like leaves from a fallen oak; a volcano on Crete decimated the capitol of the Minoans, and their culture never rose again; and once the Vandals sacked Rome, its empire began the long spiral into decline. Nothing new. Some civilizations collapsed in an hour, some decayed over centuries. Tana remembered watching the meteor descend—scientists claiming it was larger than the one that had wiped out the dinosaurs—remembered the stark terror that threatened to unknit her muscles, the utter helplessness. For months after people said that those who died of fear before the meteor struck were lucky—they never had to suffer through the blackened skies, spitting volcanoes, skin cancer, starvation, radiation sickness, endless battles.

We sat in our caves, Tana thought, *and we didn't die from lack of goods or thin air: We died from wars and poverty—from lack of composure—symptoms of catastrophe as much as the catastrophe itself.*

So Willy Transent and his people took over. Garbage and lizard eaters, creatures who slept under stars because something in their bones whispered it was right. People who would never suffer shock from losing homes and loved ones because something in their genetic makeup kept them from forming such bonds. For a time they would be the Lords of Earth, the keepers of civilization.

Tana stretched, went outside. A faint summer breeze began blowing through her hair, carrying the scent of dry grasses, bitter sage. Up near the top of the ridge, the green leaves of aspen fluttered in the wind. Tana let the breeze blow over her, just enjoying its texture on her face, in the dark, beneath the vast river of stars. She tried to imagine living without a roof over her head, without some comforting womb-like shelter. She extended her tongue, tasting the ease and freedom mingled with the wide-open horror of life outside the cave.

She could almost feel a presence out there. Something beckoning. Perhaps the voice of a dream.

A startled sparrow peeped on the ridge, and Tana looked up. Willy Transent was standing just inside the line of aspens with a few of his boys, holding a lantern in his right hand, a rifle in his left. His long silver hair billowed in the wind, and he was staring down at Tana. "Hey," Willy shouted, "Tana Rosen, I remember you!" voice hesitant, uncertain. "I remember you—from before. Are you all right?" Relief swept over Tana, more refreshing than the mountain breeze.

After a lifetime lost, someone had found her. An hour before dawn, Tana wrapped her bloody feet in rags, slung her AR-17 under her shoulder, and began the trek down the mountain to Willy's caravan.

SOLITUDE

CAROLYN NICITA

To someone millions of Earth-years old, five months is still a long time to be speared to an aspen tree. Five months of pain should seem a small moment compared to the millions of years he had endured searching for his companion, but to be so close to her, yet unable to do anything—these five months burned darkly in his mind.

His name was the image of himself. In symbolic language he might have been called Jeweled Hang Glider or Phoenix, if he had been named in space, or Harpooned, Dried-Out Manta Ray for the condition he was in now. The name Wing would do. Wing knew he must stay this way, ribs broken, metamorphosed against the atmospheric pressure which threatened to crush him, until he could access a sufficiently radiant energy source to repair him and lift him off the planet.

Those of his species explored the galaxy. They traded mental images with each other and those with whom they made physical contact, images as sharp and concrete as a satellite map. After contact, these images could be sent across the galaxy. His people stayed far from each other, a survival technique to get as diverse a view of the galaxy as possible. Their body-space, their physical comfort zone, could be measured in light years.

Wing was an anomaly among his people. They came together occasionally to make offspring. But Wing had wanted to travel with his companion, wanted to stay too long with the people with whom they had made contact. He delighted in their presence; he needed her company.

After he and his companion had produced several offspring, she made it clear in umistakable images that it was time for them to separate, time to collect disparate visions once more. He wanted to stay, to experience the images with her. What was so marvelous about having separate visions?

Nevertheless, his companion had flown away, millions of years ago. She'd left while he was drinking energy in a volcanic fissure on a gas-giant's moon and had hidden behind a star cluster until he was too far away to catch up when she fled. She had still flung images to the galaxy on her voyage, until she'd gotten stuck on this planet. A large lake between the mountains and the ocean was her last image; then silence for millions of solar years.

The human who finally found Wing was on her lunch break. Chris had answered an ad in the University of Utah *Chronicle* offering season ski passes to Solitude for students who would groom the slopes for two weeks during August. Her mother wanted her to get a real job, one that paid money, which was partly the reason Chris took the Solitude job instead.

She liked the name of the resort. When she found she had to work with others, she was disappointed. She had imagined herself riding the ski lifts, then prancing down the slopes, scooping up a weed here, a Coors can there, combing down the grass with a rake, making sure everything was smooth, ready for her powder skiing on the diamond slopes when the resort opened after Thanksgiving. She obstinately held onto that dream during her first day while she worked amid a group of sweaty people, dragging slashup off the trails and planting duck fir and spruce seedlings for erosion control. The lifts, four-legged spiders spinning towline up the mountain, were motionless in the summer, except on weekends when they lifted mountain bikers to higher slopes.

As for the people working with her, some were crude, some were puritanical, and by the end of the day they all smelled like armpits. By lunch on her second day, she decided she needed a vacation from these people. She put on her backpack and hiked up to eat in the aspen-covered hill across the highway. One of the others had said that aspens were money trees, because of their round leaves. True, in autumn the leaves shivered like pirate's treasure thrown in the air. But to her the trees talked, and what they had to say was more beautiful than human speech.

Wing saw Chris approach through the aspen, her tanned legs in denim shorts and combat boots coming toward the tree where he had been stuck through for so long. She wore no jewelry over the "I Drank Nuclear Fusion" T-shirt, except for the silver crucifix her godfather had given her at her christening.

Wing's entire outer covering served alternately as shield and sight-sensory organ as well as energy collector, and since he had contracted to fend off the atmospheric pressure, he saw her as if through a fisheye lens. He put her images into the hopeful category, binding hot pointers to it, and as she approached, as the image got larger, the pointers became thicker. Three other of these beings had come through this grove and walked on. Perhaps this one would make contact and project the last image he'd gotten from his companion: perhaps this being would know. At least she might free him and take him to an energy source.

To truly learn about a place, about its wonders and its dangers, one must see it through the sensors of its residents. Hadn't they lived there millions of years? They may have seen his companion come.

His species had developed a microorganism to aid them in gathering information. Once in the new host, it attempted to create a bridge in the mind over which images could be passed. But the microorganism must be transmitted by touch.

The human stomped closer, munching on food. Her two eyes, covered in liquid and enfolded in lids of skin, seemed to look in Wing's direction. She passed under the tree but did not stop. Instead she walked on until she was several trees away. She opened a can and slurped at the eruption of fizz.

He had tried flashing lights before, but no help had come. He reflected an intermittent amber flash, as he had seen the vehicles do on the highway.

Chris wondered what was glinting in the tree. She crammed the rest of the sandwich in her mouth and sauntered over. The thing in the tree looked not quite like an oily rag, yet not at all like a dead squirrel with a bike reflector in its mouth. She climbed the tree, wondering how the arrow got there, probably a poacher, and if the tree had grown a burl around the arrow's shaft. She tried to pull it off but it was stuck. She braced herself on a few of the limbs and stuck her fingers between the thing and the tree. The rag-looking thing looked unpromising, so she twisted the arrow out and dropped Wing to examine the arrow. He fell, bounced off a limb, and lay on the ground. Chris noticed that it had left a sticky dust on her hands which she absently tried to wipe off, but Wing's microbes absorbed through her skin anyway. After examining the arrow, she held it like a javelin and tossed it, watching it fly, imagining herself to be Diana, the huntress. Diana would have to fly on Pegasus to get a better view than this.

She noticed that she was looking at herself up in the tree. She almost fell out of the tree. It was as if she were a three-eyed creature whose third eye had plopped to the ground and was now staring back at her.

Wing saw through Chris's eyes and knew they had made the connection. It was comforting to have some company again. The ants with which he'd connected before were blind, no help at all.

He expected a pause in her actions. A being not used to this kind of communication would test out its own sensory devices. It often came over to investigate. Sometimes it would flee in terror. Occasionally it would eat him, and he would eventually pass out the other end of it. He had never encountered a response like hers, though. Chris simply climbed down the tree and walked away.

Wing could only perceive images, not thoughts. If he could, he still would have been puzzled: Chris knew that Wing was an alien. She knew he was transmitting to her. After the shock of realizing this, Chris thought, If I were a visitor to his world, I wouldn't want him to notify his authorities. I would want to be left alone. I wouldn't want him to manipulate my life; I bet he doesn't want me manipulating his life. Nobody would bother him here. Hopefully he would be free for a long time. Chris headed back to Solitude, a bit nervous that she was watching herself walk away from the back, as if at the department store watching a monitor attached to a video camera behind her.

Not that she wasn't curious; in fact she was very curious. She almost went back, then stopped herself. That's what a dog would do, she thought. That's what her co-workers would do. She would respect the alien's privacy. She would content herself with knowing that there is alien life in the universe.

What if he needs help? a stray thought asked. She imagined it was Kermit the Frog on her shoulder, asking her.

It's an alien, she thought back to Kermit. It travels through space. It can help itself.

His view still filled her head, of the aspens, and her back finally disappearing into the trees as she walked away.

By the time she was crossing the highway back toward Solitude, the image had started to change.

She walked into a white flash of fire. Not real enough to burn her, but real enough to be disconcerting.

She froze in the middle of the road, fearing that to move would be dangerous.

The image was instantly followed by a glimpse of what might have been a boat on a dark ocean, its sails edged with tiny lights.

A blowtorch-image. Several blurs of different colors, and a searing eclipse. A honk. This one was audible, a Jeep driver waving her off the highway.

As she ran, it occurred to her that the images had been silent. She visualized a VCR on fast-forward and her hand pushing the pause button.

She caught herself. No I don't want to see this. She visualized pushing the off button and, back in real life, walked to the truck bed, pulling out more seedlings to plant in the erosion-control area. She worked faster so the forewoman wouldn't think she was goofing off, like FrizzHead who came to work on his motorcycle and drove it up mountain bike trails during lunch. No one would manipulate her. But what did these visions mean?

She stomped a shovel into the topsoil and tucked a pine seedling into the gap it made. She planted one beside it to keep it company, even though when they grew they would be too close together.

The image came: a VCR, a finger pushing the pause button. Her image. Then the fire image. It stayed, as if on pause. This gave her time to get used to it. She realized there was nothing to fear, they were just visions. Her mind didn't feel as if it were warping, she didn't feel an uncontrollable urge to run towards the alien or do anything bizarre. It was only an image. A vision of fire.

When Chris started getting bored with the image, when her thoughts started to wander, the image changed, became the boat image. It stayed; it remained long enough for her to realize that what she thought was a boat was in space: a wire-frame firebird sailing on solar flares—she could see embers spraying off, outlining its wings. Then she saw a progression of images until the firebird metamorphosed into a manta, rowing through the troposphere of an orange-green planet.

She seemed to be soaring nearby, because she could see the spray blowing off herself, as if she could see in 360 degrees, though she could not see what she was. They were flying toward a volcano on the surface—

"Are you all right?" It was the forewoman.

Chris looked around. Several other people were staring at her.

One played ventriloquist. "Earth to Chris," he called.

Chris apologized and restarted her body planting seedlings, wondering how long she'd been staring at her shovel. Obviously these people had no idea what was going on. She was possessor of a great secret.

The secret image was still in her mind, and she worked and tried to keep it in focus at the same time. It was a bit like walking and chewing gum, she thought, but you have to remember to keep chewing.

She tried another image, the image of the alien himself.

The alien sent back images: An alien. It looked not quite like himself. Fire. The alien flapping into fire. The manta-firebird, much larger and glowing, flying out of the fire. Chris deduced that the fire changed these manta aliens into firebirds. So that was it, he was asking for fire. Hot fire.

Another image: A lake. A large lake as seen from space, from a planet that looked the same color as the Earth, the same as NASA pictures of Earth. It also had a large moon, like Earth.

A pointer. Zoom in on the place to which it pointed. Then: the other firebird.

Chris thought of the manta in the image, and the manta in the aspen grove. There were two of them, she realized. One had markings in a pattern on its ventral side, one had a >:' mark.

Why didn't he show them together? Chris wondered. She visualized the two different aliens sitting next to each other. Is this right? Are there actually two different aliens?

When Wing received that image he was astonished. How did she do that? How could this earth-bound human possibly have seen Wing and his companion together when they had not been together for millions of years?

Wing's people, like many in the galaxy, do not have imaginations. Their minds lay memories, like bricks into mortar, which then set fast. They recall things they have seen and felt and touch them in new and interesting sequences, making new meanings, but they cannot synthesize a new possibility. Wing and his species thought new thoughts by taking existing images and splicing them together, the way a film editor assembles a movie. He didn't know that humans had a special-effects department in their brains. Usually the inability to synthesize images was not a problem. After living several million years, one of Wing's species usually had enough images to cope with any situation. Occasionally he erased some images to make room in his memory. Hundred-thousand-year flights between solar systems usually got erased first. Wing kept all memories of his companion, and none of these memories looked like Chris's vision. So how could she have acquired this image? Time dilates, Wing knew. Time does strange things. Could this be a future image? Predicting the future seemed more plausible than completely synthesizing an image, so Wing concluded that this human was predicting the future. He stored Chris's image in a prominent place in his memory.

He sent other images to Chris. He put images together as she would put words together to make a sentence, or as film editors put shots together to make a scene.

Images from very long ago that others of his kind had sent to him of them together.

When the other phoenix bird flew farther and farther away, the images came faster. Chris figured that the other bird was leaving him.

Chris was moved. This alien was hurting inside. Attempting to ask him if he was lonely, if more were coming, Chris imagined one lone alien, then two, then several. Wing assumed that Chris had never seen several aliens flying together. He recited the vision back to her exactly as she gave it to him, no additions, no appending messages.

All afternoon he told her of his companion, how she left, how she had sent a distress message, and how he had come to find her. He showed Chris the vision his companion had sent, of the lake. He showed her where he had looked, intercut with the vision of the lake. He showed Coastal Northern California, ocean too big to be his companion's lake; Idaho, lakes too small; Great Salt Lake, no volcanic activity. Lake Mead and the Gulf of California were too far south. The visions came slowly, mournfully.

After work, Chris went back to the aspen forest. She scooped Wing into her arms and carried him to the front seat of her mother's car.

They drove down the road that mimics Big Cottonwood Creek flowing to the Salt Lake Valley. Chris was able to pick out Highway 152 from Wing's winter view of the mountains. She drove slowly, looking at the shoulders to see if his companion might be among the roadkill. The alien had not told her where his friend might be; she could be anywhere.

What would it be like to fly through space? she wondered. She imagined herself, arms spread out, visiting quasars and nebulae. I would love to do that, she thought. Maybe he will teach me how.

They approached the Lake Bonneville historical plaque.

Lake Bonneville.

Chris stomped on the brake pedal. Her interest was transmitted to Wing both by her mental calculations and her braking, which had thrown him to the floor.

Lake Bonneville. Chris got out and read the sign. It said that Lake Bonneville had existed 300 million years ago. Was it Lake Bonneville he had seen? When did it finally dry up? She knew from school and museums that the Great Salt Lake was a remnant. How could that be the lake though, when the continent it was on didn't look anything like North America? She remembered the large moon, which looked like Earth's. But nobody lives that long, she thought.

She looked at him. Who could tell? He was an alien. She reviewed the images he had sent her. She didn't have enough knowledge of science to tell how old the images were. In the visions of North America, the people she saw wore contemporary clothing. She had not seen any cavemen or Indians wearing feathers. Who knows how old he is?

She would go to the library to figure out Lake Bonneville.

She drove to the campus library, stopping only for food through the drive-in window at McDonald's.

Wing rode in Chris's backpack, watching the library's denizens through Chris's eyes. These beings seemed to be feeding off the materials of this place, letting the pages radiate onto their faces, as if deriving nourishment from them. The place evoked memories for Chris. He got frequent, disparate visions from her, some incomprehensible. Maybe touching these books and carrels and shelves made someone see the future, like touching his microbes made them see into his mind. When Chris got to the map section he transmitted an image of himself in Chris's hands. In the map area, Chris brought him out. He touched the map. It didn't bring anything to Wing's mind so he let Chris tuck him back in the backpack. He watched from her eyes since the view out of them was more interesting.

Chris watched him touch the map and tried to guess what he was thinking. She couldn't help but get carried away by the romance. This couple had not seen each other for a long time, possibly millions of years. Soon they would be together—two beings that could see each other's souls. She looked at the maps. He could travel these in a few minutes. She imagined the aliens flying together. Two of them, leaving this earth, perhaps to join others; and Chris would fly with them, exploring. If only in her mind's eye.

As she studied the maps, Chris learned that Lake Bonneville disappeared about 50 million years ago, before the Cenozoic Ice Ages. Sometimes the lake was small and sometimes it was huge, even extending into Idaho and Nevada and connecting to the Pacific Ocean. She explored the different maps and noticed where the mountain slopes had been. She searched for Wing's image and found the map that matched it most closely, a phase of Lake Bonneville about 60 million years ago that had lasted for only about 50 years. The mountains were different then as well. She compared it with the U.S. Geological Survey maps of present-day Wasatch Front. Then she put her imagination to work once more. She mentally pushed up mountains, evaporated the lake, creating Bonneville Salt Flats, leaving puddles; she rose mountains, changing the track of the Snake River, built Hoover, Deer Creek, and Jordanelle Dams, and let the runoff from the Provo River trickle into Utah Lake for him, all the time keeping track of the spot where his companion landed. Wing was in awe.

That night Chris slept in her bed, which was in her mother's attic. Wing, who never slept, watched the chaotic visions coming from her brain. He was certain she was traveling the past and future, seeking his companion, and her brain was becoming feverish with the effort. Surely they would find her, if this human survived the experience.

The spot was a quarry at the mouth of Big Cottonwood Canyon. Chris skipped work and went to the quarry before dawn. She felt a little guilty, then angry that she had allowed herself to be tied down to a job.

She looked for the spot, using the topographical map she'd photocopied last night as a guide. Though the alien had it in his mind, she had the map because her images weren't perfect, and she tended to forget and invent things.

Chris climbed over the quarry fence into the gravel pit, away from the guard station. Although there was security, she assumed it would be down the road guarding the machinery, not the piles of boulders that Wing wanted to check. Chris wondered what Wing would do if the gravel company had ground up his companion and poured her into the cement foundation of the ZCMI Mall. But evidently he felt her in here some-where. His thoughts came in staccato images.

Chris walked around the gravel quarry. She tried to go where Wing directed her by vision. He transmitted the images, whispers that looked like abstract paintings. Chris wondered if it would look like a manta or a firebird. She wondered if it would glow.

When they finally uncovered her under a pile of stones, Chris was disappointed. She looked like a fossil. Wing started moving wildly in the backpack as she picked up what he'd indicated—what looked like a fist-sized black trilobite. Evidently when they were this small and hard, the gravel crushers couldn't crush them. It had been thrown into a pile of larger rocks. Wing was ecstatic, Chris could tell from the rapidity of the images streaking past her mind's eye.

The fire visions came to her again. Did that mean they needed to warm each other up? Chris put the fossil into her backpack with Wing. Maybe they were going to kiss, or whatever they did, and they would both fly out of her backpack. She zipped up the backpack.

Fire, he sent. Volcanoes, suns, sprays of fire, hot fire whirlpools, explosions, then he repeated the image he had sent before, of his companion, as a manta, flying into fire and flying out as the firebird.

Chris remembered the images of his companion flying with him into a volcano.

Wing's companion had become dormant. She had not been injured the way Wing had, so she was just waiting for energy. Either volcanic activity would catch up to her, or the planet would explode, or it would draw too close to a dying sun. But Chris understood that they needed heat.

Where would I find intense heat, she wondered. She looked west over the dry Bonneville lake bed, now covered with houses. He's talking volcanoes. I don't think pouring gasoline over these aliens and setting them on fire would be hot enough. Where can we get heat like that? She looked around. The weather was clear now; in the winter a blanket of smog closed in over the valley because of the mountains. She thought of Morton Thiokol, the company that made rocket boosters for the space shuttle. That was an hour north in Ogden. She wasn't sure that they could survive a blast like that, though. She didn't remember any volcanoes in the vicinity, except Mount St. Helens, and she didn't have enough money to get all the way to the Cascade Range.

Across the valley were mountains whose tops had been cut off.

Kennecott, the world's largest open-pit copper mine. The planet's largest open wound. You can even see it from space. From here it looked like a volcano. She imagined lava pouring out of the mountain.

Don't they need heat to get the copper out of the ore? she wondered. What if I brought these two to Kennecott?

Chris had forgotten that security around Kennecott would be tighter than at a gravel pit. However, the guards were helpful. They told Chris that the smelter was seven miles north of the mine. She had in her naïveté imagined tractors scraping chunks of ore out of the crater and throwing them into a bubbling cauldron of molten metal. She'd just toss the aliens in, and they'd have their heat. Then they'd fly off, most probably remolded into one unified being, incidentally leaving her the secret of space travel so she could follow. But she knew that if she asked the smelter guards, "Hi. Can I throw a couple of aliens into your smelter?" they would throw her out. So what could she do? She didn't know anybody who worked at Kennecott.

One of her high school teachers, a humanities teacher who liked to talk about everything except the lesson, had proposed a theory he'd heard. He said that you are four contacts from everybody else in the world. For example: Chris might know a foreign exchange student from France, whose anthropology professor had done his doctorate in Papua New Guinea, where he had met a young boy whose shaman third cousin had discovered the plant that could kill the AIDS virus. In the case of celebrities you were three people away.

Where could she make the four-person link? Maybe she would just ask her mother, though she hated to depend on her for anything.

Her mother worked at a bank but knew a neighbor who worked at Kennecott. Chris's mother was so enthusiastic about her daughter expressing an interest in some sort of career that she immediately had her neighbor arrange a tour with one of the metallurgical engineers. That had been only two people away.

Chris kept the aliens in a cat bed in her bedroom until the day of the tour. She tried attaching Wing to a paper clip stuck in a wall socket, but the energy draw flipped the circuit breaker. Setting him on fire with gasoline did nothing, as she had supposed.

She planned how to sneak the aliens into the smelter. The fossilized alien she could stick in a pants pocket, but she would wear the larger one under a baggy shirt, in case she had to check her purse at the gate.

She tried on the costume and stood in front of the bathroom mirror. She thought she looked like a pregnant man, but it would have to do.

She knew she would get into trouble. Maybe she could pretend to be under the alien's spell, brainwashed, and she would avoid too long a stay in jail. If the Kennecott people started to suspect her, she would collapse and moan "Where am I?" While they fussed over her, she would watch the two newly-born phoenix birds sail out of view, together forever.

The tour was different from her expectations. She took it with five new employees. Chris was sweating. It was summertime, they were in a factory, and she was wearing a sweatshirt and two aliens. The tour guide droned on for an hour, and Chris still had not seen any cauldrons of molten metal, only a few places where a trickle poured into some trays.

When the group got to a Cathode-something process, the guide proclaimed the tour nearly finished. Chris realized there might not be any cauldrons. The stream of molten copper she now saw pouring out of a trough onto a moving plate might be her only opportunity. Wing had seen it through her eyes and was sending images of it back to her, as if urging her toward it.

Chris fixed her eyes on the stream. She waited until the tour guide ushered the group into the corridor to the next area. Then she crept back past the barrier to the cathode area and tossed the aliens into the stream. She saw the fire in her head. This time the fire image was live. Chris backed away to keep from being burned by the sprays of molten copper. In the stream Wing and his companion became pliable, self-locomotive, easily able to keep up with the moving machinery under them. They splashed around in the stream like waterfowl playing in a birdbath.

They glowed. They grew larger, and their movements were more flowing, swift. The light in Chris's eyes blended with the light in her head. She could not tell which was molten copper and which was alien.

A blinding light launched and crashed through the skylight, as if it had been shot from a flare gun.

Was that him? Chris wondered. No, the firelight was still in her head. It must be Wing's companion.

She looked down, trying to blink the afterimages out of her eyes.

A second light shot up, a tracer bullet, following the flare.

"Aren't you going to stay?" she yelled. She realized her sense of loss. At least they left together, she thought.

But fire from molten metal still glowed in her mind's eye. She looked back at the glowing stream. One—Wing—was still on the plate, drowning in copper. The area where he had been injured was swollen.

Then what was the other light? It must have been a baby, like the other offspring she had seen in Wing's previous images. Why isn't he leaving? she wondered. Where are the others? Aren't they at least going to wait for him?

She remembered her mental pictures of them flying away together and realized that he would have been watching, also. Now he was watching her. She could see herself in his image. He threw her image back into her mind, the one she had synthesized of Wing and his companion flying together. He showed, in rapid succession, the picture of the two flares leaving, followed by one of Chris, then the synthesized pictures again. Then Chris, live. Chris knew what he meant. Liar, he was saying. Liar.

Alarms rang. The machinery stopped rolling, the stream of molten lava shut off. The molten copper, which had splashed over the cathode wheel, solidified. It cemented Wing to the plate under the trough.

She sprang forward to break him loose. The heat warned her back. She crouched and ran back to the barrier, looking for a tool to pry him off.

She assessed the situation, wondering how she could get him unstuck before someone came and took him away. If he can't fly, she thought, at least he'll stay here.

At that moment Wing shook himself loose. He glowed but faintly. He crawled into the air, pushing himself to follow the other two lights.

In her mind Chris saw Wing's fading visions. She saw herself recede. She saw the top of the smelter, and she saw the sky. She had been left behind. Her fantasies of flying into space with them had disappeared; she despised herself for having needed those aspirations in the first place. Chris saw the tour guide running toward her. She sat, waiting for the consequences. Wing was alone. His visions of isolation made solitude intolerable. They would for the rest of her life.

She wept. The tour guide comforted her, not understanding.

Chris never gave her "Where am I" speech. When the tour guide discovered she was missing, he came back in time to see Wing's ex-companion leave. The guide had reported the malfunction and ordered the copper flow shutoff. He saw Chris huddled on the floor and feared his own negligence had gotten her hurt. Subsequent investigations were conducted without Chris.

Back home in her mother's attic, Chris tried to remember what she was feeling at the library. She felt as if she were molding destinies, participating in a timeless fairy tale. The prince finds the princess, and they fly together for the rest of eternity. For all she knew, maybe the other alien was an assassin, or maybe Wing tried to push her into volcanoes. Still Chris longed for that surrogate companionship. She felt ashamed.

As he left Earth's thermosphere, Wing checked his energy resources. He would have enough energy to get out of the planet's gravity well, out to a sufficiently low atmospheric pressure that he could become a gossamer spacefaring creature hundreds of meters in wingspan, able to tack the force of solar particles once again. He would have to sail more slowly than the others though, left farther behind every year.

The human had lied to him. He knew he could not get true visions from this planet. This was no place for his species.

As for Chris, haunted by this alien's solitary visions, assuaging loneliness would be her foremost need for the rest of her life. Chris viewed Earth through Wing's eyes. I live on this planet, with these people, she thought. She would accept that, but refused ever to be satisfied with it.

And Wing knew that his species needed to see things from different points of view, far from each other. But he refused ever to be satisfied with it.

OUTSIDE THE TABERNACLE

B. J. FOGG

very six months Zo reluctantly gathered with the faithful. Salt Lake City. Temple Square. The Mormon Tabernacle. Zo pressed shoulders with the devout to hear words from living prophets.

General conference was a tradition for Mormons. And for Zo's relatives. Every April and October his family tree transplanted to Temple Square for the weekend. His ancestors had always done the same—except they congregated in fields to hear Joseph Smith prophesy; later they stopped beside their handcarts to learn Brigham Young's plan for taming the west. A long heritage. When it came to Mormons, Zo's blood ran the deepest blue.

"It's just not right that we should have to wait in line like this," his grandmother said. She held her purse close to her chest and shook her head. "Like we're some sort of cattle."

Zo had waited in line for over an hour with Zinnie, his grandmother. The line filed slowly into the Tabernacle, past the ushers at door #22, for the final session of general conference.

"Are you cold?" Zo said. He put his arm around Zinnie and squeezed. An early October chill had settled into the Salt Lake Valley.

"No." Zinnie said. "I'd just like a place to sit—a place close to where Grandfather Richards once sat."

When Zo first moved into Zinnie's house four months ago, he wasn't sure how long it would last: a Mormon gypsy living with his pioneer grandmother.

Two of his cousins had tried living with Zinnie before. Both set-ups were disasters. Zinnie always fretted about them, as if they were children, even though one was twenty-four and had preached two years in Panama. Zinnie couldn't handle his late hours. He soon moved out.

When Zo's other cousin needed a place to stay, Zinnie had no real choice. His cousin had no other place to go except her boyfriend's house. It was disaster either way: live with Zinnie and drive her crazy, or live with her boyfriend and get pregnant. Zinnie absorbed the shock, softened the blow with the resilience that was in her pioneer blood. But Zinnie quickly found her granddaughter a cheap apartment nearby.

So when Zo told Zinnie that his marriage was ending soon and he would need a place to stay, he was surprised when she agreed. Not readily, of course. But she did agree. And that was something indeed. The next Tuesday he got a package in the mail. A fat letter written in script that looked as if it came straight from the grade school handwriting books. It was Zinnie's hand. Zo knew that. And it was Zinnie's long list of house rules. Something Zo probably should have guessed.

Zo had spent the better part of the last year getting in and out of temporal marriages. The Brethren had recently authorized this new arrangement: "temporal marriages." Mormon men over thirty-five could now wed Mormon women over thirty for a three-month trial period. This new marriage carried all the respectability of regular "eternal marriages," the traditional Mormon wedding that would last not just for this life but through all eternity. Eternal marriage: mind-boggling, yes. But also daunting to Zo and many of his generation, so at a recent conference in Salt Lake City the Brethren announced the time had come to "Strengthen the Homefront," starting with the temporal marriage covenant. And like frequent flier miles, it had a neat twist: after three months couples could upgrade their temporal marriages to eternal ones, if they so desired.

This focus on marriage was not without precedent. Fifteen years earlier, just as Zo entered his marriageable Mormon prime, the prophet issued all single brethren a new commandment: "Rise from the dust and be men." Some of Zo's buddies got engaged that very night. But many of them, like Zo, sank even deeper in the dust—eternal bachelors, destined never to reach the highest level of heaven.

The intent of the most recent announcement was of course clear to

Zo: You've got no excuse now, so get married—and *soon*. Although most Americans lived with loose—if any—family ties, when a Mormon wasn't bound into a mom-and-pop household, church leaders didn't know what to do. And too many stray cats were wandering away, especially the unattached males.

Newspapers across the country gave the announcement little press, saying the Mormons were finally giving in to what most Americans had been doing for years: living together. But to the Mormons and Zo's family, temporal marriage was a big revelation. A sign of the last days. Zo thought it wonderful—and certainly no stranger than the polygamous marriages of his Mormon ancestors.

For some reason Zo and Grandma Zinnie hit it off. He always knew he was her favorite grandchild. And keeping Zinnie company while they waited in line for general conference seemed natural, except for one thing: usually Zo and his relatives were escorted effortlessly into the Tabernacle. Door #4 would open, the usher would scan their passes, discover their heritage, and they'd be in. No waiting. But that day Mormon leaders from around the world filled the main floor of the Tabernacle; they were special guests of the Twelve Apostles. A month before, a letter from church headquarters apologized to Zo's family for any inconvenience this might cause.

Of course, Zinnie had the option of watching conference at home, like most Mormons do. The church satellite beamed the sermons into living rooms around the world. But Zinnie wanted to come in person, she said: "Tradition."

"Ritual," Zo thought. General conference was always the same thing: Men in white shirts and blue suits; women in dresses and heels. Children looking like advertisements for Easter shopping sprees. Even the music from the Mormon Tabernacle Choir, warm-up hymns no doubt, seemed another rerun. Soft tones from the pipe organ wafted as subtly as mist through the crowd. Everyone was getting ready for the Sunday afternoon meeting of general conference, the culminating session, a kind of Mormon celebration. Most of the faithful had settled down onto blankets. Scattered like confetti across Temple Square lawns, the blankets might have passed for a communal picnic.

In the past Zo had done the blanket thing with girlfriends he hoped to impress. While outside he never heard much of the sermons—there was too much life going on around him—but once, when sitting on the lawn, he almost got his picture in the official church magazine. Unfortunately, Zo got cropped out, although his friend (who was sitting next to Zo and his girlfriend at the time) appeared in the next issue. His friend looked thoughtful. Transcendent even. And it wasn't the first time a church videographer had caught Zo's friend transcending. Zo knew that the lawn outside the Tabernacle had its advantages.

But waiting in line wasn't one of them. All of Zinnie's descendants—Zo's family, his cousins and aunts and uncles—had arrived much earlier on Temple Square. They were already inside the Tabernacle. Zo agreed to bring Zinnie later, as soon as she woke up from her nap. Now standing forty yards back in line with three minutes till broadcast time, Zo doubted they'd make it inside. But he didn't say anything.

"Since I was twelve," Zinnie said, "I've never missed a session."

"Really?" Zo said, though he already knew. Zinnie had made this announcement at the start of every session for as long as he could remember. He knew what would follow: Zinnie's story about meeting the prophet Lorenzo Snow, the inspiration for Zo's first name—Lorenzo—a name he found remarkably old fashioned.

"That's right." Zinnie opened her purse and fished around. "Ever since that morning Grandfather Richards took me inside and introduced me to the prophet. I wore a pink bow in my hair—still have it, I do—and the prophet said I was as lovely as a spring morning." Zinnie wiped her glasses with a Kleenex.

When Zo first moved into Zinnie's house, she escorted him down the stairs to her basement, which was carpeted but always colder than upstairs. Zinnie held her arm out as she gave Zo the grand tour. His bedroom. His bed. A place in the closet for his clothes. His bathroom. Fresh towels there. Zo almost laughed at Zinnie's formality. He'd been coming to Utah and spending vacations in Zinnie's Farmington basement since he was a child. But those were short visits with marked departures. This time Zo didn't know when he would leave.

Zo soon realized that Grandma Zinnie had prepared herself for his arrival. On his first visit to the bathroom, he found a note posted above the toilet: "The toilet is to be flushed after each usage." It was Zinnie's handwriting in red ink on a torn strip of binder paper, something like a message from a school teacher. Under the lid he found another note, taped securely: "One should close the lid upon finishing." After a brief search he decided that Zinnie had attached marginalia to every corner of her house. And of course it was for Zo. To stop him from every possible breach of etiquette or lapse of gentility. He would later find her notes on the TV remote control, on the phone directory, in her freezer. And he obeyed them.

Since living at Zinnie's, Zo had met many eligible sisters in the Farmington congregation. Mainly school teachers and secretaries. But Claudine caught his eye the third Sunday in church. She sat alone in the pew on the far west wall of the chapel. Her face followed the words of the speaker so vigorously that Zo thought her eyes alone could interpret for the deaf.

But in retrospect Zo had to admit it was more than Claudine's intensity that fascinated him. It was her look. Zo couldn't place her. Ethnically speaking, that is. Was she black or Polynesian or Latin? Perhaps Southeast Asian? Zo couldn't tell. And he didn't really care either. A few weeks later, Zo and Claudine began talking temporal marriage, but they found one major problem: equity. Although Claudine had a job, neither Zo nor Claudine had a home.

The prelude music from the Tabernacle stopped. The ushers began to close each door, apologizing to those still in line. The people in front of Zinnie wandered away slowly, but she still hadn't noticed.

"Zinnie," Zo said. "Let's go watch conference in the Visitor's Center. It's really comfortable in there." Quite frankly Zo would rather watch conference from those plush seats. It was like an upscale movie theater.

"Visitor's Center? I'm not a *visitor* here. I'm Zina Richards Pratt. Who could ever mistake me for a visitor?" At that moment Zinnie finally noticed the line was gone. She marched up to the usher outside door #22.

"I'm sorry, sister," the usher said, his arms moving out from his sides, his palms up. "The Tabernacle is full. You can view conference in the Assembly Hall or the Vis—"

"Why should I go anywhere else?" Zinnie said. She took her pedigree pass from her purse and held it out to him. Zo had a similar pass in his wallet; it verified his genealogy. "I would like to enter," she said.

"Sister Pratt," he said, reading her name. "Please." He shrugged his shoulders, placed one finger over his lips, and bowed his head for the opening prayer. Loudspeakers broadcast a deep voice throughout Temple Square like the voice of God.

Zo closed his eyes. When he said amen, Zinnie was gone.

Claudine would be Zo's third attempt at marriage. When the Brethren announced the temporal marriage policy, Zo took advantage. Twice. Both ended quickly. At least they were convenient, Zo thought. The women he had married were both professionals. They had their own money and their own apartments. Zo had neither.

Zo's big draw was his marital status: single. Unattached Mormon males were at a premium. That's how he hooked into his first spiritual partner, Tooley. She was surplus. Bright, beautiful, wealthy—but surplus just the same. Tooley grew up in New England. Schooled in Boston. But because Mormons were scarce in the east, she rarely met Mormon men. And she was determined to hold out for the eternal partner, that "one-and-only" her girlhood Sunday school teachers had talked so much about. He would come . . . some day. They promised. So Tooley turned down date after date from the gentile men around her, and she waited.

During those quiet evenings and long nights, Tooley tapped into her creative motherlode: designing trinkets to hide in breakfast-cereal boxes. She later confided to Zo that her talent for conceiving just the right cereal-box surprise was not a talent at all—it was a spiritual gift. The gadgetry she invented—high tech but low budget—was nothing short of revelation. Kellogg's was her first major account; their sales skyrocketed. Then it was Nabisco. Soon enough every cereal maker in America was wining and dining her. But no men.

Then Zo came along.

He'd just finished a hot-air balloon safari through the last of the Kenyan game preserves when he opted for a layover at JFK on his way back to Utah. A two-day layover, time to rediscover the city. That Sunday morning in New York, Zo gathered with the Mormons in Manhattan. Tooley sat next to Zo, quite by accident; she shared her hymnal with him, quite on purpose. She smiled. Took Zo home. Fed him. Gave him her razor to shave with. She pressed a seam into all his jeans before he could say good-bye.

After a week in Utah, Zo returned to New York. To Tooley of course. The bishop there authorized the temporal marriage. Zo wed Tooley in the temple and moved into her apartment. The whole thing was fast, but no one objected—not Zo's parents, not his home-congregation bishop.

Zo was after all thirty-seven years old. And the marriage arrangement was after all only temporary.

Zo found Grandma Zinnie leaning against the cement wall that separates the temple from the Tabernacle. She was looking at the temple spires. She stared as if she were some bird of prey and the temple were a mouse she would soon pounce on. Zo stood behind her and looked up too. The temple spires cut sharply into the pale autumn sky, and Zo remembered his heritage.

Sort of. All those Sunday school lessons on temple history and Zo still wasn't sure he had it right. He remembered that they spent forty years building the Salt Lake temple. (Yes, that's right, he thought: forty years.) And not only did his ancestors donate time and skills, but at one point Brigham Young asked everyone to donate their china plates. (Now was it Brigham and Salt Lake? Or was it Joseph Smith and Nauvoo?) Zo's ancestors had cradled their china so carefully over the ocean and across the plains. But at Brigham's request (maybe it *was* Joseph) the early Saints sacrificed their only indulgence. The workmen crushed the china plates to make a coating for the temple walls—a prophet's plan to make the temple sparkle. (If it was indeed this temple, Zo thought, the coating must have fallen off.)

Zinnie took Zo by the arm, and she began to walk. She led Zo the length of the temple wall. She never looked down until they reached the gate.

"I'm going to Crossroads," she said, now looking at the shopping mall across the street.

"But it's Sunday," Zo said.

"I'm sure the mall's open just the same."

She was right. Though Salt Lake was a city full of Mormons—people admonished not to shop on the Sabbath—Crossroads Mall never rested.

Zo barely made it to the three-month mark with Tooley. He knew that now, but at the time he really thought his temporal marriage would become eternal. Sex was always good and they were friends—Zo thought. Tooley didn't seem to mind the fact that Zo didn't work or that he'd spend each day "exploring the city," as he called it.

The problem appeared much sillier: Zo was deep into his leg-weight phase. Zo's ancestors had given him their skinny-leg genes, and he was determined to beef those bony legs up. So he vowed to wear leg weights constantly for six months. He wore them on safari, to church the first time in Manhattan, to his wedding. And—yes—when Zo and Tooley lost their virginity together, Zo was wearing those leg weights, Velcroed loosely around his ankles.

He finally took the weights off two months later, the night Tooley cried quietly on the phone in the kitchen while talking to her mother. "Whatever," Zo said over and over as he took the weights off. "Whatever," he said as he floated around the apartment to Tooley's weeping, his legs buoyant like buoys. (And no, he hadn't gained a pound from all this. Just a rash.)

Despite Zo's willingness to compromise, Tooley filed for temporal separation at three months. The Brethren granted it.

"Two tickets, please," Zinnie said, sliding a twenty through the hole in the box office window.

Zo had never been to a movie before on a Sunday. He wasn't even sure what movie was showing. Zo looked at the marquis: *Forgotten Frontier.* Never heard of it. So many movies now with desktop video. Everyone was a film producer.

"What do you know about this flick?" Zo asked Zinnie.

"Nothing," she said taking the tickets. She handed one to Zo.

He knew the tables were turning. Zo once took Zinnie to a movie when he was seventeen: *Out of Africa.* Zo's brother went along, and so did a single date—for both brothers. One girl, one grandmother, and two brothers. To be even weirder, Zo and his brother kept switching seats after frequent trips to the lobby. By the end of the night, their date was visibly confused about who she was dating. She sat with her arms folded, eyes straight ahead, not responding to their comments. Zinnie thought her grandkids brutes, but she finally agreed to escort the date to her front door, while the brothers busted up in the front seat.

"You want popcorn?" Zo said to Zinnie.

"Popcorn? Yes, I love popcorn," she said. "And a Coke Supreme."

Zo spent the next ninety minutes coaching Zinnie on the movie's features: decision trees and role-playing options. All new to her. She hadn't been to a theater in nearly ten years.

When Zo and Zinnie returned to Temple Square, the Tabernacle Choir was singing. Zo hoped it was the closing hymn, because he wasn't in the mood for preaching. The movie was silly and downright bawdy in parts. Zinnie surprised Zo by choosing the raciest plots and laughing a lot. Loud. Zo laughed at her laughing.

"Let's wait by the flagpole," Zo said. Another tradition: his family gathered by the flagpole at the end of each session. There Zo would see family and friends and a lot of familiar faces—not that he knew everyone by name, but he always found the same people at the flagpole; another crowd at the fountain; others on the north side of the tabernacle. Zo realized that the bi-yearly rhythm of conference weekend marked the passages in his life, perhaps more clearly than Christmas or Easter. Everything happened either before or after General Conference.

"I hope they don't ask what we thought of any of the sermons," Zo said.

"Just say they were wonderful," Zinnie said, smiling. "They always have been in the past."

With his toe Zo began tracing the map etched into the concrete patio. The world. The flagpole emerged from the top of the world. Zo knew Zinnie was watching him, so he took grand-daddy steps from one continent to the other, just as if he were playing "Mother-May-I?"

Zinnie smiled again: Yes, you may. That smile: eerie, haunting. Too much like the look Zo's second wife gave him the Saturday he left her. That morning Zo simply waved good-bye to Margo and got in the pick-up truck. But before Zo shut the door, he was back out again. He walked slowly to Margo, who leaned against the patio railing, looking like someone out of a mail-order catalog. Without looking her in the face, Zo wrapped his arms around her and kissed her on the forehead. Chastely. As an apology. Or an affirmation. Or a thank you. Or maybe it was all those things. And perhaps none. Margo then gave him that smile, and Zo walked back to the truck and drove away. All this without saying a word. That was the end of temporal marriage number two.

For Zinnie's amusement Zo began hopping from one concrete country to the other, as if he were in a sack race, somehow hoping to overwhelm her with his buffoonery. That was when Zo heard his mother's voice.

"Oh, Zinnie!" Zo's mother said, trotting in high heels toward the flagpole. "Aren't you excited?"

"Yes, it was wonderful," Zinnie said.

Zo's mother hugged Zinnie and kissed her on the cheek. "We'll do everything we can to help get you ready. We'll have to figure out a wardrobe and then pack the house up . . . "

Zinnie gave Zo a puzzled look over his mother's shoulder. Zo shrugged slightly.

His father arrived with Zo's uncle. They both hugged Zinnie. "We're right behind you, Ma," his dad said.

"Our Zinnie—a temple missionary," his mother said, clasping her hands. Zinnie looked to Zo for help. Neither knew about any temple missions.

"You know, Mom," Zo said. "I didn't quite get what—uh—Elder What's-his-name said. We ended up the in Visitor's Center and could hardly hear a word."

"Well, the Brethren have called all members over the age of seventy to serve full-time temple missions," she said. "That means they'll call Zinnie to serve in one of the temples, and she'll live right on the temple grounds."

"For how long?" Zo said. He knew that church members had microfilmed all the available genealogy in the world, that computers had sketched out the family tree of humanity, and that technology could not solve their biggest bottleneck: Real-live, flesh-and-blood people had to perform the vicarious ordinances in the temple. Most Mormons were just too busy to sit through the long temple sessions very often.

"Zinnie will spend the rest of her life there—on holy ground," his mother said, her eyes rolled upward to the lighted temple spires.

"That's wonderful," Zinnie said with a quiver. Her hands fluttered about her face, latched onto her glasses, then brushed the sides of her hairdo. She finally clutched her purse to her chest. "That's just wonderful," Zinnie whispered, shaking her head.

While moving Zinnie to the Idaho Falls temple the next November, Zo would pack up her belongings carefully and snugly. The Brethren allowed each temple missionary to arrive with a small U-Haul of possessions. No more. So most of Zinnie's things would stay with the house. And Zo would be the guardian.

It would be Zo's house now, a place for him and Claudine to begin his third temporal marriage. Together they would take down the oil paintings and replace them with framed prints. They'd change the blinds to curtains. They'd reset Zinnie's local TV channels to satellite stations from around the world.

But Zo knew that the house wouldn't really be their home until he had detached and discarded every last note Zinnie wrote in red ink on binder paper. For weeks they'd find notes everywhere—in the pantry, on the broom handle, on the dryer door, in the fuse box. They'd trash all of these. And then one day, after two years of living with Claudine, Zo would find the very last note, nailed behind the shed door: "Wash hands after being outside." Zo would smile as he removed the paper carefully, folded it, and slipped it into his breast pocket. This would be the only note Zo would save.

SPACE PEOPLE

JAMES CUMMINGS

*T*hey have just passed the city limits sign and are beginning to cross the salt desert when Cindy says she thinks she sees a bright, white light appear just on the horizon, where the blue glow of the sunset still lingers.

Don, who's driving, says, "Where?"

Cindy leans over the front seat, pointing. "It was over there," she says. "It's gone."

Don laughs. "Cindy, you're such a hysteric."

"I am not," Cindy says. She falls back into her seat, crosses her arms. "I saw a light."

"No one else did," Don says.

"I think I did," Jule says.

"You think you did," Don says. He rolls down the window an inch and lights a cigarette. "What does that mean? Either you saw it or you didn't."

Jule says, "I was looking out the side window. I sort of caught it out of the corner of my eye when I turned my head."

"No light," Don says, "is going to just blink out of existence."

"Maybe it went below the horizon," Jule says.

"No," Cindy says, quietly. She's looking out the window. "It just disappeared."

"Why are we worrying about this?" Don asks.

A little later, when it's dark and the salt flats are gleaming on both sides of the road like an endless sea of milk, Cindy says, "I hope we see it again."

"I don't," Don says. "What I hope is that we make it to the coast in this piece of shit."

"We will," Cindy says. "Don't you worry about that."

Cindy and Jule have been friends for years, but Jule has only met Don two or three times before. Don and Cindy have been married for nearly a year. Cindy said maybe it was a risk but she thought they'd all have a blast together on this trip. In fact, she was positive about it.

Twenty minutes later, she sits up in the back seat where she's been sleeping. Jule hears her rustling, which is good because the rhythmic thump of the expansion joints on the freeway is starting to get hypnotic. He hasn't been sleeping, although he lies slouched in the corner of his seat with his eyes closed enough that Don will think maybe he is.

"This is where it was," Cindy says.

Jule turns around to look at her. Her long blond hair is mussed, sticking up. Her eyes are sleepy. "How do you know?"

"I don't know how I know. This is where it was."

Don doesn't say anything. He hasn't said anything for thirty miles.

"It was over there," Cindy says. She points vaguely ahead of them, but it looks to Jule exactly like every other spot on the salt flats. There's just pale emptiness.

"I read that book about the space people picking that guy up," Cindy says. "Those things happen."

Don takes the pack from his pocket and shakes out a cigarette. He presses the lighter button into the dashboard.

"You know what I'm talking about?" Cindy asks.

"I heard about it," Jule says.

"It was a best-seller in the *New York Times* for months."

Don lights his cigarette. "Hey, hon," he says, "relax."

Jule keeps looking at the place where Cindy pointed. It's getting closer.

Cindy says, "It's about this guy—he's a famous author, you know—and he gets taken up into their ships every now and then, and it's so frightening he can't remember it. What he keeps seeing are these packs of animals crossing the road. Finally he has this nervous breakdown. It's just too much. He has to face it. It turns out there weren't any animals. Those were the times the space people took him."

No one says anything.

"It's a true story," Cindy says. "Documented."

"It's not documented," Don says.

"Yes it is," Cindy says. "There's this statement in the book from a psychiatrist that says the guy definitely is not nuts."

"I don't think that's what Don meant," Jule says.

"I don't care what he meant. Can I have a cigarette?"

Don takes the pack from his pocket and tosses it over his shoulder. Cindy catches it. "Punch the lighter for me, would you Jule?" she asks.

Jule pushes the button and hands the lighter to her when it pops out.

"Here's your pack," she says to Don, holding it over the front seat.

"Keep it," Don says, and after a minute, Cindy sits back in her seat.

Jule wonders if maybe they can stop talking then. But after a couple of puffs, Cindy says, "It was right *there*."

Jule looks out into the desert but there's still nothing different about it at all.

Cindy says, "Could you slow down a little?"

The car slows almost imperceptibly.

"Hey," Cindy says, "a rest stop. Can we stop for a minute?"

"No," Don says.

"Oh, come on. You want to stop, Jule?"

Jule shrugs. "Don's driving," he says. "I guess it's up to him."

Cindy stares at him in the darkness. "Great," she says. "That's wonderful. Stop the car, I'm getting out." She pulls up the door handle; dry, cool air roars into the car, squeezing Jule's eardrums, tearing at his clothes. Then the tires are screeching against the concrete and Jule is thrown into the dashboard as Don swerves into the rest stop. The car jerks up to the curb next to the toilets and stops. Cindy gets out and slams the door. Jule watches her pick her way down the embankment and start walking out into the desert. He sits there, next to Don. He can't imagine what to say.

"Christ," Don mutters, "she's got my cigarettes." He gets out of the car, slams the door.

Jule is nauseated. He can't get his breath. After a few seconds he gets out and starts following Don and Cindy.

There's a strong breeze out on the flats. The air smells like dust and sagebrush. The hard white surface of the ground stretches to the horizon like a concrete stage. They walk in a line, first Cindy, then Don, and finally Jule, and no one makes a move to catch up with anyone else. They can walk forever, Jule thinks.

But after about a mile, Cindy turns around and Don starts to walk a little faster. When he reaches her, they walk side by side. Jule can't tell if they're talking or not.

Then Cindy suddenly sits down. Jule can see the pinprick orange glow of her cigarette, moving up and down. When he finally reaches her, she grinds it out in the salt and says, "This is where they were."

Jule sits down a couple of feet away. Don stands, looking out toward the horizon, his hands in his back pockets.

"Feel how warm the ground is," Cindy says.

Jule puts his palms on the salt. It's the same temperature as his skin.

"I think we should just stay here for a while," she says, and Don turns around and sits down, facing her. He says, "You believe it, don't you."

She doesn't answer. She seems to be listening.

He picks up the pack lying on the ground in front of her, lights a cigarette.

"They don't always show up when you want them to," Cindy says. "Maybe you're too stirred up."

Don watches her.

"They aren't quite on the same wavelength as we are. They have more control."

He doesn't say anything. Jule is feeling the wind.

"When they feel your mind is ready, then they come. Some people have been taken from moving cars."

"That's nasty," Don says.

"When the people come back, they're behind the wheel and everything's fine. No one understands it."

"I think I understand," Don says.

Cindy nods. "Maybe you're getting calmer. You have to be calm or they can't get through. I'm calm. Are you, Jule?"

"I'm looking at the stars," Jule says.

"Good," Cindy says.

Jule is lying on his back now.

Cindy reaches out and starts stroking Jule's arm. "Can you feel it?" she says. "They want us to be relaxed. Open. So they can make contact."

"Shhh," Don whispers.

"Talking doesn't matter," she says. "They only hear what's in your mind. That's all they care about."

The wind, and Cindy's hand on his arm, are putting Jule to sleep. It's all he needs.

After a long time, Cindy says, "You see, they're on a higher level. That's what's so frightening. They know so much. Once you've been with them, you can't be the same." She's sitting cross-legged now, palms resting on her knees. "All we have to do is wait," she says.

During the drive through the rest of the salt flats and on past Wendover, Jule sleeps. He doesn't wake up until the stillness of the car pulls him gently upward. There are bright, blue-white lights shining into it. Don is leaning half on the seat, half against the door, watching him. Jule wipes his neck and his hand comes away slick. For some reason, sleeping anywhere other than his own bed always makes him sweat.

"Where are we?" Jule says.

"Reno."

They're in a parking lot. The light coming into the car is as bright as day, but without warmth. Don's face is white.

"How come you stopped?" Jule asks.

Don shrugs. His long, Levi-covered legs stretch across the hump on the floor, and Jule realizes Don's feet are touching his own.

Jule rolls down the window. The air is cooler here than it was on the salt flats. They sit there for a long time.

Jule looks over the seat, at Cindy. She's curled up, forearms pulled in to her chest, her hands a shapeless tangle under her chin. In the glare from the parking lot lights her face is blank and smooth. She doesn't look like Cindy at all.

Later, when Don's gone into the diner to get some coffee, Jule reaches back to wake her up, but he doesn't touch her. He can't. Not when she's sleeping like that.

They get to the hotel half an hour before dawn. It's an enormous, white Victorian structure, built of wood. There are two long wings stretching away from a central section with a huge, shingle-covered conical roof. The uniformed valet takes the car, and they go into the lobby, which is all dark, polished wood and potted palms and oriental rugs. Jule and Cindy sit on a leather sofa while Don talks to the clerk at the desk. There's no one else in the lobby. A small fire burns in a fireplace with a carved, gleaming mantle. The windows are open, and

Jule can hear the faint sound of the surf. The sky, he sees, has changed from black to deep, cobalt blue. It's cloudless.

Don comes back with a key for Cindy and one for Jule. "The bellboys are busy," he says, and they pick up their bags and follow him up a vast staircase.

Within minutes, they're lost in a tangle of narrow white corridors. Cindy drops her luggage. "I'm pooped," she says. "I think we're going in circles." She looks at her key. "Are we on the third floor?"

"Read the numbers," Don says, pointing to a door which says "394." He's still holding his bags.

"I'm not thinking," she says. "I can't think anymore."

Jule says, "Maybe we're in the wrong wing. I thought this was where the courtyard was supposed to be."

"Better keep walking," Don says.

"We're lost," Cindy says.

Don starts walking down the hall.

"We'll get there," Jule whispers.

Cindy jerks her bags up from the red carpet.

They walk and walk but they don't find it. The numbers on the doors go down, then back up again. Finally Cindy throws her bags down. "This is a joke," she says. "Where the fuck are we?"

Jule can see Don's face getting blank, empty. He says, "Listen, I'll go down to the lobby for instructions."

"He got instructions," Cindy says.

"I guess we need more," Jule says.

"How are you going to find us again?" she says. "We'll just be stuck here. Don't they have a courtesy phone or something?"

Don is staring out a tiny window, smoking a cigarette. The sky is pale blue, now, Jule can see.

"Just hang on," he says to Cindy.

She's smoking now, not looking at him. Jule watches a tiny cylinder of ash drop and spatter the carpet.

Once Jule's around the corner he starts jogging and it doesn't take him long to find the stairs leading down to the lobby.

He races down, two at a time. "We're lost," Jule says to the clerk at the front desk, a boy of maybe eighteen with bleached blond hair. He's out of breath. "We're really lost."

Jule listens carefully while the clerk explains how to find their rooms, drawing a map on a cocktail napkin. Then he's racing back up the stairs. Coming down the hall he sees Cindy still sitting on her suitcase, talking in a quiet voice to Don, who is across from her, looking at the floor.

When Jule reaches them, she says, "I'm absolutely awake as hell. Want to swim?"

"Later," Jule says. "I can barely walk."

Cindy sighs. "Then lead on, leader," she says.

Jule studies the map the clerk drew.

Suddenly they're counting down the numbers on the doors, and their own rooms are in front of them.

Don opens the door.

The room is big, with pale carpeting bordered with roses. The wallpaper has garlands of roses up near the moldings, and the comforter on the bed is satin, with the same pattern on it. Near the bed is a small, round wooden table with carved legs and three matching chairs, and on the other side of the room, a matching desk and vanity.

"Oh," Cindy says. "This is something." She walks slowly across the room, looking around, and sets her luggage down by the window, which is enormous, with white shutters which have been pulled back. It looks out over the tops of palm trees to the sea. She just stands there.

"Come on," Don says to Jule. "Let's go next door and get you set up."

Jule follows him into a room which is much smaller, with a thin, faded Persian rug and rattan furniture. He sets his suitcases down on the bed while Don goes over to the window and opens the shutters.

"It's going to be a nice day," Don says. He takes a pack of cigarettes from his shirt pocket, shakes one out, lights it. "I'm sorry," he says, turning suddenly, holding up the cigarette. "Is this all right?"

Jule nods, and Don unlatches the window and pushes it open a little.

"The ocean was black a little while ago, and now it's pale blue," Don says. "It just reflects the sky. It's not any color at all."

Jule sits on the bed and starts unlacing his tennis shoes. He pulls them off, puts them together and slides them under the bed.

Don throws his cigarette out the window and walks over to a chair a couple of feet from the bed and sits down. "You look tired," he says. "I shouldn't keep you awake."

"It's okay," Jule says.

Don slides the cellophane wrapper of his cigarette pack down, making tiny crinkling sounds. "Sometimes I want to know something about people," he says.

Jule watches him.

After a minute Don gets up and ruffles Jule's hair. "Go to sleep," he says. "You need it."

"I guess I do," Jule says.

That afternoon, Jule finds the door to Don and Cindy's room ajar. He knocks.

"Come in," Don says, and Jule goes in. The room is filled with white light, and a thin, hot breeze is coming in through the open window. Cindy is gone, and Don is sitting up in bed. His skin is dark against the white sheets, exactly the color, Jule thinks, of the stone-ground bread he buys sometimes.

Jule sits in the wicker chair next to the writing desk, across from Don. "Where's Cindy?" he says.

"On the beach."

"I thought she'd get me up," Jule says.

Don yawns, takes a cigarette from the pack on the nightstand, and lights it. The smoke moves up into the sunlight, twisting. He picks up his watch from the nightstand. "Two o'clock," he says. "You're right on time for breakfast."

Jule looks out the window. He can hear the waves, but the water looks motionless, like plastic.

"What I want," Don says, "is ham and eggs. Ham steak. There's a difference."

"I'm sure they've got it in a place like this," Jule says.

In the restaurant, the waiters wear tuxedos. The place is cavernous, topped by the conical roof Jule saw as they drove up. There are fifteen or twenty people scattered among the tables. Jule wishes Cindy were here. He wishes she wasn't missing their first meal in the hotel.

Don orders ham and eggs. "Tell the cook to slice it thick," he says to the waiter, who looks to Jule like all the other personnel of the hotel, like a surfer.

"I'll tell the chef," the waiter says.

Jule orders French toast and coffee.

"You can have whatever you want," Don says.

"French toast is all right," Jule says.

"Waiter," Don calls to the boy, and the waiter comes back. "He wants ham steak and eggs instead of French toast." Turning to Jule, he says, "Don't worry about money."

Jule puts his napkin on his lap.

When they're eating, Don says, "The thing about Cindy is, you have to take her with a grain of salt."

"You do?"

"She doesn't always say what she means."

"Oh," Jule says.

"It's something you just get used to."

"How come you married her?" Jule asks.

Don laughs. "Because I love her."

"What do you love?"

Don leans back in his chair. "Let's see," he says. "I love her tits. I love her long blond hair. I love her sense of humor." He looks at Jule. "I could go on but none of that's it, really. I just love her."

"I'm not sure what you mean," Jule says.

Don sips his coffee. "You two are pretty close," he says. "You've known each other a lot longer than she and I have." He pushes his plate back and lights a cigarette. "What do you love about her?"

"I guess I love the way she tells the truth," Jule says.

Don smiles. "You're really a trip," he says.

Cindy's reading a book when they get back to the room. She's still in her bikini. Her hair, which is wet, is pressed to her head and gleams like pale metal.

"Listen to this," she says, as they walk in the room. "'Together they passed down through heat and cold, through ice and snow and wind, and then further, to the still blue place, the place where nothing moved. There they sat, for days, or perhaps years, for time could not reach them now. They sat in silence, waiting for the others. Waiting for the dance to begin.' Isn't that great?"

"Cool," Don says. He goes into the bathroom and closes the door.

"What are you reading?" Jule asks.

She shows him a fantasy novel with a silver cover. "It's about a warrior and his lover," she says. "After fighting all these battles there's nothing left to fight, so they go over the mountains and down to the Plain of Silence. Something's about to happen."

Below the window, Jule sees a courtyard full of palms. There are spots of incandescent blue—a pool.

Cindy says, "Can we for God's sake go swimming now?"

"Let's do it," Jule says.

She slams the book shut. "I could spend the whole damn day in the ocean if you want to know the truth." She picks up her towel from the bed and starts walking across the room.

Jule glances at the closed bathroom door. "We shouldn't just leave him here," he says.

"He doesn't like swimming, Jule. He's here for the tennis."

Jule is still a little confused by the twisting corridors of the hotel, but Cindy seems to know them now. "This place," he says, as they cross the lobby. "It's like something in a nightmare."

"Upstairs?"

"Yeah," he says. "Those halls."

The sea is warm. There's almost no shock to his skin when Jule enters the water. They swim fifteen or twenty yards from the shore and rest, bobbing on the swells. "I just *love* this," Cindy says. "It's paradise."

"I wonder what's down there," Jule says.

"Sharks?"

"Whatever," Jule says.

"Oh, God, Jule. Do you really think anyone's ever been attacked on *this* beach in front of *this* hotel, in all the years it's been open? I mean, it's famous. Where you have to worry is Australia." But a few minutes later she suddenly jerks below the surface, comes up gargling, and manages a half-squeal before jerking under the water again.

"Cindy," Jule says, "that's not funny."

She laughs and throws water in his face. "You can't tell what's down there," she says, looking down. "You can't see a thing."

"Will you shut up?" Jule says.

"The ocean's huge," she says. "And actually sharks are almost everywhere. Look," she says. "It could be forty feet deep. Or more. Plenty of room for big ones, even."

"Shut up," Jule says.

"The truth is, it *has* happened."

"Cindy," Jule says, "I'm going back."

"Oh, Jule," she says.

He just swims, closing his eyes, taking long, smooth strokes as if he were in the pool at the YMCA.

On the beach, he lies down in the hot sand, letting it sting his back, his legs. After a few minutes Cindy comes up and lies down beside him.

He can feel the coolness of her wet skin, next to him. Although his eyes are closed, he can still see the sun, a field of scarlet rimmed in black.

Later, when he's starting to drift, Cindy says, "This is when you wonder if maybe the space people might decide to take you up."

Jule doesn't say anything.

"It's so quiet. The sun melts you. Maybe they watch for moments like these."

Jule thinks of himself melting, like wax, mixing with the sand.

"I'm not trying to scare you," she says.

"You're not scaring me," he says. He burrows his hands into the sand at his sides. It's cooler, three or four inches under the surface. He lets his hands lie there, like great, fleshy cicadas.

Cindy begins to hum. It's a song Jule has heard but he can't remember it. She just keeps humming, and he lies there listening, floating on the sound. It seems as if the hot breeze is making that sound.

"Oh, Jule," Cindy says, after a long time. "I think they're close. I think they're right here."

But Jule is dreaming now. He's floating on a green sea under a yellow sky and there's a fin sprouting from his back which goes deep into the water, into the coolness below. He's not frightened at all.

Cindy's gone when Jule wakes up. There's no one else on the beach. The sea is like the sound of his own breath in his ears. Above him he can see a single palm frond, black against the azure sky, moving.

He's drenched. His skin, white in the glare, is mottled with streaks and pinpricks of red. He walks down the sand and into the water and lets himself hang there, his toes just touching the hard sand on the bottom.

When he's cool, finally, and starting to shiver, he walks from the water, picks up his towel and suntan oil, and walks back to the hotel, entering through a side door near the rear. The halls seem dark after the sun, silent, muffled. The texture of the carpet feels too smooth under his feet.

After changing into shorts and sandals and a T-shirt, he goes next door. Don's lying against the humped-up pillows on the bed, wearing faded cutoffs that look pale against his skin. There's a room-service tray with some dirty dishes laying on the table.

"You're pink," Don says.

"I fell asleep on the beach," Jule says.

"That's bad."

"I dreamed I was floating on the ocean and it was just like you imagine the ocean will be but it never is. It held me up. It was like a mattress going up and down. The sun wasn't too hot. It felt good."

Don lights a cigarette. "Funny," he says, "since you were baking yourself."

"I was part fish," Jule says. "I had a fin coming out of my back, one of those long, trailing fins. It kept me steady. I could feel things in the water with it."

"Creepy," Don says.

"It wasn't. It went down maybe thirty feet."

"Christ," Don says.

"If anything touched it, it was sexual."

"Some dream," Don says.

"It was different. It was like being a woman."

Don lets the smoke out of his mouth in a jet.

"I was just waiting," Jule says. "I was waiting for something to touch it. Whatever."

Don says, "What do you think it meant?"

"I don't care what it meant," Jule says. "I wanted to tell you about it."

Don rolls over on his belly, resting his chin on the back of his hand.

Jule goes to the windows and pushes them open, first one, then the other.

"I want them closed," Don says.

"It's terrible in here."

Jule sits next to him on the bed. Don's eyes are pale blue in the sunlight, almost cloudy-looking.

"I don't think Cindy will be back for a while," Jule says.

Don doesn't say anything.

Jule lays a hand on Don's back. "You're sweating," he says. "What were you doing in here?"

"Sleeping," Don says, after a minute.

"It's getting cooler now," Jule says. He reaches down and touches Don's mustache. He runs the tip of his finger along Don's lower lip. It feels cool, like the surface of a leaf.

"Yeah," Don says, "it is."

Jule is lying on a lounger in the courtyard. The pool is blue glass, the sky a mottled, milky black. The palms, knife-edged, are a darker black. Jule can feel them steadily absorbing the tepid air. In the glossy undergrowth, tubes of blue-white plasma hum. Below the surface of the pool the jets send out slow clear plumes of water. The tiles twist.

There's a wind in the courtyard, a soft one, blowing straight down on Jule. It makes the tingling in his skin go away.

Cindy comes in after a while from the row of cypresses separating the courtyard from the beach. She's still wearing her bikini and her skin looks dark, darker than Don's, as dark as mahogany. She comes over to the lounger and Jule draws up his legs. She sits down on the end.

"Jule," she says, "I love you."

The wind just keeps blowing down on them.

"If you'd been walking with me," Cindy says, "you would have gone as far as I went. I went halfway to Tijuana. Jule, this beach was *made* for walking."

Jule listens to the buzzing of the lights. It seems to be what makes the tiles twist, steadily, like clockwork.

"You can see the lights of the city," Cindy says. "The further you go, the more you can see. It just spreads out in back of you."

Jule clasps his arms around his legs, pulling his shins up close to his thighs, which makes the skin on his knees burn.

"I wish you'd gone with me, Jule. After a couple of miles I wished you were there so bad I couldn't stand it. But I just kept walking. The city got even bigger. Isn't that funny? It's huge. It's enormous."

"You should have thought about Don," Jule says.

"After a while, I wasn't thinking about anything. Not even you. I stopped looking back at the city. There's a stretch of desert. The sand goes right into the sea."

"I've been thinking about Don," Jule says.

Cindy crosses her legs. Jule can see her profile, her dark skin, shiny with oil. The lights from the undergrowth gild it.

"I'm not going back," Cindy says.

Jule can feel something unravelling.

"I've made up my mind. I couldn't tell you, Jule. I'm sorry."

"No, no," Jule says, sitting up. "Don't say it. Don't say anything like that."

She looks at him, smiles. "I'm not leaving you."

"I know."

"I'm so happy right now, Jule," she says.

Jule touches her back, strokes it.

"Jule, you'll talk to Don, won't you?"

He doesn't say anything.

"Will you do that?"

He keeps stroking her back.

"You're going to find out a lot."

He strokes her.

"I guess you have to," she says.

They don't say anything after that. They sit for a long time, in that wind coming down out of the sky. Then they walk together back into the hotel.

As Cindy and Jule walk into the bedroom, Don comes out of the bathroom carrying a plastic bag with his toilet things inside. His toothbrush falls out and he bends down to pick it up.

"Hi," he says. He goes over to his suitcase, which is lying open on the bed and tucks the bag into one corner. He's wearing nothing but white shorts.

Cindy walks over to the little table next to the bed and sits down. Jule follows her. They watch Don take his shirts down from hangers in the closet and fold them carefully and lay them in the suitcase. He walks back and forth in front of them.

"Don," Cindy says, "stop."

"Okay," Don says. But he doesn't stop. When everything's packed, he zips up his suitcase and stands in front of it. He looks at Cindy, then at Jule, and Jule closes his eyes. He hears the sound of the suitcase sliding across the sheets, and that's when Cindy does something. Jule is sure of it. When he opens his eyes, Don is sitting on the bed next to the suitcase, which is standing up on the mattress, and he's looking at Cindy. It's like his motor stopped, Jule thinks.

Jule thinks about the blackness of the sky outside the hotel, about the void that surrounds them. Anything dropped into it would just vanish completely.

"You're not alone," Cindy says.

Don just sits there, looking at her. There's a furrow between his eyebrows as if he's thinking, or trying to remember something.

"I promise," Cindy says.

She loves him so much, Jule thinks. He can't imagine it. He's almost afraid to look at her.

After a while she gets up and walks out of the room, closing the door behind her.

Jule can feel something coming into the room, like water rushing into a dam.

Don is shaking, Jule can see. He's shivering as if he were freezing.

"Come over here," Don says, patting the bed by his side, and Jule gets up and sits next to him, which is better. Then Don puts his arm around Jule's back, and after a minute, Jule puts his around Don's. They just sit there. It feels good, having their arms around each other like that.

"She's taking us somewhere, Jule," Don says.

He's not shaking so hard now. Jule tries to picture warmth going from his body into Don's. He wants to pull the blanket up around Don's shoulders.

"It's okay," Jule says.

And Don says, "Maybe it's okay."

They'll do this a lot, Jule thinks.

"What I don't understand," Don says, turning to look at Jule, "is where."

"Here," Jule says. "She's taking us right here."

THE SHINING DREAM ROAD OUT

M. SHAYNE BELL

So I buckled myself into the Driving-Simulation Unit and started connecting my head to Happy Pizza's central computer, which would connect up to Salt Lake County's virtual-reality road map of the valley, all the while looking around at the dump of a room I was in with its peeling paint on the walls and ceiling and the used pizza boxes thrown on the floor and the heat and the smell of garlic and onion in the air, but that box of a "car" I was getting into, that was beautiful to me, because I knew what it would soon turn into, and I was getting that hit-in-the-gut feeling of excitement I get just before I head out to drive and I wanted to laugh because I wasn't really going to leave the back room of Happy Pizza at all except through virtual reality in my mind, when the voice of Fat Joe, the owner of this particular franchise, came over the intercom:

"Ten minute run coming up, Clayton. If you beat your last time of 8:23 you got your raise."

Yeah, I thought, fifteen cents more an hour. "So start the show," I said.

And a virtual-reality vision of southbound Interstate 15 settled over my mind: the section just past the 600 South on-ramp and the Salt Lake City skyscrapers east and the derelict houses west and a sunset shining red on rain clouds above and rain already spattering down on the windshield and I thought, great, I'm trying to get just fifteen cents more an hour out of a stupid pizza delivery job and they make it rain.

I turned on the wipers and thought how the box I was sitting in looked to me like a car now, a nice little Japanese fast car that motored along just fine, and I punched it up to 80, even with the wet road: my tires had good traction and the road was rough enough in real-land to keep you from hydroplaning, though the city would never factor *that* into its VR road simulations no matter how many times I talked to them about it when they did their user surveys—it's like, did they really believe the state would ever get that road fixed? But they must have, because in every simulation I was ever in, I-15 was smooth, and we'd drive along on top of it like we were driving on a dream road, and you'd start to understand why Fat Joe wouldn't spring for new shocks in our real cars, not if all he ever drove was this simulation and he thought the roads out there in real-land were this nice.

I punched up the coordinates of my run, and they glowed red digital out of the dash in the dim car, dim thanks to the rain, and I turned on my lights and thought how easy can Fat Joe make this: I-15 south to the 53rd South exit, then west on 53 to the Reston Hotel, room 115? Easy run was right—it was too easy. I saw what was coming: there'd be cops along the way and stingy Fat Joe had known it, must have punched into the city files to see how many cops were on duty, maybe drove along a little on the road himself just to check it out, just to see if he could save fifteen cents an hour but happy that I'd learn more about the real-land roads and where the cops had their speed traps so I'd know exactly where to speed up and where to slow down when I was delivering pizza, and that hit-in-the-gut feeling of mine got tighter because I couldn't make 53 South doing 80 with cops on the road, so I braked my car down to 70 just to be safe, so I wouldn't get caught right away, and waited to pass the first speed trap coming up: 21st South, behind or in front of the railing along the merge lane—and sure enough, there he was, a cop just waiting for me to go by at 80 plus, but I was only doing 70 and nobody'd pull you over for that unless it was the end of the month and some cop hadn't met his quota yet.

Fat Joe must have been pissed: he'd thought a cop would get me right away, but now he'd have to sit in his VR getup, which he hated unless he was watching porn, and wait to see if one of the cops assigned to the net for a day could catch me on VR I-15, which I knew better than the back of my hand: once past the 21st South on-off ramps and speed trap I merged into the far right lane and shoved my car back up to 80—roadblock ahead, some old grandpa trying to pass the city sight requirements and motoring along just under 50 in a blue "Senior Driver" practice car—merge into the middle lane, still at 80, maybe plus—roadblock ahead, some trucker trying to get back a license after one too many speeding tickets—merge right again, back and forth, weaving in and out, always in the right two lanes, never in the far left, the fast lane, the lane cops looked in for speeders: if you weaved in and out in the slow lanes the cops would know somebody was going fast, but they wouldn't know who, the dots of the cars on their radar would all blend together if I merged in close, and sure they'd think it was probably the pizza delivery boy who'd been going a little fast when we passed them, not the old geezer trying to keep his car on the road and do minimum speed at the same time, but they wouldn't know it for sure, which meant they wouldn't come out—they'd wait for some sure prey— and you can bet I'd be a good little pizza delivery boy around all their traps.

And make my ten-minute delivery in under 8:23.

So I drove along, making good time, thinking there was a lot of traffic on VR I-15—was every trucker and school bus driver and delivery boy out trying to pass some driving test or get a raise?—when this pretty lady in a green station wagon with peeling fake-wood side panels speeds by doing 90 who knows what—and there were these three little blonde-haired kids waving at me out of the back window.

Weird, I thought. And thank goodness it was just VR—it was one thing for me to drive like a maniac in VR or real-land, it was another for a mother with her kids. I hoped she'd use VR to work out whatever was eating at her and keep it down out there on real I-15. The kids kept waving, so I waved back and changed lanes into theirs and sped up to keep them company from behind—no speed trap till around the 33rd on-ramp anyway, our only danger would be roving cops—and we hit 93 miles an hour.

I started thinking, who is the lady driving the station wagon in light rain at 93 mph and when would the wagon's engine blow, because it could, even in VR, just to teach you a lesson. Only somebody with nothing to lose or hot food to deliver would pull stunts like this, and when you looked at it that way, her speed kind of made sense: I'd heard of people coming out to check the simulation to see how well it worked, and those types would certainly have nothing to lose. So I thought

maybe the lady in the station wagon is the mayor checking up on her
VR cops and taking her kids for a joy-ride and seeing what her car should
be able to do in theory, all at the same time—I imagined that's what
somebody like her with a decent income and a crappy car so you
wouldn't look high and mighty to the voters would do on an afternoon:
hold the appointments, I've got important work coming through on the
net; then connect up, swing by the house in VR to pick up your VR kids
who'd plug in when you told them to, and off you'd go—and fuck the
city budget crisis.

We started coming up on 33, and she braked, and I braked, and I
thought this is a smart lady, she knows where the traps are, which of
course a mayor would, and I merged over into the right lane and pulled
up alongside her and looked over, but she didn't look at me: she just
watched the road and held the wheel so tight her knuckles were white.
She wasn't the mayor. Whoever she was I thought she must have some
kind of bad trouble in her life.

I merged back behind a couple of Idaho Meat-Packers' trucks
because I'd been part of a fast blip with that wagon for too long and I
didn't want to be near her when we passed 33, and sure enough another
cop was waiting there looking confused about which of us had done
what and I was happy to complicate his life. He pulled out three cars
behind me, and I didn't touch my brakes, just eased up on the gas a
little, then a little more, not wanting to look the least bit guilty and
thinking did he somehow figure out about me, and wondering how he
could have done that, and hardly daring to breathe because we passed
45 and 53 was the next exit and I'd used up nearly 5:30 of my run and
if I got a ticket I wouldn't get my raise for sure.

So I played the good little pizza delivery boy, and I watched 53 come
up ahead of us and the green station wagon take the exit and drive down
the hill and I followed her off and the cop stayed out on I-15.

But the wagon sped up down below me, and I thought what's the
lady doing? Before the intersection she suddenly slammed brakes, which
locked at that speed, and she slid to a stop blocking the exit, in front of
a red light. Real good, lady, I thought, like did she forget this wasn't the
highway anymore, then suddenly remember? Well, she'd stopped before
the red light, but any cop driving by would think the position of her car
a little strange and maybe worth investigating. I hoped one wouldn't
happen by and stop to check her out because I'd lose time trying to get
around them.

I braked to a stop behind her and waited for the light to change—she could just pull out and go when it changed—but she didn't pull out, and her head started banging around like she was being hit, though nothing I could see was hitting her in that car, and I honked to maybe bring her out of it, but she didn't even look at me.

What is she on? I wondered, and I watched her head jerk around for a minute. Then I saw that the kids were popping out of VR—they'd look at their mom, then just be gone, just not there, like they were maybe pulling out the connection and running in real-land to help her or something, and I thought: I have no choice. I have to screw this test and my raise. And I put the car in park, and unbuckled and got out and ran up to the lady's door and opened it.

That's when she looked at me for the first time, and her eyes were wide like she was scared, not of me but of something. And I said, *Lady, what can I do to help you? Can I call someone? What's going on?* And she said—

My husband's beating me.

Then she was gone, like the kids, as if somebody'd pulled the connection out of her head. The car disappeared next, and I was left standing in the middle of the off-ramp with four other cars honking behind me.

I stood there for a second or two, thinking how I'd blown the test and there was no point in going on and what Fat Joe would say, then I ran for my car and took it across 53 and up the VR I-15 on-ramp and back out onto the VR interstate looking for the green station wagon. I knew it was stupid to look for that wagon if the lady driving it was getting beaten up somewhere in real-land and I didn't know where and I couldn't even remember her license plate to stop and call the stupid police, I'd just been watching the kids in the back of a wagon doing 93 mph, I hadn't been memorizing license plate numbers, and I didn't know what to do, and I wanted to do something, something, something. Before long, but before the ten minutes of my test were up, I was past Draper and the prison and going up the Point of the Mountain doing 102 and when I hit the top, the VR blanked out and a screen came up that said "You are not a driver authorized to enter the Utah County Driver Simulation Net," which meant I didn't have the right kind of access to make the Salt Lake County net network me over to the Utah County net, and then the screen went all black in my mind: But before the words had come up I'd gotten one quick glimpse of the Utah County net, and it was all color, not city: I saw the sun glinting off Utah Lake and the green spring wheatfields and orchards around Alpine and a tall mountain south with snow still on the top and I-15 heading south to that mountain, the road looking like it had been polished and looking like it ached for me to drive on it.

"So you blew that one, Clayton-boy. You blew that one—and you're supposed to be my best driver?"

I was unhooking my head and one of the wires had stuck in the back, so I kept working at it and looked at Fat Joe who seemed just a little too happy about my fifteen cent an hour loss and said, "Yeah, so I want some practice time in VR."

And it wasn't just VR fun I was after, though Fat Joe wouldn't know that: I wanted to get back out on VR I-15 and look for that stationwagon and write down the license plate number if I saw it again.

"You can practice when you don't have runs to make in real-land, Clayton-boy. We've got one waiting for you now."

The wire came loose, and I hurried out of the car and into the kitchen: It was two pepperoni and mushroom pizzas on a Midvale run waiting for me, and the kitchen staff had already boxed up the pizzas, so I took them and ran, sat them in the backseat of my little Japanese fast car and buckled them down and slammed doors and buckled myself in and rolled down the windows while I pulled out onto 600 South heading west to the I-15 on-ramp: I never used the air conditioner because the drain on engine power would slow me down, and I was out there in real-land, which is weirder than VR: in VR you have people driving along trying to pass tests, most driving like they always meant to be good little boys and girls of the road and only a few like me driving like maniacs because we had different kinds of tests to pass—and it was only those people out there.

But not in real-land.

In real-land everybody had already passed their tests so they could all go nuts and all two million of them in Salt Lake Valley are out driving around all the time, usually heading for I-15, and you never know what to expect except lots of craziness and unpredictability and I loved it, I loved playing the game that went on in that traffic: drive a fast car fast and you'll find one or two or three others doing the same thing, and an interstate highway can become your own little VR game in real-land: slow cars doing 60 or 70 to block the road ahead when you can't change lanes left or right and the other fast cars speed past and the drivers laugh at you, but you get your turn to laugh down the road when their lane is blocked and you can speed past, and you drive, weaving in and out, and *nothing* feels like it, nothing, with the wind whipping your hair and the hot summer air off the desert blowing over your skin and no music off the radio at all because you don't need it, not then, not during the game.

And I merged out onto I-15 and shoved my Japanese fast car up to 80 plus, close to 90, because I wanted to play then, real bad, and the Happy Pizza clown head stuck on the hood of my car flapped around like you wouldn't believe, but nobody was out playing the game, just me, I was the only driver weaving in and out, getting blocked and slowing down and speeding up again and weaving in and out, and I couldn't help it: I kept looking around for the green station wagon with the peeling fake-wood side panels because a car like that existed somewhere in the valley and was probably registered to the lady or her husband and the lady was probably a hacker because how else could she get out onto VR I-15? A woman with a car like that didn't have the money to buy her way onto the net.

I wished I'd looked even once at the license plate on that car.

It was more of the predictable same-old family routine when I got home that night after work. My mother would ask, "How was your day, Clayton?" just like she did every day, and I'd say, "Fine, just a lot of driving," and I'd never be able to tell her or Dad just how I drove and the kind of fun it was and what I'd felt, and my father would look up from his paper and not say a word because he was pissed that I'd taken a pizza delivery job, not something at his bank to keep me busy through the summer till I hit the one year of college I'd get before my two-year mission preaching religion. I looked at them and wanted to try to tell them I had taken a VR driving test to maybe get a raise in the slow afternoon hours after the lunch-time rush and that I'd seen this woman getting beaten by her husband and that I didn't know how to find her to help her. But I didn't know how to tell such a story to my parents, there'd be too much to explain, so I didn't say a word about it.

"Supper's at seven," Mother said, and I just stood by the fridge getting a drink, and I looked at us and thought we all seemed like little robots going about doing what we were programmed to do, no matter what happened in our lives: Mother programmed to make supper, Dad programmed to read the paper and disapprove of me, me programmed to go up to my room and do who-knows-what till supper, my two little sisters programmed to wear expensive clothes and be little brats, and I thought, God, I'm going to break this programming, I hate it, so I said to Mom, "Let me help. I'll set the table and get the water—did you want us to drink water tonight?"

And she looked at me surprised and said water would be fine, and Dad looked at me and I knew what he was thinking: that's a woman's work you're doing, Clayton, you're a man doing women's work, isn't that a great kind of son to have? He would hardly move his arms and the paper when I tried to spread the tablecloth on the table or put his plate down in front of him, but he didn't try to stop me either because I was after all just a son who might just as well do work to serve him and we all ate supper and didn't talk much, Dad had the TV on, and I stayed behind to help Mom clean up and she said, "Well, isn't this a surprise?" But I just wanted to be close to her, and I kept thinking about the lady I'd seen in the green station wagon and what had probably happened to her.

We finished rinsing the dishes and putting them into the dishwasher and I went up to my room and stood in front of the mirror in my bathroom and played one of the other games I played with myself: Clayton, the little Robot Boy. I twisted an imaginary knob on the upper right-hand corner of the mirror to turn me on and left more fingerprints there and wondered what Mom or one of the housecleaners thought about that little circle of fingerprints that was always on that spot of my mirror waiting to be wiped off, and I said, "Hi. I'm Clayton. I'm programmed to comb my hair just like this, with every hair in place, and I'm programmed to eat at certain times and take showers at certain times and I always did all of my homework well when I was in high school so I could get good grades and get accepted into a Utah college that doesn't really care about grades, it just wants to know if you'll go to church every Sunday you're enrolled with them so you can sit and hear people talk about being a Christian, never asking, 'What would a Christian's life actually be like?' while outside the air-conditioned church building decent women are getting beaten up by their own husbands and you even see it on VR I-15."

I'd seen it.

I sat down on the edge of the tub and looked at myself in the mirror. I hated Clayton the little robot church boy whose life was all programmed for him: college, mission, marriage, kids, college, career as a lawyer or banker, and numbers and money and deadlines all my life and maybe I could even die on schedule: write it in my Dayplanner sixty years down the road—Wednesday, June 16, 3:00 p.m.: Die. Contact funeral home beforehand. Prepare final will that morning.

I stood up and twisted the imaginary knob and changed the program: I became Clayton, the pizza delivery boy, and I remembered me the first day I'd played the game out on the highway on a pizza run, the day I'd caught on to what had always been going on around me but which I'd missed because I'd always driven so slowly and predictably and couldn't see it through my slow-driving programming, but when I started driving fast I'd found a whole subculture of people who drove just that way, people who made driving to the grocery store an adventure, and driving south to Midvale an event, and if you got a ticket it was just the price of admission to the game which you wouldn't stop playing because it made you feel so alive.

That first day I'd hooked up with a blond-haired girl in a red Ferrari and a thirty-something guy in a Japanese fast car like mine and the three of us would weave in and out of the traffic and laugh at each other when one of us had to slow down and race to catch up to the others. Down by Draper we all took the same exit and stopped at a Sinclair gas station and all of us laughed about the fun we'd had, and they pumped gas into their tanks, but I didn't need to, I'd just come in to talk to them, and I said, "I'm Clayton," after we'd talked for a while, and I held out my hand to the guy, and he and the girl looked at me like I was some kind of alien and wouldn't tell me their names—and they didn't care about mine. It didn't matter to them. All that mattered was that I'd had a fast car and that I was smart enough to learn how to drive it fast and that when I was out on the road I would play the game with them. So those were the rules and I learned them and I never again tried to follow anybody off the road to try to talk. It wasn't the point.

And I turned the knob and changed the program and I was Clayton, the Peace Corps volunteer of the future, though the future was fast coming up to meet me: I'd sent in my papers and was waiting to hear back and I hadn't told my parents and I didn't know how to. They wanted me to do one set of things with my life, and I wanted to join the Peace Corps then maybe do some of the things they wanted. So I just skipped that entire inevitable conversation and imagined I looked like Indiana Jones with a shovel, not a gun, black stubble on my face and me wearing a fedora, and I was saying, "Yes, sir. I'd be glad to go to Ethiopia and show them how to dig ditches and teach them to have fewer kids," and maybe I'd actually help the people there, and I imagined I was setting off with my Bible and Book of Mormon and shovel—but I was mixing up my programs, the mission program and the Peace Corps program, and I sat back down on the edge of the tub and thought how all my programs were mixed up because I didn't have a central program to guide them: I'd just been programmed to do this or that so much I didn't know what Clayton really wanted or how to cut through the programs to ask the questions to even find out what Clayton would want to do with his life if he had ever been asked, if he'd ever asked himself. I was so programmed to want what I was supposed to want I couldn't even ask myself questions I needed answers to because the old programs would all keep running in my head and block the answers, and I wondered if any of us could ever break out of the programs that ran us?

And I looked at myself in the mirror and thought, I'm going to go tell Mom what happened today. It's not part of any of our programs. Seeing what I saw upset mine and it will upset hers and maybe we'll be able to talk to each other about more than the stuff we've been taught to think about and talk about.

So I went down and found Mom in the kitchen reading the paper, it was her turn to read it now. "Mom," I said. "We've got to talk."

And I told her what had happened, and she sat still for a minute, not looking at me, then she said, "Don't call the police if you see that lady out there again. Her husband would be a sweet angel while the police were there, but once they left he'd beat her for sure and maybe the kids. Just get her license-plate number and talk to her and see if we can help. Maybe we can send her somewhere—to her parents? Now tell me what that car looked like again and what the woman looked like." And I did and she hugged me after a while, and I thought this was a good program we were downloading into our systems. A different kind of program, because I'd made some decisions and taken some chances. When I went to sleep that night I didn't feel so much like Clayton the Robot Boy in the mirror, and I liked not feeling like Clayton the Robot Boy.

Fat Joe let me do some VR practice the very next afternoon, and he merged me out onto VR I-15 and let me loose, and who should I see driving along in her cute little red Mustang convertible but my mother, with the top down but her windows still up so she wouldn't get blown too much and her black Gucci sunglasses on and a scarf tied down around her hair. She waved and cut in front of me and took the 21st South exit and I followed her into the parking lot of some abandoned warehouse by the off-ramp. She stopped and I swung around and parked next to her with my driver's side window facing hers so we wouldn't have to get out of our cars, just roll down the windows. Mom reached over to turn down her music: she was listening to a CD of some old-fashioned group, Def Leppard or Scorpions, and I didn't even care then because I was so surprised to see Mom.

I've been looking for your green station wagon for two hours, she said. *No sign of it.*

I thought, wow, Mom—we're calling out the cavalry for this one, you and me, and I said How have you been looking? and she said *Driving up and down the interstate—Bountiful to Draper, and back again.*

I think she'll come, I said. *I think this is a release for her—maybe a kind of escape. Maybe she's even planning to escape and she knows she'll have to do it in her old station wagon, so she's practicing in VR, learning where the speed traps are, seeing what her theoretical car can do.*

Mom agreed. We went back out onto VR I-15. I went ahead fast, looking, while Mom came along behind at a slower pace, just in case the lady merged onto the interstate behind me.

I drove down to the Point of the Mountain just past Draper, right up to the Utah County net, then turned around and drove north to Bountiful, then headed back south again—when there it was, the green station wagon, merging onto VR I-15 from 21st South and going fast. She passed me, and I sped up to keep up with her, and the kids waved at me again, waving hard and laughing like they recognized me, which they probably did thanks to the Happy Pizza clown face stuck on the hood of the car, and I merged into the right lane so I could get up alongside her, but a Brink's armed car roadblocked me doing 65, and I had to change lanes again, weaving in and out till I could get up alongside her. I honked and waved and motioned for the lady to pull over and she looked at me but then wouldn't look back, just sped up.

Great, lady, I thought, I'm only trying to help you, and I followed her along till 45, and she took that exit and went down the hill, and I followed, thinking maybe we'd stop at the red light and talk, but suddenly she gunned the car again and sped through the red light, across 45, up the on-ramp, and back out onto VR I-15. I just stopped at the red light. It was obvious she didn't want to talk to me.

Mom pulled up alongside me and lowered the electric window on her passenger side. She won't talk to you because you're a man, she said. *Let me go ahead and try. Don't follow us for a while.* Then *Mom* sped through the red light and out onto VR I-15, and I just pulled off to the side of the road.

A cop car stopped behind me five minutes later, and the cop got out and asked me what I was doing.

I'm just thinking, I said.

Well, it's costing your company money for you to think in here, he said, and I told him to write my company a letter about it, which pissed him off, but since thinking wasn't illegal yet, all he could do was tell me to get my car off the side of the road and into a parking lot somewhere, so I took it out onto VR I-15 instead. I motored along pretty slow—doing the speed limit, actually, because I didn't want to come up on Mom and the lady too soon, but I never did see them. I was down past Draper and heading up the Point of the Mountain when Fat Joe broke into the VR and told me I had a run to make. Before he could pull me out, I raced my car up into the Utah County net boundary and caught a glimpse again of the country that lay beyond in VR and looking better than I ever remembered it in real-land: all green in the valley and white snow on the blue mountains and I-15 shining below me, and no sign of the big cities down there, Provo and Orem. I wondered why I couldn't see the cities.

When I got back from Fat Joe's run, which took me all the way out to Sandy, he had another waiting for me in downtown SLC, some banquet of ten pizzas, but my mother was sitting in the front diner by a window, eating a pizza of her own. "What happened out there?" I asked her, and Fat Joe told me to get out on my run, I could bother the customers on my own time, and Mom said, "Send one of the other boys. This one's making a run for me in about ten minutes," and Fat Joe looked at her as if to say "When did you buy this place so you could order my help around?" But he sent somebody else out on the run and didn't say anything. Mom was after all a paying customer, and you don't argue with those types when you're in the pizza business.

I pulled up a chair at Mom's table, and she said, "This lady is in bad trouble: her husband beats her two or three times a week and has put her in the hospital twice. She left him once before but went back to him, so I don't know what to think. You know how people in her situation are: they can't let go of the person killing them, and they leave them and then go back to them, and who knows what she'll actually do in the end, but I told her, 'Honey, you'd better get ahold of yourself and break this marriage apart before your husband kills you so you can raise these three babies. If you don't want to think of yourself, think of them.' And she thought about it in those terms and told me she'd leave her husband again. She has a sister who just moved to Baker, Nevada, who will take her in, and the husband doesn't know the sister's gone to Baker, so the lady should be safe with her. I told her we'd drive her out there. The Nevada courts can get her a divorce by the weekend. So this is the plan: she's going to call in a pizza order anytime now. You'll take it to her in my car, which is faster than yours. When you get there, she and the kids will come out to pay for it, get in the car instead, and you'll drive her on to Provo. Your Dad and I will meet you at the courthouse, where she'll arrange for a restraining order on her husband. Then we'll all go on to Baker."

"Dad?" was all I could say.

"I told him this morning what we were doing," she said, "and he's been checking into the legalities of helping this woman, which is all legal, and taking your sisters to your Aunt Cheryl's and getting us a reservation at a campground in Great Basin National Park. He's home packing his van now. He and I agree this will be a great chance for the three of us to talk. Here are the keys to my car," and she handed me her car keys.

I gave Mom my car keys and realized I maybe had some rethinking to do about my dad. Maybe I'd been running the wrong programs about him and let a few I/O errors affect my brain and keep me from seeing things right. I guess I'd find out. Fat Joe walked over, and I looked up at him. "So what's going on?" he asked.

"This boy's your best driver," Mom said. "I need his services." And she pulled out a hundred dollar bill from her purse and handed it to Fat Joe. "That should cover any inconvenience you'll incur from his absence this weekend."

Well, Fat Joe was all smiles then, and I knew my job was secure if I took off the next week, not just the weekend. The funny thing was, Fat Joe probably didn't even know that this was my own mother doing all this, and I sure didn't tell him. He came out to help me put a Happy

Pizza clown face on the hood of Mom's Mustang, and it looked so stupid there, but then, it looked stupid on any car.

When we walked back in, Mom was pacing up and down, looking at her watch, and then the phone rang. We all just looked at it till it rang again, then we all dived for it, but Mom got it and it was the lady. "Yes, I've got your address right here in my purse," and she read it back to her. "Ten minutes," Mom said, and she hung up and handed me a paper with the address on it. "Go, Clayton," she said, and I started for the door, but Fat Joe said "Don't you need a pizza?" and Mom said, "For heaven's sake, yes, but who cares what it is or if it's even cooked," so the kitchen help rushed a frozen Italian sausage and pineapple out in a box, and I ran for the car.

The address read Layton Avenue, which meant out to I-15, down to 21st South, east to West Temple, then north five blocks to Layton. I got there in seven minutes. The three kids were out sitting on the lawn, and the oldest, a girl maybe five years old, took the hands of the others and started walking them toward the car. I left the door open for them and left the car running, hoping the kids had sense enough not to touch anything, and I walked the frozen pizza up the steps to the door and rang the doorbell. The lady answered it, and I couldn't even talk for a minute when I saw her in real-land. Her eyes were both black, and her wrists were bandaged and there were bruises along her neck above her shirt collar, and her hair was a wreck. She looked at me with tears in her eyes, and I thought, Lady, don't back out now, your kids just climbed into my car. She handed me a ten, and I gave her the pizza and said I'd have to go get change from the car, could she come out for it? She nodded and set the pizza on the TV. Some man I could barely see on the couch growled "this doesn't even smell like a pizza. Where did you order it from?" But the lady just walked out of the house and followed me down the steps. She stopped and pulled a suitcase out of the bushes by the front door and hurried to put it on the floor in the backseat. The kids were in the back. We climbed in, and I started backing out and I looked at the lady again and thought how I'd known that people look better in VR because you can touch yourself up after you're in, so I should have known a woman would take away black eyes and bruises. I should have looked ahead and been prepared for seeing her in real-land, but I hadn't and it was hard to look at her now. That's when the husband ran out of the house. He must have looked in the pizza box and seen that the pizza was frozen, then looked out the window to see that his family was making an escape. I could easily outdistance him in a Mustang, and he turned and ran back to the house.

"He'll follow," the lady said. "Can you drive this thing?"

I didn't even answer her. I just took us out onto I-15 and started the game. It was all the answer she needed. She turned around and buckled the kids in, then buckled herself in.

We weren't going to have an easy time of blending into the traffic in Mom's red Mustang with a Happy Pizza clown face flapping on the hood, and I just hoped her husband was way behind us somewhere, which was too much to hope for. The lady was watching behind. "Here he comes," she said. "White Bronco, center lane. He'll want to kill you, because he'll think I've been stepping out with you."

I thought about that for a minute. "What about you and the kids?" I asked the lady, finally. "What will he do to all of you?"

"He'll just want to hurt me. The kids don't matter to him yet."

So play the game, I thought. Play it better than you ever have. He was right behind us and gaining, doing 90 plus. I sped up to over 90 and thought that this is what I would do: come up fast on the speed trap at 33rd South, get in the inside lane, then slow down fast, send the Bronco speeding past, the sure prey of any cop waiting there. We came up fast onto 33rd South, I took the inside lane and braked. The Bronco sped past in the middle lane.

But there was no cop.

"Now he's in front of us," was all the lady said.

He slowed right down in the middle lane, so I got in the fast lane and punched it. When we were alongside each other, doing 80 plus, he tried to shout something out his window. The lady wouldn't look at him. The five-year-old girl climbed out of her buckle and over the seat into her mother's arms. She looked at her dad, but didn't wave. The other two kids started crying because they wanted to come up into the front seat too, but the lady just ignored them. I punched it again to get past her husband, and he swerved in behind us—I didn't know if he'd meant to hit the back of the car or what, but he was right on our tail and speeding up behind us to maybe ram us. I shoved the Mustang up to 90 plus, and he was still gaining.

I merged right, and he followed us. We passed a Smith's grocery store semi in the middle lane and just ahead a white Lincoln was going to roadblock us doing 70. I got an idea and slowed down while the semi closed up the space between us. The lady's husband slowed down, too, though he stayed right on our tail. He didn't ram us after all. I waited till there was room for just us to merge into the middle lane between the semi and the Lincoln and did it. The semi let out a blat of horn and I sped ahead. The Bronco was sandwiched back behind the Lincoln and the semi.

We'd passed the 45th South exit and were coming up on 53rd South and one mile later the I-215 turnoff. The white Bronco reappeared behind us. He'd slowed down, gotten around the semi, and was speeding up toward us again. "I know where I can get some cops," I said.

At least I hoped I did. They were always there when you didn't want them: just off the I-15 merge lanes onto I-215 heading west toward Redwood Road. I'd gotten my first ticket there after starting work for Fat Joe and Happy Pizza. Be there today, Cops, I thought. Just be there. I didn't care if they pulled us all over and helped us sort out the mess. The husband couldn't make his wife stay with him, and he couldn't kill me if there were cops around.

So I got in the inside lane, passed 53rd South, and headed for the I-215 exit. The Bronco followed. I dropped down onto I-215, doing 80 plus, and braked. The Bronco changed lanes and sped past to get ahead of us, and a cop pulled out after him, lights flashing and then the siren started up.

We stayed well behind the chase, and eventually the Bronco pulled over. We drove past them, turned around at Redwood Road, and headed back east for I-15. The police still had the Bronco and the lady's husband pulled over when we went past.

"He's probably telling them that you kidnapped us," the lady said.

"You can straighten things out at the courthouse in Provo," I said.

We got onto I-15 and headed south past 72nd South. I realized I was breathing hard and tried to slow it down. I also slowed down the car. After all, I had a mother and her three kids in the car with me and no reason to race anymore. I dropped us down to 70 and kept it there. The lady turned around and unstrapped her crying kids and took them all into the front seat with her and held them, quieted them down. "Thank you," the lady said to me, almost in a whisper, looking straight ahead.

"My name is Clayton," I said, suddenly thinking it was important for her to know that.

She looked at me, then, but didn't smile. "I'm Elizabeth. The oldest one here is Jane. This is Amy; and my youngest is Clayton, like you."

There wasn't much else for us to say. Not then. We drove past Draper and the prison, then started up the Point of the Mountain. When we drove over the top, we could see Utah Valley. There were the green wheatfields and the orchards around Alpine, the snow on the blue mountains. I-15 stretched out below us and ahead, to the south. It all looked nearly as good as it looked in VR, though I could see the cities from the Point if I looked hard, so I stopped looking and we dropped down into the valley and I couldn't see them anymore. We'd be in Provo in thirty minutes anyway, and then my parents would come.

I thought about that and decided to tell them about the Peace Corps later that night around the campfire when it was just the three of us, after we'd dropped Elizabeth off at her sister's, the three of us without TV so we could talk, away from the things that reminded us of all the programs in our lives, out under stars in the cold mountain air and the only sounds the sounds of our crackling fire and the wind in the trees and our voices. Our lives would all seem short and valuable out there, and our dreams worth dreaming. I got that hit-in-the-gut feeling of excitement again, and it was strong because it came from being excited about talking to my parents *and* from being able to drive my mother's red Mustang down the road I'd wanted to take in the net, where the road out looked so achingly beautiful.

OTHER TIME

DIANA LOFGRAN HOFFMAN

*S*andy wandered through the parking lot of Utah Valley Regional Medical Center, sipping a carton of milk and eating a muffin from the vending machine. And wondering where she'd parked. She was tired enough that it was hard to remember anything. Her head ached. Her feet ached. She'd had three or four hours of sleep for the past six nights, juggling the demands of a sick infant, a cross toddler, a husband in graduate school, and the night shift at the hospital.

She wandered over to a trash dumpster and dropped in her carton and wrapper. Something drew her eye, something shimmering in the morning light, half-hidden beneath a pile of shredded paper. She hesitated, staring at it. Hospital dumpsters were not good places for rummaging. But the object lay near the side of the dumpster, and the paper around it seemed clean enough. She glanced around her, saw no one near, then stepped over and drew it out.

It was a ball, sort of: grapefruit-sized and divided through the middle, like a huge yo-yo. Its surface shifted from rippling greens to iridescent blues and violets. Someone's pop-art telephone or radio? She turned it over, but there were no levers, no knobs or buttons, no receiver. She pulled at it and twisted, but it did not open. She pushed and, feeling a little give between the two sides, pressed them together. They caught and held.

Silence. Sudden and absolute silence.

Sandy stiffened, her ears straining for some sound, any whisper of sound; there was nothing. *I'm deaf, I've had a stroke.*

Her hands began to shake, and she dropped the ball to touch her ears to rub them, unstop them. The ball hit the sidewalk with a harsh crack, and then there were sea gulls' cries and traffic sounds again—and they were like music.

Sandy stared at the ball at her feet and stepped backward, trembling. The ball had uncoupled with the impact. Had she only imagined? Was she, in her weariness, dreaming? Falling asleep on her feet? She shook her head, confused. She crouched down and reached out a tentative hand but then drew back. Something had happened, something utterly unnatural. *Get out of here,* she told herself. *Leave it.* But she didn't. She crouched on the sidewalk and studied the ball. There was nothing much to see, really. It lay still, apparently undamaged. It looked fairly ordinary—just pretty plastic. She reached out, nudged it with a finger. It rolled a little. That was all. *And yet . . .*

Finally, cautiously, she picked it up, but with just the tips of her fingers, as if it were hot. She stood for a long time, wondering, biting her lip. At length her curiosity prevailed: she drew a deep breath and slowly pressed in the sides of the ball. They united with a soft click.

Sound ended.

Holding her breath, hesitant, Sandy looked up—to see a world that had lost not only sound, but motion. Cyclists and pedestrians stood arrested. Birds hung in the sky. The cars on the streets lay still, as if parked in the middle of the lanes and intersections. Everything in the world had stopped, except Sandy.

She leaned over, picked up a pebble from the pavement, and threw it. It flew less than a yard, slowing and then hanging motionless in the air.

Sandy's hands grew cold, and her skin prickled beneath her clothing. *How? What power on earth could do this, could hold the world still?*

She looked down at the device (her hands were trembling again), and she pulled, twisted, and clawed at it until the sides came apart, and sound and motion returned.

The ball makes time . . . or stops it. Sandy walked back to her car and sat in the front seat in disbelief. She put the ball on the seat beside her, but the sight of it made her so uneasy she covered it with her sweater. She thought about it for a long time.

At length she drove home. Bruce had to get to his physics class. But she thought about the device throughout the day: through a morning and afternoon of weariness—she fell asleep every time she sat down to give Nathan a bottle or read Alicia a story; through an evening of colic that kept her pacing the floor during those precious few hours when she should have been in bed; and through a night shift at work when she fairly staggered through her duties.

The ball could end all that. *All those times, hundreds of times I have wished there were more hours in a day.* If only she dared to use it. But she could not even think of it without a certain rush of tension. The memory of its still and silent world made her skin crawl. It was *unnatural.* But then, so was all technology. And Sandy found that she coveted the implications of its power until she thought of little else.

She thought of it the next morning as she parked the car in front of the apartment and trudged up the walkway. She could hear Nathan starting to whimper. There would not be a moment of rest. She considered the day before her, a day just like yesterday, to be spent wandering about in a fog of fatigue. Her need for sleep consumed all pleasure, all desire, and every imperative. Yet she could have sleep now, as much as she wanted, if she dared.

Sandy paused, considering. She went to the closet where she'd hidden the ball in an ice chest and took it out. She turned it over a few times. Did it really . . . ?

She held it tightly, smooth and heavy in her hands, and she hesitated. The baby's whimper rose in pitch, becoming an angry howl. Sandy pushed inward on the ball. The wailing died. The rushing of water in the bathroom sink echoed into silence, and every other sound that should have been there fell away.

Sandy shivered. She shook her head, grinding her teeth just to hear the sound of it—of something. Grasping the ball tightly with both hands, she edged to the bathroom door and peered in. There was Bruce frozen in place, leaning over the sink with shaving cream hanging from his razor. Had his mouth just begun to open, to call to her, "I'm gonna be late; could you iron my shirt and make me a lunch while I grab some breakfast, dear?" (as he did every morning when she came home, desperate for a moment of rest before the baby woke).

Sandy stared at him with a twisted smile and said, "Not yet dear. Not for a long time yet."

She stepped to the doorway of the children's room but did not enter. Habit pressed her to check on Nathan. But he would be frozen—frozen in the very act of crying. She didn't want to see him like that. She wouldn't be able to sleep for the sight. So she left his door closed and went to her own room. She went to bed then, and slept ten hours by her watch. When she awoke it was still 7:10 in the morning (according to the clock on the wall). Bruce stood just as she'd left him, a glob of shaving cream still waiting to fall from his razor.

By the end of the week Sandy was a new woman. Her eyes were bright, the brighter for the meticulous care with which she applied her makeup. Her house was clean—really, shining clean—and the children were scrubbed, dressed and fed by eight each morning. At night, when Nathan cried, she took him into the quiet of Other Time and rocked him, uninterrupted, while Alicia stood statuesque outside the field.

Sandy sewed for herself a small waist-pack to carry the ball—the timemaker—so she could keep it with her and yet have both hands free. Throwing pebbles, she defined the boundaries of its influence. It created a sphere ten to twelve feet across, although the borders were hard to define. The pebbles slowed gradually before coming completely to rest.

Sandy found the timemaker ever more useful, and she knew she'd hardly considered its potential.

She came to do all her sleeping in Other Time (first ten hours, but later the total reached twelve and sometimes fourteen). She went jogging every day, and she did at least half of her housework within the field. Vacuuming and laundry were impossible: appliances didn't work in Other Time. Power would not come from the outlets, and water would not come through the pipes. But there was still dusting and sweeping and mopping and scrubbing and folding . . . even the dishes could be washed with brief interruptions of normal time for filling and draining the sinks.

Of course Bruce noticed the change in the home, but Sandy told him it was because the baby was going to sleep in the evening instead of crying, so that gave her a couple more hours for housework. And he believed. The work got done. It happened; therefore it had to be possible.

From time to time he did ask when she slept; she told him that work was slow, and she was able to sleep a lot while on call at her nursing station. And she said she took long naps during the day—had the children on a good schedule. He told their friends and relatives that his wife was a marvel of organization and energy.

Sandy thought she should have gloried. She had achieved her definition of the successful homemaker/career woman. But in truth she despaired, because she achieved it only by stretching every day to forty hours or more. There were women out there, she knew, that did it all in twenty-four. And once her best friend, who had three children under four, came over to her spotless home and cried and confessed she could never make it, could never be a success as a wife and housekeeper. Sandy stared at the floor. *Neither can I. It's all a façade.*

In her uneasiness Sandy tried to restrict her use of Other Time. But there wasn't really any time wasted in the first place. She wasn't watching television, or reading newspapers, or even keeping up with things like her art work or magazine subscriptions. It was just the basics of a full-time job and full-time motherhood. There was nothing to cut out.

Then came a hot summer afternoon when Sandy turned on the timemaker and went to bed, but found the heat oppressive and removed most of her clothing. She awakened some time later, groggy and congested. She stumbled to her feet, threw on a robe, and wandered into the kitchen to get a drink. But as the water poured into her glass she stared at it: the water shouldn't run in Other Time. She reached for her pack. It was not around her waist. Had she left the timemaker on the bed, and walked out of the field? She gripped the countertop. *How?* She'd thought if she left the field she would freeze, like the pebble in the air. But she hadn't.

She hurried back to the bedroom, wondering, anxious, yet unprepared. When she reached the doorway she dropped her glass in shock and stared.

There on the bed was the quilt her grandmother had made for her—pieced in the wedding ring pattern—fading, unraveling, disintegrating before her eyes; she saw the sheets crumbling into frayed pieces and dust, and the mattress shredding, pierced by rusting, broken springs. In the midst of it all the cracked and faded waist-pack settled into the wreckage of the bed, showing through its splitting seams the bulge of the timemaker.

Sandy lunged for it, lunged into the bubble of silence and grabbed the device and turned it off, and backed away from the bed in horror. How long, in dry, weatherless air, to age a bed like that? A hundred years, two hundred, three? She realized she hadn't understood Other Time. She'd thought when she activated the timemaker that normal time continued within its field, and everywhere else time stood still. Now she realized that time continued as always outside the field, and within the field it was greatly accelerated. She'd been gone maybe three minutes. And if so, around a hundred years of Other Time had passed for every minute of standard time.

The implications were terrifying. She trembled and bit her lip, comprehending what would have happened if she had left Nathan in the field—for even a moment, the blink of an eye. So many times she had fed him, rocked him, changed his diaper in Other Time. If even once she had set the timemaker down and stepped away . . .

Then another thought forced itself upon her. She *aged* in Other Time. Just like the bed. She entered it several times a day to sleep and clean house, and came out hours older. She reached up to feel the lines of her face. Her life span would be measured in hours—not in sunsets, not in birthdays. And with forty-five hour days . . . in fifteen years her children would be teenagers, her husband forty, and she would be the equivalent of over fifty. When Bruce turned fifty she would be seventy-two, and would catch her mother in age. She felt her hair, imagined herself graying, bent and tired, watching a husband young enough to be her son watch the younger women; caring for children young enough to be her grandchildren. Imagining grandchildren she might never see.

With loathing she put the timemaker down on the dresser and stared at it. It had seemed so easy, so painless to use, but the cost was terrible. If she stopped . . . how could she stop? What could she give up? Not sleep: she could cut down an hour or two, but no more. Not child care. Housekeeping? And listen to the neighbors speculate that she'd lapsed into depression, taken up soap operas, had a breakdown of sorts? "Too much stress. She just couldn't cope."

She could quit work and have Bruce take out student loans. But how could she tell him she couldn't handle work when she'd clearly been handling it so well? How could she plead stress and fatigue when she'd functioned with no sign of it? How could she ever go back?

Other Time had become an addiction—time abuse. Like the minister she'd read about who ruined his life taking speed and sedatives so he could work harder and longer than anyone else and look good. He had his drugs. She had her timemaker. It would cut just as many years from her life.

She considered showing Bruce the device, telling him the whole story. But he was desperately pressed in his studies, struggling to do well in a demanding program. If he knew of the device, he would use it—first to keep up with his classes, later to put in the rigorous hours required in an engineering firm. He would be addicted more certainly and more completely than she; and then she would be the one with the ancient companion. She would be the early widow.

She did not trust him to use the timemaker with discretion. She did not trust herself. But she *had* to use it—at least for now. To begin with, she had to replace the bed and bedding, and get throw rugs to cover the disintegrated carpet underneath. She had no money for them; she'd have to "borrow." And then she'd have to think of something to tell Bruce.

And even after that was done she wouldn't be able to cope with a sudden return to the restrictions of the normal day. But she would have to cut down her use of the timemaker.

If I only use it to catch up on sleep, nothing else . . . sleep doesn't age a person. Sleep heals, makes a person healthy, makes them live longer. I'll die a lot faster from stress and lack of sleep than from longer-than-normal days.

With this resolve she quieted her misgivings about early aging. It was not so easy to quiet her guilt, after she "borrowed" the new bed and bedding and lied to Bruce about it.

And her resolve proved difficult to keep. On Monday night when the children were both screaming, and she sat on the couch trying to bounce Nathan on her arm and hold Alicia in her lap (and both wailed), she gave in and reached for the timemaker. Better for the children. She had to get them to sleep if she was to clean house during normal time.

On Tuesday morning her sister-in-law came unannounced when toys cluttered the living room, unwashed dishes filled the sink, and muddy footprints marked the kitchen floor. So Sandy held her motionless on the front step while she cleaned for three hours in the blink of an eye.

Wednesday and Thursday she held herself to her commitment to cut back and tried to compensate with speed and efficiency. But much of the housework didn't get done. No matter how she organized or how hastily she worked, she could not keep up the housekeeping without the timemaker.

By Friday, feeling overwhelmed and inadequate, she braced herself for an attack when Bruce walked in the door, irritated already by the stress of midterms.

"I see we had a tornado today. In fact it seems this week we've had several."

She glared at him, knowing he believed all the housework could be done in two hours—for she had "proved" it possible.

"I do the best I can, with these kids."

"It seems some days are a lot better than others."

"They are."

"Well, what's the difference? Is there something special about Friday afternoon TV?"

"I *never* watch TV!"

"Well, what is it then? What's going on this week?"

Sandy struggled—unsuccessfully—to keep her voice even. "Did it ever occur to you that I spend every waking moment changing diapers and doing laundry and shopping and cooking—and I have to sleep sometime because then I spend the night working to put you through school—and sometimes there isn't any time left over for cleaning?"

"Then how come you did it all without any trouble last week? Or Tuesday? I know you can do it. I've seen you do it. And maybe it's hard. I know how it is—grad school isn't exactly too easy either. But in the end it just comes down to effort."

She could not answer—she had no answer to give—so she whirled and hurried from the room, found her timemaker, and escaped.

She cried for a while, for she could not see a way out. When she had spent herself, she slept for a while and then ate a carton of yogurt. But it didn't make her feel better. And she wasn't ready to go back.

She decided to go for a walk, so she put on her shoes and jacket. She stepped outside into the cool autumn air. The sun rested on the rim of the mountains; it would not set.

She walked down the sidewalk and across the lawn, through a world that stood silent at her command. Every person she encountered was a mime-mannequin, holding an impossible position with perfect control.

She wandered up to the back fence of the apartment complex, followed it to the base of the foothills, and climbed over it. The hillside and valley below were beautiful. The leaves were turning to gold and orange, and across the valley the sunlight silvered the surface of the lake. She wished she could see it up close, for the lake would be covered with waves, standing still.

Sandy found a trail and followed it through tangles of oak and mahogany on the mountainside. She began to see animals. She examined robins and jays and a tanager in the air, a cottontail suspended mid-leap, and squirrels and chipmunks frozen on the rocks.

And then, as she wandered higher and higher, she came upon deer. There were five of them together: four spikes and a four-point buck. They were standing about, posed as if browsing on twigs and grass. Sandy walked up to them slowly, as though she might frighten them, and studied them with delight. So close. Such detail. How would it be to see them running? She turned off the timemaker (such sudden noise!) and they came to life, startled, and sprang away from her. She froze them mid-leap, then studied them longer: their bulging muscles, willow-thin legs, open mouths—they were beautiful. She wanted to capture them somehow, at least take pictures. Why not? She could go and get her camera and they would still be here.

She started back down the mountain, wishing she had a better camera. If she did she could take pictures close up, perfectly composed, bracketed for perfect exposure, perfectly focused without telephoto distortion. They would be worth *money*. Wildlife photographers spent hours, days, even weeks walking the hills, waiting in blinds, rigging shutter-release traps. With her timemaker, she could capture in minutes what they spent weeks searching for, and do it better. With practice she could become the best. And then sell to the best magazines—*Natural History, International Wildlife, National Geographic*—and travel around the world on assignment.

She reached the apartment, fetched her little disk camera, and hurried back up the mountain. She shot all the film she had, then just stared at the deer, seeing in them a future waiting to be taken.

But she'd have to have better equipment. Of course with the timemaker she could "borrow" anything she wanted, anytime. And pay for it later—when she was successful. She wrote down a list of the things she would need . . .

It was twenty hours before Sandy left Other Time. When she finally returned, the time she had spent and the ideas she'd pursued frightened her. She could be swallowed up entirely by Other Time. And like it. But it would cost her . . . every hour of it would take away an hour of raising her children, living with her family. Being young.

When she returned to standard time, Bruce was still grouching around the kitchen, and it seemed he held awfully long grudges, though in truth his was only a few moments old.

Sandy watched him all that day and the next. She watched him snap at the children and throw his clothes in the corner of the bedroom; she watched him play with Alicia and stay up late to wash the dishes. She watched the children as well: watched Nathan howling and Nathan cooing; watched Alicia whining and Alicia skipping, with unbounded triumph, for the first time ever. Sandy asked herself what she wanted—really wanted—knowing she could have anything, for a price.

Sandy thought for several days, and as she did the days grew longer and longer. She allowed herself Other Time to sit on the balcony and study the magazines she hoped to sell to. She spent Other Time visiting camera shops and examining expensive cameras, powerful flash attachments, and specialty lenses. She checked out books on photography and read them.

The pictures she'd taken came back from the developer. She studied them, and they were good: exciting composition, extraordinary angles. But the colors were weak, the focus too soft, and there was little depth of field—limitations of the camera. She could do so much better. How she wanted the chance to try, to be not only good, but the best there was.

And she found herself growing quite comfortable in Other Time. She'd come to like the solitude and the silence, and the power to hold the world in check. At times she craved that power, and the craving frightened her.

After one fifty-hour day, she sat in the rocking chair, holding the timemaker and staring into its multicolored surface. *It could draw my whole life into this bubble where I live alone.* She closed her eyes and leaned back. Was that what she wanted—to grow old alone? She'd vowed to cut back, but lately . . . . She drummed her fingers on the chair arm. *I'm losing control; I will have to give it up altogether, or not at all.*

But it seemed impossible to give it up. And how could she get rid of it? Certainly she couldn't leave it in the dumpster, for just anyone to find. She wouldn't throw it away. Or bury it: things were unearthed too easily.

She leaned forward and rested her chin on her hand. She dared not destroy it. It seemed to have an incredible energy source. When she'd left it activated on the bed, several hundred years had passed within its field, and it still worked. She wondered how much longer it would work. Hundreds, thousands of years? And with that kind of power . . . . Her cousin had suffered third-degree burns when a can of hair spray had exploded in a trash fire. She did not want to know what a crushed or incinerated timemaker would do.

As she thought these things, Alicia came out of her room, stumbled over to Sandy, and crawled in her lap, and Sandy put the timemaker on the floor. Alicia whimpered a little about a nightmare, then snuggled down and went to sleep. Sandy sat and stroked her hair, remembering the first hug, the tentative toddler steps, the day Alicia first said "mama" and "wuv you." And how she danced in the living room as she watched *The Nutcracker* for the first time.

"Mommy," she'd asked afterward, "can I be a ballerina and still be a mommy like you?"

"Yes, sweetheart. You can."

"And when I grow up to be a mommy, will you still watch me dance?"

"Of course I will. And I'll watch your children dance too."

Sandy rocked a little faster, turned her head away, and swallowed hard.

Eventually Sandy put Alicia back in bed. Then she turned on the timemaker, took out a photo album, and pondered its pages. Would it bring her as much happiness to be a world-famous photographer as it would to watch her grandchildren dancing? To share her life and growth and future with her husband? The question made her terribly uncomfortable, and by her uneasiness Sandy knew she was losing the will to change her course. Some instinct within her whispered that real fulfillment would come from relationships, not money or acclaim. But the implications of that feeling were too hard to face.

She tried to reason that she could use the timemaker sparingly; in time her children would get older and her husband would graduate and the need would diminish; she'd be able to manage without excessive use of Other Time. She'd just use it for photography—her career. Such an extraordinary opportunity. She could hold her use of Other Time to that, surely, and not abuse the timemaker. But she knew the photography would send her away from home for weeks at a time, and might easily consume far more hours of Other Time than housework ever had. And she found herself thinking of the camera she needed, the flash and lenses and tripod, the professional-looking wardrobe. She'd have to have them to get started. She needed them *now*. And she could have them, with the timemaker. Then there was the breadmaker she wanted, the piano, the Camcorder. . . . Already she'd taken the bed and the bedding. *It had been so easy*. It was hard now to think about sending the four-hundred sixty dollars to the furniture store, when she knew they'd never ask for it, never know.

It would always be like that. Too easy to take. Too easy to postpone paying.

Sandy shook herself. The timemaker was not a gift, not a tool. It was an addiction, a temptation she could not bear. Even now she sat within its field and let it burn away the hours of her life so she could think about it in peace. But still she could not resolve to let it go.

The next morning, Sandy visited the camera shop again and spent hours there in Other Time and finally took what she wanted: three thousand dollar's worth of equipment and film. In the evening she walked up into the mountains and spent fifteen hours photographing deer and foxes and black bear in the red light of sunset against the backdrop of dying leaves.

Then she needed cash to develop so many negatives. She walked to a convenience store, waited until the register was open and activated the timemaker. She eased around to the back of the register (so no one else would be included in the field) and stared at the piles of bills in the drawers. She considered the clean-cut young cashier who would come up short when his shift ended; she stared at the balding man buying ice cream for his girls (he looked a little like her father). She could not bring herself to reach into the register. She tried three times with trembling hands. But her face grew pale and her forehead beaded in a cold sweat, and finally she backed into the corner between the wall and the video game, and sat down on the floor and covered her face.

She had let herself become a thief. She trembled with the shame of it. A thief. The timemaker had taken her integrity. If she kept it, it would also take her youth and her family.

She went home and used the timemaker to return the camera equipment to the store. She didn't know what to do with the exposed film, so she put it in the refrigerator in a plastic bag and hoped she could squeeze enough money out of the budget some day to get it developed. She needed to; she still owed over five hundred dollars for film and bedding.

She turned off the timemaker. If she was to be rid of it, it would have to be now, before she rationalized away her resolve. But what to do with it? How could she be rid of it without the risk of someone else finding it?

Then she remembered a place she had visited, two years before at a family reunion. She took her children to a baby-sitter. Then she collected a flashlight, a square of foam rubber, and a roll of duct tape.

She put them with the timemaker in a paper bag and drove north, into American Fork Canyon, to the parking lot of Timpanogos Cave. She stepped out of the car into the cooling air of the shaded canyon and stared at the mountain. The mountain was solid. And old.

Sandy took her purse and paper bag and paid the fee at the visitor's center. Then she waited her turn and paced the floor, rolling the top of the paper bag up and down, up and down, until she was finally allowed to pass the gate and start up the steep trail to the caves. It was a long climb. She walked too fast and had to stop and rest several times, and each time she wondered about turning back; she chewed her lip and worked the bag until the top frayed and shredded. But she held her resolve and pressed forward.

A tour group waited at the entrance, but she did not join them. She wanted to be alone. So she turned on the timemaker, slipped through the door and walked down, by the feeble light of her flashlight, into the very heart of the mountain. In the darkness and the damp she found herself shivering, but more from tension than the cold.

By a wall of curtained limestone she found a crevasse, as she had remembered. It was only a foot or two wide but it angled down into the depths of the earth, into depths that swallowed up her flashlight's beam and gave back no reflection. She stared into that darkness for a long time. As she had hoped, the crevasse was too narrow for most people to crawl into.

She drew the timemaker from the bag and held it, hefting its weight, stroking its smoothness. Then she began to wrap it with duct tape. It was activated—she hoped it would burn itself out eventually— and she did not want it to come uncoupled when it fell. She folded around it a layer of foam rubber so it wouldn't break, and again she taped it securely. Then she held it one last moment in the silence and the stillness it created, closing her eyes, forcing reluctant hands to hold it out, out . . . could she really do this? Fame, travel, money. . . . She opened her fingers one by one—one for Alicia, one for Nathan, one for Bruce—and let go. The timemaker fell into the crevasse with a whispered thud and rolled downward. She followed it with the flashlight beam as it bumped and slid, almost caught in a narrow place . . . but tipped sideways and finally disappeared into the darkness. After that she could hear it bouncing and rolling until the sounds faded into distant whispers, and then into the almost-silence of the dripping, echoing cave.

Sandy left the cave and started home, to struggle with her limitations, to work off the debts of her conscience, and to share life with her husband and children and her children's children.

And as she walked down the trail she pictured the timemaker. She imagined that it had wedged at the top of a terrace formation. She saw the tape crack, the foam rubber rot to dust, the water in the ten-foot bubble of time condense, drip, pool, evaporate, and condense again—and again and again. A few formations above the timemaker dissolved, and the flowstone around it thickened, creeping up and encasing the timemaker.

It should burn out quickly. Sandy calculated that thirty thousand years of Other Time could pass before she had dinner tonight. Thirty thousand years—and nature would take very little notice.

RISE UP, YE WOMEN THAT ARE AT EASE

D. WILLIAM SHUNN

*T*he jeweler tapped away at his calculator, frowned, then looked up at me. "Four-eighty-six is the best I can do," he said.

I slouched back in my chair and drummed my fingers on the glass display case that separated us. I hadn't expected more, even there at Snarr's Jewelry & Electronics, but I didn't want to seem overly eager. "My fiancee said you estimated seven to eight hundred."

"She told me it was a third of a carat, Mr. Teagarden," said the jeweler. He was a stout, sandy-haired man in his mid-thirties, which made him about ten years my senior. His face was smooth and peach-colored, without the sheen of sweat that seems to afflict so many overweight people. In fact, he carried himself in such a way that his girth was one of the last things I had noticed about him. "You watched me weigh the center marquis yourself," he said. "Point-two-eight carats is more a heavy quarter than anything."

I nodded. "They said it was a third where we bought it. Stupid to take their word for it, I guess."

The jeweler didn't respond, only pursed his lips and glanced over the cryptic notes he had jotted down as he calculated, which I had tried to read upside-down. "It's a thin stone, too," he said, "slightly yellowish, and there's a little fracture just below the bow tie. Two-sixty-six is a very good price, and the two-twenty for the setting is even better."

I knew it was the best deal I'd get anywhere in Salt Lake City, but it still hurt me to hear our engagement ring reduced to such cold figures, see it lying dismembered before me on the rose-colored velvet pad.

Some of that hurt must have shown up in my face, because the jeweler said, "Listen, the setting isn't something I normally would have bought. We deal in loose stones as a matter of course, so that was no problem, but this setting we usually carry ourselves. We use bigger stones for the side mountings, though, and *this*"—he picked up the remains of the ring between his thumb and forefinger—"I can show side-by-side with our own settings so the customer sees what difference the size of the stones makes."

I pressed my lips into a thin line.

"Is four-eighty-six not acceptable?" said the jeweler.

"Yes, it is," I said. "To be honest, I thought five hundred dollars would be stretching it."

"Well, you're more realistic than most. That's why I don't advertise the fact that I buy diamonds. People come in with such high expectations, and they end up taking a bath. But better that than letting a pawn shop rob you blind, I guess."

"I knew I was going to take a bath," I said, but then abandoned my detached pose. "At this point, the money's more important than the ring."

The jeweler nodded, as if to say he understood. "I can't give you cash, you know. It'll have to be a check."

I wondered what kind of customer would object to a check. "That's fine."

"And I hope you understand that I have to hold the ring for thirty days—just in case it's stolen. I'm afraid I *am* like a pawn shop in that regard, but it's necessary."

I shrugged. I actually still owed a thousand on the ring, but as long as I kept up the payments, no one would be the wiser.

"Then let me go type up a check for you."

While the jeweler was gone, I let my eyes wander around the store. It was large inside, with immaculate white walls and high ceilings. Expensive clocks lined the wall behind the display cases, while shelves of neatly arranged televisions and camcorders and the like occupied the opposite wall. An older man on a ladder was cleaning the fluorescent light fixtures, and only one customer besides myself was in view, a middle-aged blonde woman whose graceful features for some reason put me in mind of an Afghan wolfhound. She wore her woolen pantsuit with a casual elegance that I didn't realize was possible to achieve so early on a Saturday morning, and I could smell her Anaïs Anaïs faintly from across the room. She checked her watch with a stern look on her face, then feigned interest in a display of miniature LCD televisions, as if that would conceal her impatience, fanning herself with a padded brown envelope.

The jeweler returned after a few minutes, and seemed of a mind to shoot the breeze after I had stashed the check in the inside pocket of my leather jacket without looking at the figure. "Getting married soon, then?" he asked.

The question took me by surprise. "Uh, no," I said. "Kjirsten—the girl who showed you the ring last week—is actually my *ex*-fiancee. I suppose I should get used to calling her that."

"And she helped you sell the ring?"

I nodded.

He seemed impressed. "That was certainly good of her."

"Well, it's been what you might call an 'amicable breakup,'" I said. "It's also been a long time coming."

"So has the service around here," muttered the elegant woman, intently studying a dual-deck VCR.

"I'll be with you in just a moment, ma'am," said the jeweler with amused equanimity. He turned back to me. "I thought this Kjirsten might have been a *new* fiancee who wanted you to get rid of an *old* fiancee's ring."

I shook my head. "No such luck. Kjirsten was the one and only."

He nodded in sympathy. "What will you do now?"

The elegant woman rolled her eyes and let out a sigh that was halfway to a growl, dropping all pretense of patience. A little embarrassed by the jeweler's indifference toward his other customer, I said, "I, uh, move out. I've lined up an apartment closer to school." I patted my breast pocket. "This will sure make the first month easier."

"So you're a student?"

"In music," I said, nodding. I could have told him all about my band, and the interest a scout for Caprice Records had been showing in my demo tape, but that was when the woman turned on her heel and marched stiffly out of the store, muttering, "Tom can hock his *own* damn earrings! I don't have time for this shit!"

The jeweler watched her leave, eyebrows raised. "Huh," he said, with all the interest of a biologist examining the mottles on the back of a tree frog. "You never can tell when they're going to go off half-cocked."

I shrugged. I didn't like being part of the situation that had driven the woman off. "I'd really better be going, too," I said. "I've got a lot of errands to run this morning."

The jeweler leaned toward me. "I'm separated from my wife myself," he said with conspiratorial solemnity. "Just this month. I know how it is." He put out his hand and shook mine firmly. "Good luck to you, Mr. Teagarden. I hope things go better for you from here out."

"So do I," I said. "Thanks for all your help."

On the sidewalk outside Snarr's Jewelry & Electronics, I squinted in the bright sunlight and zipped up my jacket. It was the last week of February; the air was very crisp and cold, and shrinking mounds of dirty snow still lined the curbs. The downtown traffic was sparse, as were the pedestrians. I started north up Main, with my hands deep in my jacket pockets. The dark brick façades of the shops and the flophouses, all crowded together shoulder to shoulder, were a comfort to me, a reassuring bulwark against the loneliness settling about me like a cloak. The ring had been ransomed away, and now nothing remained to link me with any other human being in this city—nothing but the knowledge that thousands of other people, perhaps even the builders of those shops, had lived and been lonely right here on this street. The smoke-stained sadness of the city protected me.

I had not walked more than twenty yards, though, when I saw the woman from the jewelry store ahead of me, clacking rapidly up the sidewalk in her high heels and trying to flag down a taxi. She must be from out of town, I thought with a superior smile, because any native would know you can't hail a taxi in Salt Lake. They're all radio-dispatched, so you have to call the cab company and tell them where you want to be picked up.

Then my smile shaded into puzzlement, because the taxi she was waving at actually slowed down and pulled over to the curb.

The rear door of the taxi opened, but the woman didn't get in quite yet. She was frantically licking stamps and sticking them on the padded envelope she'd had at the store. She scribbled a few lines on the front of the envelope, then cast about for a mailbox. I could hear the cabbie—a woman also, which you didn't see every day—shouting at her to hurry it up.

Then the elegant woman saw me. She hurried up to me and thrust the envelope against my chest. I had to yank my hands out of my pockets to keep it from falling to the sidewalk. "See that this gets mailed," she said, with a directness and authority that I no more could have flouted than I could have willed my heart to stop beating. Her eyes were deep violet, and when they released me after a piercing moment I found myself ruing the fact that I wasn't fifteen years older.

And then I wondered if I really would have *needed* to be fifteen years older.

The rear door of the taxi slammed shut behind her. As the vehicle accelerated away, I saw that there was another woman in the front passenger seat, and two more crammed in the back along with my new friend. I imagined the five of them in that enclosed space getting on each other's nerves before long, gouging each other with their nails.

When the taxi had disappeared from view, I continued north, the woman's perfume still in my nostrils, keeping my eyes open for a mailbox. Half a block farther I passed Wyatt's Books, Magazines, and Gift Shop, then backtracked a few steps to stand entranced before the display window. The annual swimsuit issue of *Sports Illustrated* was just out, and perhaps two dozen copies of the magazine were artfully arranged in the window, with a blowup of the cover prominent at the grouping's focus. There, framed by the sapphire-blue waters of the Florida Keys, stood Vendela (one name only—why does that deepen a woman's mystique?), the most lovely swimsuit model I had ever seen.

Her body was as perfect as you would expect, clad sparely and reluctantly in a nacreous gray-blue monokini with strips that crossed just below her throat and covered only the upper hemisphere of each breast. With her hip cocked to the right and her hands casually joined behind her head, the line of her body formed a sinuous S-curve as inviting as any untrammeled length of autobahn. Her abundant honey-colored hair was pulled back in a flaxen mass, revealing a face so finely formed that I could see Patrick Nagel weeping in frustration at the deceptive simplicity of capturing it accurately in acrylics. Slightly blushing, with just the right hint of cheekbones, her generous lower lip suggesting the fullness of almost-ripe strawberries, Vendela favored me from the window with an ambiguous and inviting half-smile, but it was the intelligence in her narrowed sloe eyes and unlined brow that captivated me most completely. What secrets did she possess that could fill her eyes with such knowledge but leave the rest of her face so lush and innocent?

I find falling in love with pinups grotesquely adolescent, but that didn't stop me from going inside and buying a copy of my own.

When I emerged from Wyatt's, the sun seemed to shine a bit more brightly than it had before. I shared the sidewalks with a few construction-worker types, two or three bewhiskered panhandlers, and a group of intense young Latinos. Cars buzzed up and down the street like lonely insects, and the cold air was tainted with the faint smell of exhaust. Clutching my brown paper sack full of Vendela and my padded brown envelope perhaps full of jewelry, I found myself wishing for spring, for the girls who would emerge from hibernation, reborn, with their long, coltish legs and gravity-resistant breasts glorious like the wings of a butterfly after shedding its chrysalis. Ah, winter's end could not arrive too soon.

I kept to the west side of the street, since the east was still in shadow and would be colder. The only woman I passed was a young cash-register jockey who left the downtown Wendy's still in uniform, climbed into an old car parked in a three-minute delivery zone, and drove away. (She wasn't much to look at—so I really didn't.) I turned east at the corner of Main and South Temple, passing the historic Lion and Beehive houses as I continued up to State Street. Brigham Young had lived there a century before, with a few of his seventy-odd wives. I wondered what things had been like in *that* home.

There was a mailbox at the next corner, in the shadow of the Eagle Gate—a black metal arch that crouched over the street like a hungry daddy-longlegs—but on the verge of dropping the envelope through the slot I hesitated. The address on the envelope had been hastily scrawled, and it was difficult (though not impossible) to read. After studying it for long enough, though, I managed to convince myself that no uneducated postal worker was ever going to be able to decipher it correctly. I'll just redo the address and mail it later, I told myself, and with my justification firmly in place, I continued down the street.

It was half a block north to First Avenue, on the seam where the narrow, hilly Avenues debauched uneasily onto the broader downtown streets, then another half-block uphill to my ancient Impala, opposite the 1907-vintage apartment building I called home. I got in behind the wheel, tossing my parcels over onto the passenger seat. Then I just sat.

I couldn't go up to the apartment, not yet. My things were mostly boxed up in anticipation of the move, and I'd just bother Kjirsten puttering around on the one synthesizer that was still set up. She was a certified nurse's aide, and she worked a double shift Friday nights at the nearby LifeCare Center. She needed to sleep. Besides, if she found out that I'd gone ahead and sold the ring it would only break her heart, which had already been broken enough.

Sometimes it was so hard to know which of us was breaking it off with the other.

I shivered. The loneliness was closing in. There was nothing in this neighborhood of turn-of-the-century houses and apartment buildings to defend me from it, either. The homes all around me were filled with dreams, plans, memories, family histories, and there was no comfort in that. Worse yet, with my car parked facing downhill, the Salt Lake temple rose in all its granite majesty directly ahead of me, just a few blocks away. Kjirsten and I had planned to be married there one day, before economic necessities forced us into a forbidden mutual living arrangement. I stared at the golden sculpture of the angel Moroni atop the temple's highest spire, trumpet lifted to his lips to sound a triumphant note I could not hear, and I wept.

But not for long. I had to keep myself occupied, and my next objective was the credit union, to deposit my check. As I started the Impala, a powerful but quavering female voice blasted me from the AM radio: "And in this our eleventh hour, my sisters, can we ignore the challenge in the prophetic words of Isaiah? 'Rise up, ye women that are at ease!' proclaimed that ancient seer. 'Hear my voice, ye careless daughters! Give ear unto my speech! Many days and years shall ye be troubled, ye careless women, for the vintage shall fail; the gathering shall not come!' But the gathering *has* come, my—"

Heart pounding, I fumbled for the volume control behind the tree-shaped air freshener that dangled from one of the heater knobs, then punched the dial over to the CNN affiliate station. At the calm, modulated tones of the newsman, my pulse began to slow. The apocalyptic voice that had scared the bejesus out of me had belonged to Sister Sophia, the octogenarian doom-and-gloom prophetess who terrorized the airwaves with her prerecorded harangue for four hours every Saturday morning on KFSH, the local Christian radio station. Kjirsten must have tuned the station in as a joke when she got home from work that morning. Hah hah, very funny.

As I adjusted the mirrors, I caught a glimpse of about a dozen women emerging from buildings near the crest of the hill on both sides of the street. I craned around in my seat to watch, because I had the impression that many of them were young and attractive, and because the walk home from the jewelers' had suffered from such a paucity of female scenery. There were a couple of old women from the retirement complex shuffling across the street with valises in their hands, and a few haughty middle-aged matriarchs, but the rest were indeed delectable—most likely students or the breadwinning wives of students.

I pulled the car around from the curb in a tight U-turn, then drove precisely at the speed limit past the women as they loaded bags and a few boxes into the backs of two compact cars, a luxury sedan, and a four-by-four pickup. It was an unusual sight, but the strangeness of it didn't really register with me until later. As I discreetly tried to pick out the ones whom I would most regret never having met, the voice on the radio intruded, breaking my concentration:

". . . and in Washington at this hour, the First Lady is still missing after excusing herself earlier this morning from an informal meeting of the task force on health-care reform which she heads. Secret Service agents on duty at the White House admit that they are baffled by the disappearance, which has mobilized Treasury Department, F.B.I., and N.S.A. forces in an unprecedented manhunt throughout the nation's capital. The president has refused to publicly fault the Secret Service for permitting the First Lady to vanish, saying, 'She's a resourceful and willful woman, and if she wants to stay hidden then I have no doubt that—'"

"Damn," I muttered, punching the dial over to an FM classic-rock station. I was well past the group of women now, and it would be unseemly to linger and look back at them over my shoulder. With the sounds of Jimi Hendrix molesting a tinny electric guitar as my accompaniment, I drove over to the credit union on Seventh South.

On Saturdays the credit union was open for drive-up transactions only, from nine until one. All four lanes were full when I arrived, and the line of cars stretched out into the street. I had to wait half an hour to deposit my check (which time I spent rifling through my new *Sports Illustrated*), because, as I saw after inching closer to the window, there was only one teller on duty, an unshaven young man with dark hair and an M.C. Escher print tie. "What's the deal today?" I asked as the canister with my check, deposit slip, and driver's license whooshed into the tube.

"The tellers didn't show up this morning," said the young man through the crackling speaker. "Then the replacements they called in took off around ten-thirty. Then they got me up out of bed." His tone made clear his displeasure—and his hangover.

But something had clicked in my head, finally, and I felt a cold rime stealing across my heart. "Were they all women?" I asked, knowing the answer.

The teller nodded vigorously, then put a repentant hand to his head. "Yeah. Goddamn bitches. Oops, sorry." His apology for the crudeness was grudging, though. He opened my canister, and his eyes widened as he withdrew my transaction. "You're Reggie Teagarden?" he said. "*Of* Teagarden?"

"That's right," I said, pleased although I wished he would hurry things up a little. "Teagarden" was what I called my musical outfit, the same method acts like Van Halen or Dio had used to christen themselves (though my music owed considerably more to jazz than metal).

"Wow," said the teller. "I heard you Thursday night at the Pie. Same night my girlfriend dumped me, actually. But the music was great—kinda like Miles Davis meets Elvis Costello."

"Thanks," I said, but as soon as I had my receipt I sped away, leaving his accolades hanging. I had things to check on at home.

I ran one wheel up onto the curb in front of my apartment building, grabbed my magazine and the elegant woman's envelope, and raced up the stairs. Laverne, the toothless old souse who lived upstairs from me, was missing from her accustomed smoking place next to the ashcan by the mailboxes in the lobby, but I scarcely noticed. On the second floor I fumbled for the right key, then burst into the studio apartment I would no longer share with Kjirsten.

I threw my parcels down onto the neatly made bed, then turned in a quick circle. Everything was the way it should have been: the couch, the television with its tin-foil antenna, the potted tree, the Ansel Adams print on the wall, my Ensoniq sequencing keyboard, the carefully labeled boxes that compartmentalized my entire life. In the narrow kitchen, a week's worth of my dirty dishes were stacked up on the counter, while Kjirsten's few were neatly resting in the drainer. Nothing seemed to be missing but Kjirsten herself.

Back in the main room, I spotted the Post-It note stuck to the white keys surrounding middle C on my keyboard. The words were tiny, written in a careful, cramped hand:

Dearest Reg:

I hate to have to leave like this, but things are at last at their end. I want you to remember that you were the best of all possible men, and that everyone was jealous of me for that. You always treated me with respect (even if you didn't respect my mind), and in a curious way I did love you.

I almost wish things were different, and that we could have said our farewells in person, but of course that wasn't allowed. I'll think of you often, and I hope you won't mind that I took a few photographs from your album as souvenirs.

[signed]
K.

For a few moments all that sank in was the fact that her *i*'s were dotted rather than topped with their customary small circles. But when I had digested the note, I grabbed the padded envelope from the bed and tore it open, Privacy Act be damned. A pair of ferociously huge diamond earrings tumbled out onto the bedspread, followed less eagerly by a creased square of paper. My hands trembled as I unfolded the note, which was scrawled in the same hasty hand as the address on the envelope:

Thomas—

We're gone and we're not coming back. You'll know what I mean by the time you read this. This experiment in servitude is over and we're on to greener pastures, washing our hands of you. Try not to starve to death in front of your damned TV.

Anyway I know you ransomed your soul for these baubles so they're the only thing I'm returning. I tried to sell them so I'd be sure you'd get a good deal but there wasn't time.

Time for you to stand up and be a man. Have a nice life, you

I couldn't decipher the last word (or phrase), and there was no signature.

I sat down heavily on the bed, but before I had a chance to gather my thoughts the phone rang. "Hello?" I said.

"Reggie?" It was my father, thirty minutes up the freeway. "Reggie, you haven't seen your mother anywhere, have you?" He sounded desperate. I had never heard my father sound desperate before.

"No, Dad." Somehow I couldn't manage to put any emotion in my voice. "She hasn't been here." I paused. "I don't think she will be, either, to be honest."

That was when he broke down. "Oh, God, Reggie, she's gone, she's gone, and all your sisters are gone, too. I don't know what I'm going to do, they're *gone* . . ."

I hung up when it became obvious he wasn't going to stop crying, and then I decided to take the phone off the hook. I mean, who can sit there listening while own his father has a nervous breakdown?

I lay back on the bed, feeling a bitter aloneness that was only a foretaste of what was to come. All over the city, men must be reading notes like the ones in my hand—hell, all over the country, all over the world. I tried to picture my mother actually abandoning my father, my grandmother abandoning my grandfather, my aunts abandoning my uncles, Demi abandoning Bruce, Annette abandoning Warren, Mother Theresa abandoning all her beggars . . . and I felt like crying again myself, because they were scenarios I found all too easy to imagine.

I looked at Vendela, printed so sharply on her glossy cover stock, and her smile was no longer one of come-hither-no-stop-right-there ambiguity, but instead a baldly contemptuous smirk.

That was all we had to warm us that night, all we've had any night since—the contempt radiating from the pages of *Sports Illustrated* and *Playboy*, from the lurid covers of *Cosmopolitan* and the indexed mysteries of the Victoria's Secret catalog (or, for the less cultured among us, from the grainy half-tones of *D-Cup* and *Shaved*). It reflects right at us, like a hostile communiqué bounced off a distant satellite.

Our women have vanished, and it doesn't look as if they're coming back.

Of course, a few of them did stay behind, or missed the boat, or whatever. No one can get them to talk, though. They won't tell us where the others went, or how they got there, or even *why* they left—although the *why* isn't all that hard to guess.

Things are in a state of anarchy. There's rioting, sniper fire, blood running in the gutters. Pretty exciting stuff. We're mostly fighting over the women who stayed behind. I gave up the earrings a few days ago to save my life; the guy who took them thinks they'll help him get a wife.

He should know better.

Between skirmishes, I'm writing music like a madman. I miss Kjirsten terribly, and there's a passion in me, a fire, like I've never felt before.

I wish it had been there when my songs might still have meant something.

YOU CAN'T GO BACK

M. W. WORTHEN

I sat alone in the small iron chapel, remembering. There was a porcelain Jesus on the cross on one wall and a Star of David on the other. On the polished iron wall near Jesus were pictures of eight saints with tables and candles for each one; several of those candles had been burning at each place when I entered, and I lit one more in front of the Christ for Gus. Then I'd gone to sit in one of the pews. Like nearly everything else here on The Rock, they were made of iron.

It had been Gus Anderson who'd given me a reason to stay on Vesta, and if you look at the big picture, he'd probably kept me from eventual death. Granted, a position at a mining station wasn't exactly upwardly mobile, but there were jobs and free housing. I wasn't alone here. Jobs and housing had been scarce on Earth for a good three decades.

The problem was that when I'd been on The Rock long enough to find what it was really like, I'd decided—wrongly, I suppose—that even Earth was better. Never mind that the average temperature there was at least twenty degrees higher than a century ago, never mind that you had to wear sunglasses and cover your body to protect you from the UV during the daytime. Never mind the Hot Places from the Eight Hours War.

Never mind that my parents were dead and most of my friends had gone to Mars or Ganymede. Never mind that I'd be giving up free housing and a good job to be homeless and unemployed when I got there.

The grass is always greener, I guess.

Even if there really isn't much grass left.

Gus had been a First Class, which meant essentially that he didn't have to be here if he didn't want to—he'd earned enough points with the Company for subsidized transport to Earth and Full Retirement. It also meant that he'd probably been mining on The Rock for over twenty-five years. He'd been here for almost my entire life, and for some reason I could not imagine, he'd elected to stay here. Gus had made First Class over three years ago.

He first came to my attention as I was monitoring computer use—part of my job. He'd been using more and more space, and I couldn't figure out why any miner, First Class or not, would want that much space. I was the only one on The Rock who really had a decent reason to be using anything close to my allotted space.

Computer storage is the one thing found in abundance here, and it's a free benefit to all Company employees—which means everybody. That and the liquor and the hookers—male and female. These services provide lots of things to do when you're not actually doing the work you're contracted for, as well as keep your mind off the fact that the Company is screwing your brains out by not paying you half what you're worth.

Few people ever come remotely close to using all of their computer space. Those who did were either slowing down the machine by resaving their played-out computer games or were doing something they shouldn't, which is where the cop aspect of my job began. Lately we'd had instances of hacking that might have cost the Company lives or—worse—money. Large numbers of files sometimes indicated that kind of thing.

So when I got back to my office one day, Gus's name was flagged on my "Things to Check" directory screen. I'd installed a subroutine to let me know when someone got close to using all of their memory. The idea was to check the files to see if what they were doing merited the allocation of more memory space or if they were doing something else.

Gus was coming close to using all of his storage.

I jacked into the computer and waited while it scanned my brain-print. It asked me if I wanted the operating system displayed in virtual-reality mode, semivirtual (which would still allow me to interact with the outside world), or screen. I wouldn't be working with text or numbers, so I said, "Full virtual. Vocal input, textual response." I preferred that the computer respond in writing. Even though text could get kind of awkward in virtual-reality mode, for some reason it really bugged me when the damn machine talked to me. Call it neurosis.

As my small, metallic office faded from view to be replaced by the geometrical, semirealistic world of virtual reality, I wondered if "full virtual" wasn't an oxymoron.

I was in a small, light blue room with a huge wall screen full of menu choices. I knew exactly what I wanted. "Computer Allocation Directory," I said. "List files, Anderson, Claudius A., SSN 259-67-8927-45." All his files appeared on the screen; most had names like Provo.L, Orem.L, AmericanFork.L, PleasantGrove.L, Springville.L, and so on, and each file occupied hundreds of thousands of megabytes. The ".L" indicated that the files were linked together.

"What the hell could this old man possibly be doing?" I whispered to myself. The computer was bigger and more powerful than hell, so these huge files were perfectly feasible, but what would be the purpose? Even game files that contained their own worlds weren't this big. Even the ones that were big were chains of smaller files. This was a chain of outrageously big files.

I scanned the files again. A couple of the names sounded like cities or towns. Deciding to check this, I said, "Library Encyclopedia access."

Another big screen zoomed into view to occupy a position to the left of the one I was looking at. It had the company logo at the top, and below that, in big Helvetica letters, "LIBRARY ENCYCLOPEDIA."

I said, "Cross-reference the following words: Provo, P-R-O-V-O, Orem, O-R-E-M . . . " I read off the rest of the names in Gus's file list, except for the obvious ones, things titled "Journal," "Books," and so forth.

A window appeared at the bottom of the encyclopedia screen. "Names given are all names of cities and towns in Utah and Wasatch Counties, Utah, extant before the Intercontinental Nuclear Strike (aka the Eight Hours' War). Two of the smaller towns, Heber and Midway, still exist to some extent. No effort has been made to rebuild the others. Is further information requested?"

"No. Close Encyclopedia." The Encyclopedia display and its window faded away into the distance until it disappeared.

So Gus was naming files after old towns in central Utah.

Just then, the "Provo.L" file turned bright red, indicating that it was in use at the moment.

"File 'Provo.L,'" I said. "Source of program activation."

Another window. "Terminal 3199A. Location, room 3199, quarters of Anderson, C. A."

I wasn't surprised; I'd just needed confirmation. Now that I had it, I could make my next move. "Run program SPY," I said. "Password: GOLDFINGER. Target: terminal 3199A. Filename: Provo.L."

The text in the window changed. "File locked under personal password. Bypass?"

"Yes, bypass," I replied.

The text was replaced once again. "File is a representation of a virtual 'world.' Do you wish to observe or participate?"

At this point I thought it a better idea to remain invisible to the participant or participants in the file, so I said, "Observe." This would allow me to view the file without projecting my icon—my virtual self—into it. I would be able to see myself, but Gus and anybody else using the program would not.

My windows and room all disappeared, and I found myself standing on the street corner of another world. Forty feet in front of me was Gus Anderson. And now I knew why his files were so big. I also had a pretty good idea of why and how they were linked, and I was now fairly certain that Gus's files were harmless.

I was looking at another place, another time, and the reproduction was *flawless*. I saw a street with a number of small shops. All the shops had common walls, and most had two stories. I got the impression that the storeowners—at least some of them—lived above the shops. The street was divided, and on the median was a third sidewalk. On either side of this sidewalk were parking spaces—yes, in the middle of the street. Parked in these spaces were some fine classic cars. I saw a BMW 320i which must have been from the '90s, maybe even earlier. There were a couple of VW Beetles, a really nice old Honda, some Chevys, a Ford pickup, the latter being one of the most well-preserved old trucks I'd ever seen. All of them had gas engines. I hadn't seen a car with a gas engine since a classic car show I'd gone to in New York back in '42.

I looked up at the sky. It was a perfect powder blue—the color the sky must have been before the Eight Hours—with wisps of cloud here and there. And there were birds, sea gulls, I think. There was a hint of pollution near a horizon that was lined with the most beautiful mountains I had ever seen, brown peaks with skirts of green around the bases. One of these mountains had a huge "Y" painted on it.

I couldn't get over the perfection. Usually in a computer-generated "world," the backgrounds are either non-moving—scanned in from photographs to save space—or else just quick sketches with a few details. In this "world," it was like really being there. I could look in store windows and see people moving around, shopping and talking, and I was sure that if I were to go into one of those stores, I would hear a perfectly normal conversation. Passing cars had exhaust fumes. I could see an antique water fountain down the street spewing water into a basin. There was another across the street that seemed not to be working.

Everything had a shadow. Somehow I knew that if I came here on another day, it might be cloudy or rainy, and the shadows wouldn't be there. The details would all be different, but they would be equally perfect. I *was* here, in this small town, fifty or sixty years ago. I could understand why these files were so big, and why they were growing: the detail. Gus probably had a subroutine to keep varying the possibilities, and likely another to keep creating more possibilities.

Gus! I'd forgotten about him! I looked around, but could not immediately see him. I finally found him moving away from me down the street. He was a good block away from me.

I raised a finger that was mine and yet not mine and indicated him. "Computer," I said, "flag this icon for future reference."

A small window appeared in midair to my right. In the upper left-hand side it said "SPY," and there were menu items across the top that I could choose from if I so desired. In the middle it said, "Icon flagged."

"Close," I said absently, and the window vanished.

As I said before, I was now fairly certain these file were harmless, but I had to see more. I told myself then that I needed more proof that there was nothing funny going on, but I know now that I was just looking around; I guess I couldn't believe my eyes! It was fantastic.

Gus walked down the street, looking in store windows, and occasionally waving at someone he knew. Then he turned a corner, walked a little further and leaned into a doorway. Surrounding this doorway were little cafe tables. There was a large awning over them. He said something I didn't catch to somebody inside, and then came out and sat at one of the tables.

I smiled and shook my head. But I was also impressed. The detail was incredible. If he were to sell these files to one of the game companies, Gus Anderson would be set for life. Only one way to find out. I didn't want to invade his privacy, so I decided to wait and talk to him live. He'd be at the commissary with everyone else.

"Shut down program SPY," I said.

The next day at lunchtime, I went to the commissary to ingest my second daily share of indigestible garbage. What wasn't recycled was brought in freeze-dried from Earth. I usually tried to get as much of the freeze-dried stuff as possible, because even after ten months here, the very thought that I was eating my own recycled vitamin-enriched excrement completely turned my stomach. Occasionally I even remembered that my body wasn't the only body here on the Rock, and that usually sent me running for the toilet to provide more raw material for the food reprocessors.

I looked around and didn't see Gus, so I shrugged and found a seat. After about ten minutes, I saw him come in. He looked more or less like his icon: late sixties, full head of grey-white hair. His features were sharp and his back was straight, but he looked tired, as if he'd been mining for maybe one or two years beyond his capacity. His eyes tended to stare a bit, and he coughed a lot. I watched as he went through the line, got his food, and sat down by himself at the end of one of the long, common tables we all used to share our "lunch." I decided to ask him if I could join him. The worst he could say was "no."

Surprisingly, he said "I guess so," and I couldn't wait any longer. I blurted, "Mr. Anderson, why are you mining here when you could sell your files? You could get out of here and set yourself up for life!"

He smiled. He looked like somebody's grandpa. "Who are you, kid?"

I stuck out my hand. "Gene Richards. Computer Monitoring Office." He shook my hand. Then he continued eating. I couldn't think of anything to say, so I waited. We ate. It got uncomfortable after a while, but Gus seemed simply to be enjoying his lunch. I couldn't see how, considering what it was made of. After he finished he put his elbows on the iron table, one hand on the other, and said, "Well, Gene Richards, not that it's any of your business, but I don't want to go back to Earth. For any reason. Y'see, you can't go back. All you got is the here and now. Besides those files are special to me. I don't want them commercialized."

He stood up.

"If there's nothing else . . . ?" he asked. I shook my head. "Then I expect you'll be leaving me alone. There's nothing about those files that needs to concern the Company or your office, Mr. Richards. I have to go back to work now," he said. "The iron doesn't come out of The Rock by itself."

And that was it.

Several days later I was working on the monthly reports—keyboard input—and a note came onto my screen in the upper right-hand corner: "Provo.L file activated." I had told the computer to inform me whenever Gus ran the file. I couldn't leave it alone. He had invented a near-perfect virtual world. Why wouldn't he market it? I double-checked my temple jack to make sure the connection was clean, and exited the word processor I had been using. Then I entered virtual and used the SPY program to get into his file and interact with him there on a participating basis.

When I appeared in his world, I found him sitting on a bus bench on a street corner in a residential area. On the backrest of the bench were three stylized letters on a blue background: UTA.

When he saw me, he said, "Mr. Richards. Why is it that I'm not particularly surprised to see you here?"

"I'm sorry, Mr. Anderson," I found myself saying. "I couldn't let it go. I'm fascinated with this place you've created."

He stood up and just looked at me. Right in the eyes, for a long time. I felt as though I were being appraised. Knowing Gus as I do now, I would imagine that's exactly what he was doing.

I guess I passed the test, because he just said, "C'mon, then," and turned and walked away. We walked for maybe three blocks, and then he turned to me and said, "Wait by the car," which he indicated was in the driveway of the house he'd stopped in front of. Then he went up the walk and disappeared inside. It was a small house, traditional mid-twentieth-century red brick, the kind you find in small towns like this one. There were two trees in the front yard and a neat flower garden along the driveway side of the house. There was a little vegetable garden along the other side. From what I could see of the living-room through the front window, Gus had a lot of stuff. There were bookcases, all full, along the living room walls and little knickknacks and decorations everywhere.

Gus came out about a minute later with a set of keys in his hand.

He came and unlocked the door of the car. It was a red Mazda RX-7, late '80s model, and he motioned for me to get inside. He got in on the other side and started the car. I'd never been in one of these before and was all prepared to enjoy the ride.

Gus started the car and began to drive.

He took us through the center of town and then turned left, taking us first through a university complex and then a high-end residential area. He tersely pointed out a landmark or two as we drove. For the most part he was silent. We finally came to the bottom of a longish, uphill drive. It turned off the main road and curved up the side of a hill. For a while we were promised a nice view of the surrounding area, but then the vegetation cut it off, and there was green all around, which was also beautiful.

The sun was going down, and it would get dark soon.

We got to a metal gate, which was standing open, and drove through. Shortly thereafter the road switched back on itself, and we were going up the hill in the other direction. Almost without warning the vegetation parted and we were at the top. The road continued past a little cottage and continued to circle through several manicured fields.

We passed the house, which I assumed to be a caretaker's home, but no one was around, and continued through a field full of stone plates. Grave markers.

"Cemetery," Gus said. "Want to show you something." He drove for another moment. Past the field I could see that the cemetery ended in a sharp drop which gave onto a beautiful view of the valley we had just ascended out of. Towards the west the sun was descending in a blaze of reds, oranges and golds. Gus saw me admiring the sunset.

"Thank the steel mill for that. Without all their crap in the air, it wouldn't be half that pretty." He stopped the car. "C'mon."

He walked closer to the edge and stopped. I just watched. He looked back up at me and said, "Well? I didn't drive all this way just to strike a pose against the sunset. C'mere!"

I came, and saw what he was looking at. There were two metal plates on the ground. One read:

DAVID JULIUS ANDERSON
1957-2023

and the other

LINDA GRAVES ANDERSON
1959-2023

Between the two was a small metal marker. It said

TWO CIVILIAN CASUALTIES
OF ONE OF MAN'S MOST ANIMALISTIC MOMENTS:
MAY 28th, 2023

The Eight Hours' War. Utah had been a primary target, because of Dugway Proving Ground. Most of northern Utah was a radioactive desert. I had forgotten.

"My folks," Gus said. "This place doesn't exist any more except in the computer. I grew up here. I made the file for me. And for them." He turned away towards the valley, sticking his hands in his pockets, then continued. "Give it to a marketing agency? No. I couldn't do it."

I followed the direction of his gaze. The colors were even brighter than they had been a moment ago, though the sun was now halfway below the horizon. Almost all of the valley was visible from here, because the cemetery was perched on a hill that formed a kind of promontory out into the valley. If you turned as you looked, you could see all the way to the south, the southwest, where the lights of a small airport were beginning to wink, the west, where the lake and the steel plant were, and the north.

"I'm sorry," I said. "My grandfather was killed during the Eight Hours, too. I wouldn't want to do anything to cheapen his memory, either."

Gus nodded. "Yeah, I guess that's it. I couldn't really put it into words, so I had to show you." He was silent for a minute, then said, "I guess we should go back."

"Would you show me more of your creation?" I asked.

He turned and brightened but didn't quite smile. "You'd really like to see it?"

Would I really like to see it? I was fascinated by this place! "I wouldn't ask if I didn't," I said.

He drove me all around the valley, pointing out spots of interest, places where he had grown up, gone to school, lived his life. This time his comments were much less acerbic. I was fascinated. The details were almost indistinguishable from what the real thing must have been.

I wanted to stay longer, but Gus said he had to go and we jacked out.

The next time Gus and I got together was about a week after that when he took me to an unfinished "world." He said this one was a model of Salt Lake City. He'd just begun it, and had already set it up so we had to go to Provo first and, as with all the other files, access the Salt Lake file from there.

We'd agreed to meet in the operating system. I felt it was a little obnoxious to use my SPY program to force my way into his "world," and though he never said anything about it, I had a good idea he felt the same way. So after jacking in and logging on, I appeared in my menu room. I waited until the system registered the activation of Gus's terminal, and said, "Interface with terminal 3199A, quarters Anderson, C. A. Further request interface with virtual icon of Anderson C. A."

A window appeared in front of me with the word "accessing . . ." After a moment, the words "Interface complete" flashed at me three times, and the system replaced the window with the image of a door in the wall of my menu room. I knocked. Gus answered. Or rather, his icon did.

"I'll drive," he said. "Open file Provo.L. Location: address Gus Anderson, front yard."

The room faded, and we were standing in Gus's front yard between the house and his RX-7. He again told me to get in the car, and I did. We began driving, and after a few minutes we were on the freeway. Gus was quiet while driving; he reached under his seat and pulled out a cloth packet. With one hand he fumbled it open, and inside was a pile of antique large-size CDs in their jewel cases. He opened one in a case marked *Caress of Steel* and pressed it into the CD player. The music began, old rock 'n' roll. After a while the city buildings around the freeway became sparse, though they never completely disappeared as we went.

After about twenty minutes we came to the northern edge of the valley to a place where a mountain rose on one side of the road, and the land dipped down into a valley on the other before rising again to become highlands. It was a pass from one valley into another, separated by that incredible blue sky.

"This place is called Point of the Mountain," Gus began. "It's the northern boundary of Utah Valley and the southern end of Salt Lake

Valley. More importantly," he continued as we neared the summit of the upslope, "it marks the boundary between Bluffdale.L, which is complete, and Riverton.L, which is not."

He went on to explain that all the cities and towns of Utah Valley were free-standing files, but all the Salt Lake City suburbs were each in a big subdirectory named SLC.L. The main reason they were in the subdirectory was that they were unfinished. As he finished we crossed the boundary. It was almost as if his speech had been rehearsed. Immediately most of the colors disappeared from the world. The dazzling blue of the sky turned to a stark white, the green on the mountainsides turned a neutral grey, and the tarmac color of the road a flat black. Also everything lost its texture. It was like driving in a picture, except that actually it passed by, like driving in the real world.

There were no buildings, no grass, no trees, no other cars, no lines on the road, no detail at all. Just outlines of mountains and a black strip of road running to what my eye interpreted as a black splotch far ahead. The entire scene gave me a headache to look at.

We drove for maybe another twenty minutes, and the splotch slowly resolved itself into the outline of a skyline, which was less painful to the eye. The buildings were a bit more detailed, but a bit flat. Not two-dimensional, but flat-faced, like pictures made three-dimensional. I couldn't stand it anymore. I had to ask.

"How did you do it, Gus?" I'm a programmer, but I was never into world construction. My skills run more into operating systems and tying previously designed constructs into the mathematics. My specialty is nonvirtual programs. I really haven't followed the market for virtual stuff at all. I guess it stems from the same source as my neurosis against talking computers. "Did you use some kind of animated drawing program?"

He gave me a funny look, like I should know the answer to this already. He was right; any normal programmer would have. I'm a neurotic. Sue me.

"I used," he began, staring out the windshield and driving down this roadway from a hallucinogenic nightmare, "a program called WorldBuilder. It lets you create worlds in as much or as little detail as you like. What you do is enter the program, and interface with an information source. In my case it was the Company Library Encyclopedia. You call up the maps for the area you want. If the place is imaginary, you draw it yourself. For the scenery, skyline, and other stuff, you import some pictures. The software turns the maps and pictures into three-dimensional images.

"For the detail, you can get the computer to randomize color and detail or do the work yourself or use a combination of the two."

"And you did the work yourself."

He stared straight ahead.

"I used the combination on some places."

He showed me some places in Salt Lake he'd nearly finished. The famous Mormon temple was almost complete, as well as the not-as-famous Catholic Cathedral of the Madeleine nearby. Gus said these were a combination of old photos, paintings, and memories. They were beautiful.

"Okay," I said. "One more question. I saw you talking to some people in Provo. How did you do them?"

"Pictures and detail, the same way. The computer randomizes their actions, but looks for keywords in your speech to respond to in order to make simulated conversation. I've been trying to think of a way to make them a little more lifelike."

"AI," I said.

He twisted towards me. "Huh?"

"Artificial intelligence. The Company has one here to run some of the heavier, more complicated equipment. If we could tie into it, we could bring your people to life."

His eyebrows went up in a "that just might do it" expression.

It was again time to go back to Vesta, to work.

"You want to go home, don't you, Gene?"

It was three days later, and Gus and I had returned to "Provo.L." We were sitting at a pseudo-Formica table with aluminum legs in Gus's kitchen. The kitchen was done in varying stages of white—all very clean, but some darkening with age. The old Whirlpool refrigerator had scratches on the front. The window above the table was open, and summer sunlight spilled its warmth over our chess game. Gus was winning—with the black pieces.

"Yeah, Gus. I really do. I'm sick to death of this place."

He knew what I meant. The company treated all its workers the same. As with every monopoly the people at the top got fat, the people in the middle got by, and the people at the bottom—the ones who actually did the work—got shafted. The miners got a low wage and had to work for years to save up enough points for free passage back. I was no different. Even though I had my own cubicle and was probably one of six people on the damn Rock who knew how to use a computer for anything other than keeping records, running machinery, or playing games, I was in the same situation. Lots of people depend on me for a lot, but the only thanks I get is a too-small paycheck. Nobody notices how much I bust my ass until something doesn't get done according to their schedule.

"And where would you go, Gene?"

"Back to Earth, of course. Where else is there?" Actually there were Mars and Ganymede to consider, not to mention the L5 cylinder under construction in Earth orbit at one of the moon's Trojan points. And the other asteroid mining stations.

"Gene, you'd die. Have you got a job waiting there?"

I shook my head. He knew damn well that jobs were more than scarce. Employment on Earth was at 24.2 percent, and computer programmers and analysts were a penny a thousand. He was right. I'd die of starvation. Or exposure. There was simply *no* place to stay—welfare housing was bulging, and without a place life could get deadly. The average temperature may be up, but it could still get plenty cold, and freak storms were getting more and more frequent. If I managed to live through those things, the street gangs or the scavengers would get me for my organs if not just for relief from boredom.

Going home would be suicide.

"I wanted to go home," he said softly, "and here I am. It's the only way to go back. When your home is gone and you can't deal with the reality that is, I think it's okay to *create* a reality that you can live with. It's better than insanity."

"It's not that I want to go home, Gus. I just want to get out of here—off The Rock. Earth is just about the only other viable alternative."

"Is it?" he asked. "Is it really a viable alternative, Gene? The whole place is shot to shit."

He reached for his rook. "Check," he said. "Mate in three."

He was right.

Two days later we hiked to Timpanogos Cave. The Library Encyclopedia had registered it as a small, rather unimpressive series of caverns that lay at the top of a trail consisting of just about a mile-and-a-half, maybe two miles of partially-paved switchbacks. These switchbacks began just inside a thin canyon, so about all you could see from the trail until you reached the top was the face of the mountain opposite.

"When I—uh, when I designed this set of files," Gus had begun when we were about halfway up that trail, "I changed a few things." Gus and I were about the same height, so when we stood together, we generally looked eye to eye. When we walked together, we would at least make an attempt to maintain eye contact some of the time. Today he was staring straight ahead of him into the blue. If I followed his gaze, I could see a tiny patch of the town of American Fork through the thin notch of the canyon entrance. The sun would later sink down into that notch, creating some beautiful sunset effects. With the pollution haze on the western horizon, those effects would be positively spectacular. Either the encyclopedia had been wrong about what a hiker could see from here, or Gus had changed more than just a few things.

Gus coughed hard and went on. "The biggest changes I made were inside the cavern. Y'see, my parents were in the military before my dad retired here, so we traveled a lot. Before I saw the caves here for the first time, I'd seen some of the really big caverns—Luray and Skyline in Virginia, Carlsbad in New Mexico, the ones in Dakota, like that. So I was pretty disappointed when I saw these dinky things. I recreated them accurately in another file in a subdirectory somewhere, but what you're about to see is not what was really in this canyon before the Eight Hours. If my caves had been in this mountain, it probably would have collapsed a long, long time ago. Just thought I should tell you."

When Gus and I got to the cave entrance, we rested and went in. The whole time we toured the caves, Gus kept up a running monologue on what he had changed—what he'd borrowed or made up—and what he'd left alone. He made more noise than the tour guide, whom we weren't really listening to anyway, and after a while Gus told the computer to shut him up. It was odd to see him continue mouthing the words of his lecture without saying anything—like a video with the sound turned down.

Gus's caves were exquisite. As Gus took me through, I just looked at the colorful beauty he had assembled. There was a huge open cavern with a lake at one end, and we were completely dwarfed by it. It reminded me of what Gollum's cave must have looked like. There was a series of smaller maze-like caves with strange glasslike growths in them that looked like upside-down crystal spiders. There were colorful rock gardens with stones worn smooth. Apparently an underground river had once run through here.

At the end of the caverns—and Gus said he'd taken this part from the original Timpanogos Cave—was a simple set of passageways with traditional stalactites, stalagmites, and natural formations. They were grotesquely beautiful. I had wanted to go through Gus's dream cave again, but it was approaching his shift time. We jacked out.

The weekend after Timpanogos Cave—or Gus's version of it, at any rate—we went east. He loaded me into his car and started driving.

"Where are we going, Gus?"

Gus coughed, and said, "Just shut up and enjoy. This drive wasn't made for talking."

We drove up to Heber past Deer Creek Reservoir. He said he had doctored this one too, because as time went by and the droughts had gotten worse in Utah, the waterline had gone down, leaving boats high and dry and marinas inaccessible, so he had taken this canyon about fifteen or twenty years further back weatherwise. It was beautiful. The reservoir was high, and we could see boats everywhere, people sailing and skiing. The water was bluer than the sky. Looking up I saw a hang-glider silently following the air currents. On a nearby river there were guys in hip- and chest-waders standing out in the water fishing. On the way back we turned off the highway and went to a little place called Cascade Springs that was just gorgeous. We followed a little trail back to the springs and a little waterfall, and I saw more beauty that day than I had seen or even imagined since I had gotten to The Rock.

"You know, Gus, you've really made something here. This is just beautiful. These files could really save a guy's sanity. Maybe even his life."

He just kept looking at the road. "I know," he said softly.

It was beautiful. A dream place.

"So what have you decided, Gene?" We were driving again, this time just around town.

"I'm staying on The Rock." I grinned widely, looking straight ahead. "You can't go back. Did you know that?"

"But you can be happy," he paused as a violent fit of coughing took him. "You always have to find a place that makes you happy."

He didn't say anything for a while. We were going north on 500

West which later became State Street when we got to Orem. In Orem we turned right on 400 South. This was an area where there was a mixture of different kinds of houses.

"What's your favorite kind of house, Gene?"

This was an odd question, but I didn't even have to think about it. I'd never lived in a house, but I'd always wanted to and had one all picked out in my mind.

"Four bedroom colonial," I replied. "Like the kind they used to build in Virginia and Maryland. White with two stories, a balcony above a central porch. Two Greek columns supporting it."

We drove around some more and then went to his house and jacked out.

A day later Gus took me to the same area in Orem and showed me a white colonial with exactly the porch and balcony I'd described. We used the WorldBuilder program to flesh it out and furnish it. I put in early American furniture and downloaded all kinds of books from the library. They all went into hardback covers. The place looked like a library—the kind of place I'd always wanted to live in. I put in an antique-looking computer terminal. All the junk I'd ever wanted, I put into that house.

"Gus," I said, turning to him after we'd finished. We were standing in the front room. "Thank you. This means quite a lot."

He looked out the front window. The sun was setting.

"Don't mention it," he mumbled.

"Gene, there's something I need to tell you," Gus told me a few weeks after that. We were playing chess again, this time in a place called Kiwanis Park in the eastern part of Provo. We were sitting in a pavilion at an old wooden picnic table, and it was twilight. Gus was winning as usual.

"And what would that be?" I replied.

"Seriously, Gene. I have cancer."

This got my attention fast. I had been reaching for a bishop, but my hand fell back to my lap empty. "How serious?" I whispered.

He looked me in the eye. "Serious. It's lung cancer, and I've had it for a long time. They say I've got about two months."

"You don't look that far along, Gus."

"I am though. People usually look better in virtual than they do in real life."

It was true. I'd only seen Gus in real life once, that first day at lunch, and he had looked bad then. Tired. He must look that way all the time and "doctor" his virtual icon to look better than his real self did.

"Listen," he continued, "I want you to finish Salt Lake for me."

"But I've never been there."

He dismissed this with a gesture.

"Who cares about that. Do some research. Write some letters. Finish it for me. I want you to promise."

I promised him. We spent as much of his remaining time off-shift together as we could.

The doctors had been right. They might not have a cure for cancer yet, but they can predict it pretty accurately. The last time I saw Gus, he had been in the hospital dying. It was all right, because we had a chance to say our good-byes; I was there when he died and attended his funeral but wished I hadn't. They gave him a quick service and shot his body into space. A holdover, I guess, from those early days at sea when they buried sailors in the ocean. It was like watching one of those canned religious services on virtual.

I stood up. This iron chapel on The Rock was the wrong place to be remembering Gus, so I went down to my cubicle and jacked in. It took me only a few seconds to be recognized and select the proper file from the directory I had recently transferred to my personal allocation. Since Gus had no family, he had willed the files to me. His few other possessions went to his church back on Earth for their welfare program.

When I got to my destination, I was standing under cloudy skies at the foot of the uphill road with no sidewalk. I walked this time, and it took longer, but I didn't mind. The gate was still open, and the caretaker's house looked empty, as it always did. Today the lawns had been freshly cut, and the grave markers freshly polished. I walked to the edge of the hill, where the lawns became cliff. Even on an overcast day like today, you could see most of the valley. The lake was beautiful as usual, and the only thing that spoiled the view was the steel plant, belching fire and gushing smoke. Even so it looked as if it belonged there, and besides that smoke meant beautiful sunsets, so you couldn't damn it too much. Gus loved this place. He was gone, but I had this place to remember him by. I had this place to go to when the pressures of The Rock threatened to cave me in.

I looked down at my feet, beyond Gus's parents' markers to the new carved stone I had ordered from a monument company on State Street.

IN MEMORY OF
CLAUDIUS AUGUSTUS "Gus" ANDERSON
1982-2051
HE WANTED A PLACE THAT MADE HIM HAPPY.
HIS PLACE MADE OTHERS HAPPY.
THANK YOU, OLD MAN.

I'll finish Salt Lake City. And I'm going to find a way to tie his characters into the AI. The hell with my neurosis. Call it therapy.

THUNDERBIRD'S EGG

DIANN THORNLEY

*T*he contrails, tinted red and white and blue, shape my sand-paintings in the sky. Like those formed by my fathers on the breast of Earth Mother, the creation of my patterns requires infinite precision. Like those produced of earthy pigments, my paintings do not last beyond the moment for which they were intended. The only chant which accompanies their completion is the roar of afterburners. But many of my People say they have great medicine, and some of my People call me Shaman.

I was born in 1995, the youngest of seven children, on the Navajo Indian Reservation that stretches across the southwest corner of Utah. My father named me Betsy Ablehorse, but by the time I reached my third summer my brothers and sisters and mother all called me Asks Why.

My great-grandmother was still living then. On winter nights when the wind whistled down from the stone arches of Moab or across Glen Canyon and Lake Powell, we would gather at Great-grandmother's home. She had a tiny wooden house, and we would sit on blankets woven by her mother and listen to her tell of gods and dreams and other holy things.

Of course Great-grandmother's tales were already old when she was born in 1910, but to my young mind they might have happened just the day before. I loved the story of Lost Arrows, who had a dream of a fish that talked. He swam the Colorado to find it and learn its secrets. Lost

Arrows lived well past one hundred summers and was a Shaman when he died.

"Have you ever had a vision, Grandmother?" I asked her once.

She smiled, a little sadly, and said, "The gods haven't given dreams or visions for many generations. Lost Arrows was one of the last."

"Why?" I asked.

"Perhaps," she said, "it's because The People no longer walk in harmony with the Holy Ones. They've turned from the ways of Earth Mother."

I thought about that for a while, mouth puckered, nose wrinkled with the effort, and then I asked, "If I walk in the ways of Earth Mother, will the Holy Ones give me a vision?"

Great-grandmother smiled again. "No, no, Asks Why. Only the young men of The People have visions. A woman of The People is born knowing the path she should walk."

I opened my mouth, but Great-grandmother bent down and placed her hand over it before I could ask why.

The summer I was nine, Mother decided that I needed more responsibility, and she gave me charge of her sheep. Few among The People kept sheep anymore; most of my friends lived in the towns that had grown up around the government schools and old trading centers.

It was a very long summer. I was out with the sheep for days at a time at our grazing grounds in Monument Valley. Alone I had plenty of time to think, and most often I thought about Great-grandmother, who had died the previous winter, and the tales that she had told. And the more I thought about them, the more determined I was to have a vision.

I wasn't entirely alone. A golden eagle had built its nest in a great, crooked tree further down the valley, and one day in mid-August I spent the whole afternoon lying on my back on a sunwarmed sandstone bluff watching it glide and circle far above me. I watched it, and I daydreamed about the old times when young men having visions rode on eagles' backs and saw their futures unroll before them like the land below.

The eagle made a great impression on me. As the sun set and the breeze came up, I stood up on my bluff on my toes and stretched out my arms and leaned into the wind. I could almost believe that I was flying. I wondered how that would feel.

When the sheep were safely corralled that night and my supper fire had burned so low that it didn't compete with the stars, I found myself still studying the sky. I fell asleep watching the most spectacular meteor shower I had ever seen.

I woke to the noise of the sheep bleating in terror. Expecting a coyote, I grabbed my emergency lamp and .22 and sprang up to defend my flock.

It wasn't a coyote. Not more than one hundred yards away, flames leaped and danced like victorious warriors over a stand of sagebrush and snatched at the dry grass. The breeze sent the smoke full into my face. If I didn't put it out right away, I realized, the fire would threaten my campsite and the sheep in their corral! Trading rifle for water pail, I dashed for the watering trough, jumping over rocks and sagebrush that lay in my way.

The sky to the east was turning pale, washing away the stars, by the time the fire was extinguished. My boots and Levis were blackened with soot, my shirt smelly with smoke and sweat, my eyes running and face streaked. I stood there on that patch of blackened, steaming earth and tried to imagine how the fire could have started.

As the light increased, so did the mystery. There hadn't been just a fire. I was standing in a shallow hole almost as big around as the sheep corral. Soil and broken rocks had been flung in all directions. It looked as if lightning had struck—but there had been no lightning during the night.

Steeped as I was in the traditions of The People, my next thought was that it must have been caused by a ghost. Maybe even by the ghost of my great-grandmother as a punishment for my desire to see a vision. I shuddered and whispered a few words to the Holy Ones, invoking their protection.

Steam and little curls of smoke still twisted up—looking like ghosts themselves—from the center of the hole in which I stood. I almost ran, but practicality stopped me. Something was still smoldering there, something which could flare up again if I didn't make certain that the fire was fully out. I threw a whole bucketful of water over the spot—

—and a pillar of steam shot up with a *whoosh!*

I actually cried out with fear but I couldn't run; my feet seemed to have been planted in the torn soil. I stood there shaking, staring, waiting for the ghost to materialize in front of me.

But as the first fingers of the sun reached over the mesa and touched the earth's fresh wound, they found something that gleamed.

Curiosity overcame fear. I crept forward, still whispering for the protection of the Holy Ones. I bent down to look first. Then I crouched to look more closely. And a disappointed, "Oh!" escaped me.

The gleaming object was only a rock.

Or was it? I had never seen a rock like this before.

It was no bigger than both my fists pressed together, bubbly as boiling cornmeal, and shaped like an egg. I knelt down and studied it.

From behind me I heard the cry of the eagle. It hung eerily on the morning breeze for several seconds. Still jumpy, I wrenched around.

The great bird's shadow fell for a moment on the face of the bluff where I had lain the day before, but when I looked up there was no eagle circling in the sky.

A tingle started at the nape of my neck and made its way like a trickle of chilly water all the way down my spine. But it was a tingle of realization, not of fear:

I had seen a vision!

Thunderbird had shown herself to me!

Herself!

Even that was a revelation. In all the ancient tales, Thunderbird had always been portrayed as a warrior, striking from the heart of the storm. But Thunderbird was a mother, like the earth! Her egg lay here in the mud before me, a few inches from my knees!

With all the reverence in my young soul, I stretched out a hand to touch it, to stroke its glinting shell.

It was too hot. I jerked my hand back, crying, "Ow!" Three fingertips were reddened. I pressed them against the cool metal bucket until the smart subsided.

Throughout that day I was more vigilant of Thunderbird's egg, cooling in the mud at the bottom of the crater, than I was of the sheep. By evening I could pick it up and hold it in my hands, though it was still warm. I brought it back to my campsite, gently washed the mud from it, and placed it in the nest I'd made in my floppy felt hat. And all through the night I held it close to my breast, warming it with my body as Thunderbird would have done.

The next time I took the sheep home, I couldn't suppress my smugness.

"You look as if you have a secret, Asks Why," my mother said.

"You've been smiling ever since you came home. Can you tell us what it is?"

I hesitated. Two of my brothers, Raymond and Thomas, were standing nearby. They would surely make fun of my story. But Mother asked again, "What is it, Asks Why?"

"I had a vision," I blurted out.

Mother turned away from her stove and looked at me with the same sad smile that Great-grandmother had always given me. "Women of The People don't have visions," she reminded me. Her tone bore gentle correction. "You know that; you know all the sacred tales."

Raymond and Thomas, twelve and fourteen, were snickering into their hands. "Maybe she did have a vision," said Thomas. He took an empty whiskey bottle from the top of the recycler's bin. "Uncle's been looking for this all week! I think Asks Why took it with her and drank it!"

"If you really had a vision," Raymond challenged, "where's your gift from the Holy Ones?"

I had brought the egg with me, of course, but I kept it concealed, carefully wrapped in my bandanna. In the old times when a young man had a vision and received a gift—like the silver scales Lost Arrows received from the talking fish—he kept it in a tiny leather pouch which he wore on a thong around his neck. Only he could ever take it out and look at it; he was never to show it to anyone else.

"You know I can't show it to you!" I told him.

Thomas waved the whiskey bottle. "I'll show you! It's right here!"

I went outdoors so I couldn't hear their laughter. But that night, when my three sisters were asleep in the little room I shared with them, I unwrapped Thunderbird's egg and stroked its shiny surface and prayed.

When I was fourteen we had a unit on astronomy in science class at the government school. We learned about the stars and the planets and their moons. We learned to recognize constellations and to plot the movement of the stars and planets. And we learned about asteroids and comets and meteors.

"Sometimes," the white teacher said, "meteors enter Earth's atmosphere. Usually they're small enough to be completely consumed by the heat of entry and they never actually reach the ground." He paused. "A large amount of meteor activity is called a 'meteor shower.' Did anyone read the extra material in the blue box on page 185?"

Only one hand went up, at my left. I rolled my eyes: Teddy Many Bears.

Despite the image conjured by his name, he was not plump and cuddly-looking. He was lanky, he wore glasses, and he should have been called Knows Everything. "Two of the major meteor showers happen during the summer," he said. "They are the Delta Aquarid meteors in late July and the Perseid meteors in the middle of August."

"Have any of you ever seen a meteor shower?" the teacher asked.

This time, mine was the only hand up.

"Will you tell us what it looked like, Betsy?"

I wasn't sure how to describe it. I settled for, "It was kind of like—the sky was raining bottle rockets."

The class laughed.

The teacher didn't; he seemed genuinely interested. "Where were you when you saw it?"

"Out in Monument Valley," I said. "Herding sheep."

My classmates, including Teddy, stared at me with a mixture of awe and disbelief. None of them had ever herded sheep. I added, with the air of an expert, "It's easy to see meteors out there. There aren't any city lights to get in the way!"

"And what time of the year was it, Betsy?"

"August," I said. I thought of that night five years ago—and of the fire the following morning, and Thunderbird's egg, tucked safely into my belt pack with my plastic lunch card and my pens.

The teacher nodded. "Then you probably saw the Perseid meteors," he said. With the next breath he continued his lecture. "Occasionally meteors aren't completely vaporized during entry and they strike the earth. Does anyone know what these are called?"

Teddy Many Bears raised his hand again. "Meteorites!" he said.

"That's right. Have any of you ever seen a meteorite? Several have landed in this part of the country over the years."

No one would admit to ever having seen a real meteorite, even in the Museum of Science. So the teacher brought out a display case and passed it from table to table.

"You'll notice that they don't all look the same," the teacher said. "Some look like lava from a volcano and others look metallic. Many of the metallic ones have a high nickel content."

I craned my neck, trying to see the collection, until the case reached my table. And then I practically recoiled.

There in the center of the case was something that looked like Thunderbird's egg.

At first I felt betrayed. Cheated. I was useless for the rest of the day. After school I took a long walk, leaving the town behind. Yes, even my family had moved to town by then. Mother had sold her sheep, and she and Father had bought a used Ford pickup truck with air conditioning, a CD player, and a double cab so Mother and my unmarried sister and I wouldn't have to ride in the truck bed.

I climbed up on a rock, drew up my knees and wrapped my arms around them to make a chin rest, and looked out over the desert.

A golden eagle was flying. I watched it for a long time, until it came around in its circle, dipping down as it passed over my head. For a moment I was cooled by its shadow. I heard the rush of its feathers in the wind. "Just believe!" they seemed to whisper.

And something occurred to me.

It only made sense that Thunderbird should lay meteorites for eggs. After all Thunderbird wasn't an ordinary bird; she was the deity of the storm and the heavens!

Besides, the tokens brought back by others who'd seen visions had all come from nature, too: a puma's tooth, a Gila monster's tail, the silver fish scales of Lost Arrows. It wasn't the object itself which was significant; it was what that object represented.

I cradled the bulge in my belt pack as I walked home.

Raymond enlisted in the Aerospace Force the next year, and my parents and I drove him to Lackland Aerospace Base in Texas to enter basic training. There was an air show going on in San Antonio at the time, and we spent half the day watching the aerial circus.

Every moment of it thrilled me. But the show that made my heart race as if it had wings itself was the one performed by the Aerospace Force's official demonstration team: half a dozen F-22 fighter aircraft painted red, white, and blue with a stylized representation of Thunderbird painted on their undersides! Their loops and climbs and dives, their head-on passes with only inches to spare replayed in my mind long after the show ended.

Sometime during the night, I realized what my vision meant.

"What do you have to do to ride a Thunderbird?" I asked Raymond the next morning.

"First," he said, "you have to be a pilot."

"How do you do that?" I asked.

He laughed. "You have to join the Aerospace Force. But you have to be an officer. That means you have to go to college. You've got your work cut out for you, Asks Why."

I was fifteen by then, and everyone in my family still called me Asks Why.

Getting to college, I knew as well as Raymond did, would be a feat all by itself. My family was as poor as everyone else on the reservation. Very few young people ever got to go to college.

"If you can make good grades," the counselor at the government school told me, "you may be able to get a scholarship. I suggest you put your emphasis on mathematics and the hard sciences."

The sciences were hard, all right. Math was even worse. Sometimes the studying made my head ache; sometimes it made me feel rebellious. What did math have to do with flying, anyway? When I couldn't stand it anymore I'd run to the outskirts of town and out into the desert.

Feeling the wind in my face reminded me of my goal; watching the golden eagle soar overhead reinforced it. And when it dipped low over my perch, its flight feathers would whisper, "Work and believe!"

I wondered if Lost Arrows had had to work so hard to achieve his vision.

I didn't graduate from high school as valedictorian, but I was near the top of my class. "You have every chance in the world of getting a scholarship," my counselor had said when the time came to consider such things. "You just need to apply for one." He added, "I know of one you might be interested in. Aerospace ROTC at Brigham Young University has a new four-year scholarship available only to native American cadets."

"Why?" I asked, wrinkling my nose. "That's the Mormon school, isn't it? The one with the good basketball team?"

The counselor nodded. "I guess Mormons have a warm spot in their hearts for their Lamanite brothers," he said in answer to my question.

"Lamanite?" I asked.

"That's the Mormon name for you native Americans," he said.

I asked, "Why?"

He shrugged. He wasn't a Mormon either, and he didn't know anything else about it. Instead he said, "BYU ROTC also has a good history of getting pilot billets. I thought that would interest you the most."

"Definitely!" I said.

So I applied, and I received my scholarship, and in the fall I moved north to Provo.

It was like moving to another country—maybe even to another planet! No coed dorms. No smoking, no drinking—you couldn't even get a soda pop with caffeine on campus! And with the kind of hours I spent at my studies, I really could have used a little caffeine from time to time.

I majored in physics—the hardest of the sciences in my opinion. But physics also answered questions I'd pestered my mother with as a child. Why is the sky blue? What are rainbows made of? What makes ripples on a puddle? How does an eagle glide? I also learned what mathematics had to do with flying.

The only question physics didn't answer was why girls were not supposed to have visions. Not that it mattered anymore. Many times at night, while my roommates were out late with their boyfriends, I'd get my Thunderbird egg meteorite out of the back of my dresser drawer and unwrap the bandanna to stroke its metallic surface.

I was commissioned a second lieutenant in the United States Aerospace Force on April 25, 2017. I was twenty-two. Three months later I entered Undergraduate Flying Training at Williams Aerospace Base in Arizona.

The hours of study required in college were light by comparison to UFT. Even with fewer pilot allocations available than in years past, the wash-out rate averaged 30 percent. I thought that was murderously high—until I learned that in those same years past wash-outs had reached 50 percent.

The classroom work was tedious, the jump training only marginally interesting—but the instructors had to make sure we'd know how to escape a dangerous situation before we got ourselves into one.

As part of jump training we went parasailing. Some of my fellow trainees called it waterskiing on air. Wearing full flight gear, including an open parachute, each of us took a turn on the tow rope that trailed behind a military truck. When the wind caught the 'chute, you went airborne. When you reached two hundred feet, you dropped the rope and began your parachute descent.

I always took my time descending, maneuvering to catch the best thermals so I could ride the wind for as long as possible. If I closed my eyes I could imagine myself as an eagle, flying wingtip to wingtip with the golden bird which had borne my dreams on its back since I was nine. And if I ignored the snugness of my jump boots, I could feel the nudge of the meteorite egg lying in a leg pocket of my flight suit.

My instructor wasn't pleased. "Ablehorse," he said—at least he didn't call me Asks Why—"if you keep this up you're gonna find yourself flying hang-gliders for some air show instead of fighters for the Aerospace Force!"

The desert of central Arizona reminded me of the one in southern Utah where I'd grown up, with cacti and canyons and even a golden eagle who let us share his sky. On my early morning training sorties, when the air was still crisp enough to make you shiver as you taxied out for takeoff with the canopy raised, I could imagine the joy the eagle felt rising to meet the sun.

A few times, practicing maneuvers, I was doing aileron rolls when the sun edged over the horizon, and I would hang there inverted for a moment, watching from this unusual perspective as it rose completely. Even the eagle couldn't do that!

I was two months from graduation when the accident happened. Returning to the classroom for debriefing after my own sortie, I found my instructor pacing. He only did that when he was severely agitated; I'd seen him do it when my tablemate failed a check ride.

My guts knotted up. "I hooked it, didn't I?" I said.

He shook his head. "No, you passed your ride. But somebody didn't. I saw the crash trucks taking off as I was heading back here."

A little later we learned that neither student nor instructor had escaped the disabled craft.

"Bird strike," someone reported. "Big one. Crash crew said the canopy was smashed in and there was blood and feathers everywhere. Both men were probably dead before the trainer augured in."

"It was probably that eagle," suggested someone else, adding a string of adjectives the like of which I'd never even heard back home. "I've watched it for a few months now, hanging around right in the flight path. If the wildlife backers weren't such fanatics we could've shot it when it first showed up and maybe this wouldn't have happened."

I suddenly felt as if I was going to vomit; I whirled around and left the room.

I spent the rest of the day searching the sky for my eagle.

It never appeared.

Pilots are as superstitious about flying accidents as my People are about death in any form, but they deal with it in a different way. That evening my classmates drove into Phoenix to a bar called Wings, a legend among pilot students. They took a holocube of the dead lieutenant and added it to the collection stacked on a shelf behind the bar, then they spent the rest of the night getting fall-down drunk and making jokes about canopy ornaments shaped like eagles and picking feathers out of the pilot's teeth. I didn't go along, as I usually did. I heard the jokes from the lieutenant one door down from me in the quarters when she came staggering and giggling in at three in the morning.

That was the morning I reported to the commandant.

"I have to leave, sir," I told him. I stood at stiff attention.

Colonel Haversack had bushy eyebrows, and he drew them together as he told me to be at ease and take a seat. "Why, Lieutenant?" he asked. "From what I understand, you have a fine record here. You're in the running for Distinguished Grad, and you have less than two months to go."

I steeled myself. "It's the eagle, sir," I told him, unable to meet his gaze. "Its death is an omen. Some kind of evil is following me."

Colonel Haversack didn't laugh. He furrowed his brow and considered for several minutes. And then he said, "What drew you to become a pilot in the first place, Lieutenant Ablehorse? It had to be something momentous. I don't believe I've ever seen a native American woman come through UFT in all my years here."

I drew a deep breath. And I told him about the eagle I had watched when I was nine and about the vision which had come the following morning. I told him of the Thunderbird show I'd seen in San Antonio, and how the meaning of my vision had made itself plain. He smiled a little at that, but not unkindly, and so I told him of the eagle which had been my strength through high school and how the eagle here had lifted my spirit when the demands of the training might have crushed it.

He listened to it all, nodding occasionally; and when I finished he leaned back in his chair and thought again.

"Lieutenant," he said at last, "in the mythology of your people does the eagle or the thunderbird have greater medicine?"

"Thunderbird, sir," I said.

"Is the thunderbird's medicine great enough to ward off whatever evil the eagle's death has brought?"

I hesitated. Then nodded. "I think so, sir."

"Then don't give up your dream, Lieutenant," he said. "If you're meant to fly a Thunderbird, then your thunderbird will get you there. Stick it out."

Colonel Haversack was a wise man, I thought as I strode down the corridor from his office. If he were one of The People he would probably be a Shaman.

Returning to my room I removed Thunderbird's egg from the back of my dresser drawer and placed it on my desk where I could see it while I studied. But the next morning I slipped it into the leg pocket of my flight suit.

My hands shook all through my flight preparations: running through the system checks, firing up the engines. My instructor watched me from beneath gathered eyebrows. "Are you all right, Ablehorse?" he asked.

"Yes, sir," I said. But I wasn't sure of that.

"You filed a different flight plan from the one we briefed in the classroom," he said.

The original one would have taken us over the area where the accident had happened. Nothing in the world could make me fly out there. I only said, "Yes, sir," and looked straight ahead.

He studied me for a long moment before he shook his head and muttered, mostly to himself, "Crazy Indian!"

It was the hardest training sortie I ever flew. I think I had my teeth clenched the whole time. But as I banked the craft around on the final approach for landing, I glimpsed its shadow skimming over the ground before me. It wasn't shaped like my aircraft; it was shaped like Thunderbird.

I finished UFT as Distinguished Graduate, pinning on my wings on 29 May 2018. There followed another year of lead-in training with the F-22 before my first duty assignment took me from Luke Aerospace Base in Arizona to the Middle East.

Desert Storm had been part of my military history class at BYU, and my instructor, Major Carson, had shaken his head as he talked about it. "That conflict was the first in which we played a major role in the Persian Gulf region," he said. "If events continue as they have, many of you may well see duty over there." The Mormon cadets had exchanged remarks about something called Armageddon and the prophecies in their scriptures.

I hadn't set much store by Mormon prophecies, but on my first day in Dhahran, trying to get some crew rest in quarters with faulty air conditioning, I wondered if my being there would be enough to qualify Major Carson as a prophet.

I served in two Middle East conflicts, Desert Fist and Sand Lion, before I pinned on major. By the time Sand Lion began, I was a senior captain recently selected for promotion, and I was a flight commander.

We were returning from a predawn attack on a target just outside of Esfahan, Iran, skirting Qomsheh and heading for the Gulf, when my wingman was hit by a surface-to-air missile. Our warning gear detected its launch and we took evasive action, but the SAM kept its lock on my buddy's bird.

I can still see the explosion of its impact, still remember how I thought I would suffocate before I saw the billow of his opening parachute—and only then realized that I had been holding my breath. I radioed in for the rescue 'copter, ordered the rest of the formation on home, and began to orbit my downed wingman's landing site.

Captain Eddie Fox was a Sioux from South Dakota. Though the languages and customs of our respective Peoples were as different as they were from the white culture, we still found we had much in common. We shared histories and legends, and in time we discovered that we were in love.

"In the old days," I had asked him once, "was it just the young men of your people who had visions, or could girls have visions, too?"

Eddie had laughed at that. "Among my People," he said, "if a girl claimed to have a vision, she'd be accused of drinking too much whiskey! Why? Do Navajo women have visions?"

I remembered fourteen-year-old Thomas waving Uncle's whiskey bottle. "No," I sighed. "Everyone would accuse a Navajo woman of being drunk, too."

So I didn't tell Eddie about my vision or about my goal, but I loved him anyway.

The sand of the Iranian desert was pale compared to the red and orange sand of southern Utah, and the smooth faces of dunes reflected the rising sun like mirrors. The glare kept me from actually seeing Eddie below, but I knew where he was and I could see an Iranian truck heading in his direction. The E model of the F-22 has a multibarrel twenty-millimeter cannon and I put it to good use, stopping that truck. My fighter took a few rounds of antiaircraft artillery in the process, which ripped up my port stabilator some, but I kept up my orbits.

I kept an eye on my fuel readout too, knowing that when it reached bingo I'd have to leave whether the Search and Rescue ship was there or not. Maybe it was just my tension and I was checking it more often than I thought but that readout never seemed to change.

—until I headed back to base with Eddie safe in the SAR ship behind me. Then my readout plummeted. I touched down at Dhahran with too little fuel left to even taxi in, and for the next hour or so my ground crew crawled all over my bird, examining its shot-up stabilator and speculating on fuel consumption. I heard about it when I got back from my post-flight debriefings.

"No way that flap shoulda functioned, ma'am," my crew chief said, jerking a thumb toward the stabilator. "One of those hits clipped a hydraulics line; you lost a lotta fluid. And we still haven't figured out the fuel thing. We thought maybe your fuel gauge was faulty, but—" he shrugged, "—it checks out okay." He could only shake his head. "We shoulda been picking you out of the Gulf, ma'am," he said. "That bird shoulda been swimming!"

I had to agree, but deep inside I had a feeling about what had happened.

The news pool heard about it, of course. Eddie and I found ourselves cornered by a couple dozen people with microphones and cameras, and we spent the next hour and a half answering their questions.

"Captain Fox," someone said, "what was going through your mind during the time you were stuck out there?"

Eddie laughed self-consciously and ran a hand through his sweaty black hair. "This is going to sound kinda strange," he said. "Maybe it was the heat or something. I knew I could hear F-22 engines, but every time I looked up all I could see was a giant bird, and I thought, 'I'll be all right. Thunderbird is protecting me.'"

I remembered the fuel readout and the way my F-22 had soared and circled so effortlessly over the place where Eddie waited, despite its damage, and I felt a thrill run up my spine. That night I told him about my vision. He didn't laugh or accuse me of drinking too much.

Half my clan was waiting at the airport when I arrived home from Dhahran. They had seen my story on the nightly news; I was a hero.

I was more than that. The tribal elders sprinkled me with sacred corn pollen and called me Shaman.

That meant more to me than the Distinguished Flying Cross, which was presented the same day I pinned on my gold major's leaves. "Well, Major Ablehorse," my commander said as he shook my hand, "I expect after this you could ask for just about any assignment you wanted and you'd probably get it—short of Chief of Staff!"

I didn't want to be Chief of Staff. I knew what I wanted. And when I submitted my next "dream sheet," I asked for it.

The U.S. Aerospace Force demonstration team still uses the F-22 for its aerial shows. I put in more flight time now than I did even as a combat pilot. And I do a lot more traveling!

We recently did a show in Dhahran. Going back there gave me an eerie feeling, as if I were taunting the Holy Ones who direct The People's fates. So I went out to the flightline early, while only the ground crews were there, and I sprinkled sacred corn pollen over the swept wings and the bubble canopy of my aircraft.

I think every sheikh in Saudi Arabia was in attendance. It was a proud moment for the U.S. Aerospace Force.

But today is prouder still—at least for me. I've come home. Today the Thunderbirds fly over Hill Aerospace Base in Ogden, Utah, and my whole family is there, from my parents, whose hair is now white with the snow of many winters, to Raymond, who wears the proud stripes of a chief master sergeant. Eddie, my husband, is there too, on leave from his test-pilot post at Wright-Patt.

With the ritual precision which is the soul of this tradition, I mount my aircraft. My crew members secure my harness, my crew chief hands me my helmet.

The scream of the jets sends a ripple through the crowd filling the stands. I speak to my wingmen as my craft rolls forward and they follow, one by one.

The sky over Ogden is very blue today. So clear that if you look long and hard you can see eternity. This is my sand floor, the surface on which I will paint for my People. As one, my team and I activate the contrail dye.

Red billows from the exhaust nozzle of my aircraft. The color which the sun paints across the sky as it sets, the color of the desert's rock and sand. The color of The People. This sandpainting in the sky is for them.

I smile under my oxygen mask as the pattern takes shape: a great bird with red and white vapor for wings. In the pocket of my flight suit, Thunderbird's egg presses against my leg. The smile widens when I think of how my family greeted me at our reunion yesterday.

They didn't call me Asks Why.

They called me Flies With Thunderbird.

SCRAP PILE

MELVA GIFFORD

aker, please let her hold together till we land," Paul Turner pled as he felt the starship vibrate, signifying the first stages of exit from hyperspace.

"Why does it always have to be like this?" he murmured, pressing his long frame against the pads of the chair. Around him the various pieces of furniture and equipment in the lounge began to quake.

A low whistle continued to penetrate the entire ship. No crew in the long and "glorious" history of the Galactic Star Fleet vessel, *LaVerkin*, had ever been able to stop that confounded whistle. You had to become a heavy sleeper to survive a tour on this ship.

In the back of his mind, Turner knew he should be terrified. It wasn't safe for a craft to shake so badly every time it exited hyperspace. It wasn't all that safe when it shook entering either. But, Turner thought, the continuous repetition of the events, coupled with the various other minor catastrophes he had experienced while on this tour, had dulled his sense of fear.

He was a veteran.

A startled gasp over the ship-wide speaker caused Turner's stomach to tighten. He listened to the message for the captain.

"Captain!" came the voice of crewman Gwen. "She's starting to do it again!"

"Gwen, we can't chance having that blasted fuel dump right now!" Captain Liebing's voice was tight as it echoed through the audio system.

"Close down the ducts. Isolate the lines. Do something! We're entering orbit. If it ignites—"

A slight jolt ran throughout the ship just as the first gentle lift was felt from the edge of the atmosphere, and Turner knew, with a sinking feeling, that the fuel had dumped into space just as they contacted the first traces of the air below. Turner cursed, wishing he knew the names of more Gods. As usual all the efforts of the ship's engineers, Gwen and Thell, were useless. The ship did as it darned-well pleased.

Captain Liebing, knowing what must have happened, responded with his own long array of colorful metaphors, followed with a voice of resignation, "Get out the spacesuits and pumps everybody. We'll try to delay our descent as long as possible."

Turner unlocked his restraints and jumped up from his seat in the lounge. This was an example of why, though the ship was recorded as the *GSF LaVerkin* in all Fleet logs, her true name to the crew and sister ships in the fleet was *Scrap Pile*.

He hated risking his life but knew they had no choice. Three times the *Scrap Pile* had for some unexplainable reason dumped her fuel, twice just before entering a planet's atmosphere. The only thing they could do now was gather it back up by going outside in their spacesuits and chasing the viscous fluid with their pumps.

Outside the ship they could see the fuel slowly oozing away in a long thick stream.

With resignation showing in every line of their space-suited bodies, the crew headed for the farthest edge of the spill, knowing from their past experiences that the quickest way was to work toward the ship—and it was imperative to work quickly—not only to prevent the fuel from dispersing into space but to save their lives. They needed to prevent the fuel from igniting, but they also needed it to maneuver the *Scrap Pile* to a safe landing.

Part of the fuel was already beginning to glow as the friction from the upper atmosphere began to take effect. The crew worked quickly and efficiently, each one doing his or her part, using as little time as possible, then heading for the airlock when they had gathered as much fuel as possible.

They had no more than removed their helmets and begun to congratulate each other on a successful run when the ship's alarm began to blare. What now?

Gwen's voice, calmer now that the fuel had been collected and sounding apologetic, came over the speaker, "Turner, the nav computer's misaligned again. You'll have to come up to make exact coordinates."

Turner banged his way to the top levels of the ship. Sometimes it definitely did not pay to be chief navigator.

"Damn computer!" Turner murmured. He sighed as he settled himself in front of the navigation computer and contemplated his fate. The craft was not nicknamed the *Scrap Pile* without cause. It had gained a well-documented (and widely known) reputation for being able to claim every system failure possible.

The worst curse bestowed on a member of Earth's starfleet was to be assigned a tour of duty on the *Scrap Pile*. That's why they were now orbiting Earth, preparing to descend past the satellite Tamiuw II. Tamiuw II marked the precise location for the space window that would lead to Utah's planetary shipyard. The base possessed some of the most highly advanced equipment and skilled repairmen.

Now their reputation would truly be put to the test.

The old navigational center was the only room in *Scrap Pile* with large portals lining every wall and the ceiling. It offered magnificent sights—if one was in the mood to appreciate them.

Turner wasn't.

He immediately set about taking readings and manually adjusting the controls to their proper settings. He could clearly see Tamiuw II pass by the aft instrumentation screen as the ship made its final approach.

The ship's inner vibrations began to subside as they lowered through the atmosphere, and Turner relaxed. The primary settings were all laid in, but he knew better than to leave. The computer had a tendency to choose the worst times to be uncooperative—he'd probably have to remain up here until they made planetfall.

"Hey, Turner, don't you have anything better to do than baby-sit the nav controls?"

Turner looked up to see the smiling face of Scoop, his best friend, just poking around the doorway.

The navigator smiled, glad for a visit. "Come on in, Scoop. Take the load off your mind."

"Cute," he replied.

Scoop walked to the seat near his friend and gratefully lowered himself into it. The communications officer tended to be the best-natured crewman on the ship—with his almost bald head and stocky body, he had to be.

He stretched with obvious pleasure, lifting his legs up to rest on the console before him, settling in with a sigh. "Ahhhhh, a great load off my mind."

His name was Errick Paylor, but everyone called him Scoop. He said it was because as communications officer he knew all the news before everyone else. Actually it was because the top of his head resembled an upside down ice-cream scoop.

"Mother's going to be calling you," Turner reminded him.

"So nice to be loved."

"Loved, hell. What will you wager it'll be over twenty pollution citations this time?" Turner pulled out a pad from his uniform jacket ready to peel off a few credits.

"No way—I'm saving my money for shore leave."

"Provided we get there."

"Tut, tut." Scoop vigorously scratched his dry scalp with both hands, voice fluctuating in rhythm to the movement. "This ship will get us there one way or another—in one piece or several."

"Paylor, get down here!" a voice boomed over the com system.

"Mother calls," Turner said.

Scoop rose with reluctance, haphazardly rubbing at the heel smudge on the console. "Capt'n's cheery tonight. I wonder why?"

Turner leaned back in his chair, temporally glad he was the navigator and Scoop would have to help handle the coming trouble. "This landing ought to create the longest citation list ever—and you thought MarCinn 4 was bad! Utah's *fanatical* about its air control. Good luck appeasing the local officials—"

"Paylor!" the captain's voice shouted over the com, a full octave higher.

The communications officer fled the room, leaving Turner to attend to his duties alone.

As the craft descended into the atmosphere, it shook under the onslaught of changing pressures. Crew members kept watch over their separate positions as the ship quickly dropped to Earth below. Distorted images of landmass became more distinct, and the ship spewed out a trailing path of smoke and stench above it.

The stone cliffs of Zion National Park opened up to show a spaceport, with attending ships and a neighboring complex occupying half a small city.

It took four minutes for the port authority to clear enough of the black exhaust from around the landing gear for it to be safe to open the outer hatch.

As the nine men and four women exited the ship, with their duffel bags, they were greeted by an applauding welcoming committee.

Turner and Scoop exchanged glances. After their many tours of duty on the *Scrap Pile*, they were used to the looks of amusement aimed at them or more specifically at their "ship."

They both bowed, their mood matching that of the snickering assembly.

The other crew members, not yet used to such a reception, ignored it.

Turner and Scoop recognized some old friends they'd both served with a couple of years before and sauntered over to that part of the reception committee and shook hands.

"What's she held together with, Turner?" a familiar voice asked, "Gum?"

Turner searched the crowd. "Hi, Vic," he said. Then he turned and greeted the others. "Hello, Brawn, Hayes. Berra, it's been a while. How are you doing, Vic?"

"Heard you had an interesting trip, this round," Vic noted with a chuckle. The laugh lines around his eyes showed that he enjoyed humor. "You two have got the longest-standing survival record on that ship, not counting your captain. Any of your transfer requests come through yet?"

"Not yet," Scoop sighed.

Three port personnel approached the group. One, the stockiest of the trio, was holding a clipboard. "Any of you Captain Liebing?" he asked.

"Nope," responded Turner. "We'd never claim that privilege. Mother—er—the captain's waiting for you inside."

While the port personnel talked to Turner, Scoop casually leaned over to glance at the thick pad of computer printouts clipped on the board. Citations—in triplicate.

The trio nodded in unison and turned to ascend the ramp.

Berra nudged his friend. "Hey, Turner, getting pretty free on the nicknames. Aren't you worried that Liebing will hear you?"

Scoop spoke up, "He knows he's a mother hen to this pile of scrap."

"He's from Utah, isn't he?" Berra asked. "Heard tell it was through him you were able to bypass the shipyard's two-year waiting list."

Scoop leaned close, and his secretive act made the others huddle around. "An opening came up. The *Entrim* never made it here—lost both ship and crew. Mother arranged for us to take their slot."

He smiled proudly. "Times like this, I'm definitely glad for the captain's connections. It's helped us out this round at least." Scoop's voice fell away as he suddenly took in the sight before him. He was looking through the entrance of the neighboring national park. The port itself was positioned tightly between the park and Springdale City.

What he saw was nearly indescribable. The terrain was ragged and angular, a harsh beauty. A series of stark cliffs portraying a wide tapestry of reds, whites, and browns rose from an earth littered with a maze of sand, rocks, and sandstone hills. Towering cliffs climbed to a vividly blue sky.

Nestled at the base of a range of cliffs and hills—but outside the park—lay a wide collection of lush trees and shrubbery, unnatural next to the bare rock of the desert.

"Your first visit to Utah, I take it?"

Scoop nodded, open mouthed. Finally words returned. "Where did all the red come from?"

Vic snorted, amused at the expression from the two crewmen. "The locals call this area Zion." He pointed a finger at one of the more prominent stone figures standing as sentinel against the blue sky. "That's called Angel's Landing."

Turner nodded, still mute.

"And it's natural?" Scoop added before the others could ask.

Turner and Scoop were both obviously perplexed that, after traveling to other worlds in search of adventure and beauty, they'd find one of the most beautiful scenes they had ever seen, on Earth, in a gallery of stone and cliff.

The new arrivals were told of Checkerboard and Sting-Boat Mountains and the Narrows. Much of the conversation centered on the natural architecture as they departed the landing field.

Berra, reverent to the moment, said: "You should see Goblin Valley. It looks like a place where God had a beach party."

Turner turned to his old friend. "A what?"

Vic interrupted. "Come on, I'm thirsty."

"Isn't this supposed to be a desert?" Turner asked.

Berra wiped the perspiration off his forehead with the back of his hand. He pointed out some transparent tubing that framed part of the horizon.

"The state has an irrigation system that pulls water right out of the air. Look at all the plants. It's helped their growing seasons for the last century. I think their atmospheric irrigation and recycling systems are part of the reason so many engineers are attracted to Utah. There's a lot of experimenting going on, and Utah's the guinea pig."

The conversation fell away as the group left the yard. They headed for one of the bars that ringed the spaceport. A high, nearly transparent defense wall framed the back of the port's recreation buildings, presenting a definite barrier between the bars and the interior of Springdale.

A cloud of dark smoke, compliments of the *Scrap Pile*, had begun to gather against part of the shield, creating a growing blemish that would require a hard wind or air purifiers to dissipate. Turner knew that the cost and manpower required to conduct such an activity would eventually end up on the ship's expense reports.

"Came here to see if she could be fixed up, eh?" Berra asked, returning to their original conversation. He began tugging at an ear irritably.

Utah was humid and hot, contrasting with the normally dry air of the ships. The difference made everyone feel as if their skins were crawling.

"We're hoping these engineers can do something for us," Turner admitted.

"Miracles are possible, so I'm told," Hayes returned snidely. Her blue eyes sparkled as she looked at the two men.

"You'll have one of the best engineers of the Fleet working on your ship," Brawn cut in, her long brown hair catching in the slight breeze.

Turner and Scoop smiled, their expressions brightening for the first time since being assigned to the *Scrap Pile*. No more constant whistling throughout the night. No more vibrations before and after hyperspace. No more malfunctions continually cropping up throughout the ship, keeping them forever busy with never a moment of relaxation. It would take time for them to adjust to running a perfect ship. But they would certainly be willing to change.

"So there we were, in our spacesuits, a waterline broken in the storage unit spilling all that water on the deck, and with the insulation problem, what else would you get but ice? So we thought, well since it's here, why not a good game of space hockey? There were so many dents in those walls already . . . "

Scoop let his sentence hang, enjoying it. His audience's imagination took over, and they laughed. The bar was loaded with members of different crews, each enjoying a nice evening planetside.

Scoop originally intended his story just for his companions, but it attracted other ears as well. Their table soon became surrounded with men and women intently listening to the woes and adventures of those aboard this infamous ship.

"You had insulation problems and a waterline break at the same time?" one thin voice asked from the circle.

"Yep," Scoop returned, enjoying the attention they were getting. He couldn't resist adding, "It happened soon after we reactivated our malfunctioning gravity controls. Now that was fun!"

The amazed exclamations encouraged Scoop to continue. He and Turner both knew that their catastrophes did not regularly occur so close together, but neither of them could resist promoting the legend and reputation of the *Scrap Pile* to recruit looks of amazement from their audience.

They would become men to be remembered as two survivors.

Of course no life had been lost on the ship—yet. The crew had always been able to correct the malfunctions before they took a life.

The *GSF LaVerkin* was one of the few older Epsilon-model vessels that had made an "adequate" transition to the newly invented hyper-drive, requiring Earth's fleet to still use the ship for transport, much to the crew's consternation. The crew often dreamed about sabotaging the hyper-drive.

"One would have to be suicidal to remain on that ship," someone said.

"Being aboard her gives me a warm feeling right here," Scoop said, pounding his chest dramatically.

"Yeah, heartburn," Turner finished, getting a laugh from most of those listening. The few bar customers intent on their own drinks and company now looked over at the growing circle.

Turner poured his fellow crew member another drink as Scoop expounded on their past adventures. He told his audience about the time of the oxygen leak, the pressurization imbalance, the fuel dumps—

He was a good storyteller, Turner admitted to himself. Why did it all sound fun when the crew actually had to risk their lives, time and time again, to keep the ship going? The knots in his stomach were not something he remembered fondly. So Scoop's almost favorable report irritated him.

It was insane: combating one problem after another was no way to spend your time aboard a ship, all the time wondering if you would get to port in one piece. Their companions in contrast reported their own ships to be near trouble-free, giving them time to read books, watch the visro waves (when they were in range), and to just relax and enjoy life.

Turner glanced at his cup, trying not to let his growing irritation spoil the mood of the party, for it was surely turning into that. He sighed and tried to laugh with the others at whatever Scoop was saying as the night pressed on.

Two days later the entire crew of the ship stood assembled in the engineering room, looking down at the casing now covering the main computer line that ran throughout the ship.

It lay new and glistening like a snake that had just shed its old skin.

Captain Liebing stood proudly near the new equipment, his face beaming. He eagerly began his explanation: "Gentlemen, we find ourselves at an historic moment. The *GSF LaVerkin* will never again be called the *Scrap Pile*.

"Apparently the problems we've been experiencing have been the result of an electrical chain reaction originating from here." He pointed a hand excitedly toward the computer line. "Once the source of the problems was identified and corrected, everything else linked up. The ship will no longer give us problems."

"Doesn't seem possible, Capt'n," Turner said eyeing the new machinery skeptically.

But Liebing, ignoring the doubt Turner was expressing for most of the crew, dismissed them to prepare for lift-off.

Five days out Turner sat on his bunk staring up at the ceiling. He still had a half shift to wait until he was on duty. Maker, he was bored. None of the books in the computer appealed to him, and with so little practice at having to hunt for things to do, he was at a loss. So he sat.

He glanced up when he heard raised voices in the corridor. Thell and Horan were at it again. They had been at each others' throats ever since lift-off.

Turner shook his head.

He'd never noticed their animosity before. They were usually occupied with keeping the ship from falling apart. Now they were debating whose turn it was to baby-sit the nav computer. Yet so far the computer was behaving perfectly. They remained on course and would reach their first assignment in seven days.

So why baby-sit a perfectly behaving nav computer? Turner got up and stepped into the hall to find the two men facing one another.

"Problem?" he asked.

"Stay out of it, Turner," Thell warned, standing straighter as the tension increased.

Turner spread his hands before him in a token of peace. "Hey—if you—" he began, but Captain Liebing bolted into the corridor, stopping Turner from making peace.

The captain glanced at the trio curiously. "Is there a problem here?" he demanded.

"No, sir," Horan answered stepping back with a small smile. His lanky frame filled the passageway, and he had to press himself against the wall as Liebing nodded and passed on. When he was gone Horan's face hardened and he turned back to his opponent. "Look, Thell, just because you're the chief engineer doesn't excuse you from taking the same amount of duty time as the rest of us."

Turner headed for the lounge. This was already becoming an old argument. He stalked into the lounge, only glancing up to see who was there as he turned through the door. All that greeted him, however, was a thrown fork that seemed intent on skewering him. He instantly jerked his head aside and watched as the projectile hit the door that closed behind him.

Snickers rose from within the lounge.

"Little slow on the timing there, Leach," Scoop critiqued from the sidelines.

Leach, a stubby fellow, was standing in the center of the room next to one of the tables. He nodded with mock seriousness. He turned back to his projectiles, which just happened to be the entire complement of the ship's eating utensils, and moved the next one over.

They had been carefully and precisely lined up on the surface of the table in an apparent order of importance: first the forks, then the spoons, last the knives.

Turner walked away from the door, making a wide berth around the concentrating Leach.

All eyes were centered on Leach, who aligned a spoon with about half its length hanging over the edge of the table. Then with one swift, practiced hand swung down, the projectile flew across the room, hitting the same spot as the fork.

"What is this, the flatware Olympics?" Turner asked.

Scoop looked up from his chair. "C'mon, Turner. It's boring as hell here. You know that. We need something to entertain the masses."

Turner pulled up one of the chairs to sit down, also watching the concentrating crewman. Another spoon was now being placed into position.

"If Mother were to come in—" Turner began.

Scoop looked up, sudden humor lighting his eyes. "Hey, now that's an idea—a moving target!"

"Isn't there something more constructive to do in your spare time?"

"Look, Turner," Joy Gubler said, "this ship is cramped. Thell snores in his sleep. We're too far out to catch the visro waves." She sighed wearily, "And Gwen's jokes aren't that funny."

Another of the crew, short and thin, looked up from the library disk he was reading. "What about my jokes?" he asked.

"We've never had the time to relax before." Scoop said. "How were we to know this ship lacked all the little extras other ships take for granted?"

Joy snorted. "I spent all leave hiking Angel's Landing while listening to my friends praise free time." Joy looked around the room and shook her head with clear reproach. "I wonder if they were trying to convince me or themselves?"

"We never realized how much time it took to keep the ship together before," Turner said.

Gwen turned his attention back to his book, not pressing the issue about his unappreciated jokes.

Turner was thankful the man was more even tempered than most. But he had a strange sense of humor. Who knows what Gwen would come up with as a response to a crew member who insulted him, but he was certainly better tempered than Horan or Thell. As if on cue Turner heard raised voices from the hall.

"Those two still arguing?" Ina Bundy asked, her thin form draped across three chairs.

A voice from above hollered over the com system. It was Mother.

"Thell! Horan! It's now both your turns to baby-sit. Get up here and take over."

"Guess that's settled," Turner said with a sigh.

"Those two have always had a hard time getting along," Scoop said. "Never became a problem until now." He turned away for a moment to applaud Leach's bull's-eye with the spoon.

Turner nodded. He pulled a storage box in front of his chair to prop his feet up and leaned back, folding his arms behind his head. "Never knew how loud Thell snored, either, until the ship got so quiet. The walls don't provide much of a buffer, do they?" He looked over at Scoop and leaned forward, stealing a glance at the preoccupied Gwen. Turner whispered, "Gwen's singing in the shower is as bad as his jokes."

"You're telling me!" Scoop said, nodding for emphasis.

Turner chuckled at the sincerity of his friend's reaction. What was there to do now when there was nothing needed to keep the ship from falling apart? Everyone was becoming irritable, snapping at friend and foe alike. Many of them were having trouble sleeping. With nothing to do who got tired?

Friends back in port had generously detailed the virtues of a normally functioning ship, but they neglected to state what occupied one's time while crossing the long expanses of space between ports. He found himself noticing the various dents scattered about the dull surface of the far wall. Unable to think of other entertainment, he began to count them.

Two days later everyone had assembled in the Rec room. The captain had called a conference on the growing issue of low morale, and Liebing hadn't accepted any excuses for nonattendance.

"Capt'n—Thell's and Horan's constant bickering is driving me up a wall," Gwen stated as he stood in the center of the lounge. His arms were folded.

Liebing sat, straddling the back of a chair. His gray temples accented the deep creases of his face, a face that now looked sternly over his crew. The captain was, however, known for his fairness—seven growing kids at home apparently helped—and he now listened carefully as the crew took turns detailing the trying behaviors of their companions. Scoop's complaint surprised Turner the most.

"Turner screws up the food processor every time he uses it, Capt'n."

Turner looked at his friend as if betrayed. Scoop had of late lost much of his good mood and was becoming a grouch. Turner himself became defensive. "Yeah?" he rebutted, "What about when you—"

"All right, all of you," the captain's tone commanded silence.

"I must admit all of you have been a royal pain in the butt ever since we left Earth." The crew remained silent, but the looks on some of their faces clearly indicated that their captain had not been much of a blessing himself.

"We've had too much free time on our hands," Liebing observed, "and we've been getting sloppy." He glanced around the room catching each person's eyes.

"We don't function like a team anymore," he said. "Before we've had to work together to keep the *Scrap Pile* from falling apart. We probably know more about how to keep a ship together than any other crew in the fleet. Now we've all gotten lazy, including myself."

"So what do we do about it?" Turner asked. "I'll be the first to admit it—I'm bored as hell."

In response Liebing stood up, indicating that the others were to follow him. Curiously, looking at one another, the assembly complied.

The captain led his crew to the place where the Utah engineers had recently conducted repairs. It looked the same as before, the new metal casing that shielded the main computer line still looking out of place next to the old, worn fixtures.

Liebing walked over to it, then waited until they had all surrounded the unit. He cleared his throat to gain their undivided attention.

When the crew were all looking curiously at him, he swung a firm foot against the new shield. The force of the impact vibrated throughout the entire room, leaving a large dent in the computer line.

As the noise of the impact receded, another more familiar noise began. A sound they had not yet forgotten: a low whistle.

It had been a good seven days since they had heard that noise. The vessel seemed to quiver slightly, as if in accompaniment to the whistle. A red light began blinking on one of the monitors from a wall console.

Turner smiled, as did the rest of the crew.

Maker, it was good to be home.

SIGNS AND WONDERS

KATHLEEN DALTON-WOODBURY

The phone woke Tevita in the night. He kicked at his sheets, freeing his long brown legs so he could run into his mother's room. The call had to be from the hospital—about Grandpa.

"What? Right now? Do you know what time it is?" Suliana listened for a moment and then held the phone away from her ear, staring at it. Tevita reached out to take it from her, but she shook her head and waved him back. "Yes, I'm still here. Where's the nurse?" Tevita could hear Grandpa's deep Tongan voice as his mother moved the phone away from her ear again. "All right. Don't shout—you'll wake the whole hospital. We'll go look. You go to sleep now. It's—" She turned to look at her clock-radio. "It's after two in the morning, and you need your rest. Yes, we'll go look. Then we've got to get back to bed too. I'll come see you after work. No, I'll talk to you about it then. Good night, Papa." She hung up and sat blinking as she stared at the phone.

Tevita cleared his throat and ran his hand through thick black hair, wanting yet not wanting to hear what crazy thing Grandpa wanted now. Suliana sighed and gave her son a tired smile. "There's a comet. He said he saw it through his window and knew we had to see it too." She shook her head and stood up. "Get some pants on, and a jacket." Putting on her robe, she shooed him out the door of her room.

When Tevita came into the living room, he found Suliana crouched at the front window, trying to see the sky beyond the roof of the porch. "Where is this comet supposed to be?"

"Over Olympus Cove. Papa's room looks east."

"Well, let's go outside then." He opened the door. "I just hope no one sees us." He stepped to the front of the porch and forgot about anyone else. There, hanging in the sky, small enough to cover with his thumb, was a comet: a bright smear of light, a blot of white paint brushed through and spread upward toward the stars. No roar, no movement, just light and silence. Tevita felt the chill of the autumn morning enter through his bare feet and creep up his legs, but he didn't care. Wait until he told the guys about this. Had someone already said something at school and he hadn't been listening? This was really something.

He felt his mother standing next to him, heard her shuddering breath, knew she was crying. He put his arm around her. Good thing it was so early and no one could see him.

He lifted his other hand and barely covered the comet with his thumb. It was so huge, burning its image into his memory forever. He sighed. "Wow."

Suliana nodded. "Wonder what Papa is going to say about this."

"Signs and wonders, Mom." Tevita pulled his gaze away from the blaze of glory and looked down at her. When had she gotten so short? She smiled up at him and shook her head, then started for the door. Tevita followed her. No need to glance back; this was something he would never forget.

When football practice ended, Tevita found his mother waiting for him outside the gate to the stadium. Glad that his complexion hid the blush that heated his face, he waved his friends on and walked over to her. "Mom, what are you doing here? I don't need a ride home like some kid." He glanced over his shoulder, certain the guys were laughing at him, then thought of Grandpa. "Has something happened?"

Suliana gestured away his question. "Papa just wants to talk to you. Do you want to go home first and clean up?"

"Do I have to go see him?" Tevita started toward the car, knowing that it would be useless to argue. "You know how I hate hospitals and being around sick people."

Suliana gave a barely audible snort. "You're his only grandson and you haven't been to see him yet."

Tevita held out his hands for the car keys. "Okay, Mom; but I'm doing it for you."

Tevita stood in the sonic shower and let the vibrations remove the football grime. He wished they could afford a water shower, but this did the job and he had to admit he enjoyed the tingle on his skin; besides the low hum made it easy to relax and remember.

Poor Grandpa, he went through life doing the best he could and hoping for something better, and when the something better didn't come the way everyone had expected it to, then what did he do? Tevita had only been a kid when the century had turned, but he had still sensed the disappointment in the adults around him. Where was the Millennium they'd been hoping for? Tevita wondered if Grandpa had been crazy before then, or had that been when it started? "We must not be ready yet. There has to be something we still have to do." But the heart seemed to have gone out of most of the adults back then. Even Tevita's religion teachers acted like deflated balloons, going through the motions, tired and puzzled.

Only Grandpa still burned with the fire. "I've got it! The City of Enoch! Didn't Joseph Smith say it was at the North Star? Where will it go when it comes back with the Lord? It has to land somewhere, right? But it can't land on all the people, all the cities." Grandpa's grip on Tevita's little-kid arm was as strong as a vice. "Remember that guy who thought the rock pictures spread out on the ground in—where was it? South America?—were for people from space? That's what we have to do. We need to make a picture for the City of Enoch, so they'll know where to land, so they won't land on Salt Lake City." Tevita rubbed the bruise on his arm after Grandpa released him. "We can go up to Idaho and get lava—Max Morrison has acres of it—and spread it out on the salt flats. We'll make what—a fish? Something big enough to be seen from space."

"Why a fish, Grandpa?" Even though Tevita really didn't care.

"Early Christian symbol—fishers of men." Grandpa waved away the question. "Doesn't really matter, they'll know it's for them, whatever it is."

It had taken years. Tevita had grown up and grown strong helping Grandpa arrange the lava across the salt flats, putting each chunk of rough black rock where the old man directed, and it still wasn't complete. He shut off the shower and stepped out to flex his muscles before the mirror. Well the effort had been worth something to him after all.

Tevita followed his mother as slowly as he could down the glaring white halls of the hospital. His nose burned at the smells of pain and disinfectant. He didn't need this.

His mother led him to a small room off of one corridor. The slatted shades were pulled up to expose a large window full of Wasatch Mountains and sky. No wonder Grandpa had seen the comet. Tevita imagined the night sky framed in the window and saw the glory once again. "Does it have a name?"

"The comet?" Grandpa harumphed. "What difference does that make? They name it after whichever *polongi* saw it first." He lifted an IV-trailing arm and pointed at Tevita. "I name it Warning. You saw it. Didn't you feel it?" Without waiting for an answer, Grandpa harumphed again and folded his arms across his chest. "'They seeing see not; and hearing they hear not, neither do they understand.'"

Tevita tried not to stare at the old man in the bed. He'd only been in the hospital a few weeks, but the change in him was more amazing than the sight of the comet had been. The once large man—larger than Tevita even—seemed to have shed all his muscle and left only bones hung with yellow-brown skin. The dark wires of hair had turned white overnight. Tevita thought that only happened in stories.

Suliana tugged on his arm. "Sit down, Tevita, so Papa doesn't have to wrench his neck to look at you."

As Tevita sat in the chair, he noticed that Grandpa had turned toward him, his still-bright eyes watching, waiting. "Tevita, you know what this means, don't you?"

Tevita glanced around the room, looking at the blood-pressure gauge attached to the wall, then at other machinery arrayed around the room; anywhere but at Grandpa. He really didn't need this.

"Tevita, answer me."

"What what means, Grandpa?"

"The comet. It's a sign." Grandpa leaned toward him. "The *polongis* think it's just a ball of ice and rock, but it's a sign for you and me, Tevita. For our people."

Tevita sighed and looked down at his clenched hands. An old scab curled away from one of his knuckles. He picked at it and it fell away easily.

"Look at me, boy. You know what you've got to do."

Tevita finally raised his face to the old man and met the fiery gaze with his own unbelieving one. "I've got school and football practice every day, Grandpa. You don't want me to quit school, do you?"

"You don't have to quit school—you didn't have to quit your job this summer, did you?" Grandpa leaned back on the bed, his face turned toward the mountain. "You can do it on Saturdays, the way you did in the summer. This is my dying wish, Tevita."

It was Tevita's turn to snort. "You're not dying." But the figure in the bed already looked more like a cadaver than something alive. What if Grandpa really was dying? He'd never been sick before the heart attack. What if the only thing keeping him alive was this crazy idea? "It's not your job—or mine—to make a landing place for the City of Enoch, Grandpa."

Grandpa waved away Tevita's statement. "We've been over this before. You know what year it is. You know the Millennium didn't happen at the turn of the century." Dark eyes narrowed at Tevita, and he couldn't look away. "The Tongans accepted the gospel and came here and to Independence, Missouri, so we could meet the Lord when he came again. After all, the Tongans in Missouri are building houses for him. They know we are the people who must prepare the way." The burning gaze seared right through Tevita. "You give me a better reason for no Millennium. You show me that everything is ready for him to come back."

"But we'll never be ready, Grandpa." Tevita stood up. They had been over all of this before. And Tevita had quit going to religion classes when Grandpa had had the heart attack—if there really was a god and Grandpa was doing his work, why would God strike him down in the middle of the job? He turned his back on the bed and the mountain. "Maybe the Second Coming was all a big story anyway."

Grandpa didn't even ask what he'd said. The old man had always had excellent hearing. But either Tevita's hearing had gone bad, or everyone in the room was holding their respective breaths. Before Grandpa could recover and react, Tevita decided he'd been there long enough. "I've got to go." He pushed out of the door and down the hall, expecting at any moment to be pierced through the back with the sound of Grandpa's roars.

Every morning after that, by 2:30, the phone shrilled out its wake-up call. "Go see if you can still see the comet." Tevita and his mother would stumble out onto the porch to gaze at the sight that burned deeper into their memories with each viewing. And the comet blazed over Olympus Cove, a harbinger of something, though Tevita refused to even think about what it could be. He also refused to return to the hospital. That thing in the bed wasn't Grandpa. It was some kind of special effect, and he didn't want to think about it either. He was a sophomore on the varsity team and he had three good seasons ahead of him. He didn't want any Second Coming to get in the way of that. And he needed his sleep.

Then one morning Tevita woke on his own. His clock-radio said 2:45. Had he slept through the phone call? He tore out of the sheets and into his mother's room. The bed lay empty and the clock-radio read 2:46. He hurried into the living room and looked out the windows. Suliana saw him from the porch and opened the door. "Tevita? Get some pants on and come out here."

When he joined her, she turned from staring at the sky to face him. "Come look."

What now? And then he saw the sky over the mountains, grey and menacing with clouds that reflected the city's glow and hid the comet's light. The air crackled with angry energy.

"Is that why Grandpa didn't call this morning?"

Suliana unwrapped her arms from around herself and put them around Tevita. "I don't know. I hope so, but I'm afraid."

And then the phone rang, a distant shriek. But Tevita knew in his heart it wasn't Grandpa. Grandpa was gone, gone like the comet, gone with all his wild and millennial dreams. Tevita sat down on the porch stairs. He didn't want to hear about it.

After the funeral and *pola*, Tevita's mother asked him for the keys. "I'm driving. We have somewhere special to go." The sun glinted off of the Great Salt Lake as they headed west on North Temple Street. Could she really expect to see anything? But they took a turn he didn't recognize, away from I-80, and he realized they were going to the small plane airport. Tevita shook his head. What was the point? Too bad they didn't believe in cremation; he could have scattered Grandpa's ashes among the lava. "Grandpa left us money to fly over his masterpiece, didn't he?" Suliana nodded. Good, he'd been wanting to see what Grandpa had made him work on for so long. It was Grandpa's money. Just one more part of his craziness, Tevita guessed.

How big did something have to be to be seen from space? And would a plane get them high enough to really see it? One time when the work was done for the day, he had climbed a nearby hill and still seen nothing but lava. And Grandpa didn't even have a map, carrying the whole picture in his head. Tevita was willing to take this one last look, but Grandpa was going to be disappointed if he thought this would change his mind. Besides how could Tevita finish something he couldn't visualize? But maybe that was the purpose of this flight.

As the plane rose into the sky, he squinted into the glare of whiteness. At least the lava would make a break in the monotony of salt. The pilot turned to glance back at Suliana. "You'll have to tell me where to go, Ma'am. Your father's instructions weren't very clear."

"Ask Tevita. I've never been out there."

"West. How high can you get? If you follow I-80, we ought to be able to see it fairly soon."

Below them green, yellow, and rust-colored water lapped against Black Rock, the lake high again in its cycle of rise and fall. And to the west, the salt flats beckoned with their latest, unfinished works of art. They passed over the concrete "tree" and the metal "tower of technobabble" and all the other "statements" that mingled with billboards along the shabby, hole-pocked interstate.

And then something besides grey mountains and green-yellow-rust interrupted the whiteness. A black smear to the north of the ribbon of road beckoned to them. "That way. Do you see it?"

The plane banked and left the road behind, putting the sun over the pilot's shoulder. Tevita strained to see a fish as the splatter of lava moved toward them, but the picture wouldn't resolve itself. "Can you get any higher?" The plane tilted again and carved a circle in the air, a crown over the lava spread below. Tevita frowned. This didn't look like any fish, unless it was a jellyfish or something. It looked more as if someone had dumped a large blot of black paint on the salt flats and then swished a brush through it, spreading it outward toward the sun.

Then Suliana's gasp echoed the chill that went through Tevita as he realized what he was looking at. He and Grandpa had created a black comet against a white sky, a sign and wonder for the heavens, a message to those who waited above. And it wasn't finished. One section of the comet's tail was missing, making the whole thing look lopsided.

"Wow! That's really something." The pilot banked the plane some more, craning his neck to see past Tevita. "Why's it so big?"

Tevita glanced at the man, one of Grandpa's scorned *polongis*. "It's supposed to be seen from space."

"Really? But we aren't sending people up any more. Or do you mean someone else? I thought they'd decided no one is out there, or else they would've answered all those messages we've been beaming out to them."

Was there really no one out there? Tevita still wondered. Was this picture nothing more than a crazy dream, a last desperate gasp of hope rejecting the environment of despair? What if there really was someone, something? What if they waited, watching, for the completion of the sign, a signal that it was time to come back?

Which was better, accepting *polongi* reality or believing in something no matter how crazy? Tevita remembered the light that seemed to shine from Grandpa when he talked about the picture. It made him stand out among all the dull, colorless men around him, the men who had given up. Which kind of man did he want to be?

Tevita realized that the pilot was waiting for an answer. "Maybe they were looking for the right message." He shrugged. There was really only one way to find out. And besides it would be a fitting monument to a man who wouldn't forsake his dreams.

Grandpa had kept his beliefs, stood tall and strong against the despair in others. It didn't matter if that made him crazy. Tevita realized now that the dream was the important thing. He blinked at the tears he hadn't been able to shed before. "How much time do we have?" Staring out the window at the unfinished part of the comet, he made sure he would know it when he got back on the ground. It would take, say, three or four truckloads of lava to finish it, at least.

"Time's almost up. But we've got plenty of gas, and I'm willing to stay a little longer. That's pretty spectacular. You say your grandfather did it?" The pilot shook his head. "He must have been some kind of guy."

Tevita glanced at his mother, who smiled at him through her own tears, and he smiled back. Then he turned back to the pilot. "Thanks, but we've seen enough. And, yeah, Grandpa was a real wonder."

SONGS OF SOLOMON

VIRGINIA ELLEN BAKER

t's midnight. There's a strong snow outside. Blowing against the window, against the pane of warm glass where the flakes cling and then, for one brilliant second, crystallize. When they melt, the light from the street lamp outside strikes them and they glitter there like tears.

Holding my love in this rippling light, in the darkness where the snow falls like stars beyond us, I pray in secret, in a closet of my own making.

I lie awake, watchful; as always. I tell myself they won't come, but in my heart I know they will.

They always do.

Somewhere between the falling of the snow and a bell tolling deep in the city, I feel myself going. Slipping into it. Trying to clutch at David, but no longer having arms or legs to hold him with.

Fighting it this way, I go into my dreams.

"You always were the rebellious one," Grandmother tells me. She holds me with a hard hand around my wrist, even though she's been dead for thirteen years.

As she shakes me, shakes my arm hard enough to bring the tears, another face overlays this one, and suddenly I have two Grandmothers: one, this mask Corrections wears; the other, the overlay, the real Tante, but sadly as I last recall her. I stare, fascinated, as this last face overlaps the first and becomes more defined. More solid. Startling. Such a clarity. I see every line: pale, her face, the color of snow under a grey cloud, surrounded by the casket's silk pillowing. Her eyes are closed, her mouth sewn shut. The pain in my wrist, in my chest, is the same when I see it: the same as the day they lowered her into the earth.

Hearing her voice like this, so sharp and strict, so unlike the truth, is like that pain to me.

Briefly: I wonder if this is not deliberate. My own dreams have never been so sharp, so brilliantly defined. So solid. Tante's closed mouth. The x-crossed stitches on her lips. Still, I hear the ranting behind it. The script is the same. Every night. It doesn't change, no matter how much I cry, how much I beg them to stop.

But tonight there is the face of her death. And though the pain of it is bad, there is something else: something of me that makes it sweet.

I realize suddenly that I am holding my own.

Then the face behind *her* face, the one with such deep lines and dark furrows at the top of the nose, intrudes, and I know someone has seen, has been sharp on the job, and has adjusted the programming.

Grandmother disappears entirely, leaving me with their rendition of her: The Grandmother-Construct. Horribly familiar. Every line the same. But her hair and eyes wild. The soul of a Fury in her face.

"You listen to me, you little shit," she says, hissing behind her teeth (which I know are false), and in that instant I know there is a man behind this vision of her. A simple programmer. Or maybe just the semblance of one. A visit from Corrections. I am on parole, and they know it. "Try that again," Grandmother says, "and I'll drop-kick you into the next world. And you know that isn't far from here."

I know. At any given moment the dream-scene could shift; at any point I could find myself flying over a gorge or being dashed from the top of the Goosenecks or falling from Dead Horse Point into the river below it. They know I hate to fall.

I look away from the Grandmother-Construct to see that she and I are standing on a plain filled with poppies. The plain is a low bowl at the belly of Mt. Olympus, and the city of Salt Lake, as I have come to know it, shimmers beyond us. In this dream I see it as a mirage of light. The sun glints off the windows of a multitude of homes, bright orange fires that dot the hillside. But it is the poppies that I want to see. Bright red and pink, their heads are tossed by a light breeze. Each petal is so thin, so delicate and fragile, I take a small moment to fear for them.

The Grandmother-Construct slaps me hard, hard enough to put me into the dirt of the mountain trail we are on.

"Look at the city," she says, and commands me where to look, exactly, by extending a long finger and pointing into the city's heart. For one crazy second I half expect fire to come from her fingertip and think, *Oh God, she'll kill us all.* But nothing comes, and I follow along the line of her pointing finger and look.

Before she says it I know the worst part is to come: "Write about the city," she says. "Write the song of the righteous."

Once again I begin to cry. The sun is still setting. I can see the angel Moroni on fire with it. He raises his trumpet and this, I think, is where the penance really starts.

Waking in the morning I see that David has covered his pillow with blood. His face too is washed in the color of it, a bright swath of red against his pale face. His nose and eyes are clotted with it. For some reason it does this to the men. Women bleed in other ways.

"Was it bad?" I ask him, though this has become more of a ritual than a need to know. I know. I know how bad it is. The blood tells me everything.

To my horror, he begins to cry. They have never gotten him to do this before.

I touch the gently pulsing point at the base of his skull and feel nothing. Of course. Hidden, only those of us who wear the pain of Correction know they are there. My fingers curl into a fist. I wish I knew who they were. Where they were. I would kill them, if I could.

I wash David's face as gently as I can. He does not resist, doesn't really move at all. Just sits on the edge of the bed. His tears streak the blood before I can wash it completely away.

"We could go to the park," I say. "Buy some coco from the vendors. Ride the carousel. If you'd like."

David lifts his head as if to nod, then stops, looks out the window. I know what he's thinking: That it is beautiful. That he could capture it in oils with all its light and subtle shadings. If he could still paint it. *If.*

A covering of snow lies on everything outside. White. Thick. The cars are buried under it, the high metal fences, the leaves of the trees; bark encased in crystalline carbuncles.

Under the wild oak that grows beyond our bedroom window, an orange-swirled cat sits in a high bough, washing its face.

"You could bring your easel to the park," I tell him. "You could paint. You *could.*"

He sits as still as the snow outside. The cat has lifted its head from its upraised paw and stares at him now. Its eyes are pale gold. I watch the two of them watching each other, both of them frozen, like the tree, like the buried cars in the parking lot. I just watch. What else can I do?

A heartbeat, maybe even more than that, and the cat suddenly winces. It puts down its paw, puts all four paws down more firmly on the bough of the tree. Then it hisses at David and jumps down from its place, down onto one of the cars and out into the lot. It leaves dark imprints in the new snow, its paws sinking more than an inch as it minces away slowly—taking a step and shaking off the snow, the wet off from that one paw, then stepping again. Though I can't see its face, I can imagine its deep disgust; it is written in every line of its long body.

Finally David shakes his head. "I can't go to the park. Listen, I'll stay home and read. It's a good day for it. See? I could build a fire. You go."

I nod because I know there is nothing more to do for him. They have been running scenes of a beach in his mind at night. A tropical beach with a television preacher and a choir singing spirituals. They play it so much, he hardly dares go out anymore, though I tell him there isn't a tropical beach within a thousand miles.

He so loved the snow when I first met him. On my way out I glance back to see that he hasn't left the bed. He is still sitting there, his skin pale as marble in the winter light, looking out of the window at the snow.

Out in the park I am permitted to go only so far, only to certain places. Friends say I could disregard my programming. Just last week Sally Hobart said, "I don't think I even believe it happens. They took you in to examine your art, then let you go. That's all."

I told her to touch the back of my head. She did. Tells me it's nothing, that she can't feel a thing. Just hair and skin.

I can't tell if she can or can't, or if she's just being Correct. You never know. I can only feel it a little myself. A slight, spongy mass just under the bone. I can't feel it on the outer skin so much as on the inside, when I touch it. Reminds me of a loose tooth. But I can feel the softness there, inside.

Finally Sally put her hands in her lap, palms up, and looked somewhere hard beyond me.

"And anyway, you knew it would happen," she said. "I think you wanted it to."

Wanted it?

To fight the Commission, yes. To be declared subversive, dangerous, a criminal—*maybe*. If it would do any good.

But mostly, to make something of some worth, of some beauty. As I saw it.

Now I have this. No prison sentence, no barbed-wired fences or cells or bars to contain me.

Just this. The dreams. The pain. And oh God, the fear.

How can I explain it to my friends? We are all programmed after all. They feel a tickle in their noses and sneeze. I see green and begin to cry, a "sneeze" of hysteria that grows worse for every minute I do not go back inside. The one time I tried to stay, I clawed furrows into my cheeks that bled for days. I have the scars. See?

For now I am glad only that the park is warm and white, that the green is covered and that even the cold is tempered. Drops of water fall sporadically from the surrounding trees and buildings, but the sound of it is muffled. It is quiet. So wonderfully quiet. Like a church made for one.

While I am looking at a mural (actually fairly well done; they're getting better at this, which is the worst for me, I think), a woman comes up to me. She is dressed in the standard outfit, the ubiquitous pantsuit in dark colors, the cuffs below her wrists and the collar pulled up around her neckline. If she has breasts it is impossible to see.

"He does such wonderful work," she says. "I can't imagine anyone who wouldn't want to come out and see it, even on a day like this."

She looks at me for the response, the expected reply that has replaced ritual for so many here.

I have no choice but to nod, but I close my mouth up tight, until my teeth hurt with the effort of it.

A frown draws her eyebrows close. For a moment she reminds me of the Grandmother-Construct in last night's episode.

(Corrective dreams. So sorry. *God.*)

Having control of myself (for this struggling instance), I look at the woman in her drab clothes and think, *This could only happen in Salt Lake.* We used to say so all the time. That didn't make it true. It only started here, I think. Here and other places like it. Wherever people were just too damned afraid. Of everything that was not like them.

Suddenly I'm very hot; my skin is burning. The heat wells just under my cheeks, and I wonder that the woman can't see it moving under the skin there.

It's happening everywhere, I think, and the panic is so deep I can hardly see, can hardly breathe. *Everywhere*.

The woman is looking back at the mural. I have no choice but to look with her. I am programmed, now, to do it.

It is a very Mormon painting. Though I know in other places the scenes would be different. For here, for this place, it is epitomal.

A family of wives stands against a sunlit horizon. Their backs are strong; their faces are plain and hard, but the austerity itself is its own beauty. Their hands are huge, like the hands of their men.

Or their *man*, rather. Though this singular male is not illustrated in the picture, he is implicit in it everywhere: in the women's waiting eyes, watching the deep russet skyline for a sign, for any sign of his coming. The little dusting of homespun cottages scattered along a river. The unsullied white of the clouds. The butter-yellow of wheat that has been blessed, growing in such straight lines that not a furrow, not a stalk, is out of place.

A strand of hair is flying loose from one sister's tightly pinned bun. The sister next to her, glancing toward her; her hand reaching up, forever reaching, forever halfway there, to put the escaping strand back in its place.

But at least it is not the *Ten Virgins* again.

And I say to the woman, "I like the *Ten Virgins* best." Inside I curse my lack of vigilance. Helpless now, as the faces of all Ten Virgins are recalled to me. Five of them are all the same: coolly knowing, more shrewd than wise, I think. What they know makes them *choice*. And in some odd way, they are both sad and glad that the rest of us do not know it.

The other five are all different and seem, in their variety, to represent every sin a woman could aspire to: the Glutton, the Sloth, the Bitch, the Whore. The Heretic.

No need to ask which are the wise, which are prepared in just this way and thus acceptable to the Bridegroom, and which are not.

The woman's face lights up. "Now *there's* a lesson," she says, nodding. "I have a copy in each of my daughters' rooms." Her smile is more relaxed now, though I know I have not passed all the tests, not yet. "Which ward are you from?" she asks.

Ahhh, I think. Here it comes. So I try. Try to tell her I have no ward, no stake, no church, no faith at all anymore. There is so much to say, so much to tell her. So much, and I cannot even open my mouth.

Inside the images begin to reel out behind my eyes and I see the green—acres and miles and worlds of it. The tears begin. The salt of them chaps my skin. It's cold in the park after all.

The woman, expecting any answer but this, looks more closely at my face. She sees the furrows, the marks of my previous, uncontrollable anguish. That I am damaged. Not like those wise virgins, whose composed and knowing faces are all clear and younger and lovely. Whose eyes say they possess every touchstone needed to pass. That the others do not. That they *know.*

Can you not see? they ask. The righteous, they should *see* the outward signs and *know.*

Like this woman. She backs away from me, smudging the snow on the sidewalk so that her footsteps are no longer clearly human marks. With a furious glare, she turns her back and walks quickly away.

At home I dry my face on a clean towel and draw a bath. The water, so hot it steams, blurs the mirror. All I can see in the mirror now is a smudge of black hair under a rainbow beret and a pale oval underneath, as swirled as a thumbprint in the glass.

I got the beret in Moab, where David and I went together for Memorial Day weekend years ago. The red of the rocks there warmed the evenings when the sun set and made a fortress of dark, upraised wings for the love we made by the fire at night.

We have not made love for months. Not since.

But that same vital orange-red is woven into the beret. I sweep my hand across the mirror and see it more clearly, as though under water, but water that is clear: that vital red and vibrant blues and greens.

I touch the throbbing softness at the base of my head and laugh.

That woman should have known. My beret should have told her everything.

Still laughing, I go into the bedroom to tell David my little joke. As poor as it is, he would understand it.

He's on the bed. His pillow is soaked with blood. There is more blood there than I have ever seen, from him or in my life.

"David?"

I whisper his name into the hard grey darkness that is coming on, not daring to turn on the lights. Then I go to him. His skin is cool, not quite cold yet.

"*Oh, God,*" I say; and it hurts to say it, hurts horribly in angry bursts that flare along my head and settle, like stinging nettles, at the base of my skull.

But it hurts even more not to say it.

I gather up David's head and see that the blood has come out of his nose, from his eyes. All the blood.

On the floor beside him is his easel, his brushes scattered like a match stick gathering of wild colors. Blues and greens are smudged on the hardwood floor where the brushes fell.

He has painted me, nude; naked and smiling. The smile as fragile as poppies. Like the first time we made love.

He even managed to finish it.

Holding him close, I close my eyes. It isn't long before they come for me. Grandmother again, the Construct with a man's voice behind it. Flying over the poppies, their red and pink spotting the deep green field like a virgin's blood on her marriage bed.

You are not prepared, they tell me. *The Bridegroom knows you not.*

The scene shifts. Abruptly. My stomach rolls with it, and I am slammed into: a meeting house. It is huge; an eternity of walls that go on forever. Windows everywhere.

The tabernacle on Temple Square.

I'm sitting in a pew, right up front. The *Christus,* the only statue of Christ left in Utah, stares down at me. The hollow eyes are stern. They have moved him there, out of the Visitors' Center (where anyone could come to him) and into the tabernacle. I don't know why.

He stands behind the old wooden pulpit. It's much too small for him.

The sacrament table is just below. It is covered with a white cloth. A myriad of small bloodstains splotch the fabric, and I wonder just what it is that this sacrament represents.

The *Christus* intones, though his mouth does not move, "Take. Eat. This is the flesh of my body. My blood."

I shake my head. This is *not* His sacrament. This is nothing like it.

The face of Christ is harder than the stone he is made of. "Where was your oil?" he says. His voice loses its vast, tonal quality. Takes on the shrill tones of the Grandmother-Construct. "Where were you while I tarried?" he asks.

Why? I think. *Why do they always come to me in visions of the things I have loved?*

But I am still holding David, I realize. He is in my arms, his blood on the pew, on the plain brown carpet underneath. And I know I am half in and half out of the dream. I look up at the statue's white stone face. The hands are outstretched; the whole attitude of the thing is that of looking down. He is bigger than me. But he is not the god they would make me think he is.

Tired. So damned tired. David's blood smeared on my hands, sticky as it dries.

But still I say what has bothered me all along, all this terrible time, of Virgins.

"Where were *you?*" I ask. Crying. Ignoring the Construct. Giving this image of God more of my soul in anger than I have ever given in love. "*You* were the one who tarried. *You* were the one who wasn't there. *Where were you?*"

Grandmother again, slapping my face. "Who do you think you are? You aren't any *kind* of virgin, much less a wise one."

But I don't want to be a virgin, I tell her. I am getting hysterical again. But this time, it is of my own making. I am still talking past them, past the familiar Grandmother-face and into the face of the stone Christ, which I force them to make kind, the way I remember it. The way it was *made.*

The program is slipping. It is not the strength of my fighting that makes it go; I know that right away. It is that I am going as David did: Out. Beyond their range. Where *I* am. Where the *Christus* still stands in a swirl of stars, and smiles. Just barely. It is a small smile. A *Mona Lisa* smile. No mocking or even mystery. So small, you could almost miss it.

But they can't take away what I've already seen.

And I am flying. Suddenly I am flying, but not afraid. No heights, no gradations of high or low. No place to fall to. I am going straight up on a gentle curving stream of air. Everything is pale, like the snow outside my window as it passes through the brilliant glow of the lamps.

They give it one last try: The mural of the *Sisters* blocks my way. Panoramic, curved around all sides. Stretching out around me. I keep flying, thinking, *Surely I will break through.*

But then I have *become* the thing. See that I am *in* it, a part of it. My back is straight, a tendril of hair escaping the bun that is bound so tightly to the back of my head. The woman next to me comes to life, moves her hand to put that elusive strand back in its place.

And I have a revelation: *that if she can move, then I can too.*

A deep breath and I come to life, lifting my plain brown skirts high around my knees. Bounding toward the crops. Legs long and bare. Flashing past the winter wheat.

Thinking of David, whose gentle face I see so much like that pale smiling stone. I send a swarm of locusts into the straight gold-and-green fields. I send it from my heart; with my thoughts I send it. I am the white roe. I am the breast of my love. I sing the Songs of Solomon. Dancing with a tambour. Crying out the songs.

Everything melts then into swirls of color and light that are free and strong and just waiting to be made.

Far off I can hear the voices of a dozen Constructs. Fainter now. Cursing God, cursing me. I am still connected, but fading fast. This is good. I look upon it and see: That it is good.

Above the bed, above the bodies slowly cooling there, I laugh a song of great delight, and dance.

PUEBLO DE SIÓN

CHARLENE C. HARMON

Vibrant orange, red, indigo, and green blazed across the sky while the sun set, as though textured with a palette knife by an angry god.

Appropriate, Marisa thought. The sky even looked a little bloody, as if millions of droplets of blood tainted the atmosphere. For all she knew they did. Maybe the blast, like a volcanic eruption, would leave the atmosphere tainted for months. She stared at the colors of the sunset, trying to see inside them, memorize them, lose herself in them, until they faded and died.

Finally Marisa closed her eyes and allowed the anguish she had held back all day to engulf her, drown her with its blackness. With the blackness came her memory of the great burning wind, exploding across the sky of her mind with the force of a hundred tornadoes, terrifying her senses as strongly as its reality had the day before. The stench of burning nitrogen was so strong she could taste it. Marisa curled into a fetal position and bit into her arm. She would not cry out. Not this time. Then the storm vanished, leaving a silence so heavy she could hardly breathe. Slowly the voices of her father and the others in the Anasazi pueblo filtered into her numbed mind. With reality came a renewal of the void left by the death of her mother and sister, her friends, her town. Her world.

She pulled her windbreaker more tightly around her to ease the chill still lurking in the spring air and looked down the hill to the pueblo. It was breathtaking. Even in Marisa's emotional state, she appreciated its majesty. Built inside a giant, shallow cave, the pueblo stretched two city blocks wide and nearly one block deep. Most of it still bore the ravages of time: broken-down kivas, roofless dwellings, caved-in walls. But the part where they now lived was beautifully restored. Marisa concentrated on looking at the pueblo, examining it in detail to rid herself of the memory of the storm that had screamed overhead, destroying everything above the canyons. She saw the open doorways and windows, the rough surface of the adobe, the way the colors of the clay blended with the reds and oranges of the canyon wall. She thought about Martin and Janet Smith, the only other people they had seen since they had entered Quetzal Canyon several weeks ago. The Smiths had been touring Canyonlands when the blast came. They were having a picnic near the rim of the canyon, had seen burning debris whip through the fiery wind roaring over their heads as if they were under an invisible floor looking up. They went to the surface and found nothing. No cities. No homes. No people. Nothing but sand and the canyons. The Smiths stayed at the pueblo long enough to discuss the possible cause of the desolation and beg some food. No one really knew what the blast had been, or if there was any radiation. They had no way of knowing how far the blast extended, whether a few hundred miles or a few thousand. There was still a lot of atmospheric interference, so radios were useless. Her father thought the blast was due to the N-Cycle testing in New Mexico, at a facility built by the government specifically for highly controversial and dangerous experiments. They were testing a new bomb that was supposed to ignite the nitrogen in the atmosphere. The Smiths thought the blast was divine retribution, that the Second Coming was at hand. They argued for a while, and left to find other survivors and convert them to their point of view, mumbling something under their breaths about "blind fools."

Somehow that memory brought Marisa to tears. She didn't know why the Smiths would make her cry, but the crying eased the void in her soul. Since Marisa was alone, she let her tears run unchecked. Marisa cried for the death of her mother and sister. She cried for the loss of her friends. She cried for her older brother who had died in the Great Mormon Migration of 2047.

"Why, God, why were we called from Mexico to die in the deserts of Zion?" Marisa didn't understand why a loving God would call his people together to kill them a short seven years later.

Her father had declared a day and a half of mourning. After that they would get to work so they could make a new life in the abandoned Anasazi pueblo. Her father said they had too much to do to survive. Marisa was sure that Olga, whose emotions resembled an ice floe, would have no problem.

"*¡Mariposa! ¿Donde estás, hija?*" It was her father, calling her from the pueblo to ask where she was.

Marisa quickly dried her tears and took a deep breath. The air smelled so stale and sanitary now. It would be hard to get used to. She wiped her eyes again, not wanting her father to see her crying. "I'm here, *Papá.* I'll be right down." Good! Her voice sounded fairly normal. Marisa took another deep breath and climbed off the rock she had adopted as "hers" and slid carefully down the hill.

Marc was the first person she saw when she got to the pueblo. He was the youngest member of the team, only a few years older than Marisa. He was tall and blond and built like a football player. He was also kind. He treated her like a legitimate member of the team—unlike the others, who only tolerated her presence because she was Pedro Ovando's daughter. "Hi, Marc. Did I miss anything?" She hadn't wanted to hear all the arguing. She'd rather wait and hear the *Cliffs Notes* version.

"Not much. Tim's been on his soapbox. He's sure we'll all die of radiation sickness in the next few days, so we should all give up and await our fate. Your father's set up a work schedule for tomorrow. Olga's just there as usual. She hasn't said much, just nodding agreement with everything your father says. That's about it. Where have you been?"

"Watching the sunset, and thinking." Marc caught the undercurrents of pain and didn't ask any more questions. He just gave Marisa a quick hug and walked on. Marisa watched him for a moment as he crossed the compound, a small smile on her face. They had all become a lot closer since the blast, not knowing if the western half of the United States was gone or if the blast had been small, covering a few hundred miles. Hopefully the air would clear up soon so they could get some sort of news. Even if it came from Radio Havana it would be something. They only had enough gas to drive to the nearest service station, which no longer existed, and only enough food to survive a few weeks. Whatever the cause of the blast, they were stuck.

The pueblo was their best option, since it provided shelter and more than one source of water: a small waterfall in the back of the cave and a river not far away. Each person had his or her own room on the ground floor around a large courtyard or plaza. They were protected from the elements by the cliffs above and behind them and had a good view of the valley in case anyone came.

Marisa walked over to where her father, Tim, and Olga were seated around the fire pit in the center of the courtyard. Tim was thirtyish with stringy brown hair and a perpetual frown. Olga was older. Maybe forty or fifty, Marisa wasn't sure. She kept her Swedish blonde hair pulled back in a bun and had a quiet air of snobbishness. Marisa didn't like her. She reminded her of the KGB spies from old 2-D television shows. Then there was her father, the team leader. He was in his fifties and still took pride in his large, bushy mustache. He thought it gave him character, especially among all the gringos. Marisa thought it made him look like Groucho Marx.

"*Mariposa, hija,* where have you been?" Even after seven years in America, and years before that teaching in both Spanish and English at the Universidad de Magdalena, her father spoke English with a heavy accent.

"Out. Watching the sunset," Marisa replied with patient exasperation.

"You didn't go near the surface?" Her father looked at her sharply in sudden concern.

"No, *Papá.*" Sometimes her father made her angry, treating her like a child instead of an eighteen-year-old adult. He had forbidden her from going to the top of the canyon for any reason. If there had been radiation, the fallout would get them anyway. She wondered if it was his way of dealing with the firestorm or if he was in some form of denial.

Marisa sat on a block of rough adobe and poured herself a cup of Brigham Tea. She didn't know the name of the plant it came from, just that a lot of it grew around the pueblo. It smelled bad and it tasted awful. She took a swallow and grimaced in distaste. It *was* hot and soothing, she kept reminding herself. Sort of. Maybe. Okay, it was just hot. She drank it more for something to do.

"*¿Qué piensas, Mariposa?*" Her father's voice interrupted her thoughts.

Marisa looked up. "What do I think? About what? I'm sorry. I wasn't listening."

"We are going to see if we can start up the irrigation system and get some of the wild grain harvested. Most of the fields were on top of the canyon, but there are one or two smaller ones nearby. There might be enough wild grain there to be of use. It is early enough in the season that we could have a harvest before it snows. I would like you and Marc to work on that tomorrow."

"Okay." She was glad it was Marc. She'd rather work with him than Olga or Tim.

"It doesn't matter," Tim said. "We'll all be dead before we can harvest anything. Why bother?" He'd been going on about death and dying since the blast. The Smiths hadn't helped. They believed it was the end of the world and God was cleansing the Earth before the Second Coming. Tim believed them, and since his past was far from spotless, he was sure he was a goner. He wouldn't even help collect water. He just sat in the courtyard and preached gloom and doom. But for all his words, he wasn't adverse to eating with the rest of them.

"Tomorrow, Tim and I will go hunting," her father continued as if he hadn't been interrupted.

"I'm not going hunting," Tim said. "If we catch anything, it'll be so full of radiation we'll die all the faster."

"Unless you want to starve to death first. You help or you do not eat. It is your choice."

Good. It was about time her father laid it on the line. He was beginning to irritate her. He was such a lazy good-for-nothing, work would do him good. Marisa had no idea why he'd been selected for this dig. He'd had nothing to offer.

"What about Olga? She never does anything, and you treat her like royalty," Tim complained, stuffing a roll in his mouth. Olga was an anthropologist. She spent a lot of time with Dr. Ovando, "studying his technique" and learning more about the Anasazi. Olga did whatever Marisa's father told her to do without a murmur. Marisa thought she was a little too obvious. It was disgusting. Especially as her father was married. Or had been. Marisa bowed her head and clenched her fists for a moment, controlling the pain.

Her father chose to address Marisa rather than Tim, who probably knew already what Olga would be doing but asked just to be nasty. "Olga is going to look around the pueblo. There is a good chance there are some sealed rooms we have not yet found. Other sites have had them. If there are, there may very well be some things we can use."

Marisa poured herself another cup of Brigham Tea and stood up to go to her room. She had been told what she needed to know. Now she wanted to be alone. "Sounds good. I'm going to bed now. Good night."

"Buenas noches, hija," her father replied. Olga merely inclined her head. Tim mumbled something about dying in her sleep. Marisa pulled her mini halogen floodlight out of her pocket as she went into the adobe and clay room that was now her home and shined it around, checking for snakes. She picked up her military sleeping bag by the bottom and shook it out vigorously. It was one she'd bought a few years ago at an army surplus store. It was warm and comfortable and had been with her on many camping trips. Once she was sure it was empty, she carefully straightened it out again.

Her books and writing tablet were sitting on a "shelf" in the wall, just below a painting of men hunting antelope. Her two pairs of jeans, T-shirts, and other personal items, including a 3-D holograph of her family, decorated other parts of the room. It didn't make it seem any more like home. Nothing would. Marisa wondered what they'd do for clothing when theirs wore out. The thought of wearing animal skins made her itch. Marisa set her still-full cup of Brigham Tea on a shelf. She didn't know why she'd brought it into her room. She wasn't going to drink it. She pulled out her Book of Mormon. Maybe it would help her feel better. She sat down on the hard floor and read for a few minutes, then settled down into her sleeping bag and tried to sleep. Even with the pad under her, the ground was hard and cold. She moved around a bit, trying to get comfortable. Finally she settled her derriere in an indentation in the floor that wasn't too awkward. She turned out the light and snuggled down into the bag to sleep, and the nightmare started.

She was standing on a sandstone formation that looked like a small stegosaurus, watching the sun rise above the sandstone cliffs, spreading light and color, when the great firestorm came. It darkened her mind and filled it with a hungry roar. The searing wind burned her flesh, but left her chilled to the marrow. Suddenly a giant hand reached out of the storm and grabbed her, pulling her into the swirling darkness. Marisa screamed, trying to pull away from the hand, but it was too strong for her. In the maelstrom she saw her mother clawing and screaming. Then her mother burst into flames and scattered into the wind. Marisa screamed again and again, but the wind ripped her voice from her and threw it away.

Marisa felt something warm holding her tight, enfolding her in its arms. She fought and struggled to get free, afraid that she too would burn. "Marisa! Wake up!" Hands shook her, then slapped her across the face. Again the arms held her close, and she felt herself being rocked back and forth by the wind. "It's okay, Marisa, wake up." Slowly the storm faded. Someone was holding her, comforting her, making her feel warm and safe. She buried her head in the soft sweatshirt and cried. She didn't care anymore if her father knew. At least she assumed it was her father.

"*¡Mariposa!* Marc. *¿Qué pasa?* What are you doing?" her father demanded from the doorway of her room.

Marc? Of course, it had to be Marc. As much as she loved her father, she hadn't felt warm in his arms in a long time. And he would have spoken in Spanish. A dull red spread up her neck and across her face as she pulled away from the comfort of Marc's arms to address her father, but Marc spoke first.

"She was screaming, sir. I came to see what was wrong." Marc quickly stood and walked over to face her father. "She had a nightmare. I was trying to comfort her."

"Marisa?" She knew he was angry. He only called her Marisa when he was displeased with her. Otherwise he used her childhood nickname, Mariposa, or butterfly.

"*Es la verdad, Papá.* It's true. I was having a nightmare. *Nada ocurrió.*" Didn't he know her well enough by now to trust her? She was embarrassed enough having cried all over Marc. She didn't want her father treating her like a teenager.

"*Bien. Lo siento.* I am sorry. I was on the other side of the compound with Olga, we were talking about what could be done to the pueblo, and saw Marc go into your room. I was too far away to hear you. I naturally assumed . . . I was concerned." He turned to Marc and nodded his head. "*Muchas gracias.*" Feeling he had explained enough, he turned and walked out the door. Marc went to follow him, then paused.

"It's okay, Marisa. I have nightmares about the storm, too. If you need to talk, let me know." With a smile and a wave, he was gone.

Marisa sat for a long time, staring out the door at the night shadows. Marc was nice. He'd known just what to do. He hadn't made fun of her nightmare. Otherwise she would have been too embarrassed to work with him. Thinking about Marc helped her sleep.

The next morning neither her father nor Marc said anything over their ash cakes and Brigham Tea about Marisa's nightmare. After they cleaned up Marisa and Marc walked in silence, enjoying the peace of morning as they headed east along the canyon to where an old grainfield and irrigation ditches remained.

The sun was just coming up behind them, making the reds, yellows, and oranges of the sandstone brighter, the leaves on the trees and the plants greener. She had always liked morning in Canyonlands and Zion National Park. It was so full of contrast: bright colors and deep shadows. Many times she had spent the night in the bottom of one canyon or another to rise early and take pictures. Her pictures were never as good as ones she'd seen in tourist brochures or magazine covers, but they weren't bad. Her camera was in her backpack at the pueblo. She'd taken a few shots since she'd been here, but she had no way to develop the film now. Marisa closed her eyes for a moment in pain and stumbled over the rough terrain.

"Careful." Marc reached out a hand to steady her. She thanked him, and assured him she was fine. As they started walking again, Marc asked, "Did you sleep okay last night?"

"Yes, I slept okay." As okay as she could under the circumstances. "Thank you for your help last night."

"No problem. I haven't slept well either."

Marisa thought she'd done a good job of covering her feelings. She would have to try harder.

They talked a bit about the area, the flora they encountered: the sage brush and cottonwood trees, the sego lily and wild onion. Plants they could use later for herbs and clothing or food. Marisa had heard that cottonwoods could be used to make clothing, but she wasn't sure how. The sage would help if they had to cook wild rabbit. Marisa noticed that it was quieter than usual, as if the insects and animals were in mourning. The canyon didn't sound like what she was used to. She took a deep breath and sighed in disappointment. It would take her a while to get used to it. Even the plants and trees around her couldn't cover up the sanitized smell from above the canyon. Marisa shook her head and thought about something else.

The first thing they did when they got to the grain field was to survey the area and see what was still growing from the Anasazi. Most of the grain had died and been taken over by sage and rabbit brush, but there were still quite a few patches of wild wheat and barley and an occasional squash. They walked the perimeter, noting the size of the areas they could reclaim. In the northeast corner they found what looked like an old creek bed that had been an irrigation ditch. They decided to follow it and see if it connected with a viable water source. If they could trace it to a river, they might be able to divert water back to the field and start growing crops again. If not they'd have to find another way to get water to the area. It took them most of the day, but the creek bed didn't die out. It went to within a few yards of a tributary of the Green River. If they could dig a trench the rest of the way, they might be able to irrigate. They discussed the various possibilities and opted to try digging a small trench between the tributary and the creek bed. They ate a late lunch of MREs and Kool-Aid. She had the Beef Stew, and Marc got the Chicken à la King.

The team had come prepared to stay for several weeks at the pueblo, doing the final surveys and studying any remaining debris before opening it up for tourists. They had brought along several weeks' worth of MREs, as well as pancake and Kool-Aid mixes, cookies, granola bars, and candy. Her father brought a first aid kit, a water purifier, and a small Bunsen burner. He liked to be prepared. Marisa thought about winter. They hadn't brought any clothing for cold weather. Even though no one said anything, it was pretty obvious that unless a miracle happened they would die during the long, cold winter.

After lunch they dug and cleared until they had made a trench big enough for water to flow through and slowly fill the old creek bed. It would take a while before they knew whether or not they were successful, and it was already after dark.

"After last night my father is going to have us both put on KP," Marisa quipped.

"Not when we tell him what we've accomplished," Marc said. He was always philosophical when it came to dealing with other people, angry fathers. Marisa wished she could be so optimistic.

They hurried back to the pueblo, arm in arm so Marc could keep Marisa from stumbling and so they could combine their mini floodlights to help them see better. Just before they arrived at the pueblo, Marc stopped.

"What's wrong?" Marisa hadn't seen or heard anything unusual.

"Nothing. I just wanted to let you know that you did a great job today," and he kissed her. It was brief, over almost before it began, but Marisa liked it. When she didn't say anything, he kissed her again more slowly, giving her a chance to respond. Then he started walking back to the pueblo, practically dragging Marisa behind. She wished he'd give her a little more time to assimilate this new turn in their relationship. Then again, if her father caught them . . .

It was nearly midnight when they got back to the pueblo and found Marisa's father and Olga waiting for them at the dying campfire. They were pouring over a diagram of the pueblo traced into the dirt. When her father saw them, he jumped to his feet.

"Where have you been? *¿Hija, por qué te portas así?*" Why was she behaving like this? Behaving like what?

Marc quickly explained about the fields, the creek bed, and what they had done.

"*Bien,*" her father replied, pacified at Marc's explanation. He should be, Marisa thought angrily, it was the truth. "Tim and I caught nothing today," her father said. "I almost had a deer, but Tim scared it away. *Tonto!*" Her father stomped around the fire, gesturing expressively with his hands while he talked. "Then he said he wanted to try to shoot a rabbit. I say okay. I give him the gun. I find a snake and try to kill it with rocks. I look back, my gun is on the ground and Tim is gone with my bullets. *¡Loco! ¡Idioto!* I tried to find him. For three hours I looked. Nothing. Then I come here, and he is sleeping. I wake him up. He says the bullets are gone, buried somewhere. He does not remember where. I could have strangled him. *¡Basta!* I can no longer tolerate his behavior." He paced around a bit more, calming himself before he continued speaking. "Olga found a sealed room behind the complex. Inside we found pottery, tools, some leather goods. We will show it to you tomorrow. It is late and we need to get up early." Marisa's father helped Olga to her feet. They both started toward their rooms. He stopped and turned back to Marisa. "Ah, yes, we have more company. A family with eight children. The father is a Mormon bishop, which is good. Maybe God is on our side. But enough talk. It is late. Go to sleep. We will talk more tomorrow."

Marisa poured herself a cup of Brigham Tea and took a couple of rolls and a cookie out of the cooler, then sat on a block of adobe by the fire, absently staring at the drawing of the pueblo. Her father had never been a man of many words. His philosophy was to say just what is needed and go on to the next item of business. She wondered about the family, where they were from, if they were staying. They must have walked, because she saw no vehicle outside the pueblo. And why was Olga with her father? She hadn't said two words, and there had been no apparent reason for her to stay up with him. They could have discussed the pueblo any time. Marisa didn't like it. Tomorrow. Her father would answer her questions tomorrow. While she was brooding, Marc came and sat beside her, a cup of Brigham Tea and a sandwich in his hands.

"You came in the Mormon Migration didn't you?"

"Yes. The prophet said come, so we did. We sold everything we couldn't carry."

"You walked? Why didn't you drive? Surely, with your father's position . . ."

"Yes, we walked. Along with most of the others. The border patrol was turning away anyone without the proper papers. My father didn't bother to get them. He said it would take too long. He didn't think the government would let him leave anyway. They didn't want a major exodus, and my father was "too valuable" to be allowed to immigrate. He knew they wouldn't let him go. They would just come up with excuses, paperwork, anything to keep him from leaving. My father also didn't want to let them know he was planning on leaving, or they would have stopped him."

"How could they have stopped him if he was determined?"

"Oh, the government has ways. Many people have disappeared because they didn't do what the government wanted. Or their families disappeared."

"So you sneaked over the border?"

Marisa nodded, not wanting to talk about it. She especially didn't want to talk about her brother, who'd died at the border. She rubbed her hand back and forth across the bottom of her mug to soothe herself.

"Then how come he's working with the Bureau of Land Management and the National Park Service if he's not here legally?"

"He is legal now. The BLM pulled a few strings and made us all citizens."

"I thought it took years to get naturalized."

"Usually. But they wanted my father to head this project."

Marc finished off his sandwich and asked, "Isn't it a little unusual for a Mexican to be an expert on the Anasazi?"

"No more than for a German to be an expert on Olmecan culture."

Marc got up, rinsed out his mug, and put it back where it belonged. He then walked over to Marisa and stopped. "Umm, Marisa, you didn't mind that I kissed you, did you?"

Marisa blushed. "No. I didn't mind."

"Good." He leaned down and kissed her again before walking to his room. "Goodnight."

"Goodnight."

Marisa sat by the fire for a while longer, thinking about the day's events, about Marc and his apparent interest in her. Mostly about Marc. She knew she should go to sleep, but she was afraid of having another nightmare. Maybe she could talk to Marc? He'd understand. And he'd told her to let him know if she needed to talk. No. It was late, and she didn't want to disturb him. Besides if her father woke up and saw them . . . And she couldn't go to her father. Maybe if she stayed up until she couldn't keep her eyes open she would not dream. It didn't work. At least this time, she didn't scream.

Marisa was still a little groggy the next morning over breakfast. But she was acclimatizing to her new life. The bitter herb tea didn't taste so bad today. Neither did the ash cakes, although they still tasted like soot.

While they were speaking Marc commented that he had turned on the portable radio last night, just to see if anyone was out there. "I got some station in Spanish. So at least we know the blast was local. I couldn't get a clear reception, so I don't know if any rescue parties are being planned, but at least the air is clearing. In a few days we might be able to get something local."

When everyone heard the news they were ecstatic. It was the best news they had heard since the blast. Maybe with some careful planning and a clear radio station to guide them, they might be able to walk out of the canyon before it got too cold.

"This is all good, but we still have a lot of work to do," Dr. Ovando cautioned. "If rescue teams come it may take months for them to find us once they are sent out. We need to proceed as if nothing has changed." They all agreed not to dwell on the radio until they got a clearer station and more concrete information. The dishes were cheerfully cleaned and put away, then Olga and her father led Marisa and Marc to the sealed room. Tim chose to skip the work, and food, and stay in his room. He said if he lived to dinner, he'd help skin whatever they caught. Otherwise it wasn't worth getting up.

The room they went to was at the back of the pueblo. They climbed up to the second level, walked back to the cliffs, then climbed down through a circular hole in the roof into one of the rooms thought to be a council chamber. Along the wall that supposedly ran flush with the cliff face was an opening large enough to climb through. Her father took the Coleman lantern, now being saved for special occasions. The room was not very large, and the air was still musty, though the room had been open all night. Stacks of pottery were neatly arranged along one wall; piles of skins that looked brittle and ready to fall apart decorated another; arrowheads of obsidian and flint were grouped in another area along with what looked like spears and plows; mummified cornhusks dotted the floor, much of the corn rodent-eaten. There were several other tools that Marisa couldn't identify placed here and there, as well as some woven shoes and decorative clothing that would probably crumble to dust the minute they touched them.

"How did you find it, *Papá?*" Marisa queried.

He gave her a stern look. "Olga found it." She had forgotten that her father told her last night that it was Olga's discovery. "She noticed this room was different from the others along the cliff wall. She and I cleared the opening last night while we waited for you." He added the last part to make Marisa feel guilty.

"This is great!" Marc enthused. "Is any of it usable?"

Olga answered him in her careful English. "Most of the pottery is. And most of the tools. The corn is useless. The cloth and skins are either rotten or too fragile to use—at least, what we have seen. The woven materials we shall merely use as a pattern. I don't want to try touching it, it's too fragile. The rest . . . we shall see."

"That is what we would like you to help us with today. We need to categorize all that is here. Then we will know what we have and what we can use," her father added.

"Yes. Pedro and I will work with the skins and leather. We want you and Marisa to catalog the pottery and tools. As we will probably be using them, list only what is still in good condition. The potsherds you can ignore. For now. If we ever leave here, the shards can be studied. Put the usable items in the center of the room, the rest can stay where they are. Much of it will go to museums—assuming we are found." Olga addressed Marc. She didn't even look at Marisa. This was the most Olga had said in Marisa's presence since they'd come on this trip. Marisa had assumed it was because she didn't speak well, but she spoke English better than Marisa's father. And when had Olga started calling her father Pedro? Marisa walked over to where Marc was inspecting the pottery. When Olga's back was turned Marisa made a face at Marc, imitating Olga's mannerisms. Marc turned his head and tried not to laugh. Marisa's father coughed. She looked up and found him glaring at her.

She didn't want to apologize. She didn't like Olga or her attitude. Instead she shrugged her shoulders, sat on the ground, and began to sort through the pottery. She knew her father would be angry, but she didn't care.

The four of them worked several hours, sometimes talking about trivial things, sometimes working in silence. When Olga and her father did talk, it was about the pueblo and the condition of the materials in the room and what it would mean to their chances of survival. Marisa enjoyed the work more than she thought she would. The pottery fascinated her. Some of it was decorated in a braided pattern, and all of it was utilitarian. It was thick and sturdy enough to be serviceable. Other pieces were decorated with bright colors and intricate designs. They even found a few ceramic effigies, male and female, that they carefully set near the wall where they wouldn't be disturbed. They also found one wall covered in a bright mosaic of colored tiles and some turquoise jewelry that they hoped to look at more carefully at a later date. The tools were still in good condition. When Marc and Marisa began to search through them, they found that the Anasazi had also left chunks of rock and tools for making spears and knives.

When they had done as much as they could, they crawled out of the room, bringing a few knives and some pottery with them. The leather was too old and brittle.

Over lunch they met Mel and Bonnie Hammond and their family. The Hammonds were from Idaho and had been on vacation in Goblin Valley. The oldest daughter was just a little younger than Marisa. They were a happy, talkative group, and lunch was a lot of fun. They had all cleaned up the area and were preparing to go to their separate jobs when Bonnie noticed a large group of over a dozen people walking toward them. In the lead were Martin and Janet Smith. As they got closer they hailed Marisa's father.

"Brother Ovando!" Marisa backed away from the rest of the group and watched from a distance as the Smith Company encircled the Hammonds, her father, and Olga.

"*Señor* Smith. I thought we had said all that was necessary the last time you were here."

"Ah, Brother Ovando. Even the worst sinners deserve another chance, so why not you?" Martin Smith smiled. It was an oily smile that made Marisa cringe inside. "Come. Surely you won't turn away weary travelers. Won't you offer us a drink?"

"I can make some Brigham Tea if you'd like," Olga quickly offered, putting the kettle on the fire. She collected a stack of Anasazi pottery to serve as mugs.

"Sister Svenson, you are most kind." Martin Smith glared at Marisa's father.

Mel and Bonnie Hammond introduced themselves, trying to break the tension. "Where are you from, Mr. and Mrs. Smith?"

"We are messengers from God. He has revealed to us that the Second Coming is at hand. The earth has been cleansed, and Jesus Christ is returning to reclaim his people. We have been chosen by him to prepare Zion." Martin Smith sat down on a log, as if he were addressing lesser mortals.

"But the scriptures say Zion was to have been built in the tops of the mountains," Mel reasoned.

"Yes, but the world has become corrupt, an unworthy vessel, a den of iniquity. God has revealed to us that he will build Zion in the majesty of Zion National Park."

"But this is Canyonlands," Marc muttered under his breath. "Zion is on the other end of the state. You need a geography lesson." Marisa looked at him and tried not to laugh.

"Are you claiming to be a prophet?" Mel asked.

"The earth has been cleansed. The mountains have been brought down and the valleys, or the canyons, will be raised up. I have been chosen to usher in the Millennium." Martin leered beatifically at those around him.

Marisa looked curiously at the rest of the company. No one but Martin Smith had said a word. They reminded her of turkeys standing in a rainstorm looking up with their mouths open.

"The scriptures clearly state that before the second coming of the Lord the sun will be darkened and the moon turned to blood. That hasn't happened yet," Dr. Ovando pointed out.

"Ah, you *have* read the scriptures, Brother Ovando," Martin Smith sneered. "But there you are also mistaken. We were near the top of the canyon when the blast came. The sun was indeed darkened. Have you looked in the sky? The moon is red, bathed in the blood of a million souls."

"Not all are dead, Mr. Smith," Dr. Ovando said. "Marc was listening to the radio last night and heard a broadcast.

"Ah, Brother Ovando, you are mistaken. The words young Marc

heard last night were merely leftover transmissions still retained in the atmosphere. You will see. In a few days the atmosphere will clear and you will hear nothing. Then perhaps you will believe us. But then it may be too late. For God is choosing his messengers from those who survived and only a fortunate few who heed his call will be saved. Those who do not will be cast out forever. Doomed to outer darkness."

Marisa, seated next to Marc on top of the first floor of adobe rooms, put her hands over her face and tried not to laugh. She peeped through her fingers at Marc, who had such a mischievous twinkle in his eyes that she could barely restrain herself from laughing out loud.

"My brothers and sisters, you must not let your mind dictate the path your soul will follow. The carnal mind will lead your soul to hell. You must follow your heart. The Lord has cleansed the Earth by fire, as he foretold. 'For the day cometh that shall burn as an oven.' That day is here. We are a special people, hand picked to usher in the millennium. You and your pueblo are a part of the eternal scheme of things. Repent of your sins and follow us. God will forgive you if you truly bare your souls and follow him. Join us in this divine calling."

Mel had brought out his Book of Mormon and his Bible as if he wanted to continue the debate, but he remained silent. Marisa thought she understood. The Smiths weren't listening to anything and had worn out their welcome.

"It has been foretold that the earth shall burn with a fire and all the wicked shall perish. The elements of the earth shall melt in the heat of his displeasure. I have been to the surface. I have seen the desolation. The sand has become glass in the cleansing fire. The Earth is being prepared to become a giant Urim and Thummim, a divine crystal ball to show us the way. I have seen the future in the crystal sands. We must preach the word today, for tomorrow will be too late. We must prepare our hearts now to accept him as our God," he paused dramatically. "We ask you to heed the call of your Savior and join us in this divine calling." Marisa kept quiet, knowing if she spoke she would only make him angry.

The entire Smith company looked around expectantly, as if waiting for the others to fall on their knees and bow to them or something.

No one moved or spoke for several minutes. Finally Martin Smith shook his head sadly. "My friends, my heart is heavy with sorrow for you. You have been taught the word of God and have failed to heed his calling. If you do not join us, you will spend eternity in the bowels of misery knowing that you can never pass through the pearly gates into heaven. I appeal to you one last time, out of the goodness of my heart. Repent of your sins. Give up your pride. Join us in welcoming the Savior."

"We have listened enough, *Señor* Smith. We do not wish to follow you. We would like you to leave," Dr. Ovando said, rising to his feet.

Martin Smith stood very still for a moment, then he seemed to erupt like a volcano. "Very well, Brother Ovando. You have made your choice. You have condemned yourself and your people to eternal damnation. Be warned: You have not heard the last of us. We will return, whether in this life or the next. And when we all appear before the judgment seat of God to be judged, we will testify against you and say, 'I told you so.' Then you will be hard-pressed to have a reason why you did not follow us, why you should be exalted when you condemned the messengers of God." With a mighty flourish Martin Smith dusted off the dirt from his shoes as a sign of condemnation, turned, and led his company west out of the canyon.

When the Smith company could no longer be seen, the group, with the exception of the younger Hammond kids who had long since retired to their rooms to play, gathered to discuss what had occurred.

"I don't know if you saw their faces when they left," Steve, the eldest Hammond boy, laughed, "but they looked like lobsters. I'm sure they wanted to move into the pueblo. They were really pissed." Mel gave his son a look of reprimand. "Well, they were."

"Tim's gone," Marisa's father interjected. "I checked his room, and he's gone."

"Well, the Smiths forgave him his sins. I can't really blame him for following them, considering the state he's been in," Bonnie said.

"He's complained so much and done so little, I'm glad he's gone," Steve added.

Marc and Marisa sat quietly. They were glad Tim was gone but didn't want to say anything. They were rid of him. They should leave it at that.

"I hope he's happier with them," Bonnie commented. Even though Tim did nothing but complain, she felt sorry for him.

Three soldiers, privates on maneuvers with the National Guard, had been with the Smith company out of necessity. But when they found the pueblo, they chose to stay. Karl, the most talkative of the three, was tall and thin with a receding hairline. When there was a lull in the conversation, he introduced himself. "I'm glad we finally found someone sane. They were really starting to get on our nerves. They found us a few days ago. They took our Scotch and told us to repent. Man, we were hungry enough we didn't care at first."

"So," Bonnie asked, "how did you escape the blast?"

"We were tired of marching and formations, so me, Jeff, and Bob climbed down into a hole for a few drinks. We had a break before starting the next phase of training. Bob had some Scotch. We figured we deserved a little fun. Besides, nobody'd care if we were gone until roll call that night, and we'd have been back by then."

Jeff, a middle-sized blond in his twenties, looked a little nervous as Karl spoke. "Are you sure we should be telling them all this?

"Why not?" said the third of the party, a portly man who looked about the same age as the other two. "What are they going to do? Report us?"

"The main thing is that we're away from those kooky Smiths," Karl said. Addressing the party, he continued, "They had us up at dawn, prayin' and doin' meditations. They said they were cleansin' our wicked souls. Then we spent the rest of the time walkin' around lookin' for other people. The Smith Company wouldn't ever stay in one place more'n a day. Their mission was to find as many people as they could and go somewhere to start their new Zion."

"I told you they wanted the pueblo," Steve chimed in.

"Every time we encountered someone, Martin and Janet would begin their spiel about all of us being saved to prepare for Christ. And anyone who didn't listen would be damned. We're just glad you guys are here so we don't have to take any more of their crap. Man, they were worse than any preacher," Karl continued.

Marisa's father and Olga explained to the three men about the pueblo and how they were trying to revive the lifestyle of the Anasazi so they could survive here. The newcomers said they didn't mind working if it was for a good reason.

Groups for gathering water and wood, hunting game, and collecting edible plants for dinner were put together. Each group then left to find what was needed. Marisa went to gather firewood. She was glad she didn't have to kill and gut any animal, even a snake. The thought made her sick.

After dinner the last packages of cookies were passed around as daily chores were discussed and assignments handed out. Marc, Marisa, Mel and Bonnie Hammond, and their boys were assigned to the grain field. The two youngest boys wouldn't be able to help much, but with all the work that needed to be done, they were better off with their parents in the fields. Their group was to restore, tend, and eventually harvest what grain and squash they could. That was fine with Marisa. She loved gardening. Each year she had helped her mother with the family garden.

Just as they were getting ready to go to bed, Dr. Ovando came storming into the courtyard, cursing in Spanish.

"*¡Estupido! ¡Tonto! ¡Brujo! ¿Quiere matarnos todos? ¿Qué está pensando, éste typo?*"

"*¿Papá, qué pasa?* What happened? Who is trying to kill us?"

"Tim."

"Tim? I don't understand?"

By this time Marc, Olga, the Hammonds and the three soldiers had come out to see what was going on.

"The radio. It is broken, useless. I went to listen to the radio, see if I could get any news, and it was broken. Parts torn out and strewn across the ground outside the Van. I could kill Tim!"

"*¡Papá!*" Marisa said sternly. She knew her father couldn't kill anyone, no matter how angry he got, but the others didn't.

"I know, *hija,* I know. I would not kill him."

"*Papá,* enough."

"She's right," Mel interjected. "What good would it do to go after him now? The radio can't be fixed. Besides, maybe it wasn't Tim."

"Not Tim? Only one who would take bullets to not kill animals when we are starving would destroy a radio when we need to know what is going on outside. *¡Loco! ¡Bastardo!*"

"*¡Papá!*"

"*Lo siento, hija. Perdóname,*" he apologized.

Dr. Ovando stomped around the courtyard, occasionally picking up rocks to throw into the darkness outside. Olga tried to calm him, but he wouldn't listen. Marisa quietly told everyone that he would be fine. He needed to vent his frustration. By morning he would be over his fury. Silently she hoped Tim didn't return or she wasn't sure what her father might do to him.

"There's nothing we can do," Mel told the others. "We need to sleep and continue with our work. If a rescue party comes, it comes. If not we need to prepare for winter and survival. Mel stopped speaking and smiled suddenly. "Wait a minute! We have a shortwave radio in the RV.

It ran out of gas a few miles from here. We should be able to listen to any transmissions from there. Why don't Marc and I go out there now and see if the battery's still working?"

"That's a great idea!" Marc said. "Maybe we could contact someone and let them know we're here."

"Can I come too, Dad?" Steve asked.

"Sure. Why don't the rest of you go to bed, we may be gone a while."

After the three men left, Marisa went to tell her father about the RV. Bonnie put the younger children to bed. No one else wanted to miss out on any news when the men returned, so they sat around the campfire and waited. Olga had some hot Brigham Tea sitting next to the fire for the men, since they would be cold when they returned. They expected a long wait, but the men were back in just over an hour.

"Well?" Marisa asked, impatient to learn what happened and why they were back so quickly.

"The RV's gone," Mel said.

"Are you sure you went to the right spot?" Bonnie asked.

"Yeah. The Gameboy we made Michael leave behind was still on the ground nearby. It looked like someone dragged off the RV, but I don't know how."

"I bet it was the Smiths," Steve said.

"We don't know that. It could have been anyone."

"Not just anyone could have drug off an RV," Jeff replied.

"Yeah, and the Smiths would probably use it as their personal throne room," Bob said acidly.

"So, we still have no radio. No way of getting any word from outside," Dr. Ovando said dejectedly, summing up the obvious.

"Look, we have rifles and we can track them by the tire tracks. Why don't we go after the Smiths and get the RV back?" Bob suggested, a vengeful gleam in his eye.

"No. It's not worth it. We have much to do here. Let them go. What good will it do them to haul a dead RV around?" Marisa's father said quietly.

"Dr. Ovando's right. There's nothing we can do. The RV is gone, as are the Smiths. Even if we did find the RV, the radio would probably be broken as well. They have no desire to learn that life goes on outside the canyons."

"I suggest we all go to bed. We have a lot of work to do tomorrow," Marisa's father said quietly.

Marisa knew he was right. They had to put the loss of the radio and the RV behind them and move on. The Smiths were better forgotten.

A pattern developed over the next few days. Breakfast and dinner were foraged from nearby plants and game, supplemented by ash cakes and Brigham Tea. While the different groups were out during the day, lunch was provided from what provisions they had left from before the blast. Marisa and her group spent the day in the fields, redigging trenches, weeding out sage and grass, and coaxing what grain remained to grow. Olga and the four Hammond girls practiced making pottery and weaving when they weren't out collecting sego lily, cattails, wild onion, Brigham Tea, sage, and other useful plants. They frequently came to the grainfield to get silt and clay from the creekbed or to give Marisa's group plants to cultivate in the fields. The girls also did the laundry under the supervision of Olga. They'd make a game of the washing, splashing and playing. Olga didn't like it, but as they were getting the work done, she couldn't complain. They also practiced weaving grass and straw. They first tried some shoes patterned after the ones found in the hidden room. They were uncomfortable, but come winter, they would be better than frostbite.

Marisa and Olga avoided each other as much as possible, which was fine with Marisa. The soldiers went out each day to hunt for snake, rabbit, and deer. They said they felt more comfortable doing that, since they didn't have much knowledge of gardening or pottery making. Once they came back with a sheep, boasting about their increasing prowess as marksmen, until the poor animal was found to have a broken leg. Her father worked on the pueblo itself, fixing up the rooms and making sure they were sturdy enough to live in. He refortified the parts of the pueblo that were crumbling and taught himself how to make a credible adobe and clay plaster. He also cut timber and collected grass and mud to make roofs so more of the structure could be lived in. Everyone helped collect firewood and prepare meals. Marisa and Marc spent little time together outside of working in the field. She didn't know if he was still interested. She hoped so.

From time to time supplies would disappear. Each time they carefully searched the pueblo and found nothing. It was thought that either Tim or someone from the Smith company was sneaking in and taking food, pottery, and knives. They never took much, and they never came at the same time of day. Provisions were moved to different locations, but things still disappeared. As much as they tried, they couldn't catch anyone.

One night Karl had had enough. "Why don't you let me, Jeff, and Bob go after the Smiths? We can make them give us back our stuff."

"No, it is not worth it," Marisa's father tried to explain to them, but they remained adamant.

Mel stood up and walked over to where they were arguing. "Supposing you did manage to find the Smith company—which wouldn't be easy. What would you do? They've probably eaten the food, and the pottery and tools are easily replaced. Would you shoot them for that?"

Jeff was convinced. "He's got a point, guys. It's not worth it." With everyone against them, the other two capitulated.

On Sunday they rested. Church services were performed in the open courtyard. The soldiers weren't interested, so they stayed in their rooms or went for a walk. The rest of the day was spent visiting and relaxing, getting to know each other and talking about their families before the blast.

It had been one week since the blast, and they were starting to adjust to their new lives, to cope with the new challenges. The Smith company hadn't returned, except for the occasional stealing. Nor had any other people wandered by. After a relaxing dinner they all sat around the fire and sang songs. No one had felt much like singing at first, but one by one they joined in. After two hours had passed and it was time for bed, all were in better spirits. That night, for the first time, Marisa didn't have a nightmare.

Monday things continued to get easier. The fields were clear of all but the wild grain and more was being planted. Marisa wasn't sure what they'd do when it started to snow. It would be too cold for much. And they wouldn't have time to stock up on food and clothing. Especially if the Smith company kept stealing what little they had.

Tuesday they finished early in the fields. They weeded and watered and then decided to take a break. Some went off to explore the area some more. Marisa went back to her room. She got out her writing tablet and sat by her window. She knew there was a lot that needed to be done, and she could always help Olga and the girls, but she wanted a break.

She had been told throughout her life how important it was to keep a journal, but she'd never had anything to say. Marisa felt it was time to start. If they died of radiation poisoning or starvation this winter, at least whoever found them would know who they were and what they had tried to do. Her father would forgive her not helping out somewhere else if he knew what she was doing. She wrote until almost sunset, then, after watching the sunset, she felt guilty and went to help Olga and the others prepare dinner.

They were all returning from their various duties the next evening when the helicopter came. At first Marisa thought it was another, smaller blast, but then the noise clarified and she could see a black speck in the fading light, coming east down the canyon. Everyone raced out into the open, hoping to attract the attention of the pilot. When it was almost on top of them they could see it was one of the new military Wolves with a large "search and rescue" painted on the sides and bottom. The helicopter landed, and the blades slowed to a stop. Everyone eagerly raced forward as soon as the whirling dust had settled and two men dressed in khaki flight suits stepped out. They barely cleared the cockpit when they were besieged by people, all trying to talk at once. Marisa's father and Mel took charge, getting everyone to go back to the courtyard where they could all sit down and hear what the two men had to say.

It was just as they had assumed. An N-Cycle test in New Mexico had gone awry and "leaked" into the atmosphere. But its effects weren't as bad as suspected. The bomb had devastated a 300-mile radius and caused damage for another 200 miles. Those who were on the lee side of the mountains and in deep valleys and canyons were untouched. In Utah the cities of St. George and Cedar City and Kimball were gone. Mesquite in Nevada was gone, as were others in Arizona and New Mexico. Marisa bowed her head in brief mourning for those who had died. Then a thought struck her and she began to giggle. Her father looked at her sternly. *"¡Cállate, loca!"*

Marisa couldn't be quiet. "I'm sorry, *Papá*. I was thinking about the Smiths. I wonder how they will feel now to know the truth?" The rest of the group looked at her for a moment and started to laugh too. They really shouldn't be laughing at the Smiths, but they had been so pompous, and now it was all for nothing. The two men from the helicopter looked on in confusion. Quickly Mel explained who the Smiths were and why they were laughing.

"Oh, yes. We picked them and their group up yesterday. They were pulling an RV. Why, I don't know. There were nearly two dozen of them, and the RV wasn't that big. They called themselves the Smith Company. They weren't very happy to see us. One couple, the Smiths, I guess, looked really put out.

"They were mumbling something about the wrath of God and starting up a colony on the salt flats," the co-pilot said, cracking a smile. "I wish I'd have known before I picked them up."

The men talked about what had been going on since the blast and the relief efforts that had gotten underway once it was determined there was no radiation. The Mormon church, the federal government, and the Red Cross had organized a joint relief effort that would ensure homes and jobs for the survivors and the eventual revitalization of the affected area.

The pilots listened with admiration and surprise at how well the group had coped. They said an LCAC, a large military hovercraft, would be by the next day around mid-morning to pick them up and take them to Salt Lake City.

"We've got a survival kit with some basic provisions if you'd like it," the pilot offered.

Mel politely refused for the group. "No, thanks. We still have some of our original supplies, and we'd like to "live off the land" for our last evening here. But thanks anyway."

After the helicopter left there was a lot of hugging and crying. Olga brought out some Kool-Aid and the men cleaned and prepared a couple of snakes they had killed. That night they sang and danced and talked. Everyone stayed up late, not needing to rise with the sun and work. They discussed their plans for the future and promised not to lose touch.

Marc pulled Marisa aside later in the evening. They found a quiet spot and sat side by side and talked for a while.

Marc put his arm around her, "Why don't you come study archaeology at BYU?"

"I would love to, but I don't have any money. I don't even have transcripts. Everything I had was at Southern Utah University." She had thought about BYU when she was applying for college but chose to stay closer to home so she could be with her family. Now she wouldn't be able to go anywhere. No school would accept her without high school transcripts and her placement tests.

"You can get a scholarship. My father's dean of the department. If he and your father write letters of recommendation, you're a cinch to get in."

"I'd love to go." She hadn't thought about school since the blast. It would be great if she could get her degree and work with her father and Marc.

"We could spend more time together, if you'd like," he said hesitantly.

"I'd like that." Marisa smiled shyly at Marc and blushed. Marc squeezed her shoulders and changed the subject.

They talked a bit longer, then Marisa went to look for her father to tell him her plans. He and Olga had disappeared and she didn't find them that evening.

The large hovercraft arrived as promised mid-morning. There were already a few people inside, looking much the worse for their experience. Two of them wore military fatigues like Karl, Jeff, and Bob. Marisa sat down next to her father and Olga and looked out the window as the hovercraft lifted above the rocks. She would miss this place. And its beauty. It had come to mean a lot to her. She would return often, she promised herself.

Marisa hadn't had a chance to talk to her father all morning, so she quickly told him her plans to attend school, and Marc's offer of help.

Her father looked relieved. *"Bien, hija.* BYU is a good place. You will be happy there." He smiled smugly. "And Marc will take care of you." He paused for several seconds, looking at his hands. "I also have news. Olga and I talked last night. We are going to go back to the pueblo to live." Marisa sat for a moment, stunned. She would love to be able to help out with the pueblo, maybe in the summer when she wasn't in school. But did Olga have to go with him?

She smiled. "Sounds great." She turned away and looked out the window to watch Quetzal Canyon slowly shrink into a small crack in the colorful canyons, which in turn shrank into the vast wasteland left by the bomb. She knew everything had been destroyed, but the reality of nothingness stabbed her like a knife. There was nothing but dirt and sand to the edge of the mountains, where strings of foliage could still be seen repelling the mountain cliffs. Some areas looked as hard as glass, as though the heat had fused the sand. The colorful hills of her former home looked washed out and barren. Everything on ground level was gone. Only the canyons and a flash of green here and there, on the lee of the hills or deep valleys where the blast had overlooked a spot, remained untouched. It was hard to believe that life continued on elsewhere as if nothing had happened. Other people were still going to work or school, watching cable and laughing with friends. The past week seemed like a moment plucked out of time or a bad dream.

Marisa closed her eyes and rested her head on the back of the seat in front of her. The shock of going back into society where the blast was only a horrible news story would be greater than adjusting to a simpler life. Marc, sitting in the seat in front of her, turned around and gave her a reassuring smile, letting her know that he understood. Marisa smiled back, then looked out the window as the Rocky Mountains rose majestically in front of her. They were far enough away from the center of the blast that the pine trees were still green and snow clung to dark crevasses and mountain peaks. As they flew over the Wasatch Mountains and descended into Utah Valley, Marisa could see the cities spread out before her. Buses and shuttles dotted the highways like little ants. A monorail, like a silver snake, wove its way above the streets. Marisa leaned her head against Marc's seat again. This would not be easy. She had just started to accept her new life. Now she had to move back into the "real world." A world without her mother and sister. A world where life remained the same, but she could never go home. Marc whispered a few words of encouragement and gently squeezed her hand. She smiled her thanks, not feeling like talking. Tonight she would see if Marc would drive her up into the mountains so she could see the sunset properly. Watching the sunset always helped her think clearly. It helped put things into perspective. Marisa looked out the window again. The atmosphere was still thick with debris and microscopic dust from the blast. A string of clouds accented the horizon. It would be another glorious sunset.

A FOREIGNER COMES TO REDDYVILLE

ELIZABETH H. BOYER

*M*y grandfather, B. Y. Green, died three years ago, so I can tell this story now. I never really thought I would, but when Christmas is coming, I start missing him. Christmas was his season as long as I knew him, but it never was the ho-ho-ho kind of Christmas at his house. He had a little tree on the table and presents for us kids, and Grandma made fudge and divinity and peanut brittle and fruit cake for the grownups.

But what I remember most was star-gazing on Christmas Eve. He used to call me outside to look up at the furiously-cold Idaho sky, skinny old Grandpa standing there in his old jeans and flannel shirt with the beak of his old hat tipped back just looking up at all those stars. The colder it was, the more stars filled the black dome of the sky. I'd shiver and shake, but he'd just keep on looking with the kind of awe you feel when you look into something limitless, when you know you'll never understand, nor humankind ever understand, with all their machines and inventions and intelligence.

"Betty Jean," he'd say, "just look up there at all those stars. You and I will never know a fraction of what's going on up there. Not a fraction."

He had a reverent note in his voice that always made me shiver, even when I was sixteen and thought I knew twice what he knew. Then maybe it was that black dome shot with a zillion stars that reminded me who I was, and how long I'd be here. Then maybe it was because he knew something most people don't.

He told me his story when I was twelve. I was in the sixth grade at McCammon Elementary and Miss Thornleigh was my teacher. She was mean and strict and walked with a cane, which she also used to point like a gun barrel at any kid who dared utter a peep out of turn. My best friend since kindergarten had moved away, and I hadn't found a niche yet, and the adolescent kid groups were pretty tight-knit in the little towns of Arimo and McCammon. Nobody moved in, hardly anybody ever moved away. Friendships were made young and usually lasted through high school.

It was fall after Halloween and after the potato picking was over. Grandpa Green lived in a little old square brick house on one of the last streets in McCammon, not far from the gravel pit and the cemetery on the north end of town. Our house was in the next block behind the defunct McCammon news office. The streets were gravel then, every intersection had a streetlight, and none of the streets had names. Sometimes after dark I got this itchy feeling, sick of Channel Three and too bored to do homework, so I'd slip out of the house and race down the street to the next streetlight just to get some wind in my hair and stretch my legs and wonder what life was going to be like when I grew up. Sometimes I'd keep going past the pool of streetlight and tap on Grandpa's door. Loud usually, to be heard over the roar of the television.

This night we'd just had our first two inches of snow and I had to race out in it, coatless, and leave my footprints, flying up to that spotlight under the old street lamp. I wondered where the footprints of my life would lead. I vowed I'd leave McCammon and everyone in it and never come back, except rich and famous, and wouldn't they be sorry that they were so mean when I wouldn't even talk to any of them. I didn't feel much like talking to anybody, but I saw the dim light behind Grandpa's curtains. Grandma had died about two years ago, so he was alone. They'd been married fifty-six years, but he never complained about being lonely. Maybe he felt like I did—all choked up inside with a big cold lump of something that wouldn't go away. I trotted up to his door. Besides I'd run out without a coat again, and I was feeling cold and a little wet where the snow was melting on me.

He was always glad to see me, and he always had a bag of store-bought cookies. He also had his little wood stove in the living room heated up almost red hot, and his beat-up orange cat was melted on the floor in front of it. I sank down in his old red couch with the big fat arms. I guess he could tell I was feeling down. He just kept telling me funny little stories about what he and old Tiger had done that day and what he got in the mail and how Mrs. Harris brought him an apple pie, still hot. That's what I liked about him—he was deep-down happy with his life, even though he had plenty of problems himself, being old and sick and alone and living pretty lean. As long as he could rake his leaves and poke around in his little garden, he was whistling away and talking to folks walking by and enjoying himself. Pretty soon I was eating a piece of apple pie and telling him about my problems.

"You're going to be all right, Betty Jean," he said. "I know you can be or do just about anything you make up your mind to do. This minute, right now, doesn't matter a whole lot, except in what it does to make you different tomorrow. Life has a way of turning out a whole lot stranger than you think it will. It's a wondrous place out there, and nothing in it is more amazing than you. Run ahead of the crowd, don't get stuck in the middle of the herd. Most people are too scared to take a different direction. Don't try to be like all of them, or you'll never be happy. As soon as you think you fit in, something changes. If you're not afraid to be alone, amazing things will happen to you."

I guess I mumbled something about not having any choice about being alone, and I wasn't happy about it. I was already alone, without a best friend to sit with at lunch, and nothing amazing had happened to me.

"Let me tell you a story," he said, settling back and looking into the little red isinglass window of the stove, and this is what followed.

When I was a young man, I used to herd sheep out to Reddyville for old man Harkness. It was getting close to Christmas time—one of the coldest winters anybody could remember. I was grazing the sheep along Marsh Creek where they could find willows and brush and a little grass. I had a sheep camp, a team, a saddle horse, a rifle, three dogs, and two dollars' worth of groceries. Every few days somebody would ride out to check up on me and bring me a sack of flour or beans or something. I was sixteen and all alone in the dead of winter with two hundred head of sheep. No roads, no telephones—that was being alone, and I didn't like it much either, only I didn't have any choice. My daddy was dead, and I had to earn some money for the family, and this was my chance. I got paid five dollars a week.

At night there were coyotes and cougars after my sheep, so I got into the habit of sleeping light. When the dogs started barking and growling, I rushed out with my gun and sometimes got off a shot or two. But one night after they barked, they just sort of clung to the wagon instead of chasing off to hunt the intruder. They acted like they were scared, which was unusual, especially for old Brick. I've seen him tear after a pack of coyotes, barking and snarling—but never far enough that they would turn around and get him. He was smart; he had a lot of collie in him. This time he leaned against my leg and I could feel him trembling while he whined and growled.

That was enough for me. If a grizzly bear was after old man Harkness's sheep, he could have as many as he wanted. I wasn't fool enough to fight a bear for some other man's sheep. Calling the dogs in after me, I crawled back into the sheep wagon and shut the door.

Funny thing was the horses. Pinky and Doc were still standing quiet, tied to the wagon for the night. I'd seen them get a whiff of a cougar more than once, and they'd like to tear the wagon apart getting away. During the day I'd hobble them and let them forage where I could watch them. They could travel almost as fast with hobbles on as off, and I didn't want them to end up back at the home ranch and leave me stranded. I had a sack of grain to bribe their loyalty with, which came in handy when I wanted to catch them. I could hear them sighing and shifting their feet around, calm and relaxed, not snorting and jigging around trying to see something to get scared at. If something was out there, they would've smelled it and raised a fuss.

I looked at old Brick, and he rested his chin on my knee, looking worried. His ears were still pricked up and twitching, like he was hearing something I couldn't. I wasn't enjoying this much, I can tell you. Not that I was any more superstitious than the next person. My mama was mortally terrified of Indians, and she'd put the same fear into me as a child. Even though I knew the Indians had moved on out of Marsh Valley, I couldn't help remembering some of her bloodier stories of what had happened to the early settlers of Reddyville and other little forgotten places now buried under the sagebrush. I knew Fort Hall was too far away to protect me now.

Then I thought I began to hear a sound, high and far away like a big wind. It got louder and louder, real fast, until it went screaming by one side of my wagon in a ball of blazing white light and heat like the middle of July, then it was gone as fast as it had come. The horses jumped, making the wagon rock, but after they finished jerking around, I couldn't hear a thing. The sheep bleated and moved around a bit and started settling down again. I opened the door and looked out. I couldn't believe my eyes. A trail of fire led straight along the ground not a hundred feet from my sheep camp. The juniper trees and sagebrush were burning, in the middle of the night, in December, with a foot of snow on the ground. I could see where the fire ended in a ravine about a half mile away.

I don't know how long I stood there staring, but when I shut the door and came back to my little sheepherder stove, the wagon was almost as cold as it was outside. The dogs whined and didn't show any interest in getting out of the wagon. I sat and stared at my little stove awhile, trying to think, then I jumped up to look again. Only a few little patches of fire still showed in the treetops. It was so quiet and cold and by the light of the stars, I could see the sheep huddled up in clumps, sound asleep. It was so quiet it was like nobody was left on earth except me.

I waited until daylight, but I didn't sleep much that night. Every crackle, every snort from a horse jolted me wide awake, and I'd listen to that piercing silence and think about that track of fire. I wasn't overly religious, so I wasn't thinking along the lines of signs from heaven. This was something I just had no explanation for, with the knowledge that was available at that time.

When it was light I put on my buffalo coat my father used to wear and walked out to look at what I thought I'd seen. At first I hoped I wasn't going to see anything. Then I found the track where the snow was melted away down to bare ground. The sagebrush and trees were burned, charred black, and the ground was bare. It started just at the tops at first, then more and more of them were burned, then the tops were sheared off like a haymower had gone through them. Pretty soon the trees were plowed right down, snapped off and burned like someone had planned it. Even the lava rocks looked scorched. I knew something about volcanoes, since so much of this land was lava beds, but I couldn't see how that had anything to do with what I was seeing.

By the time I reached the edge of the ravine, I was shaking. The burnt trail went over the edge and down into a thick stand of junipers. I saw something down there in a tangle of tree limbs and rocks, so I climbed down. The dogs stayed on the ridge, looking down at me and whining.

The thing I saw was made out of metal and rounded smooth. I first thought of an automobile. I'd seen a few automobiles in McCammon and everybody thought they were pretty fine and modern. Rich people were getting them in the big cities, but I thought they'd never take the place of horses for country folks who had real work to do.

When I got a little closer, I could see this thing was no automobile. By then I'd decided anyway there was no way it could be an automobile, this far out in the rocks and junipers. It didn't have any tires or seats or anything like a Model A, which was mostly what we saw in McCammon at that time, but I'd seen pictures of Hupmobiles and Studebakers and other fancy automobiles. I couldn't see any sort of opening, so I assumed it had to be upside down. I climbed down alongside it and just looked at the things on it, funny manufactured details I'd never seen anything like before—nor since either. Everything looked like an iron skillet that had been burned in the fire. I didn't understand any of it. I don't mind telling you I was scared half to death at the idea there was something this strange to my knowledge. How limited my knowledge was and the world's knowledge was at that time wasn't even as clear to me yet as it soon would be.

Then something caught the corner of my eye and I turned my head, sort of slow, not really wanting to see something else I didn't understand. It was almost a relief to realize it was just a man, crawling out from the other side of the burnt machine.

"Hey, did you see this thing last night?" I said, all in a rush of relief at having someone to talk to. "It almost ran over my sheep camp. There was this big light, like the headlight of a train."

The man looked at me, saying nothing except for a funny gabbling sound. I looked at him, and I saw that he looked kind of strange and dirty—covered with soot actually, and my first impression was that he was really old and shriveled, like old people get sometimes. His face was little and wrinkly, and his eyes were kind of sunken away deep, and his skin had a grayish color. He wore a padded coat and pants that were made together, one piece.

"Are you all right?" I asked. "What are you doing here?"

The man made a feeble gesture with his hand and made sort of a moaning sound. He took a tottery step forward and almost fell, like he was weak. I caught him before he fell, and I noticed how light and frail he felt, like a real old person. He was shivering too. This was something I could handle, I thought.

"Come on. I've got a nice warm fire and some coffee in my sheep camp. We'll get you fixed up, and then you can tell me where you belong."

I wrapped him up in my buffalo coat and pointed back the way I'd come and made as if to carry him. He insisted on crawling back into the machine, which gave me a few anxious moments, then he came out carrying a little suitcase. It was real heavy, but I carried them both back to the sheep camp. He didn't say much except more moaning and gibberish. I thought he looked a little better when he got warmed up by my little stove, but I couldn't get him to do more than taste the coffee. He made a face and put down the cup. I couldn't really interest him much in my boiled beans either. I figured he was nearly frozen the night before and needed some rest, so I went out to look at the sheep and take the horses down to the water. When I got back he was sleeping, breathing real slow and sort of rattly. I was concerned. The nearest doctor was in McCammon about five miles away. I could take him to somebody's house in Reddyville and borrow a wagon. If he took a real bad turn it would mean riding to McCammon to get the doctor, then back to Reddyville. I wasn't sure how much time this old fellow had. I didn't like the grayish color of his skin or the faint blue tint of his lips. Then there was the matter of paying Doctor Goodenough for the call.

After I went outside to check the sheep, I gathered up some wood and cow chips and came back into the sheep wagon. The strangest thing was the dogs. They wouldn't go anywhere near the wagon now, when before they couldn't wait to get inside by that stove. They growled and whined and hung back with their tails curled down between their legs.

My visitor was awake, looking at me with his dark, sunken eyes.

"Feeling better?" I asked. "Sure is cold out there."

He answered in that peculiar gibble-gabble, scattered with odd clicks and sighs like I'd never heard before. All of a sudden it struck me that he must be a foreigner, French or Italian or something.

"You're from France?" I said, hoping he would recognize the name of his country in English. "Italy? Germany?"

He just looked at me, his expression empty and mournful. He didn't even shake his head or realize I'd asked a question. I named all the countries I could think of, which wasn't many. I wasn't educated, and I was only sixteen.

Then he started to talk to me in that strange language, going on faster and faster. I just sat there feeling stupid, and not that I would admit it, a little bit fearful.

"I just don't know what to say or think," I said to him, although I knew it didn't do any good. "I just don't understand your talk."

But even animals know from your tone whether you're friendly or angry, so I resolved to keep talking to him so he would know he was with a friend. I only hoped I was with a friend too.

I offered him whatever I had to eat, when mealtimes came around, but he only tasted the biscuits and beans and coffee and didn't look real interested. Mostly he slept, so quiet it was hard to tell if he was breathing or not.

For two days we went on, talking our own language to each other. He seemed to be getting weaker, even though he often came to the sheepcamp door and looked outside while I was tending to my chores. I had to come to some decision, because the browse along the creek was running out and I would soon have to move the sheep.

According to my calendar, it was the week before Christmas. As the sun sank down behind the white mountains each night and those cold hard stars shone down, I thought of my family and I felt a little low in my spirits. I wished with all my heart I could be at home with my mother and my two younger sisters on Christmas Eve. But I was the man of the family now. I'd asked Mr. Harkness to pay my wages of five dollars a week directly to my mother, so she and the girls would have as many of life's needfuls as it would buy.

I didn't have one thing of Christmas in my wagon, so I decided to carve a little manger scene for my little sisters. I would give it to them whenever I saw them next, or maybe Mr. Harkness's foreman would take it by the cabin for me. I got some dry juniper and set to carving a Mary and a Joseph and a baby in the manger. They turned out pretty good, so I went on with a sheep and a donkey. All the while I talked to my foreign friend, sitting up and watching me like a wrinkled-up old monkey. He jabbered back once in awhile, but not as much as he used to. I knew he was getting weaker, and I would have to do something.

It was Christmas Eve, and I was whittling away at my manger people. I was getting pretty pleased with my little creation. It sat in a box turned on its side to represent the stable. I added some sticks and bits of hay and rocks and twigs off the junipers. I now had a couple of shepherds and I had one of the three wise men done. I finished the second one and put him in the scene. I went to carving the third one, aware that my stranger's eyes were open and watching me. I even made little boxes and urns for the precious things the wise men brought the baby Jesus. When I put the third king in the row beside the others, he opened up his mouth and gave a cry that raised the gooseflesh on me. He raised up his hands and clenched his fingers into fists and went on giving that strange cry, and somehow I knew he was weeping.

"Here now, old timer, what's the fuss?" I said in a soothing voice. "Are you wishing you were home for Christmas too?"

As if in answer he reached for a bit of wood and held out his hand for my knife. After a shameful moment of hesitation, I gave it to him and he started carving. All I could do was stare at him with my mouth open. He was better at it than I was, and in a little while he had a figure made. Slowly he reached out and placed it in the manger scene, lined up beside the three kings. I only stared at him, and I guess I managed to look completely stupid. He picked up the figure and held it out so I couldn't avoid taking it. His deep, sad dark eyes watched me as I studied it. There was no mistaking the identity. He had carved a rough little figure of himself in his odd gray clothes, kneeling and holding a gift for the infant.

I went on looking stupid. Struggling to his feet, he went to the door of the sheep camp and opened it up, letting in a frigid blast of night air. He pointed out to the sky, extending his shaking hand. Again he gave that strange wailing cry that made my hair stand on end.

"Here now, close the door, we're going to freeze to death," I said, my voice shaking. Here was a fellow human creature in the most terrible despair, trying to communicate with me, and I was as dumb as a brick wall.

He gave me a mournful look, tottering back to his bed. I shut the door, plenty relieved, but still pained by his sorrow.

Later that night his breathing got strange and sputtery. I couldn't let him just die, but if I left my sheep, I could lose the job my family needed so sorely. After wrestling with my conscience, I finally decided what I would do. I wrapped him up in my father's buffalo coat and stoked the fire with cow chips. Then I saddled up my riding horse and rode down the creek to Reddyville.

"Mother," I said when she opened the door, all glad and astonished, "I can't stay. I've left the sheep. You've got to send someone for the doctor to come to my camp. A foreigner has fallen sick, and I'm trying to tend him—but I think he's only getting worse."

She made me come in for an hour or so to unthaw my hands and feet and drink some hot tea. I'd had the forethought to bring my manger scene for my little sisters, and they were as excited as anything you can imagine at getting woke up in the middle of the night with such a present. They knelt by the stove in the red light coming through the little windows, putting each piece in its place.

Mother threw on her shawl and went over to the neighbors' about half a mile away to get them to go for the doctor. When she got back I was half asleep and warmed through.

"B. Y.," said my littlest sister Lydia, looking up from the manger scene, "why have you got four wise men? There's only three, isn't there, Mama?"

"I don't know," I said. "My foreigner carved it, and he made it to look just like he does. I don't know what he meant by it. Maybe where he comes from, they have four wise men at Christmas time."

"There's really only three," said Emily.

"No, there's Melchior, the fourth wise man," said my mother. "He was traveling to Bethlehem too with a present for the baby Jesus. But he stopped along the way to help some poor people and by the time he was done helping them, he had spent all his money and sold the wonderful gift he had brought. So he never made it to Bethlehem, but he was specially blessed for helping the needy people."

I went back to my camp as fast as I could go, afraid I'd find my foreigner had died while I was gone. He was still alive, I could hear his breath just barely wheezing in his throat. When I lit a candle, I could see how bad he was. I wished I'd sent for the doctor earlier, but I knew the doctor would charge five of my precious dollars for his ride from McCammon to Reddyville.

I sat up for the rest of the night beside my foreign friend. It was the only thing I could do. When the daylight rallied and I could blow out the candle, he opened his eyes. Weakly he struggled against the buffalo coat, trying to loosen his arms.

"Just lie easy, can't you?" I said. "The doctor is on his way. Heaven knows how I'm going to pay for it, but I know my daddy wouldn't stand by and watch a stranger die. I'd have a tough time facing my conscience if I did. So it doesn't make any difference. It's a small price to pay to be able to say I did everything I could. I just wish I'd done it sooner, old timer."

I swear he understood me. He looked with his old tired eyes right into mine, and I felt that everything was all right with him, however it turned out.

Then he began struggling around, looking for the little suitcase, which he always kept close to hand. I lifted it out from under his bunk and put it beside him. He unlocked it by some means I couldn't see. Then pushed it toward me, but he was pretty weak and could scarcely budge it. Then he pointed to my little box I kept beside my bed for my pocket watch and my daddy's old worn-out Bible and other things that were important to me. I put the case beside my bed, by the box. That was the last thing I ever did for him. I went outside to chop some wood, and when I came back, I knew he would breathe no more.

I waited until almost noon for Doctor Goodenough. He rode up horseback with his bag tied on behind.

"I'm sorry, but it seems I called you too late," I said. "My friend has died."

"Well, let's have a look at what he died of," said Dr. Goodenough, "and make sure it isn't something catching."

He climbed into the wagon and I waited outside, since there wasn't any abundance of space and I was feeling like I'd let down the poor little foreigner. After a long time, the doctor opened the door and beckoned to me.

"Come in here and look at this," he said.

He'd taken the clothes off the foreigner to get a better look at him. It made me a little angry that he could be so cold-hearted, but I suppose death was nothing to him, as much of it as he'd seen.

"Have you ever seen anything like this?" he said.

I never had. I forgot about being angry as I looked at the remains of my foreign friend. It came to me slowly that there was some sort of deformity about his withered little body. He just wasn't made like you and me. His head was too big, and his ribcage wasn't shaped like any I'd seen. His skin was more like leather, and there wasn't a hair on him anywhere.

Dr. Goodenough questioned me closely. I guess I was in some sort of shock, although I'd never heard of it then.

"B. Y. Green," he said to me finally, "I knew your father. I tended to him in his last illness, and I wish I'd saved him. But if I had, he'd be grieved to see his son keeping secrets from a man who means only to help him. Now I can tell there's something you're not telling me. If I go away now, this will always be a hard spot between us. You know something that I don't."

Dr. Goodenough was the most educated man in McCammon. He'd been to a university back east to get his medical degree. The idea of his not knowing something that I did was amazing to me. Trouble was I couldn't tell him anything to relieve his ignorance, because I was in the same ignorance myself.

"I'll show you something," I said, wondering if I was doing the right thing. "But I can't say what it is, because I don't know."

While we walked through the junipers, I told him about the fireball I'd seen burn a path through the trees. I could tell he was skeptical, until I found the blackened trail. We climbed down into the ravine and he looked all around it. Then he took out a notebook and drew pictures of it. I waited for his explanation. He never said anything. He just followed the trail back, heading for my sheepcamp. When he got there, he went in and studied my poor foreign friend a long time, making some notes in his notebook.

"B. Y.," he said, "make no mention of this man or his means of conveyance if you want to enjoy the rest of your life among your fellow man." Then he began wrapping up the stranger in one of my blankets.

"But who is he?" I demanded.

"Better ask what is he," answered Doctor Goodenough. "But whatever he may be and wherever he may be from, this world is not ready yet to know about it."

I never thought much more about it after he overwhelmed me by refusing any payment for his visit. He took away the little foreigner, leaving me and my sheep alone again.

After he was gone, I remembered the heavy little box the stranger had given me. When I opened it I started to shake. My own staring face looked back at me from a bar of solid polished gold the size of a brick. It had writing on it, but it wasn't English. I didn't know what language it was. I'd never seen anything but English written.

I left the sheep again and went to talk to my mother, taking the little heavy case with me. My sisters were at school, so the one-room house was quiet, except for the ticking of Mama's clock as I told her about the foreigner, all the while turning his little wise-man carving over and over in my fingers. I cried then too, thinking how he'd come so far on his journey with his gift, only to die by misfortune in the hands of strangers. Mama never said anything, not even when I showed her the bar of gold.

When Daddy died she was like that, sort of going inside of herself to find the answers she needed.

"Brigham," she said, "I recognize the truth of what you are saying. But your little stranger didn't die in vain. He traveled from afar to bring a gift, and he gave it to you. It will never get to where he intended, but it's up to you to see to it that his gift is used for the best purposes."

"Who was he, Mama?" I asked, setting the figure on the table between us. "Do you really think he was a wise man, traveling to find another Christ-child somewhere on another star?"

"We know there are worlds without number," said my mother after thinking a moment. "I find it impossible to stand under the sky and look at the stars and believe that there is no one else in the universe except us." She tapped the little wise man with her finger. "He wasn't all that different from us, was he, Brigham?"

"No, not so different. But Mama, if he was traveling to some other world, if a Christ-child was born somewhere else, what does it mean? Wasn't our world the first? I never thought it could happen again."

"Or if the Savior came back again," said Mama, almost as if she were talking to herself, "why didn't he come back to our earth? Or is there more than one Savior? How many times, in how many places, has our old familiar story happened?"

Like I said before, I'd been rebellious and never very churchy, but I began to feel frightened by the smallness of my own existence. "Mama, I think this is something we shouldn't talk about. Maybe it isn't something religious at all. Maybe this stranger only wanted to do what I was doing and carve a little figure too. If we could speak his language, we'd know what he really meant. We're only guessing and trying to make it look like what we understand. Maybe he was on his way to pay a debt or buy something. Maybe my manger scene didn't make any more sense to him than the writing on that gold does to us."

"But maybe it did, Brigham," said my mother. "Maybe that was the only thing about this world that did make sense to him. You certainly couldn't talk to him."

Mama was a sensible woman, and as it turned out, a good businesswoman. We sold up everything we had, which wasn't much, and moved to McCammon, where there wasn't anyone who knew us to wonder where the poor unfortunate Greens got their money. Mama took the gold and made investments. She bought a house, some land, some other houses which we fixed up and rented. My sisters grew up and got married, I met the woman who would share the rest of my life with me. We never turned away from an opportunity to help someone in need. I don't know exactly how long it took to use up all the gold bar. By then, thanks to my talented mother, we never missed it when it was gone.

A few years after we left Reddyville, Doctor Goodenough was drowned in the Portneuf river when his buggy turned over. I went back once and tried to find the place where the trees were burned. I guess I was still ashamed that I never got the doctor there soon enough to save the stranger's life. But I couldn't tell one gully from the next, all the sagebrush and cedars looked just alike. Nothing was left of Reddyville. Everyone had moved to McCammon or Arimo or Downey or Pocatello, looking for an easier life. I always wondered if anyone else ever found that strange machine from the stars and wondered what it might be, or if a landslide covered it up, or if the land just gradually healed around it.

During all the business of getting grown up and married and settled and going through World War II, I struggled to educate myself. I began noticing there were new writers who fancied writing about rocket ships to Mars and invaders from outer space and traveling to other planets. At first I read them sort of secret and ashamed. Most of them I could tell were made-up stories, but there were some I thought could be true and some that sounded a lot like what had happened to me that cold December in Reddyville.

I never got real religious, even afterward, but I came to believe in many different things. I never forgot what my mother said that night in Reddyville. It troubled me, and does yet, to think that if he came back after he was here, that he didn't choose us again. And it's hard to feel lonely when you know you're not alone. A lot of people flat out deny that life could exist on the stars. And while they're doing it, standing on this little pinpoint of light we call Earth, there's probably a million other tiny little fools on other pinpoints of light saying the same thing, that they're the only ones in the whole big universe, like they're some sort of bigshots running the whole show. Now just look up there at those stars, Betty Jean, shining down here in Idaho and all the rest of the whole world and who knows how many others. Some of them don't even exist anymore, and here we are looking at the light they made millions of years ago, just for us to see by. Some day somebody might be looking at the spot of light we left behind. Kind of puts all our problems in perspective, doesn't it?

I miss my grandfather most at Christmas time. I'm not twelve anymore. I'm happy to report that I survived adolescence and have negotiated into the waters of middle age without too many mishaps. Maybe something about his Christmas story stuck in my head. Whenever I'm thinking my problems are the end of the world, I remember those cold Idaho nights, looking up at the stars with him and feeling my world expanding, taking in the Milky Way and all the constellations, all the universe, and him pointing up to the stars, like he knew we have friends out there.

My mother said she never heard this story, and Grandpa probably made it up just to entertain me when I was feeling down. He was on medications too for high blood pressure.

"Then where did Great-grandma Green get the money to buy houses and land in McCammon?" I demanded.

"Oh," she said, "they had family back East."

I just figure Grandpa B. Y. knew what he was doing when he decided not to tell any of his family his story, except me. He outlived his sisters, and none of the family knew what I was talking about when I asked what became of the manger scene with four wise men.

SNOOZE

DAVID DOERING

A Mormon once thought of using alcohol for something good. It was at my dad's wedding to his boyfriend James. The Mormon was me. The something good was Snooze.

By now everyone knows about Snooze. Seems you can't have a baby today without first picking up a dispenser or two. Revolutionized parents' lives, I'm happy to say.

I was researching at that time theta endorphins at the University of Utah. I suspected that these endorphins were part of the brain's sleep mechanism. Professor David Webber of Stanford put me onto the subject. He'd wanted to do the work himself but was too deeply involved in a project of his own on human cycadic rhythms.

Like most scientists about to make a major discovery, I wasn't aware of anything unusual. My dad's wedding was the biggest concern in my life that week. I suppose I could have left things to my dad to handle, but I was worried about him. I just wasn't sure if Dad should marry again so soon after Mom's passing away. He also had commitments at work. I wanted him to take some time off. Go somewhere.

Not Dad. He said that love strikes when it will and now it had. So I gave him the only thing I could: time by himself so he could think things through before the ceremony. So he could be sure. And I would handle the wedding.

That's why I hadn't spent a lot of time at the lab those last few days. I left Robyn Moody, my grad assistant, supervising most of the experimental work. I was certain nothing was going to happen with the sample reactions I put her in charge of. They were part of a baseline study on the effects of theta endorphins on pigs. Regular doses. Doses subjected to enough heat to simulate fevers. Doses mixed with common proteins. That sort of thing. No surprises. Robyn could handle it.

In the meantime, I was anxious for the wedding. A spring wedding in Salt Lake City seemed romantic, and I wanted it to be perfect. I had expected to have to handle the decorations myself along with everything else. I hadn't expected James to do such a wonderful job decorating the McCune Mansion for the ceremony. Turned out he had taste.

It wasn't that I disliked James. It was just his timing. And maybe that there just isn't anyone good enough for my father. Maybe that's why I wanted to take charge of things at the wedding. So I could keep busy and get over my jitters.

When Saturday came the mansion was crowded with guests. Someone called it the city's social event of the year. (Okay, so I was the one who said it.) Even the mayor showed up. The minister finally called the house to order with a "Brothers and Sisters, let us begin."

Mary Beth, who worked for Dad in the mayor's office, and the little knot of people with her moved into their seats with a swish of taffeta and lace.

Dad and James moved down the aisle. They had settled on traditional white tuxes. James's fit better over his husky build than my father's over his lanky frame. They were both handsome.

No sooner had I gotten comfortable in the wooden seat than I felt the vibration of my purse phone. I eased myself out and found a vestibule.

"Yes?"

"Kim? It's Robyn."

"Robyn? What are you doing calling me now? You know I'm in the middle of my dad's wedding."

"I'm sorry. But I knew you would want me to call. I wouldn't have done it if I wasn't worried."

"What's up?"

"I came in after lunch and found one of the endorphin experiments running a little hot. I'm not sure who set it, but it's at eighty-five degrees."

"Eighty-five? How long has it been that high?"

"About two hours. I had to take care of the specimens, so lunch took a little longer."

"Well, I don't think we can do anything now. Lowering the tempera-ture won't help. The compounds must have broken down by now."

"Sorry. I'm not sure how the thermostat got reset."

"Don't worry about it for now. I've got to get back. Just keep the rest of the dishes down to forty."

"Hope your dad's having a good time."

"Bye."

I got back in time to hear most of the ceremony. When I heard "You may now kiss . . ." I looked straight at my dad. He never looked happier. I could see now that he wanted to be married again.

I ducked out to the pavilion where the caterer was setting up. She was putting the finishing touches on the luncheon. I overheard a couple of helpers discussing the punch. One suggested that a bit of alcohol might calm the crowd down and liven things up. I told him that he ought to take his liquor and calm himself down.

Otherwise, I was happy. By then the guests were moving out of the house and onto the lawn. I saw Dad coming my way. I wasn't sure what to say to him. Should I just be polite and tell him I'm happy for him? Or should I tell him I wished he'd waited?

My dad didn't reach me. My phone vibrated again. I walked behind the pavilion.

"Yes?"

"Robyn again. I'm sorry. But the overheated endorphin solution is unstable."

"So what? Look, if we have to rerun this test, we'll rerun the test."

"I'm sorry. I know I'm just the grad student, but you insisted that we account for every drop of this solution."

"Okay, then, why don't you calm it down with a little alcohol?"

"Alcohol?"

"I've got to get back to the reception. Bye."

I don't know why I said that about the alcohol. I hardly expected Robyn to go through with it, but she did. Chalk it up to faithful grad student instincts. Not only that, she also followed through diligently administering the unstable samples to lab animals.

We soon realized that the solution which produced the most profound effect was the one that overheated. The alcohol acted as a catalyst to alter the theta endorphins' structure. They now induced a mild sleep in the test subjects within a few moments of application. We found few side effects.

The first use of theta endorphins was as an aid to relaxing overactive infants. One whiff and they slept for several hours. I don't suppose it would surprise you that Snooze proved to be a big seller for moviegoers around the world.

My dad got a divorce three years later. He thanked me for not gloating. He said he was proud of me. So I didn't have the heart to tell him that if I had followed my instincts I wouldn't have been at a wedding to come up with the idea for Snooze in the first place. He promised me that if he ever thought of marrying again, he would ask me. I think Dad's the greatest.

SHANNON'S FLIGHT

GLENN L. ANDERSON

Before the turn of the century, mustang herds ran wild on the mesas near Dead Horse Point, which provided a natural corral for enterprising cowboys. Once driven onto the promontory, horses could escape only by passing through a narrow neck of land which the wranglers controlled by fencing. After roping and breaking the most marketable mustangs, cowboys shipped the horses back east for sale, leaving unwanted culls or "broomtails" behind to find their own way off the mesa.

The Point gets its name from one such incident. According to legend, cowboys left behind a band of broomtails that stayed on the promontory. Although the corral gate was left open, the horses failed to make their way back to the open range. Remaining on the Point, they died of thirst within sight of the Colorado River, 2,000 feet below. To this day, the reason for their apparent entrapment remains a mystery.

–Del MacCrae, "The Story of Dead Horse Point," *Tour Southern Utah*

*S*omething rustled, and Shannon Call spun in the darkness. Behind her the moon shone on empty desert. Just rocks and piñon pine and scattered cactus. No sign of the apparition tonight. Not yet anyway.

Shannon sat still and hugged her arms. She couldn't decide whether it was exhilaration or just a case of the creeps that had raised the gooseflesh there. Probably some of both. What did it matter anyway?

She turned back toward the drop-off. Two thousand feet below, moonlight sparkled silently on the switchbacks of the Colorado River. A cool wind washed a fragrance of sage up out of the chasm and across her face, where the tears had not yet begun to dry on her cheeks. She'd been thinking about Ronny tonight, as she had every night for the past two weeks. Her trips to the state park had become a sort of ritual pilgrimage. But in spite of her persistence, Shannon still had not yet begun to make sense out of the relationship she had fled from. Even so her nightly trips to Dead Horse Point had not been wasted. She found she could sit and gaze out over the spacious canyon, and just for an hour or so she could feel free.

She stood and stretched some of the stiffness out of her legs. Then she headed back along the narrow asphalt trail toward her aging Toyota Tercel. Even in the open air of the desert, she began to feel trapped again, stuck in limbo between the pain of the present and the terrible uncertainties of the future. She was married, but not really. Her man lived with her, but was never there. He was in and out of her house, in and out of work, in and out of jail.

And where was she? Where was Shannon? Not sure about that one. Actually, she mused bleakly, for the past six years she had never thought much past her husband and where things stood with him.

Another rustle, and Shannon glanced out across the flat again. Something dark skittered and disappeared at the base of a twisted juniper. A fox, perhaps.

She continued around the deep shadows of an empty pavilion until she spied her car, looking lonely and deserted. Earlier in the season other vehicles might have shared the parking lot. But by this late in October, even weekend sightseers were scant, and campers seemed on the verge of extinction.

She turned onto a gravel footpath. Ronny's voice ran on in her head as she walked. She was the only one he really loved. Couldn't she see that? It was all over with Julie. Sure it was. But before that it had been all over with Chari, and before that, with Nanette. So why was his undershirt full of Julie's perfume again? Oh, that was her imagination, wasn't it? She could still hear him, railing. She was paranoid. Neurotic. *Sick*. And so damn controlling. Why couldn't she stop clinging? No wonder he drank. No wonder he couldn't handle staying around for more than a couple of weeks at a time. Couldn't she see that it was all *her*?

Then he'd be burned out again, and back at her door. It was over with Julie now. Really over, for good this time. Besides, he hadn't wanted Julie. Shannon should have known that all along. Women flocked after Ronny, and what had he ever done to bring it on? Anyway, this time it was finished. All of it. The women, the booze, the cocaine. Even the gambling. No more. He was coming home, now. He had been so foolish, he had taken her for granted. He loved her so much. He just needed her to keep working her night job to tide them over till he could find decent employment, and then they would move out of their trailer. Maybe leave Ogden altogether. Find some place better, some place she deserved.

Shannon paused halfway to her car at a water spigot with a drinking fountain on top. Touching the handle, she could feel her fingers tremble slightly against the metal. She ran some water into her mouth, across her cheek and over her eyes. They burned.

Oh yes, Ronny had known what she wanted to hear. She had wanted it so very badly she had ached for it. And that, precisely, was why she had to get away. Because her want was so big there was no getting out from under it. Ronny had his women and his nose candy and his José Cuervo; Shannon had Ronny. The addiction was swallowing up her life, and before long there would be nothing left of it. So, not for the first time, she had run.

She allowed the water to wash across her forehead, and she shook her hair back from her face. California would have been better. Or somewhere back east. But Moab offered Uncle Howard's winter home, and he and Maxine wouldn't be back to take up residence till after Thanksgiving. Rent was cheap, and math tutors were scarce in town. So here she was, living a day at a time, hoping Ronny wouldn't catch up to her too soon. Praying that he would just stay away for a while.

Because there was still that part of her that was drawn to him so powerfully. And if he showed up on her doorstep again—here, now—what would she do? Just how in heaven's name would she handle that?

Shannon skimmed the water away and opened her eyes. The breath stuck in her throat.

The stallion stood before her, so much closer this time, scarcely ten feet away. The same silver Appaloosa she had seen twice before. The one with the long corkscrew scar on its flank.

The ghost-horse.

Shannon stood frozen, a single droplet creeping slowly down her cheek. Her heart was a jackhammer. The mustang studied her with eyes that were bottomlessly dark. Its mane and tail swam in the moonlight like banners of slow-motion seaweed. Both gaunt and majestic, it took a cautious step forward. Then back again.

For a single magic instant, alongside the thrill and the terror, Shannon seemed to feel something else. A beckoning, a kinship. Reflexively, she extended her hand.

The horse whirled away. Shannon sucked in a scream and fell backward. In a single motion, as fluid as ground fog, the animal fled, galloping a wide circle along the lip of the canyon. Shannon scrabbled to her feet to watch and gasped again. There in the distance, just barely perceptible, were more mustangs. Six, ten, a dozen or more. All running together, leaping and flying, cascading like a river of lost souls over the uneven terrain.

Then they were gone.

Shannon stood staring after them, sucking wind and feeling the skin prickle in waves across her ribs. She had never been so frightened in all of her life, and yet never so high. It was a moment of pure, exhilarating wonder.

He wouldn't believe it when she told him. He would come unglued. Ronny would come absolutely un—

She stood staring blindly into the darkness then, trying not to think, trying not to feel. Finally though, something inside her seemed to buckle and collapse, and she started to cry. She tried running for her car but didn't make it. Instead she dropped onto the asphalt and held her hair in her fists and sat in the dark and wept.

Porter's Desert Souvenirs sat amid a jumble of sandstone tablets and old wagon wheels. A column of rusty mine cars stood mustered near the shop's front door, some filled with coal, others with hunks of colored rock.

Shannon sat in a back room of the building, near some stairs that led to the apartment above the store, tutoring Trish Talbot. Their tabletop was a single slab of fossil-pocked shale.

"It's out on the edge of the canyon. Dad first saw it from the bottom with his binoculars." Trish let her pencil doodle a rubbing at the edge of her math paper, where a trilobite made a bump under the page. "He says there's big bones there, and that means big bucks. But first he has to get a permit 'cause it's on state park land. Out by Dead Horse Point."

"What?" Shannon asked and blinked. She hadn't been paying attention, her thoughts vacillating between Ronny Call and the Appaloosa, almost as if there were some connection between the two. But Trish's last few words had cut through the haze.

"The new fossils. The ones my dad found last weekend."

"Oh." Shannon glanced dully at Trish's worksheet. Out of thirty problems only two had answers beside them. "I'm not doing you much good this afternoon, am I, Trish?" Shannon rubbed her eyes. She hadn't slept. And now along with all of her other feelings, she felt a wave of guilt. "You could do this on your own time and save your dad some money. It's all review."

"And they don't give permits to just anybody," Trish went on, oblivious. "But if he can work a deal with the U. of U., he can dig for them on their permit. They'll pay him really good. We might could get a new truck, and I could get at least two new outfits and maybe my own phone."

Shannon gave her a look of mild skepticism.

"I haven't asked him about that last part yet." Trish looked defensive. "But I'm old enough for a phone. I cook dinner sometimes, and I can drive the truck by myself too. With the clutch and everything, if I stay in first. Dad showed me how."

Shannon mused blankly. Her own phone. She had once asked Ronny for a second phone. Ronny had said no. He'd been jobless. Shannon had been teaching full time and tutoring part time, making all the money. And Ronny had said no. Even now, Shannon still didn't own her own telephone.

Trish doodled down to a second bump. A flowery crinoid began to appear. "Jenny Burton has a phone."

Shannon wasn't thinking about telephones anymore. Her thoughts had returned to the Appaloosa. She studied her pupil's face for a time. "Trish," she ventured finally, "do you believe in ghosts?"

Trish looked up, her own expression blank for a moment. Then her eyes brightened. "Yeah. I thought I saw one once, and it scared the crap out of me. But it was just my white sweatshirt hanging on a shovel handle by the back window. Do you?"

Shannon nodded. "I think I saw one."

Trish's eyes brightened some more. "Cool! When?"

"Last night. Out on the Point. It . . . " Shannon hesitated for just a moment. Not because of the outlandishness of what she was about to say. There was total acceptance in Trish's ten-year-old gaze. But Shannon's guilt was still there. She wasn't being paid to tell ghost stories. Then again, she wasn't getting much teaching done in her current frame of mind anyway.

Fine. She would deduct the time.

"It was a horse," she said.

Trish's face slackened. There was no skepticism. Just total and immediate absorption. "Nu-*uhhh*."

Shannon nodded. "I think there are others. A whole herd." And she related everything.

Trish listened hungrily, leaning over her math book and chewing on a fingernail. "They're the broomtails!" she finally exclaimed. In Moab, it seemed, the legend of Dead Horse Point was common knowledge.

"They might be," Shannon answered.

"Sure they are. And they're still trying to find their way off the Point, huh?"

Shannon smiled. "I see you have this all figured out already."

"Sure." Trish had run out of fingernail. She started on her pencil eraser. "My grandma read me this story once in *Reader's Digest* about this old man who was hit by a train at this crossroads place. For years and years after that, people would go by late at night and see this spooky light. It was supposed to be the old man's ghost, holding a lantern and trying to keep his own accident from happening."

Shannon's smile dimmed a bit. She had heard similar stories herself.

"And when the train didn't run anymore," Trish went on, "they pulled up the tracks and built a mini-mall. And the lights stopped."

"Because with the train gone, there was nothing holding the old man at the crossroads," Shannon finished. The pair stared at each other for a moment, reflecting.

"Right," Trish affirmed. With an air of finality, she spit out a little pink eraser chunk. "So what do you think's keeping the broomtails on the Point?"

Children were marvelous, Shannon mused. At this point an adult would be trying to determine why Shannon had seen something that wasn't there. But Trish was trying to figure out why the ghosts had hung around long enough for Shannon to see them.

"I don't know," she said.

The two sat in contemplation for a few moments more. Then Trish's eyes focused, intense with excitement.

"I want to see one. Take me out there!"

Shannon laughed. "Your dad would like that. I'm supposed to be helping you catch up on your math and instead I take you out in the middle of the night on a ghost hunt."

"He wouldn't mind! He'd probably want to come along. Please!"

Shannon straightened in her seat. "I think not," she said, even though, knowing Porter as little as she did, she suspected Trish might be right. "Besides, we've wasted a half an hour here already. Time to get to work."

Trish groaned, and Shannon finally agreed to let her finish the last half of the worksheet on her own time if she kept quiet about the ghost story. Trish agreed without hesitation.

"Not a word then." Shannon pointed her finger. "Your dad would think I'm crazy, and nobody wants a crazy person tutoring their kids."

Trish's expression grew serious. "He wouldn't think that. He likes you. He wants to take you out, but he says you think he's just a dumb rock hound."

"I don't think that, Trish."

"Then why won't you go out with him? He asked you, I heard him."

Shannon sat staring at the girl, searching for some neutral response, hoping all the while that her face was staying nondescript.

Because I'm married, Trish. But don't ask about the man I'm married to, or why I'm here without him. Those are the kinds of details we don't fully divulge, even to family and friends, let alone pupils and their parents.

"You think he's ugly?" Trish's face was expectant. "I told him to get a haircut and shave his beard. My grandma thinks his beard is gross."

"I think his beard is just fine," Shannon answered, and she was telling the truth. While Porter Talbot was not precisely striking, he was not far from it.

"Then why don't you come with us tomorrow? Out to take pictures of the bones. Dad would like you to come. He said I could ask you."

"I don't think so, Trish," Shannon began, but she couldn't really think of a good reason why not. After all, where would Ronny be? Out with Julie or Chari or Nanette or some other nameless Barbie look-alike? And Shannon couldn't even let go long enough to spend an afternoon with a little girl and her dad. What did she have keeping her at home anyway? A half-hour's worth of papers to grade. If that.

Her look must have betrayed some vulnerability. "Make you a deal," Trish ventured. "You come, and I'll do two extra worksheets. By tomorrow morning. Promise." And she followed up the proposition with her most charming smile.

Porter Talbot hunkered down at the canyon rim, which zigzagged to form an outcropping some forty feet away. He motioned to where a layer of stone had fallen off. Trish and Shannon sat beside him on a rock, fanning an occasional gnat.

"That's where the section fell from. When I found the first bone fragments at the bottom, I was sure they came from the middle somewhere." Porter gestured halfway down the canyon wall, which dropped spectacularly before him. "No way to get at them. But then I got scanning with the binocs, and here it was. Right at the top. About as pretty as it gets."

Shannon squinted, trying to see what he was talking about. "Am I looking in the right place?"

"Probably." He motioned her over. "Come here, you have to know what to look for."

Even looking into the sunlight, Shannon could see the pale amber of Porter's eyes, which shone lighter than the deep tan the desert had baked into his face. His beard was trimmed short. It was the same tawny gray color as his hair, which the breeze stroked back and forth across his forehead.

Shannon felt an unexpected swell of attraction. She had been wrong, she decided. Perhaps Porter Talbot *was* striking after all.

"See?" He pointed, tracing shapes on the cliff face. "Those darker forms above the main fault, where the new stone's exposed." She scooted closer so that her eyes could follow his finger. His fragrance was rich and male, a fragrance of sweat and lingering aftershave and sunbaked denim. She found herself resisting it, edging back a bit.

"I see it, Dad!" Trish's voice piped up just behind Shannon's head, making her jump a little. "It goes up and then bends, like an elbow!" And then Shannon saw it too. The shape was not much darker, but it was there. And next to it what had appeared at first to be striations in the rock now stood out clearly as a set of ribs. Continuing on, similar shapes formed a pattern that streaked and dotted the stone for several yards.

Porter mopped the back of his neck. "Some kind of big vertebrate.

Could be camptosaurus, allosaurus. Maybe ceratosaurus. Could be more of them. Where you find one, you tend to find a whole graveyard."

Shannon drew back from him a bit more. "You can tell what *kind* they are?"

"It's the period," Porter explained. "A Morrison fold runs through this side of the canyon. Upper Jurassic." He looked at her as if to assess her understanding. She found the terms vaguely familiar. "Shoptalk," he shrugged and gave an easy smile. "Let's get some pictures for the university boys and see if this is worth anything to them." He chuckled knowingly.

From behind them came a growling whinny and a sound of hooves fidgeting in the dirt. Shannon turned. They had left Porter's trailer at the park entrance and had ridden in along the edge of the mesa, surveying for other sites. Now their horses stood tethered in the shade of three separate trees. One of the animals, a black mare with a white spot on her nose, shuffled nervously.

"What's wrong with Maggie?"

"She doesn't much like it out here, Trish." Porter rose to his feet. "Don't know what the devil it is. Was like this the last time I brought her, but not so bad."

He stepped over to calm the mare, and Shannon felt a light shiver run along her arms. She let her eyes scan the landscape. The animals were tethered about a hundred yards outside the narrow neck that separated Dead Horse Point from the desert beyond. The place where Shannon's ghost-horse had first appeared was less than a half-mile away. She turned to look behind her, half expecting to see something again. There was nothing.

"Hey, easy, babe. Easy, girl." Porter was cooing to Maggie. He slung the strap of his Canon around his neck, still trying to settle her as he rummaged through his saddlebag. Nearby Trish stood beside the young Palomino they called Shortribs, unloading several cans of pop. Shannon eyed the horse. It also seemed skittish but less so. Only Doc, the thick-boned Morgan Shannon had ridden in on, seemed unaffected. He stood by sleepily and twitched an ear. Shannon scanned the desert again.

"Trish, honey, didn't I send you for some film?" Porter shuffled to keep up with Maggie as she edged and circled, straining at her reins. "Where is it?" He tugged back against the horse, armpit deep in the saddlebag.

"It's in there," Trish called back thickly over a bag of Doritos she held in her teeth. Her arms were full of Pepsi. "I put it in this morning."

Shannon trotted over to help with Trish's load. On her way, out of the corner of her eye, she saw the movement that made everything go crazy. It might have been a big lizard or a small ground squirrel. Whatever it was, it darted through the sand between Maggie's legs.

A whinny broke from the mare's throat like a scream. Porter flung himself backward, fighting to free his arm from the saddlebag. Maggie reared wildly. With a crack like a gunshot, the branch she was tethered to broke and flew, clubbing Porter in the head. He swore, dropping and rolling to get out of the way.

"Dad!" Trish screamed, and all of the pop cans tumbled.

Porter cried out, jerking in an outstretched hand just as a hoof dropped hard to meet it. He rolled again. A ragged mesquite stump snagged his shirt and tore it wide. Wheeling in the opposite direction, Maggie galloped off at full speed, trailing a dusty jet stream. In moments she was out of sight.

Trish hobbled over on one foot. Her load of Pepsi had dropped on the other. Shannon followed. They reached Porter as he rose on an elbow. Trish dropped to her knees and hugged his head, ready to cry.

"Are you okay?" Shannon knelt beside him. She could see no blood. "That looked awful." Her heart was racing, partly out of concern for Porter, and partly, she realized, because of past experience. If this had been Ronny, he would be screaming after the horse, maybe threatening to kill it, lashing out at anyone within earshot for no good reason at all. Yet Porter looked unharmed—and for the most part unruffled—except for his tattered shirt and his left hand, which he held stiffly above the ground.

"Hell yeah, I'm okay," he grunted through his daughter's hug. "My own fault. I should've given up on the film and let Maggie calm down." He gave one of Trish's arms a pat and eased it away so he could look around. His camera lay on the ground near where the horse had bolted. "I'll heal, but that thing costs money. Go grab it for me, Trisher. Let's see how bad it is."

She ran for the camera. Porter gave a grunt and a sigh and rolled onto his seat, propping his back against a mound of sandstone. Shannon was still looking at his hand.

"Can I see that? It looks broken."

Porter smiled weakly. "You a part-time nurse, too?"

Shannon took the hand gently. It was badly scraped, and there was color under the skin. "I've handled my share of broken bones. Playground first aid, you know. Can't move that at all, can you?"

Porter's fingers trembled and his body tensed. "You got that right. Which's gonna make it pretty damn hard to shoot those pictures. Which I need today if I'm gonna get them developed by the time I head for Salt Lake on Monday."

She turned the hand, studying it. "You're lucky. It doesn't look crushed. You must have pulled it out of the way just in time."

"Teaches math, nurses wounds." Porter teased a crumpled weed from his hair. "You're a woman of many talents, Ms. Call. Can I ask you something?"

She glanced at him. "Mmm-hmm." In his weary smile she found a mixture of appreciation and unconcealed attraction. His torn shirt gaped. The skin there was as tanned as his face, his chest and belly sculpted with muscle. They were covered with the same tawny hair that colored his beard.

"Do you wear tinted contact lenses, or did your eyes get that deep and blue all by themselves?"

Shannon felt herself blush. "I don't wear contacts," she said, smiling back in spite of herself. She explored Porter's knuckles just a bit more firmly to change the subject. It worked. He winced.

"You ought to have this x-rayed," she responded, still smiling. "We need to get you back to the emergency room at the hospital."

A shadow fell onto Porter's shirt, and Shannon turned. Trish had returned with the camera. Her face was stricken. Porter winced again.

"She totaled?" he asked.

Trish shook her head. "No. It looks okay." But as she dangled the camera toward her dad, she looked again as if she were going to burst into tears.

He took it from her. "Then why—"

Out of Trish's overall pocket she drew two small boxes with Kodak labels. "I thought I put them in the bags, Dad. I really did." Her voice broke.

Shannon stiffened.

Porter stared dully at the film. After a moment of total silence, he burst out laughing. Trish's expression began to soften as his laughter trailed off. Finally breathing heavily, he held out his good hand and Trish put the boxes in his palm. He stared at them.

"I wanted Fuji," he said.

They all burst out laughing then, Porter propped on a rock, Trish collapsed over his legs, and Shannon still holding his broken hand. They laughed till tears rolled down their faces. And for Shannon there was something about that moment that was very nearly as magical as the appearance of the ghost-horse the night before.

In the end it was Shannon who took the pictures. Porter showed her how to focus the lens, operate the zoom, and use the meter, and then he coached her as she framed the shots. His confidence in her seemed complete and matter-of-fact. His patience was astounding considering his hand, which was beginning to swell darkly.

And yet, aside from this, there was something more. In the half hour that he called directions to her as she picked her way across the rocks with his camera, Shannon felt the oddest feeling, and she wasn't sure she was comfortable with it. Always with Ronny there was a clear distinction. He was a man, she was a woman. But here she and Porter were just people, working together. No, more. Friends.

By the time they were finished, Shannon decided she liked that. She liked that very much.

Before long they had arrived back at the trailer to find Maggie, grazing patiently and awaiting their return. There Porter asked Shannon out again. Something inside her screamed back in anger and sadness when once again she felt compelled to decline.

Shannon was home by 5:30. Exhausted she fell asleep on the couch while she waited for some leftover Ragu and noodles to heat through in the microwave.

As she slept she dreamed.

The desert lay cool and moonlit before her, and she flew over it on the back of the silver Appaloosa, which glided with hoofbeats as soft as mist. They led the ghost herd as they fled the Point, straining toward the slender neck of land that separated them from the freedom of the open range.

Yet as she rode Shannon's anticipation began to ebb, replaced by an awful dread. Something lurked there, in the dark, just past the narrow passage. Something enormous and terrible, waiting to fall upon her.

The Appaloosa charged ahead, and though the terror throbbing beneath her ribs grew thicker with each passing second, Shannon held on. She tightened her jaw and held back the screams until she was certain the terror alone would kill her, but she held on anyway, fighting the urge to let go, to leap off, to flee with all of her strength in the other direction.

Then against the deep purple blackness of the midnight sky, something blacker reared to fall upon her.

Shannon jerked awake, smacking her shin on her aunt's glass-top coffee table. The phone was ringing.

She fumbled for it with one hand and rubbed at her leg with the other. She found the receiver, lifted it to her ear, and cleared her throat, still trying to shake off the lingering fright of the dream.

"Hello," she gargled, and when the deep male voice on the other end spoke, she saw that she had the receiver turned the wrong way. She juggled it around. *Porter*, she thought sleepily.

"Hello," she said once more. She was about to ask how the injured hand was coming along but was cut short.

"Hi, babe. Been missing you." The voice on the other end of the line purred. It was like warm water to cold bones, almost impossible to resist. Shannon was instantly wide awake.

"Ronny," she whispered.

Her heart began tripping, partly in alarm, partly as that old longing for him abruptly kicked in. Oh, it kicked in hard. She had forgotten how real that part of her was. The feeling was instantly heady, almost intoxicating.

"You didn't have to leave," the voice went on, "but I know why you did. I don't blame you, really, babe. But I told you, it'd all be different. And it is, honest to God, I just been sitting home worried sick about you. I thought maybe you'd tried to call, but I wasn't here 'cause I'm working two shifts."

Because she could think of no other response, Shannon asked, "Where?"

"With Barry, out at the wrecking yard. As long as I want it, but that's just temporary. Got some other things cooking. Big things. Good ones, for you and me."

Good things for you and me. Such an old story. And yet it was in Ronny to do it. She knew it was in him, and that was what was so hard, wasn't it? Knowing it was there and hoping this time it was really coming out, for good.

The old feelings were caving in on top of her. Soon she'd be in over her head. She fought them.

"How's Julie?" she asked. Her voice broke.

"Hey, babe, don't do that to me. I told you it was over, and it is. I don't have the slightest idea how she is. I don't care. She's out of my life, I haven't seen her for . . . " He hesitated for the briefest instant. "I don't know. I can't even remember. Come on, babe. Give me a break. I need you, I can't do it without you, you know that."

Shannon closed her eyes. She wanted out.

But she wanted him.

"How did you find me, Ronny?"

"Max told me you'd gone south. Tina said you had these relatives in Moab. I got their number from information."

Shannon sighed. Tina. She probably gave him more than just the number. Shannon had suspected for some time that her brother's wife had developed a thing for Ronny too. Max still didn't know. In reality Shannon wasn't sure how much there *was* to know. Maybe nothing. Maybe she was being unfair to both of them. How could she tell?

His voice purred in her ear again. "Shannon, you still there, hon? I called for you yesterday before I left, but I couldn't get any answer."

Adrenaline sent a jolt into Shannon's chest. "What do you mean, before you left?" Suddenly she was trying to catch her breath.

"I'm at that Maverick here, just inside town—"

"I don't want to see you, Ronny." Shannon's words flooded out, driven by panic. The receiver in her hand was slick with cool sweat.

"Oh, come on, babe. I came all this way, I have to see you. Just to talk, that's all."

She struggled to calm herself. "Not tonight. Really. I can't."

"Look, just give me the address. I can get it from the phone book anyway. I just want to see you, I *have* to see you tonight. You don't know how I've missed you. I've been crazy without you, baby."

"No, Ronny, please."

"Honey, you don't know how hard it is. I'm clean two weeks now, but I need you by me or I can't make it. You're my life. You know that. You have to know that."

She was slipping away. She could feel it. The guilt, the loneliness, the fear, the longing, they were like chloroform. They were pulling her under. She couldn't shake them off. "Ronny look, I . . . I just need to be alone right now." Her thoughts felt jumbled. The words didn't want to line up. "Maybe, later. Okay? Maybe tomorrow. I'll talk to you tomorrow."

"What do you mean, tomorrow? Where am I supposed to stay tonight, in my car?" An edge of anger seemed to creep into his voice and slip away again. "It cost me everything I had just to drive down here. I only did it for you, why else would I be here?"

Maybe he was right. Even after everything they'd been through, what kind of a person would she be if she wouldn't even see him for a few minutes? Would that even be fair?

She was losing it. She had to go.

"Ronny—"

"And now you won't even talk to me? You wouldn't do that to me, babe, I know you wouldn't. You can't just close the door on me after all I've done for you. I've given up everything for you—"

She let the phone clatter onto the hook switch. It took a bounce, and she slid it back with a shaking hand.

He would be arriving soon. There was no stopping him. She couldn't allow herself to be home when he came. Or any place nearby where he might find her. Not tonight.

She ran for a jacket and checked both doors to be sure the house was locked. Then she got in her car and drove. Taking back roads to make sure he wouldn't pass her on the way, she headed out of town, toward the turnoff to Dead Horse Point.

Shannon was scarcely two miles from the state park entrance when nightfall overtook the desert. A sky full of thunderclouds cast a pale luminescence at the ground. Wind tugged at the sage lining the road.

As her Toyota plowed through the dust clouds raised by the gathering storm, Shannon's thoughts roiled. What the hell was the matter with her, anyway? She had run nearly five hundred miles to keep Ronny from finding her, and now she was running again. Why didn't she just end it? Why didn't she just go find a lawyer and fill out a few papers and be done? There were no children to fight over, and he could have everything else, including the trailer. Why couldn't she just stand her ground and tell him it was over and then move on?

That was one part of her talking. Another part was still in touch with all those feelings that had flooded back when she'd heard his voice again on the phone. It was the same part that worried over him and wanted to take care of him and give him some place safer to sleep than his car. Yes, she was attracted to him, but there was so much more. He had been right on at least one count, hadn't he? She was sick. She wished it weren't so, but here she was.

Something capered into her headlights, like a goblin. Shannon gave a little cry, her foot jumping to the brake. Then she saw it was only a tumbleweed. It somersaulted twice and disappeared.

Her heart pulsed in her throat. She tried to calm herself, but the fear ran much deeper than the momentary start she'd received. The fear was at the base of her sickness, she knew that. The fear of letting go of him, of what it would mean to be unmarried and unloved and forever unable to feel his warmth beside her in her bed. The fear of what he would do if she abandoned him, of how angry he might get and how out of control he might get. What would he do to her? Or to himself? Could she bear the monstrous guilt of leaving him alone to fend for himself with no money and no home and a monkey on his back? What if he overdosed in a fit of desperation? Or killed himself outright, what then?

Yes, the fear was always there, waiting, and tonight she battled to keep it at arm's length. It would do no good to engage it, as she had so many times before. The future held hundreds of dark eventualities waiting to be explored. It was just like the dream, wasn't it? Somewhere up ahead, beyond the limits of her vision, all of her worst anticipations merged and reared, dark and terrible and unknown. Ronny behind her and the future before her, and she was held immobile in between. And there was really no way for her to get past that. Perhaps there never would be. The more she thought about it, she knew, the deeper into despair she would descend. She knew because she had done it before, time and again. So tonight, she just drove. She just drove and tried not to think and scanned out the windshield, watching.

She knew what she wanted. With increasing desperation she wanted to see the Appaloosa again. She could still feel that vague beckoning, as she had the night before.

Within minutes the parking lot appeared in her headlights. She sidled her car up to the familiar water spigot and shut off her engine. She knew how to call the stallion. It was the water that had lured the horse so close. Even in death it was still trying to survive, just like the old man and his train.

Shannon turned the spring-loaded handle and opened the valve. Beneath it a tiny pool began to form. After twenty seconds or so, she shut off the water and waited.

The storm was closer now. Lightning scattered splashes of blue light against the backs of the clouds crowding the horizon. The wind came in tepid gusts, sending tiny waves across the puddle. Shannon found a smooth spot and sat, brushing a handful of pointy gravel out from under her seat. Then she waited some more.

Five minutes. Ten.

Shannon reached up and turned the valve again. This time she didn't let go. The water came in a steady stream.

Gradually the air grew cooler, filled with the damp herbal smell of rain on dry grass and dusty bark. The first echoes of thunder lumbered over the wind. Shannon peered at her watch. Fifteen minutes had passed from the time she first drew water from the spigot. She watched the stream now as it fell and broke, fell and broke in the pulsing wind. The sound was pounding, rhythmic, like trundling hooves.

She glanced past the stream.

The entire herd stood staring, spread along a nearby shelf of stone like faded statues. Shannon tensed and caught her breath. The Appaloosa stood out front, mane waving in lazy oblivion to the now blustering wind. It was perhaps twenty feet away.

Shannon let go of the valve, and it snapped shut. She rose slowly, her chest again heaving with a thrill of fear and wonder. The animals were other-worldly, beautiful. A flash of lightning lit the desert, seeming to erase them momentarily before the darkness painted them back onto the landscape again.

Shannon straightened fully to her feet. Against her careful movement the lead stallion stood his ground, studying her with his bottomless stare. Then he turned and trotted a few paces into the desert before turning back and eyeing her again. Several others in the herd echoed the Appaloosa's movement. Yes, she thought with growing excitement. They want me to follow.

As if they heard her thoughts, the horses fled *en masse*. In a single motion like a river of pale silk, they swept out across the sand and flowed along the shoulder of the road.

Shannon scrambled to her car and ground the starter, revving it to life. She bumped over a pothole, spun the wheel, narrowly missed the spigot and gave the herd chase. Only then did it occur to her where they were going.

The horses were racing toward the narrow neck leading to the open range. Shannon followed at top speed. They were about to show her what had held them captive for over a hundred years.

Shannon overtook the ghost herd just as they veered away from the road and headed off toward the canyon's edge. She swung the Toyota onto the shoulder and skidded in the dirt. As she threw the door open to follow the horses, the first big drops of rain began popping onto the roof of her car.

A blast of thunder crackled from the sky. Shannon ran, the wind now tearing at her clothes and her hair. She leaped down from a small rise, raced across a pebbled wash and climbed up a stand of rock that looked like a tipped stack of giant dinner plates. Barely visible in the distance, still galloping full tilt, were the horses. They were looping back toward the road, where the asphalt cut a narrow path across the neck of land that led off the Point.

The animals were making a run for freedom.

Water seemed to fall in a blanket from the sky. Lightning came in bursts, searing the desert with white light. Behind the curtains of rain, the horses flickered in and out of being in time with the lightning.

The lead stallion reached the asphalt. Abruptly he reared.

Just as suddenly all of the other mustangs changed direction. They were coming back now, not in a flowing mass as they had begun but in broken frenzy, spreading out in every direction at once. And close behind them something was charging across to give chase.

Something huge.

Shannon's eyes widened, her heart slamming jets of terror from beneath her ribs and up into her throat. She would have turned to flee if her legs had any movement left in them, but they had suddenly turned as fluid and insubstantial as the rain.

She had been wrong. Earlier that day she had attributed Maggie's skittishness to the lingering presence of the ghost-herd. But now she saw that an entirely different apparition haunted that end of the mesa. It stood two, maybe three times taller than the frantic steeds trying to get out of its path. And as it grew closer, looming through the gray veil that the rain had drawn before it, Shannon realized with a mixture of awe and utter disbelief what this beast must be. *Merciful heaven,* she thought, and almost laughed in spite of the fear that welled in her chest. *This couldn't be. This was crazy.*

And yet on it came. It loped after the horses on the elephantine legs of some impossible hybrid ostrich, its eyes mad with primitive hunger. It was a phantom risen from Porter's Jurassic graveyard.

The thing darted after the nearest ghost horse, dipping low. The mustang's hooves stuttered, almost dumping the animal over before it could swerve to avoid the monster's jaws. Other horses leaped and milled in mad confusion. With terrifying quickness the beast doubled back in mid-lunge, snapping at another animal. This one fell. Shannon's own scream covered the shriek of the fallen horse as the monster pivoted and dove, all teeth and raking claws. Then the scene evaporated with the darkness in a flash of white light.

The thunder was simultaneous with the lightning, an explosion so loud it knocked Shannon backward. Her buttocks made a wet plop on the rock, and she sat staring out into empty darkness again. Rain pounded around her. The wind whipped it in her face. She rubbed a mat of soaking hair away from her eyes and scanned the desert. All of the apparitions were gone. She was alone.

Shannon sat panting, blowing rivulets away from her lips. She finally rose on stiff legs only when the rain began to ease up and the cold had seeped deep into her bones. Still numb with amazement, she waded through the wash and ascended the shoulder back up to her car.

The vehicle looked wrong sitting at the side of the road. A dented Toyota didn't belong in a place where ghost-dinosaurs chased ghost-horses across a haunted mesa. No, that prop just didn't fit this part of the movie. What did the ad say? *Oh-oh-oh, what a feeling.* They had no idea.

This night had been insane, unreal. And as Shannon climbed soaking wet and shaking behind the wheel of her car, her thoughts still seemed to be flowing in kind. In the depths of her mind, she could feel it. A plan was already beginning to form there, one that would rescue the ghost-horses and lead them to freedom.

Shannon awoke the next morning about 9:00, naked under the padded warmth of her aunt's electric blanket. When she opened her eyes to the sunny bedroom, decorated in mauve ruffles and floral wallpaper, she felt the same odd disorientation she had felt the night before while staring at her car. The room felt mundane and otherworldly compared to the phantasms still chasing through her head. From downstairs came the sound once again that had originally awakened her. Someone was knocking at the door.

She tensed at once.

Upon returning the night before, she had noted with relief that Ronny had not been camped out in her driveway. As was typical he had managed to find a bed some place else. She had taken the phone off the hook to avoid another call, but she had known even then that she would not be able to avoid him for long.

She stepped over the wet clothes still piled on a throw rug beside the bed and crept to the window. Furtively parting the curtain, she peered down at the driveway and felt a wave of glorious pleasure and relief. Porter Talbot stood beside his truck and waved sheepishly in her direction.

With care Shannon slid the pane open, squinting against the sunlight. "Hi," she said a little dreamily. Then she remembered she hadn't a stitch on and hugged herself close and low against the sill.

"Sorry to get you up," Porter called. "I tried phoning, but your line was busy. Wondered if I could talk to you a minute." He smiled up at her.

She smiled back. "Sure. I'll come down, wait a second."

"Better get something on first," Porter said. He gave her a little-boy grin. On another face she might have found it either irritating or embarrassing. On his she found it somehow charming.

Shannon closed the window, threw on a robe, and spied a mirror on her way out. Her hair was a clump. She gave it a few quick brush strokes, saw it would take at least a half-hour to do anything with, and swore. She saw too that her nose was running, courtesy of her midnight field trip. She grabbed some tissue and headed downstairs, trying to rearrange what hair she could with her fingers.

"How are you?" she asked, opening the door to Porter. She drew the robe closer around herself. "I look terrible this morning."

He smiled in at her matter-of-factly. "Wildflower's still pretty," he said, "even when it's waiting for the sun to open its petals. Do you have just a second?"

Shannon felt herself blushing again and didn't care. It felt so good to have this man standing on her doorstep instead of the one she had anticipated only a few moments before. She glanced past Porter into the street. A part of her almost wished that Ronny would arrive. Right here while she was standing with nothing on but her bathrobe, talking with one of the most handsome men she had met in recent memory. That wouldn't quite be poetic justice, but it would be close.

Shannon drew the robe a little tighter. "Come in," she invited. "What's going on?"

"Well, I have to leave for Salt Lake this afternoon, and I just got a wrench thrown in the works." Porter stepped inside. "I don't know if you can help me or not, but Trish's grandma was going to stay home with her while I was gone, and she got a call this morning from her sister. They had some quilts accepted in a show in Utah County, so she has to go up there to get them hung. I could postpone my trip, but I hate to put these guys off. University money evaporates like gin at an Irish funeral."

With growing delight Shannon saw where this was leading. It was just what she needed: a place to disappear to for a day or so. In the meantime maybe Ronny would just fade back to Ogden for a while.

"I should be back by Wednesday night," Porter went on. "I can pay you some for your trouble."

"Oh, I wouldn't dream of that," she said. "Actually it would work out really well for me too, as long as you don't mind me bringing in a couple of other tutoring appointments."

"Not a bit." Porter smiled appreciatively. "I owe you one, Shannon. I'll leave a number where you can reach me if need be." Looking relieved he brushed some hair back from his forehead with a cast-covered hand.

"How's that doing?"

Porter examined it. "Better." He nodded back out toward the driveway. "Had some trouble shifting in the truck. I got a friend changing the U-joint in my little Mercury automatic so I can drive it." He eyed her. "You doing okay? Sounds like you might be coming down with something."

Shannon dabbed at her nose. *No kidding*, she thought. *It's what I get for chasing ghosts in the rain.* With the thought she realized that the intensity of the previous night's experience had begun to fade. The memories had started to feel out of place with her immediate surroundings instead of the other way around. She looked into Porter's face and saw an unexpected measure of concern.

"Oh, I'm fine," she said. "Just a cold." And as she looked at him, she marveled. How could she be feeling so comfortable, standing here talking to this man in her bathrobe, wiping her nose and looking like a hurricane victim?

"You probably picked it up from Trish," Porter suggested. "She's had the sniffles ever since she jumped into the canal to save Tony Whitefeather's guinea pig."

Shannon felt a giggle forming and raised her eyebrows in delight. That sounded like Trish. Within minutes, Porter had finished the whole story, and Shannon's laughter had moved him on to another. From there they both seemed to lose track of time. They talked into the late morning, Porter sitting on the arm of Aunt Maxine's big couch and Shannon curled on the cushion. Porter talked about his own childhood adventures, Shannon about summers on her grandfather's Arizona horse ranch. Before long she was talking about where life had led her from there, and within just a few minutes, she arrived without warning at her reason for being in Moab.

She felt a rush of panic. For a moment she considered dodging the issue but realized things would be even more awkward if she did. The grim truth was, she now saw, that her marriage to Ronny was a reality there was no running away from. Even here, for a few moments, five hundred miles away from home in her aunt's living room.

"We're separated," she said. She ran her fingers along the piping of the couch cushion. She didn't want to look at Porter's face. "We have been, off and on, for three years or so." Odd, she thought. Separated. In all this time she had never phrased it that way, even to herself.

Tightening inside she glanced up at Porter. She expected to see shock on his face. Perhaps a degree of betrayal. Maybe even disdain or revulsion. She saw in fact none of these. Instead he just nodded with a kind of detached sadness.

"I hear you," he said. "Trish's mother was like that. Never could decide what she wanted. We weren't living together either the night I got the call from the UHP. She died in a rollover coming back from a party in Green River. Some guy was driving." With that the pain in his face seemed to become more immediate. "Never knew whether there was something between them, or if she'd just caught a ride. With Rita that was always hard to get a handle on."

"I'm sorry," Shannon offered. She felt a sudden urge to gather this man into her arms and hold him, to soothe his pain in a way she had never been able to for herself.

"Yeah, it was bad." Porter cleared his throat. "Seems like Trish has come out of it okay, but she's shoved a lot of things down deep. I suppose they'll have to come out some day." Porter's eyes studied Shannon's with a mixture of compassion and appreciation. "You know how it is, I guess."

"Ronny and I have no children," she answered. "But, yes, I think I know how it is."

Porter wiped his sleeve away from his watch. "Oh, hey, I need to go," he said apologetically. "I've kept you forever."

"No, it's been good," Shannon said, and she meant it. She wished they could visit into the afternoon. There was suddenly a whole world of things she felt like she wanted to talk about.

"Make yourself at home at the house," Porter said as he stepped to the door. "There's an elk roast in the freezer and melons in the fridge. Take the horses out if you like. Trish can show you some trails."

Shannon regathered her robe and followed him. "We'll have fun together. I'll be over a little past noon."

"Wish I was going to be there," Porter said, and the sincerity in his voice was tempered with just enough flirtiness to keep things comfortable.

Shannon smiled at him. "We'll have to get together and visit again."

"That we will," Porter answered. "See you on Wednesday." He turned out into the sunlight toward his truck. Shannon sat back on the couch and watched him through the front window. She didn't think he could see her until he gave her a wave as he pulled away. She waved back and watched until the truck was out of sight.

On the chance Ronny might still show up, Shannon took no time leaving the house. On the way to Talbot's, she passed by City Market for a few groceries and then stopped at the library for a couple of novels to pass the time.

In the hush of the book stacks, the plan that had begun to form out on the Point the night before presented itself to Shannon again. She realized abruptly that everything had been set in place. If she were actually going to do something, she would have to do it tonight, wouldn't she?

She laughed to herself. It was outlandish. Too absurd even to think about.

Perhaps too dangerous as well.

But as she put her car in gear and headed for Porter's Desert Souvenirs, she found herself thinking about it, all the same.

"Please take me out to see them. *Please*."

Trish was an old master at begging. Shannon could see that from the start.

"Trish, I have a responsibility here. To take care of you, not to go running around the desert after dark."

"But it's okay. My dad told me to take you out on the horses while you were here."

"In the middle of the night?"

"He said we could take a night ride. He did. Just if we don't go too far."

"Trish. The Point's more than twenty miles away."

"So, we take the trailer, and we're never more than a mile or so from the truck. No problem."

"The horses are skittish out there."

"Only Maggie."

"Trish, . . . " Shannon let out a long breath. The interchange was taxing. But the real trouble was, she was fighting her own urge to return to the Point as hard as she was fighting Trish.

"*Please.*" The little girl scrunched her whole body with exertion. "I'll do seven extra sets. I'll finish the whole chapter. By the weekend I promise. That will put me *ahead* of schedule!"

"Trish, I don't know. It might be dangerous." Shannon knew immediately this would only add fuel to the fire, but the words were already coming. "There's something else out there."

Trish's face became the picture of delicious excitement. She leaned across the dinner table. "What?"

Oh, this was going to sound so bizarre. Even to Trish.

Looking ravenous the ten-year-old leaned closer. "Tell me. What?"

Shannon nibbled at her lip. "I found out what kept the horses on the Point." She took a breath. "What still keeps them there. It's another ghost. Another kind of animal."

"Nu-*uhhhhhh!*" Trish's grin vanished.

Shannon felt her own face go stiff. The statement had sounded more than bizarre. It had sounded ridiculous. "Actually, it looks like a prehistoric animal," she went on. Oh, boy. Oh boy, it was sounding really bad, and it was about to get worse.

"I think it must be some kind of dinosaur."

"*Nu-UHHHHHH!*"

Shannon winced. "I know it sounds crazy, but I saw it. Chasing the horses. Right about where your dad found that big fossil bed out there."

The intensity on Trish's face blossomed into a broad smile. "That's not crazy! It's awesome! When did you see it?"

Shannon stared at her for a second or two, nonplused. Then

beginning slowly and gathering speed, she described the experience of the night before. Before she was even finished, Trish was sprinting downstairs into the shop.

"Let's get the field book! My dad's got a field book!"

She returned with an encyclopedic volume bearing drawings and color plates. Together they leafed through to the section labeled *Jurassic.*

"This is the part where the big mean ones start. The meat-eaters." Trish pushed the book at Shannon, leafing pages one by one. "What kind was it?"

Shannon eyed the tome doubtfully. Identifying bones was one thing. But looking up a ghost in a fossil field book was like searching for the Flying Dutchman in a merchant marine directory.

"Trish, I don't think . . . "

Then she saw the picture and got very quiet. "Oh my Heaven," she whispered. "That's it."

The illustration showed a massive two-legged reptile. It had leaped onto the back of a larger but less fortunate creature, which looked to be in its death throes. Two similar predators were approaching from the background like wolves in a pack.

Trish beamed. "It's an allosaurus! Cool!"

Shannon stared. Somehow, seeing it there made it official. Official and unsettlingly real.

"So why do you think *it's* been hanging around all these skillions of years? Huh?"

Shannon was still gazing at the picture. "You got me. Maybe it's just trying to find something to eat."

Trish tipped her head. "Yeah. The food ran out, and it starved. So now it's trying to eat the horses, huh?" Then a look of skepticism stole over her face. "But why are the horses so afraid of it?"

"Wouldn't you be afraid if it were trying to eat you?"

"But that's different. I mean, they're already dead. What've they got to lose?"

Shannon set the book on the table. "I don't know," she said. "Maybe nothing. Maybe they just think they have something to lose."

"Well, it can't hurt us. Ghosts can't hurt you, my dad said. You can't even feel a ghost because when you try to touch it your hand goes right through like smoke and that's how you can tell it's a ghost."

Deep in thought, Shannon was only half listening.

"So," Trish went on, "there's no reason we can't go out and see them, is there?" She turned. "I'll go hook up the trailer. I know how. I'll just need a little help."

Shannon's eyes focused as Trish reached the doorway.

"You wait just a minute, young lady." Her voice was even firmer than she had intended. Trish stopped, her shoulders drooping, just short of admitting total defeat.

"Come *on*," she begged. "We gotta go out there."

Shannon just sat and looked at her. Why did she feel such an intense compulsion to do precisely what Trish was asking?

The image from the dream seemed to drift from the back of her mind, and for a moment Shannon was flying through the night once more, riding the Appaloosa to freedom.

They stared at each other.

"*Please?*"

Slowly Shannon closed the field book. "I think if we go, we should do more than just look at the horses." Even though she had begun to feel her heart pulsing at the base of her throat, she allowed a smile to steal across her face. "I think we should try to help them. Don't you?"

There was an unearthly stillness outside the window after Shannon docked Porter's truck in the parking lot. A sound of tires munching gravel, a final stutter of exhaust in the muffler, and then nothing. No wind, no crickets. The silence on the Point seemed complete.

"Is this where we see them?" Trish's voice was mostly breath.

"Yes," Shannon answered. "Stay here." She opened the door and peered into the night before making her way to the horse trailer.

She'd been having second thoughts ever since they'd hit the turnoff. Maybe this wasn't such a good idea after all. Not at all. Her mind kept asking what Porter would say about all this. Or aside from that, what her own mother would say. Yes, weird as it was, that thought had seemed most persistent. Given the necessity, how could she explain this to her mother?

Actually, Mom, it's not that complicated. See, Trish is going to lure a big herd of ghost-horses to freedom, while I act as a decoy for a prehistoric monster.

That much had been more than enough, and her brain had gone to work immediately to change the subject. So much for the explanation. Good thing Mom was in Flagstaff.

Shannon swung open the trailer. Doc stood placidly inside, already saddled. She stepped inside and grasped his reins. In spite of her misgivings, here she was. And after all of the effort she and Trish had exerted to get here, she would feel too foolish turning back now. She guided the horse out onto the pavement.

A whisper erupted at Shannon's elbow. She jumped. Doc blinked.

"You see anything yet?" Trish asked in a low voice.

"Trish, I asked you to stay in the truck."

"I'll stay close by, I promise. Let me get the water thing ready."

Trotting around the trailer, Trish hopped into the bed of the pick-up and came out with a twenty-gallon washtub. She lugged it toward the nearby spigot while Shannon checked the cinch on Doc's saddle.

"Fill it about halfway," Shannon said. "Any more will be too heavy. Then you're back in the truck." She had considered the child's safety already and decided she should be okay as long as she spent most of her time in Porter's pickup.

Shannon slipped Doc's bridle over his halter. The horse's safety was another issue. In many spots the mesa was like a natural obstacle course. Yet if she kept her distance from the allosaurus and chose her route carefully, the risks should be minimal. At just past full, the moon would give them enough light to see, and the Morgan would be sure-footed enough to handle himself.

Shannon thought about the picture in the field book. How safe would she be herself?

Ghosts can't hurt you, my dad said. You can't even feel a ghost because when you try to touch it your hand goes right through like smoke and that's how you can tell it's a ghost.

She let Trish's assertion run through her head as she recalled the fierceness and speed with which the beast had attacked the fallen mustang. Porter's declaration might be reassuring to Trish, but in Shannon's view his expert opinion ended with paleontology. Who knew what the rules were here? If indeed there were rules. And what if this thing weren't a ghost at all? What if it were some other sort of paranormal boogey-creature that nobody had ever heard of before, let alone labeled?

Such comforting thoughts.

She felt a tug on a belt loop. "It's full," Trish said.

"Okay," Shannon answered. Her mouth had grown dry. "Let's load it in."

Together they hefted the tub and staggered with it, finally banging it onto the bed of the empty trailer. Puffing, they stood side by side, scanning the dark desert.

"Now what do we do?" Trish whispered.

"We leave the doors open and wait." Shannon gave her shoulder a pat. "Me out here, you in the truck. Go on." She walked over and took Doc by the reins. For the first time he seemed a bit edgy.

Perhaps they would see nothing. That had occurred to Shannon from the start, and it was the most disturbing risk of all, wasn't it? The risk of discovering that Shannon's apparitions existed only in her mind. Might she be just a little sicker than she thought? Could this whole thing with Ronny be pushing her over the edge? What if the horses appeared again in all their supernatural splendor and Shannon was the only one who could see them?

What then?

At her side, as if in reply, there was a tiny strangled sound. Trish's fist locked onto Shannon's arm like a clamp, her eyes swelling like dark silver dollars.

"Oh, crap," Trish managed, and pointed. "It's them."

Shannon hurled a gaze out across the mesa.

Three pale shapes emerged over a rise, shadowless in the moonlight. Others spilled over the top after them. Half-galloping, half-flying, they streamed through the desert toward the open blacktop of the parking lot.

Something made a low rumble in Doc's throat. The horse snorted once and took a step backward. Shannon gave Trish a shaky nudge toward the truck.

"Hurry," Shannon said. "Start up the engine before they get here." Trish clung to Shannon's arm like a bug transfixed by some king-sized light. Shannon shoved harder. "Go *on*," she urged. "Stay on the road, keep it in first, and make sure they're behind you all the way. And don't go too fast! *Scoot!*"

Trish turned and ran. Shannon grabbed Doc's reins and slung herself into the saddle. Behind her Porter's GMC roared to life and ground into gear. She patted Doc on the neck. "Let's go, boy," she whispered and gave a kick with her heels. The Morgan lowered his head, humped his back, and raced out onto the mesa.

Threading a path across the broken landscape, Shannon flew. Beside, on her right, the ghost-horses shot past like a torrent of fog, rushing toward the departing water tub. Doc veered, giving them a wide berth. Shannon guided him out around the lip of the canyon. Then she turned him north and whipped him with her reins. Leaving the pickup far behind, the Morgan thundered forward, weaving through rocks and trees and finally breaking back out onto the road.

A jolt of panic sent a lump into Shannon's throat.

Before her, distant but closing fast, the narrow neck sat bathed in moonlight. The *déjà vu* was undeniable. This was the same scene that Shannon had looked upon before, riding the Appaloosa in her dream.

She felt her limbs go watery. In that instant, weak with fear, she felt an almost irresistible urge to turn back. But she couldn't turn back. She wouldn't, not now. Instead she sank into the saddle and clenched her teeth and kicked at Doc's flanks with all of her might.

That was when, from just beyond the passage, a behemoth shadow lurched from the darkness and spread cavernous jaws.

Doc pulled up and reared. Shannon tipped, grappled, and managed to hang on. A terrified squeal erupted from the horse's throat. The animal wheeled around, regained its footing, and sped off the roadway into the desert. Shannon hurled a quick glance back over her shoulder. With a thrill of terror she realized her plan was working. The shadow was coming. The beast was after them.

Shannon felt Doc take to the air. She snapped her head to the front and let her body move with him. Beneath them a gully slipped past in a blur. The horse came down smooth on the other side. He cut left between two junipers and out onto a clearing of sage. There was a splintering crash immediately behind.

The junipers! Shannon's thoughts reeled in confusion and fear. *That sound was the trees! It plowed right through them! How on earth could it be so close?*

She turned again to look. Panic slammed the breath from her lungs.

The allosaurus tore through the darkness with unbelievable speed. Its legs pistoned like enormous pile-drivers, and in two quick lopes the thing was towering at Shannon's side. She could hear the thud of its footfalls, see the sinews ripple in its neck as it turned its undulating head toward her face. White breath jetted from its nostrils into the cold night air. The thing curled back scaled lips to show its teeth.

This was no nebulous phantasm. This was a living, breathing monster.

Merciful heaven, Shannon's mind screamed, *is this real? How in heaven's name could this be real?*

Recoiling its head, the beast lunged and snapped.

Shannon screamed out loud. She toppled from the saddle. The ground bounced savagely against her side, pounding the breath from her lungs. Doc's hoofbeats retreated into the night. Shannon rolled, fighting to breathe. Her heartbeat roared in her ears. She looked up.

The allosaurus took just one more leap after the fleeing horse. Then it dug an enormous claw into the earth and pivoted, its tail sweeping in counterbalance. For a moment it stood poised, scanning the darkness, sucking huge draughts of air. Shannon froze, but the beast spotted her anyway.

Doc was gone. But she would be easy prey.

Still fighting for breath, Shannon scrambled to her feet and ran. Behind her the allosaurus let out a hissing snort. She could hear it coming. To the side a cluster of rocks jutted skyward. A crevice split them down the middle. She slipped inside as her breath returned, and her lungs responded with a wavering scream.

A foreleg swept into the crevice, groping. Claws rasped against stone. Shannon fell forward and into open air on the formation's far side. She tried to get up but her legs buckled in fatigue and fear. Her strength was gone.

Above her a dark shape blotted out the moon. The allosaurus had rounded the rocks. It crouched above her now, its tail slithering, dry and heavy. The beast peered down with tiny, glinting eyes and tipped its head like a bird. Then it bared its teeth for the last time. Shannon opened her own mouth to scream again. Nothing came out but a shuddering moan.

The monster fell upon her.

Like a gust of wind from some primordial bog, something rank and humid hit her squarely. Shannon grunted with the weight of it, then gasped to feel it pass through her chest and disappear. She lay coughing, trying to expel whatever it was from her lungs. Then she found there was really nothing there to expel.

Panting, she rolled onto her side. After a while she stood.

The desert was quiet again. The allosaurus had disappeared, just as it had in the burst of lightning the night before. Still shaking, Shannon made her way to the other side of the formation and scanned the desert to make sure.

The monster was nowhere to be seen. What was more it had left no signs behind to indicate its presence at all. No claw prints scarred the clearing. No shattered trees littered the gully.

Astonished, Shannon breathed something that almost sounded like laughter from her lungs. Everything had been an illusion. It was all a trick of the haunt. In the end Trish had been right. The beast that had seemed to shake the earth in its deadly pursuit had been as impalpable as smoke. In spite of Shannon's terror, the monster had possessed no power to hurt her at all.

She stood blinking numbly at the horizon, trying to grasp the full meaning of what her mind was telling her.

"Shannon! Shannon!" A small voice warbled faraway behind her. Shannon shook herself out of the daze and found enough strength in her legs to climb to the top of a stony mound. Thirty yards away Trish had parked her father's truck and was standing in the headlights. Doc stood beside her. Shannon called back, waving her arms. They felt very heavy.

"Shannon, look!" Trish cried. She motioned away to the north. "They made it! Do you see them? They made it, they got away! They're free!"

Despite her exhaustion Shannon felt a rush of jubilation. She looked into the darkness, past the Point's neck, far out into the open range. Barely visible, like a ripple of moonlight on flowing water, the ghost-herd ran free. Shannon felt tears brim in her eyes. No wonder she had felt so compelled to help them escape. Somehow a part of her seemed to have been freed along with them.

She waved just once after the silver Appaloosa. Then she began her weary trek back to where Trish waited on the road.

Two days later, scant hours after Shannon had returned from her stay with Trish, Ronny Call appeared on her doorstep. When she spied a clock later, Shannon found that their conversation had lasted nearly thirty-five minutes. She was surprised that he had stayed so long without being asked inside.

Ronny had done most of the talking. Shannon had mostly listened, the bulk of her responses confined to a single word.

"No."

Ronny's demeanor had shifted, slowly at first but with increasing speed, from promising and conciliatory to plaintive to desperately abusive. Finally, ranting threats and obscenities, he had stomped to his car and squealed away.

Shannon had closed the door, walked up to the bedroom, lain on her aunt's comforter, and cried. Her pain was dark and bitter. It was a pain so vast, she feared, that in venting itself it might tear its way out and leave a wound too enormous to heal. She found instead that as the tears began to thin, they left an aftertaste of unexpected sweetness and relief.

After a while Shannon opened her eyes. Her world was still intact. Aunt Helen's florid walls stood quietly around her, painted in autumn sunlight. Shannon lay still in a broad amber shaft, feeling the warmth on her arm and her face. She watched the shadows of the curtains play on the closet doors and thought about ghosts. From there her thoughts drifted back and forth, and finally a wave of euphoric happiness washed over her. She realized that for the first time in years, she had been thinking about where she would go and what she would do instead of where Ronny's life would take her.

Shannon allowed her mind to wander until it began straying too far into the future, then called it back. She had no idea what the upcoming days and weeks would bring. She had already resolved not to concern herself with those until they arrived. She had made that decision yesterday morning, when she had called the State Bar Association for a legal referral.

After a while she looked at the clock. School would let out in an hour, and her tutoring appointments would begin. If she left now she would have just enough time to go downtown and back. There was a sidewalk sale at the shop on Second South and Main. She had noticed it the previous afternoon on her way out of the attorney's office. She had enough to buy a new blouse. If she was going to dinner with the Talbots tonight to celebrate Porter's contract with the university, she would want to look nice for the occasion.

RUMORS OF MY DEATH

LYN WORTHEN

was sitting in my usual booth at my favorite diner, casually reading the *Deseret News*, while I sipped my sugar-free, imitation orange-flavored breakfast drink, when I spied a picture of myself on page B-5. Not the kind of guy to look a gift horse in the mouth, I decided to see what the *News* had to say about me this time.

They said I was dead.

This came as a bit of a surprise, so I read on to see just how my demise had occurred. According to the obituary, "popular columnist Kim Taylor"—that's me—died in an aircar accident on the Bonneville Salt Flats two days before. I was survived by my "wife, Chris Taylor, who was currently out of the country," and my urn "could be visited at the Little Cottonwood Crematorium for the next three days before being shipped to the grieving widow." Apparently in my *Instant Will* I had bequeathed "all my assets and properties to Deseret Industries," thus neatly avoiding death taxes.

Well, aside from the most obvious fact that I was sitting there, very much alive, reading all of this, it was perfectly clear to me that they had really screwed up this time. Not only had I not been to the Flats in at least a month, maybe two, I have an excellent record and have never wrecked my aircar. Well, not seriously. OK, not seriously enough to have killed me. Yet.

Also Chris wasn't out of the country. She was simply on the other side of it, visiting relatives in Nantucket. Indefinitely. I don't think she would have appreciated being billed as my "grieving widow" either.

The tip-off that this was somebody's idea of a joke was the idea of the crematorium. They had been promising us for years that the technology was "almost to the point" where someone near death could be frozen and later repaired and revived. I had signed up two years ago. I figured they'd have to practice on somebody and it might as well be somebody who didn't care instead of someone who had a real reason to come back from the dead.

I did like the touch about having left everything to Deseret Industries though. I hadn't thought of that myself, but I wished I had. Those people distribute things in their multistate thrift-shop network so efficiently that Chris wouldn't be able to recover a fraction of her belongings by the time she flew back from Nantucket.

Well, I had enjoyed the practical joke, but it was time to find out who the perpetrator was so I could start planning my revenge. I popped out my phone, but there was no dial tone, only a mechanical voice repeating "This number has been disconnected" and instructing me to call the Cellular business office with any inquiries I might have.

Fine, that would be my second call. In the meantime I slid my Call-Anywhere card through the payphone reader to make what should have been a simple call. The vid-screen blinked through a series of messages about card privileges having been revoked and if I still wanted to make a call would I please insert the proper change into the machine?

I never carry cash.

Since I'm a regular customer, I was able to talk the waitress out of enough change to call the newspaper where I was given some song-and-dance about not being able to give out the information I was requesting over the telephone and if I would like to come to their offices in person, with proper identification as a relative of the deceased, and fill out the necessary paperwork, then perhaps my question could be addressed. Good God!

I put breakfast on my account (I guess no one at the diner knew I was dead yet), and headed to my aircar, both impressed with my tormentor's skill at pulling off this joke and determined to do him one better, or her. But first I would have to determine the extent of the joke. I didn't think the *Deseret News* would print an obituary without some verification that the deceased in question was actually dead, so I headed over to their business office to pull a few strings and find out who had submitted the obit.

As a syndicated columnist I don't really work for the *News* and therefore don't rate a parking space. But I do have friends, and one of those friends owed me a favor once upon a time, a long time ago, and I've been one of the privileged few who doesn't have to fight for parking in metropolitan Salt Lake City ever since. Until today. When I arrived at the garage, I found my usual parking spot all right, but there was some guy there putting somebody else's name on it. Even as I sat there and watched him do it, another aircar pulled up, took my space, and settled down for its long winter's nap, the owner strolling off to the elevators as though he owned the place. I was speechless, struck completely dumb for perhaps the second time in my entire life. Not one to let minor inconveniences slow me down, however, I maneuvered my aircar into the nearest empty space, hoped the guy was on vacation, and went into the building.

I stopped counting the number of people who did double-takes as I passed them after one of the newsroom secretaries threw an entire stack of papers in the air at the sight of me. Mumbling something to the effect of "not yet" to various incarnations of "aren't you dead?" I traversed the circuitous route to my desk and did not stop to chat about it.

Whoever it was had gotten to my cubicle too.

A re-recycled paperboard container sat in the walkway, my name-plate neatly taped to the lid. Other than that there was no sign that I, or anyone else for that matter, had ever occupied the cubby. Even the whiteboard had either been bleached or replaced, because there were no stains from the times I had accidentally grabbed a permanent marker to write notes to myself. Every tack had been removed, the floor had been cleaned, and I was sure the tops of the cabinets would pass the white-glove test for the first time in several years. I didn't have a glove, so I didn't bother to try.

This was getting out of hand.

I suspected I was dealing with a pro, so I wasn't surprised when I tried logging onto the computer and was rewarded with an "invalid password" message. But journalists are an inquisitive bunch, so I just typed in one of the many passwords belonging to other *News* reporters that I happen to have "noticed" over the course of my association with the paper. Once in I dug into the obituary files—they're not locked because the reporters use them for research—I took a look at mine. It looked perfectly normal, complete with pertinent vital statistics, the information the paper had printed about the accident, a partial transcript of the *Instant Will*, and the verification of death, which is all I had wanted in the first place, so I dumped a hard copy to the nearest printer.

I couldn't get into the Personnel files, but I did take a look at my latest column, downloaded via the syndicated network for whom I officially am—was?—employed. It had a very touching editorial note appended to it:

This is the last column submitted by Kim Taylor before his tragic demise over the weekend. We will not only miss the wit and wisdom of his columns, but his actual presence around the *Deseret News* offices as well. The editorial staff joins with his grieving widow in wishing him the best of whatever the next life holds.

I couldn't believe it. Somebody had gone to a lot of trouble. All of a sudden I got this chill—it started at the base of my neck and chain-reacted its way down my spine, spreading out along my arms and legs until it hit my fingers and toes. What if I was really dead, and just didn't know it?

Absurd.

Dead people didn't borrow money, drive aircars, and use computer terminals. At least not according to any theology I know. No, I was definitely not dead. And I wasn't ready to admit that I was until I saw the coroner's report. So I congratulated the assembled gawkers on their collective effort and asked how many of them it had taken to pull this hoax off. After being met with a bevy of blank looks, I headed off to the morgue in search of a "Dr. M. Jordan," to see what he had to say.

Dr. Jordan, when I finally found him, was working on a body. I was hesitant about interrupting, but he seemed glad for the break. "It happens every now and again," he said, rummaging through a stack of diskettes for the one with my death recorded on it.

"You talk to dead people?"

"Sure. Someone will come in and say, 'Hey, I'm not dead.' And I'll say, 'Sure you are,' and show them their death certificate. I suppose you want a hard copy?" He was sending the document to print even as I nodded my response. "Anyway, they'll look at the certificate, usually take a copy, then leave. I guess some people just don't want to admit when it's over." He handed me my certificate, complete with his official seal and signature and reached for a new pair of rubber gloves.

I looked at the certificate. It seemed official enough, but I still wasn't about to take the word of a piece of paper and go quietly to my grave. "Who's this?" I asked, pointing to the name of the guy listed as having identified my remains.

Jordan peered at it, then consulted his computer. "According to the police report, Steven Carter was the person on duty on the Flats when you wrecked. He identified you there. I never met him."

"What about the body?"

"What about it?"

"Did it look like me?"

"I wouldn't know. When they brought in the wreckage of your aircar it was mostly a blob of polyurethane with a few bone and metal fragments and a slightly damaged *Instant Will* chip sticking up out of it like a flag. I pronounced it dead. In other words there wasn't much left for the crematorium to dispose of, and your urn probably contains as much of the car as it does of you."

I sighed. Investigative reporting was never really my strong point. That's why I make my living doing humor and satire. Still unless I wanted to roll over, I was now going to have to track down this Steven Carter guy and find out what made him think I was dead. I was on my way out the door when Jordan called me back.

"One piece of advice."

"Yeah?"

"Stay dead. Once the system thinks you're out, it's a whole lot easier to stay out than to get back in."

"I'll remember that."

Stay dead. Sure, Doc. There was one problem with that: aside from the occasional lousy moment, I rather liked being alive.

I dug up a telephone on the temporarily vacant desk of an out-to-lunch city employee. My vid-screen Tele-Directory search turned up listings for two-hundred and eighty-four Carters, but only twenty-seven individuals named Steven, not counting alternate spellings and individuals listed simply as "S." I spent the next thirty-some-odd minutes calling each and asking if they were the Steven Carter who worked out at the Flats. When I finally struck gold, it turned out the guy was at work, and his wife said she didn't expect him back until sometime that evening. Next stop, Bonneville Salt Flats.

Steven Carter was a college student who spent six hours a day, five days a week sitting behind the counter at the Flats, studying. Occasionally the job required him to look up from his books and help someone. Today that someone was me.

"Oh, sure. I remember that accident," he said. "It was a meltdown."

"Yeah. The death certificate said you identified the body."

"Mm-hmm." He sounded wary.

"May I ask how you did that?"

"It wasn't my usual shift," he said as he reached for a large book on the counter and turned a few pages. "I was filling in for one of the other guys, and it was a busy day." He tapped at the page, which had 'Saturday 7/14' written in big letters at the top. "Everyone who comes to speed-test has to sign. Here it is: 'Kim Taylor, SLC, Sector 17, 2:30 p.m.'"

"At 2:30 p.m. last Saturday, I was losing a racquetball game. I was not at the Flats," I said acerbically.

"Hey, look, I just showed the police the register. I'm not responsible for what they did with the information."

"I don't suppose you remember the name of the officer who made the report?" I was fishing, but it was worth a try.

"Sorry."

I was beginning to see what Jordan had meant about it being easier to stay dead. Steven and I consulted the Tele-Directory and found a number of Taylors—not quite as many as there had been Carters, but a sizable number nonetheless. Probably the result of years of polygamy. My listing had already been deleted, and there were no other Kim Taylors listed, which probably explains why the police had decided I was the deceased in question. There were five other "K. Taylors," however, so we called them. The first four were Karla, Kathleen, Kathryn, and Keira, none of whom had ever even been to the Flats. The fifth was picked up by a sultry-voiced answering machine which informed me that "Kim wasn't able to take my call just now, but if I'd like to leave a message she'd get back with me as soon as she was able."

Beep.

"Hello, Kim Taylor. This is Kim Taylor," I said to the machine, "and theoretically one of us is dead. I don't think it's me. I hope it's not you. I'd leave my number, but the phone company thinks I'm the dead one. I'll be calling you; hope you're in."

Beep.

I made a note of her address.

Steven couldn't tell me anything more since the other Kim Taylor had checked him- or-herself in while he was outside talking to another driver. But that and the voice on the answering machine got me to thinking. It had never occurred to me that the occupant of my urn might be a *female* Kim. Why couldn't my parents have jumped on the Jacob-Jared-Jason-Joshua bandwagon, anyway?

At least now I knew this wasn't somebody's idea of a joke. There was actually a dead body, and it wasn't mine. I even had a pretty good idea whose it was. All I had to do now was convince the entire U.S. government that they'd made a mistake. Simple.

By the time I got back home, the utilities had been shut off, and Deseret Industries workers, with their usual industriousness, had cleaned the place out. Everything was gone, including the partial roll of toilet paper in the bathroom. As I sit here writing this, I am indebted to the computer industry for making notebook computers with lightweight, long-lasting batteries, and to my foresightedness in always carrying mine along.

The ATM swallowed my cash-card.

My Master-The-Possibilities card was confiscated when I tried to get a cash advance.

I don't carry American Express, but my guess is that it would have been revoked too, since I left home without it.

I finally went to Kim Taylor's apartment. The other Kim Taylor. It seemed the logical thing to do. She still had a functioning telephone. And a well-stocked kitchen.

I called my lawyer. I called my accountant. I called every public official I knew, to no avail. They all tried to be helpful, saying nice things like, "I'm really sorry about that, Kim. Maybe if you called so-and-so over in such-and-such a department they might be able to help you."

I even called Chris. I got through this morning.

"I thought you were dead."

"A misconception, it seems."

"What a shame. I rather liked the idea of being a rich widow."

"Not so rich, I'm afraid. My possessions were left to D.I. They collected them while I was out researching my demise. Didn't you read the will?"

"Well, what about *my* possessions?"

"They took those, too."

"Thanks a lot!"

"Anytime. Look, Chris, I'd love to sit here and bicker with you, but this is long-distance—"

"If you're dead, who's paying for the call?"

"Kim Taylor."

"I don't suppose you'd care to explain?"

I explained. I don't think she believed me at first, but she had already deposited the check for the life insurance and wasn't too thrilled with the idea of having to give it back. Or the new car.

"Well, sweetheart, as much as I wish I could help you out, just talking to you could get me thrown in jail for insurance fraud."

"Chris!"

"Where would you like your ashes scattered?"

"Chris, this is serious!"

"Really, Kim, it was so nice of you to die when you did. Saves me the cost of a messy divorce. Besides it's much more fashionable to be a widow than just another divorcee."

"Chris!"

"And you left me so well cared for. The insurance ought to be enough to replace all that stuff the D.I. people took."

"Chris, will you be reasonable?"

"I think I'm being perfectly reasonable. Good-bye, darling. Have a nice afterlife."

She hung up.

I suppose it could have been worse. I mean, I could have really been dead and she could have been grief stricken and all that. At least this way I get to have the pleasure of haunting her occasionally and letting her explain me to her friends.

I haven't figured out what I'll do next. I can't stay here indefinitely—sooner or later someone will come looking for the other Kim Taylor. Besides I'm running out of groceries. I continue to submit my daily column to the network in hopes of getting my old job back, but I haven't seen any of them in print.

The *Instant Will* people are advertising their chips as a next-generation product that can take a meltdown and using a photo of my melted remains in their current campaign. I called to let them know that their chip wasn't accurate, but they said since I was dead I didn't have any legal rights in the matter. Nor was I entitled to royalties.

In school our teachers told us of the old days when bureaucracies got bogged down in the shuffling and filing of pieces of paper stuck together with red tape. Now a person's life can be erased in the time it takes to type DECEASED next to the nine-digit number that represents everything you have ever done. Maybe Dr. Jordan was right after all. Lose your number and you cease to exist. Still there are ways to get other numbers. Perhaps I'll just stay dead and create a new identity. Maybe one named Jared.

FINALE

PAT BEZZANT

*J*essica Taylor slipped into the computer alcove off the kitchen to call up the latest weather forecast, hoping a winter storm would provide an excuse for skipping the New Year's Eve party.

She heard the sudden clatter and clang of pots and pans pulled from the kitchen cupboards. At least it provided a noise trail. Her seven-month-old daughter was safe—for now.

Scanning down to the local forecast, Jessica read, "Weather for the Wasatch Front, December 31, 1999: clear and cold, with overnight lows expected in the high teens. Tomorrow—" Who cared about tomorrow? More out of habit than for any real interest, Jessie punched up headline news: "Millions prepare for world's end tonight."

She hit the power switch, and the screen went blank. Jessica stared at the monitor even after the low moan of the computer fan died.

"Jessie, what are you doing? We're going to be late."

Jessica turned from the blackness of the screen to face her husband. Seeing Eric in a tuxedo was a rare enough event that she looked at him as if they were newly met, feeling a rush of pride in her spouse. He stood in the doorway, his blond hair shining under the hall light, as he struggled with the red bow tie that matched his cummerbund.

On her way to the kitchen, she paused long enough to straighten his tie. "I hope the red isn't too flamboyant."

The baby looked up at the sound of her voice and wiggled her delight, grabbing another lid. Jessica pulled the aluminum lid from her baby's hand and began replacing the pots and pans. It was like running up the down escalator as Erica pulled one out for every two Jessica put in.

"You've got to be kidding," Eric said, following her into the kitchen. "With Greg Peyton always stirring things up, a junior partner in a red tie isn't going to shock anyone."

"Don't think you can get away with nonsense the way Greg does," she said, standing to face him. "You're not the pampered nephew of a senior partner, thank God."

"I think I look great in red."

Jessica ignored him to return to her pans, Erica now clearly ahead in her race to empty the cupboard. "It seems the business world is getting more conservative every day, and you don't want to do anything to—"

"Arriving late isn't exactly what I'd recommend for a good impression," Eric said.

Jessica stood up, the baby riding on her hip. Eric put his arms around them both and whispered. "Or are you going in your bathrobe?" He slipped a hand along her neck, lifting her long dark hair to kiss her behind her ear.

"Here, this will help." She handed him the baby and bent down to finish putting the pans away.

"Ushering in a new century is a once in a lifetime experience," he said.

"Not for our baby." She stashed the last pan in the cupboard and took Erica from her husband. She lifted her up and cooed into her face, "You're going to live to be a hundred so you can go to a twenty-second-century party, aren't you sweetheart."

Erica smiled with her mouth wide open and grabbed two fistfuls of hair. Eric pried open the little hands. Jessica hugged the baby to her, saying over and over in her mind, "You'll live a long and happy life. You'll live a long and happy life. You'll live a long . . . "

"I'm leaving for the sitter now," Eric said. "Hurry and get dressed."

At that moment Jessica felt cold fear rise up to crowd out her ability to rationalize it away. She stood still, willing herself to breathe slowly, calmly, but the fear wouldn't be fought off. She followed her husband into the living room. He was putting on his coat.

"I don't know about tonight," she said.

Eric continued buttoning his coat, "What do you mean?"

"I mean, I don't know about going out tonight."

Eric gave up buttoning. "What are you talking about? You spent weeks lining up a sitter. You spent $500 on a black dress."

"I know."

Jessica felt ridiculous trying to put her feelings into words. She almost decided to ignore her apprehensions and send her husband for the baby-sitter after all. But she couldn't.

"I don't feel right about leaving the baby."

"Oh, I don't believe it! The party's with all our friends from the firm who said you'd disappear if we ever had a baby."

"I know."

"We're going to show them life goes on after parenthood. It's all planned." He smiled at his wording. "No pun intended."

Jessica smiled and even managed a laugh. If he were in good humor, maybe he would be open to compromise. "We could take the baby with us."

She freed her hair from the grip of the baby's hand. She'd spent hours curling it so she would project the image of an attractive, intelligent woman instead of a harried housewife and mother. She turned the squirming baby loose on the carpet.

"Jessie, it's New Year's Eve. You can't keep the baby out that late. Besides children are definitely not invited."

She could hear the beginning of a whine in Eric's voice. She hated it when he whined.

Jessica left the living room for the basement. She called behind her, "Don't let Erica fall down the stairs."

When Jessie returned with the portacrib, her husband had taken off his coat and was seated with Erica on the blue floral sofa, busily thwarting the baby's attempt to put his silk tie in her mouth. When he saw the portacrib he groaned. "Oh, no. You're joking, right?"

"I'll get myself ready and pack the diaper bag while you run over and pay the sitter. It's only right since we're canceling out at the last minute." While she talked she took Erica from her husband and started down the hall to the bedroom. The portacrib stood in the middle of the floor, a monument to Jessie's determination to take the baby.

Half an hour later Erica sat in her car seat bundled up in a pink snowsuit decorated with an embroidered bunny. Eric hadn't said much to Jessie after returning from the sitter's. She promised herself she would cheer him up.

Jessica reached across to Eric with both hands and gave his arm a hug. "It won't be so bad having Erica along. She'll go right to sleep."

"I guess we could say our sitter canceled out at the last minute," Eric said.

She smiled. "With a mind like that, it's a good thing you went to law school."

"I'm not the only lawyer here."

"If you go in there with that story, someone will tell you to sue the girl for breach of contract and hustle to take the case."

Eric laughed but sobered quickly to ask, "What's with not leaving the baby? You've left her often enough before. In fact, judging from the sitting bill you ran up doing Christmas shopping, I'm surprised Erica remembers who you are."

She gave his arm another squeeze. "Well, it *is* an 'End of the World' party. We'll just tell everyone we wanted to all go out together!"

She tried to end with a laugh, but it wouldn't come.

Eric groaned. "I hope you're joking."

She let go of his arm and stared out into the clear winter night. "Of course I'm joking." Then she added quietly, "I hope."

"Come on." He turned east on Eleventh Avenue, glancing at his wife between each statement. "We've laughed for months over all the hoopla for the year 2,000—the hysteria about the world's end. That's the whole point of the party. Hell, we planned it last New Year's Eve."

"I know."

She concentrated on her hands.

"Jessie, you've never been religious. When did you start worrying about Armageddon?"

"It's not just the evangelists. Almost every day there is a guest on one program or another— "

"You've been watching too many talk shows."

Jessica put her hand on the dashboard and looked back. "Why didn't you turn on Terrace Hills? It's shorter."

"I thought it would be nice to drive by the cemetery. It will get us in the mood for the party."

Jessie looked out her window at the tombstones in City Cemetery. The monuments looked gray against the snow. The somber white of the Memorial Mausoleum hemmed the left side of the road. Up the hill Jessica could see the bright lights from the Jamesons' house, still five minutes away by the roundabout route her husband had selected.

"How would you feel if something horrible happened when Erica was with a sitter? What if there was a landslide or an earthquake or a tornado or . . ."

"I don't believe I'm hearing this! Where's that hard-nosed attorney I married?"

He reached over to take her hand, but she snatched it away. "Don't patronize me!"

Erica started fussing in the back. Jessie turned around and patted her legs. Eric made a left at the top of the hill. They would be at the party soon. She didn't want to go in with an unresolved quarrel between them, but how could she get him to understand? He probably thought her brain had eroded during postpartum blues.

"I can't explain in a logical way how I feel," she said. "It isn't logical. I don't know. It's like being afraid of the dark or something. Don't worry. I'll get over it."

Eric took his wife's hand and gave it a squeeze. "I hope so." When she looked at him, he smiled at her. "If not you'll cause a crash in the baby-sitting industry."

Jessica laughed.

Eric pulled their Toyota 4-Runner into a small parking place near the house. "I hope the Jamesons like babies."

"Oh, I forgot to tell you. I called Mrs. Jameson when you went to the sitter's. She said she would just 'looove' to see Erica."

"That's a relief." He got out and opened the back to get the portacrib. Jessie took the baby and the diaper bag. Mrs. Jameson answered the door wearing a lovely, floor-length black dress, her gray hair piled high on her head.

"Jessica, dear, how wonderful to see you. It's been such a long time. Now let me see that baby. How clever of you two to name her after you both. Oh, David, have you seen the Taylors' baby? Her name is Eric-ca, get it? Named for Eric *and* Jessica. Isn't it wonderful?"

Mrs. Jameson's run of patter kept Jessie well occupied while she led them up the stairs off the entryway to the room where they could stash their coats and the portacrib. "The baby will be all right in here, don't you think, dear, unless you think it's too cold? I always keep the house cool when we have a party. You know how hot it can get with a lot of people drinking champagne. Do you think the baby will need a blanket?"

"I brought her things, thank you, Mrs. Jameson."

"Well, we've got plenty. Do let me know if I can help. If you need milk or anything, just ask Martha. I'm sure you've met her. She's been with us for years. With all the food for the party in the refrigerator, she's the only one who can find anything. Oh, my, there's the doorbell again. Will you excuse me?"

Eric had escaped during the speech. Jessie finished taking off Erica's snowsuit and hung it over the portacrib. With a glance in the hallway mirror, Jessie took Erica down the wide curved staircase to the party. She waved to Bob and Julie as they came through the door. Now that she'd taken her extended leave of absence, Bob and Julie were the only husband-and-wife attorney team at Rollins, Jameson, Cleveland & Grow.

"Well, well, what have we here?" Greg Peyton appeared at the bottom of the stairs, cornering Jessie more quickly than usual. "The lovely Mrs. and Miss Taylor!"

Jessie had hoped that motherhood would lessen Greg's amorous attentions. Instead it seemed to have increased them.

Eric saw them come downstairs and crossed over to join his family. He put his arm around his wife. Relieved not to be alone with Greg, she commented briefly, "How nice to see you, Greg. And what an interesting tie." Looking at the patterns of green and blue more closely, she said, "Oh, it's a fish!"

Jessie let her husband escort her through the large arch into the Jamesons' spacious living room. Everyone had worn black, as requested. With the art-deco furnishings, the party looked like a scene from a movie—figures in black arranged carefully in a white and black set. Only Erica in her pink, stretch sleeper was out of place. Mozart's *Requiem* permeated the house through large speakers built into the walls. The music was soft but penetrating. Ceiling-to-floor windows were staggered along one wall of the two-story room.

Jessica stood next to a window to admire the view of Salt Lake City, the brilliance of downtown surrounded by lights stretching out in all directions. Erica started slapping at the glass so Jessica moved away. Just then Mr. Jameson walked by.

"Nice to see you, Mr. Jameson," Jessica said. "The view is splendid. It's a lovely house for a party."

"Why, yes," he said. "We thought it would be marvelous to watch the destruction from up here." He spoke loudly to be overheard by those around them, and he got a good laugh, as expected. As a senior partner, any attempt at humor was successful in this crowd.

"Let me get you a drink, Jessica." There was Greg again, ever attentive. "No one should die sober."

"No, thanks, not till I get the baby to bed. She'd have her hands all over it."

Greg accosted Eric. "You're quite a slave driver, old man. Too cheap to hire a baby-sitter? Jessica, darling, you married the wrong guy." With that parting comment he crossed the room to stand by a tall, lovely blonde.

"I don't know why you ever went out with that guy," Eric muttered.

"Greg's not so bad when he's not trying to annoy someone."

Jessie could see by her husband's erect posture that he didn't like his wife defending a former beau. She teased, "And if I recall, the tall, handsome attorney I married had another girlfriend at the time I was seeing Greg."

Eric smiled down at her. He kissed her forehead lightly and was rewarded by Erica who grabbed his hair with both hands.

At that moment Bob and Julie walked over. "I've heard of families getting into your hair," Bob said, "but this is the first time I've actually seen it!"

Eric freed himself with some help from Jessie. "Hi, Bob, Julie. You both look stunning in black."

Julie groaned loudly. "Don't lie. It's horrible. I've never worn black before, and I'll never wear it again. I look like a corpse."

"That's the whole point, Julie," said Bob. "This is the big night!" He slapped Eric on the back and laughed.

Jessie could see Eric's unease with the topic of conversation, and she knew it was her fault. Did he think she was going to get hysterical or something? She joined in the spirit of the conversation more for his sake than her own. "I hope you both have all your affairs in order."

"What affairs? Julie, have you been talking?" Then Bob laughed again. "No, actually, this is the best way to go. All at once. No worries about whether or not you took out enough life insurance, or how long the estate will be in probate. One big bang and that's it."

Julie covered her ears. "Let's change the subject."

"I've got a better idea," said Bob. "Let's change the music. Violins give me a headache. Where's the CD player?"

He addressed his question to Jessica. She glanced at Eric as she answered.

"The player and turntable are in the den just across from the kitchen," she said, wishing everyone would forget that she knew her way around the house because of Greg. "But I wouldn't touch that system without talking to Mr. Jameson first. It's his baby."

"I like the music," said Julie. "What is it?"

"Mozart's *Requiem*," Eric said.

"*Requiem?*" Julie asked. "How dismal! And wearing black was a terrible idea. It makes everyone so gruesome."

"But this is a great place for the party," Bob said. "This house sits between two cemeteries."

"Two?" Eric asked.

"City Cemetery is at the bottom of the hill and LDS Cemetery is up the hill."

"We drove past the city cemetery, but I didn't know about the other one. I never noticed it," Eric said.

"That's the only reason that hillside isn't filled with houses," Bob said. "Prime real estate—all used up by a bunch of corpses."

"Corpses!" Julie shuddered. "I'm standing by Erica. She looks cheerful in pink."

Julie played with Erica, babbling like another baby instead of an attorney. No one seemed to mind the baby. Jessica hoped Eric noticed and wouldn't be angry. When Erica eventually got fussy, Jessica took her upstairs to bed.

She locked the bedroom door before nursing her so they wouldn't be disturbed. After the baby fell asleep, she held her a few minutes longer. Then she laid her gently in the portacrib. Jessie tiptoed to the door even though she knew Erica was a sound sleeper. She turned and smiled at the sleeping baby before turning out the light.

Jessica returned to the party. Time moved along on the sounds of flirtatious conversations and clinking glasses like countless other New Year's Eve parties. Everyone Jessie talked to had a joke about the end of the world. She heard the particularly good ones repeated again and again, as well as several plans to run up personal debt. Being lawyers they debated whether it constituted credit fraud if one really expected creditors to perish. They toasted the end of the world, mourned it with laughter, celebrated with jocularity, but never showed signs of expecting it. Jessie couldn't understand why she of all people felt fear. This was her social circle. She was as well educated as the others in the room, just as intelligent.

But was there a false ring to their laughter? Surely she only imagined it.

Jessie regretted wearing a watch. After 11:30 she looked at it every minute. By 11:45 she knew if she heard one more pun about doomsday, she would embarrass herself and her husband for life—a life she hoped would go on after this stupid New Year's Eve party.

Eric returned to her side and took her hand. "Your hand is clammy," he said. "Do you want another glass of wine?"

Jessie's empty glass surprised her. "I'd better not. I've had too much already."

"How about some water?"

She smiled. "That would be nice."

Eric took the wine glass, but she gave his sleeve a couple of quick tugs before he left. "Don't be gone long."

"Not a chance. The first kiss of the new century is mine!"

Jessie began to relax. Eric had a way of making her feel better. But then it was 11:55, and Eric wasn't back. She started for the door to look for him, but Mrs. Jameson intercepted her.

"I'm so glad you brought little Erica. It's been so long since I've been around a baby. I wish that nephew of mine would settle down and have a family. You and Eric seem so happy."

Happiness was the farthest thing from Jessie's mind. It was 11:56, and Eric wasn't back yet. "Yes, Mrs. Jameson. I'm looking for Eric. Have you seen him?"

"Don't worry about Eric." Mrs. Jameson took Jessie's hand in both of her own. "He will be here by the stroke of midnight, I'm sure. I've noticed the two of you tonight. He never lets another man get you cornered."

Jessie smiled but her face felt tight, as if she posed for a still photograph.

Someone shouted, "Two minutes to midnight!"

Mrs. Jameson released Jessica's hand. Jessie looked at her watch. It read 11:57. It must be slow. How could her watch be slow tonight? She made a beeline for the door without excusing herself from Mrs. Jameson. She literally ran into a man she vaguely remembered as a new client.

"Pardon me."

Jessie had been walking quickly when he had accidentally turned into her path. He took her in his arms to steady her. He was none too steady himself. He must like free champagne.

"This calls for a kiss," he said. "Happy New Year!"

"My turn!"

It was Bob.

He had started to kiss Jessie when Julie gave her husband a quick punch on the arm.

"No fair! You can't kiss Jessie unless Eric is here to kiss me." She took Jessie's arm and began to propel her back toward the center of the room.

"Where is Eric?" Julie asked.

"I'm just going to get him. Excuse me, please!"

At that moment, the countdown to midnight began. Jessica thought "It can't be that close to twelve. Someone must have started the countdown early."

"Ten! nine! eight!"

Jessica looked toward the door. There was no sign of Eric.

"Seven! six!"

Maybe she ought to run upstairs to check on Erica.

"Five!"

Everyone in the room shouted the numbers. Jessie couldn't think.

"Four!"

Maybe Eric was with the baby.

"Three!"

Jessie stopped breathing.

"Two!

"Oh, God!" she thought.

"One—"

The room exploded with the combination of cheers and shouts of Happy New Year. Everyone kissed everyone else.

Still there was no Eric.

Midnight had come and gone. She had been a witless fool to get so tense.

But where was Eric?

Jessie's fear had climaxed into nothing. It left her exhausted and empty with the void rapidly filling with anger.

Where was Eric?

Mr. Rollins rapped on his glass for attention. The room became quiet. Too quiet.

Mr. Rollins, as a founding member of their successful firm, commanded complete attention. But the stillness felt deeper than that. Then

Jessica realized there was no music. It must have been turned off during all the shouting when no one would have noticed. She reasoned it was the absence of music that made the room so deathly still.

What a relief to hear Mr. Rollins. He was certainly no doomsday prophet.

The crowd moved forward when Mr. Rollins called for attention. Jessie stood back near the entranceway to the hall. Rollins spoke in a strong, deep voice. He complimented the attorneys, the staff, and their families for their contributions to the firm.

Jessica jumped when Eric came up from behind her and took her arm. "Jessie, I have to tell you . . . "

"Shhh." Jessica bit back her desire to grill him about where he'd been when she'd needed him. One didn't whisper to one another when Mr. Rollins gave a speech.

"Listen, Jessie . . . "

Jessie felt her cheeks flush when Mr. Jameson turned around to tell them to be quiet. She couldn't believe it when Eric started to whisper again.

"Greg is . . . "

Jessica felt cold fury. Why had Eric been with Greg, whom he didn't even like, when he knew she needed him with her? She pulled away from him, giving him as nasty a glare as possible.

Rollins was saying, "At the beginning of the twentieth century, the world was a very big place."

Eric moved to Jessica's ear again. "Come on out to the hall."

Rollins deep voice said, "Economic systems were only loosely connected with light international trade . . . "

Eric tried to lead Jessica out, but she shook his arm off. Why didn't he get the message to shut up and shut up quick?

"Economic integration has had its negative side," Rollins continued. "As our planet has shrunk . . . "

"Jessica, come now!"

"But if we could peek in at a party a century ago and listen to a speech like the one I am giving now, what would have been said?"

Jessica allowed herself to be led away to stand by the windows more as a way to hear the speech than to listen to what Eric wanted to say.

"Would anyone have dared hope that in the twentieth century London would be but a few hours from New York by transatlantic air travel? That machines small enough to fit in a hand would do equations in less than a second that once took men hours? Would anyone have dared dream that the twentieth century would land a man on the moon? I think not.

"We are in difficult times. The space age has been declared dead by the economic woes of men who can't afford to dream. But surely the twenty-first century will move man to the stars."

Rollins paused then. No one spoke.

Eric turned Jessie to face him. Just as he opened his mouth to talk, she heard a distant rumble. The lights flickered off, then on, then off as the room boomed with the sounds of thundering destruction. Jessica covered her ears. A woman's scream barely pierced the roar. The floor vibrated. The house would fall down! She had to get upstairs, to Erica!

But she couldn't move. Eric held her tight. She fought to get free. From behind him she could see the motion of bodies, unheard above the cracking rumble, as people pushed one another and fell.

Jessie fought to free herself from Eric's embrace. She must get to Erica. He was shouting in her ear, but she could not sift his words out from the roar that made her head feel like it would pop. She had to get to her baby!

Eric yelled again, "It's a joke! Nothing but a dumb joke!"

Jessie stopped struggling against her husband. The violent noise faded as if a thunderstorm moved away. A joke? Jessie heard weeping and groaning.

Then she realized that light filtered in from the lights in the yard. Someone had just flipped a breaker switch to throw the house into darkness. Below them the lights of Salt Lake City shone without wavering.

The sound of a needle being carelessly lifted from a turntable was picked up on the speakers. Then the lights went on.

When Jessie stopped struggling to get away, Eric relaxed his grasp of her. Now she pulled away, looking at him as if he were a stranger. A joke!

He reached for her again, and she was too numb to move away. Hugging her close he said, "Don't think I had anything to do with it. I went to the kitchen to get your water. There was Greg running an extension cord from outside into the den for the sound system. I used every argument I could think of to talk him out of it. At least I slowed him down so he didn't make it right at midnight. I came out to tell you, knowing you were nervous anyway."

Jessica's eyes looked over her husband's shoulder. Bob and Julie were just crawling out from under the grand piano. The archway to the hall had about ten people, mostly men, crowded under it. Jessica gasped as she saw Mrs. Jameson. She was on her hands and knees and was having trouble getting up.

Eric turned to see who Jessie was looking at and immediately left her to help Mrs. Jameson. Apparently someone had knocked her over in the darkness. Her iron-gray hair, always perfectly arranged, had been crunched in on one side. Had she actually been stepped on? Eric helped her to a sofa.

Jessie knew she ought to help, but she was part of the frozen scene around her. A floor lamp had been knocked over. Wine and champagne glasses were on the floor, many broken, their contents spilled out on the white carpet. Looking at the room and its occupants, one would think there had actually been an earthquake. Many of her friends, her former colleagues, were in tears. Mr. Rollins had an arm around his wife. She had been standing near him for his speech. He at least still had his glass in his hand.

TJ, one of the junior partners, had a bloody nose. He stood in the center of the room, oblivious to the blood creating a dark spot on his black coat and staining his shirt red and dripping onto the carpet. Jessie looked away.

"Happy New Year!"

Greg's voice boomed into the room. When people in the entranceway moved so he could see into the living room, he stopped in mid-stride.

The doorway crowd recovered first. There were a few embarrassed chuckles, but mostly sheepish grins. A few even had the presence of mind to forget their own awkwardness and help those injured in the panic.

At their movement Jessie roused herself and picked up some napkins from a table. She crossed to the center of the room to help TJ get his nosebleed under control. When she handed him the napkins, it was as if she awakened him from sleepwalking.

"Oh, Jessica, thank you," he mumbled through the napkins. "Someone slammed into me in the dark."

"You'd better sit down." She tried to lead him to one of the many sofas.

"No, no. Let me get to a bathroom."

Jessie walked with him. Everyone in their path gave them wide clearance. She turned on the cold water faucet for him and took the soaked napkins, throwing them into the trash. She snatched a guest towel from its ring with a fleeting regret about ruining Mrs. Jameson's towel. A few ruined towels were insignificant when compared with the mess in the living room.

TJ mumbled through the towel. "I really appreciate your help. I don't know what hit me."

"Someone's idea of a joke."

Jessie didn't add that she knew whose idea it had been.

"I'll be all right," he said. "You can get back to the party."

"Not much of a party, anymore. Are you sure you'll be all right?"

"Yes, thanks. You're terrific." Coming through a layer of cloth, it was a muffled compliment.

She smiled at him. "I'm going to check on the baby. I'll see how you're doing in a few minutes."

Leaving TJ, Jessie went upstairs, opening the door to peek in at Erica. The light from the hall shone on her sleeping child. Jessie shut the door again, trading the tranquillity of one scene for the confusion of another.

Mrs. Jameson was not up to telling everyone not to worry about the mess. Her husband sat beside her on the sofa, helping hold an ice pack on the left side of her face. Their maid Martha took charge of supervising the clean up, not bothered at all that men and women in formal clothing were cleaning house. Jessie picked up broken glass and the scattered glasses that remained intact, cleaning wine off a couple of wood tables.

As everyone worked together she felt a camaraderie develop that she'd never experienced working with these people in the office. The feeling of good will may even have extended to Greg and the date who had served as his accomplice at the breaker box. Greg, on his knees, scrubbed the white carpet stained from TJ's nosebleed as if to wipe his own conscience.

The room was in order within half an hour. Only the carefully constructed façades of confidence and sophistication were left damaged.

Some of the guests got ready to leave, but Mr. Rollins called for their attention again. He cleared his throat. "I'm not sure whether I ought to finish my speech." He paused for the nervous laughter to disperse. "But I did want to wish you all the happiest of New Years and prosperity and peace for the next century."

And then he began to sing in his rich baritone, "Should auld acquaintance be forgot, And never brought to mind?"

Everyone joined him, but Erica. She slept.

DEALER

MICHAELENE PENDLETON

eBarron's jackals took their time beating the shit out of Brackett. They enjoyed it. They told him what they were going to do before they did it. Frank, the one with no front teeth, would hold him while the tall blond with a Death From Above tattoo on one bicep worked on him for a while, then they would switch.

Death From Above was imaginative. Frank concentrated on kidney punches and blows to the chest. Death From Above worked over Brackett's face, closing both eyes, breaking his nose, clapping both hands over his ears until they ran blood. He was especially good at groin punches that just missed Brackett's genitals. They didn't break any major bones, and they didn't mash his nuts. Brackett figured they were saving that for the next time.

The beating fell into a rhythm. Closed off in his head, Brackett orchestrated it to the Crusader's Chorus from *Alexander Nevsky*. That kept him together, disconnected from the pain. Until the music ran out.

After a while he stopped feeling any new pain. His body was one red haze of agony and nothing they did to him mattered any more. Death From Above must have recognized that. He called Frank off. Holding Brackett upright with one muscular forearm around Brackett's neck, he said, "Had enough, Dealer? Ready to cooperate now?"

Brackett managed to shape his split lips into "Screw you."

Death laughed. "Maybe later, sweetheart. You're not too pretty right now." He dropped Brackett to the cold concrete floor. "We'll be back.

You don't deal with Rulon, we can keep this up for a long, long time. Think about it."

Brackett couldn't see much with his eyes swollen shut. He heard the door slam and the lock click over. The room, a basement storage unit in what was once the Hotel Utah, felt empty. One part of his mind, sitting way back trying to be divorced from the pain, urged him to try to find a way out. The rest of him just lay there and hurt.

Maybe what hurt most was losing the Kallinikov. He'd had a standing order for that piece for more than two years. It wasn't easy to find. Kallinikov's *First Symphony* was reasonably common, but the *Second* was a rarity. There weren't many copies of it even before Sweep Night when the National Guard and army reserve units had confiscated all foreign music, books, clothes, cars, electronics, every item of foreign manufacture, everything on the proscribed lists that hadn't been voluntarily surrendered. These days, the *Second* was as valuable as the Mormon Tabernacle Choir's Easter chorale set to the *Feuerzauber* from *Die Walküre*. He had a buyer for that one, too, if he ever found it.

He'd finally tracked the Kallinikov to a chemistry professor at the U. They met this morning at a restaurant on Foothill Drive, the prof looking guilty as hell, his nervousness so obvious that Brackett almost backed out of the deal. He watched the prof, potbellied and balding and twitching in the booth, ignoring a cup of what passed for coffee these days, and scanned all the other silent, eye-shaded customers for a long time before he decided the place was clean.

The buy went down quick. He passed the prof's table, caught the man's scared gaze, and jerked his head toward the men's restroom. Eight thousand in old bills to the professor and, in return, a digital audio tape tight-wound on a small spool wrapped in a thin baggie. Brackett stepped into a stall and, after checking the seal on the plastic, shoved the spool up his ass. The charlies at the Sugarhouse checkpoint were fuzz-cheeked kids who seldom had the nerve to body search.

It was more than four miles from Foothill to Sugarhouse but Brackett walked it. Taking the bus made you a target, said you had money to waste. It was easier to slip into the crowds of unemployed homeless that milled along the broad main thoroughfares, passing under the Buy American banners that stretched over the streets, three to a block and flapping in the wind that came from the west, carrying with it an acrid tang from the copper smelters at Magna. He wondered why they bothered hanging the banners; it wasn't as if you had any choice.

The crowds were thick today, soft spring air drawing them out of their shacks and dens, just roaming around in the sun before the soup kitchens opened at noon. Brackett smelled their unwashed stink, saw their drained and empty faces. The old anger, usually only a background noise, surfaced. It pounded through his head with the force of Stravinsky's percussion.

Patriots' Public Radio said that the unemployment rate was holding steady at 23 percent, but Brackett knew they lied. After the economic collapse that followed the nationalization of all industry and the forced divestiture of foreign holdings, the jobless rate had shot up to 47 percent. Yet Brackett saw more sad, hopeless men and women on the streets now than there had been eight years ago when Insulation became national policy. Unemployment had dropped some when all foreign nationals, including those married to Americans or naturalized citizens themselves, were deported; but as the country completed its withdrawal from world markets, the reality was that there were no jobs.

Brackett's anger was bone-deep. The worst of it was that he didn't see it reflected in the faces around him. They only milled and waited for their soup. The angry ones had already been gathered up.

Brackett used the *Largo* from the New World Symphony to keep his own anger off his face. Slouching along with the crowd, his ragged jeans and black windbreaker no cleaner than theirs, his brown hair just as shaggy, dirt lined in the creases of his knuckles, he melted into their sullen silence.

There was nothing wrong with his planning. He just ran out of luck.

"Jackals." The word whispered through the crowd and sliced through the Dvorak playing in Brackett's head. Instinctively, he hunched his shoulders, making himself shorter. An eddy formed, pressing people in on Brackett, no one willing to move.

The woman in front of Brackett, a stringy-haired blonde with a skinny baby on her hip, said, "Are they blues?"

Someone snarled, "Hell, no. It's goddamn state maroons." The woman whimpered and backed into Brackett. But there was no place to go. Farther back, where the word hadn't reached, the hungry mass surged forward, carrying them toward the checkpoint. Brackett kept his head down and shuffled along with everyone else.

The two jackals sat on the hood of a long, black Lincoln, strafing the checkpoint line with cold faces. They were shiny with polished silver buckles and buttons, their expressions hidden behind reflecting sunglasses. Their short-sleeved gray uniforms were sharp-creased and bloused into mirror-bright black jumpboots. The angle of their maroon berets claimed an arrogance that set them above run-of-the-mill checkpoint charlies.

Chainlink fencing funneled the crowd into a grocery store parking lot, clearing the streets for approved traffic. Brackett had no place to go but straight on. The jackals could have been looking for anybody, but the hair on Brackett's neck stood up and prickled. Without being able to see their eyes, he felt their attention rivet on him as the line moved forward. He jammed his hands in his pockets so he wouldn't wipe the sweat that slid down his cheek.

The jackals watched him hand his ID card to the young charlie who, smug with his small handful of authority, took one look at the red striping that labeled Brackett as unemployable because of unAmerican activities and immediately ordered him into the stripsearch canvas tent.

Even though the lump in his rectum felt as big as a baseball, Brackett held himself calm and loose as three stripsearch charlies checked the labels on his clothing and shoes and watch. They went through his wallet and turned out the labels on his shorts and T-shirt, seeming disappointed to find Made in America tags on everything. They matched his Social Security number against his retinal pattern in their computer files. When it cleared, they let him put his clothes back on and stamped the date and time on his daily papers. Brackett released a tightheld breath and walked out of the tent right into the cold grins of the two gray jackals.

"Mr. LeBarron wants to see you," Death From Above said. They shoved him into the deep back seat of the Lincoln and drove to what Brackett still thought of as the Hotel Utah, even though it had been turned into an office building several years before Insulation. Frank slung the big car across 21st South and up the wide, mostly empty expanse of State Street while Death From Above hung one arm over the back of the front seat and watched Brackett with a silent, baretoothed smile. Brackett saw himself reflected in duplicate from the sunglasses and tried to ignore the sudden fear that etched its way up his backbone. He reached for the music, but nothing came into his head.

Rulon LeBarron held no elected office, his name wasn't on any official letterhead, but neither the governor nor the state legislature made any moves that Rulon LeBarron wouldn't like. It was said that he was a jack Mormon renegade, but even the LDS church left LeBarron alone. The church may have had to rent him space in their office building, but they disassociated themselves from him, as far as it was safe to do it, anyway. Of all the people Brackett didn't want to meet, Rulon LeBarron topped the list.

Frank parked the Lincoln in the red zone in front of the building. The two jackals marched Brackett through the landscaping of tulips and daffodils and into a foyer of wine carpet and dark heavy furniture massed with brass fittings. Men in business suits and secretaries in crisp white blouses looked away, suddenly busy elsewhere. With both elbows held in a grip that threatened to numb the nerves, Brackett had no choice but to grit his teeth and move where he was dragged.

LeBarron's suite took up the top floor, displacing what had once been a restaurant. The view from the plate-glass windows encompassed the city from Emigration Canyon and the Uinta Mountains on the east to the islands in the shrinking Great Salt Lake. When the elevator disgorged Brackett and his guards, LeBarron was standing, hands laced behind his back, looking down on the golden statue of the angel Moroni with his trumpet topping the temple that raised its semi-Gothic spires across the street to the west.

LeBarron let them wait in silence for a time before he turned, a smile on his ruddy, affable face. He was a big man, broad with authority, solid in his power. Despite the smile, his eyes were as dead as a snake's. He came around a teak desk the size of a dining table to stand in front of Brackett.

The jackals dropped Brackett's arms. LeBarron made a couple of sucking noises through his front teeth, then said, "I've been told you deal in contraband music, Mr. Brackett."

The fact that LeBarron knew his name scared Brackett more than anything so far. Brackett ignored the swirl in his gut and shook his head. He matched LeBarron's smile. "You've been misinformed. I'm just one of the great unwashed."

LeBarron's smooth forehead creased. "You're a smartass. I don't like smartasses." He nodded to Death From Above. The blond jackal stepped away from Brackett then backhanded him across the mouth, snapping his head back. Brackett felt blood trickle from a split lip.

LeBarron said, "Let's try again. I know who you are. I know you make your living dealing proscribed music. I want to talk some business."

Brackett slowly raised one hand and wiped his chin. "I don't know what you think I can do for you. You've got me mixed up with someone else."

LeBarron exhaled a sharp breath. "I'm not going to waste much time with you, Mr. Brackett. Give me the tape you picked up this morning."

With his mouth gone suddenly dry, Brackett understood why the chemistry professor had been so nervous. "What tape?"

"Get it," LeBarron said.

Death From Above jerked Brackett's arms behind his back, up between his shoulderblades, and bent him double. Frank pulled a surgical glove from a pocket and slowly stretched the tight rubber over his right hand, grinning into Brackett's face. He dragged Brackett's pants and shorts down and dug for the tape.

Brackett tried to keep his rage and shame off his face and knew he failed. "You son of a bitch."

Frank stripped the plastic baggie from the spool, dropping the baggie and glove into a trash can, then handed the tape to LeBarron. LeBarron juggled the tape in his palm. "Kallinikov, I believe? Russian." He shook his head sadly. "Garbage. But, it does establish your profession beyond doubt. Now shall we talk business?"

Through clenched jaws, Brackett said, "Have I got a choice?"

LeBarron laughed, a jovial, friendly sound. "No, Mr. Brackett, you do not. Now that you understand that, our relationship will go much easier. You may put your pants back on."

Brackett felt better with his dick covered up. LeBarron strode around the desk and sat in a high-backed chair. He plucked a cigar from a teak thermidor and let Brackett wait while he went through the ritual of smelling, clipping, and lighting it. Exhaling a corona of sweet blue smoke, he said, "I was dining with a business acquaintance recently. In the course of our conversation, it came out that he is planning to purchase from you a certain piece of illicit music." He drew again on the cigar. "The *Ninth*, by Von Karajan and the Berlin Philharmonic, I believe."

The bastard was playing with him and Brackett didn't like it. "So?"

"So, I want that piece, Mr. Brackett."

Brackett felt his blood slow down and get heavy in his veins. Dealing illegal music with Rulon LeBarron had the earmarks of a suicide run. He'd geared himself up to face jail, but he wasn't ready for this. Several different responses flitted through his mind, none of them of much use.

LeBarron had him, and had the power to do just about anything he chose. Brackett settled for, "I can't sell you that piece. I've already taken money for it. If you know I deal, then you know I deal in exclusive sales. Your 'acquaintance' has already bought the *Ninth*."

"But you haven't delivered it."

"Makes no difference. I gave him my word. We have an agreement."

"Break it, Mr. Brackett."

LeBarron's smooth assurance fired Brackett's resistance. "If I slide out of a deal, my reputation goes to hell. If customers can't trust me to deliver an exclusive product, my business suffers."

LeBarron chuckled. "Reversals happen to every businessman, Mr. Brackett. What you have to decide is if your business reputation is worth your life."

Death From Above slid his arm around Brackett's shoulders. His voice came soft in Brackett's ear. "Pay attention, sweetheart. This is where it gets interesting."

"I want that piece of music, Mr. Brackett."

Brackett shook his head. "I can't sell you that piece. I do have a version by George Szell and the Cleveland—"

"Trash. Von Karajan defined Beethoven for all time. I won't settle for an inferior recording. I'll be generous. I'll double the price you asked for it. That should salve your conscience, Mr. Brackett."

At the smug repetition of his name, emphasis on the *mister*, Brackett felt his good sense snap. Raw anger seared along his nerves. "Do you really think you can buy me that cheap? You bastards took my job. You took my country. You took the rest of the world away from me. You took everything I believed in and twisted it, made it shit. Well, fuck you, *Mr.* LeBarron. This is one time you're going to be disappointed. You don't get the *Ninth*." He set himself, stomach tight, waiting for the jackals to move on him again.

LeBarron's smile never wavered. "Defiance. People of your sort never learn. We'll talk again tomorrow. You may think differently then. Gentlemen, escort Mr. Brackett to the basement. Discuss the matter. See if you can persuade him to be more agreeable."

Now that the jackals' discussion was over for the time being, Brackett didn't feel agreeable. He just hurt.

After a time, the cold of the concrete floor got through the pain.

Shivering hurt so he forced himself to stand up. It took a while. Once he was up, it felt good to lean his battered face against the chill of the wall.

Helpless rage twisted in his gut, hot enough to burn out the fear. He wanted to kill someone. Rulon LeBarron or Death From Above, it didn't much matter which. Preferably both. He reached for the music and pulled in *Götterdämmerung*.

That smooth bastard could have his balls for breakfast before he'd give in.

Brackett broke after the third session. The music was gone, his head empty and echoing. Death From Above proved that the relatively mindless beating they began with was minor compared to the pain that could be inflicted by a truly original mind with access to psychogenic drugs and electric leads. Old methods, maybe, but effective. The most Brackett's pride could manage was to sway on his own two feet as he squinted through blood encrusted eyelids at Rulon LeBarron, and said, "The *Ninth* is yours."

They sat him in a chair in LeBarron's light-washed office. A warm rag rubbed gently at his face and he smelled a tropical flower perfume. A woman's voice said, "Jesus, you really worked him over. It's going to take a while to fix this."

LeBarron's rumble cut across her protest. "Don't worry about it, Lela. Just make him presentable from a distance. I want to get this business over with."

Nothing was making much sense to Brackett. He flinched as a needle slid into the soft skin inside his left elbow. When it pulled out, the pain was already flowing out with it. He floated, silly-happy with the relief.

Lela's breath was warm on his cheek. "Hold still, babe. Going to fix you right up." With one hand she held his head back and dropped an ice pack over his eyes and nose. She took the ice away and put a warm cloth in its place. After a few changes back and forth, Brackett found his eyes would open some.

Lela's face filled his vision. Big, dark eyes and hardlined red lips. Olive skin stretched tight over fragile cheekbones. A lot of black hair and golden hoop earrings. Brackett found himself grinning foolishly at her while she dabbed at his face with a makeup sponge. She set a pair of heavy black plastic sunglasses on his broken nose. "There you go. Ready to face the world."

Things started to come back into focus. Death and Frank were standing behind his chair, Rulon LeBarron ensconced behind the desk with Lela sitting on one corner. LeBarron's easy affability was gone. He didn't need it anymore. "Lela, you drive the car. I have another task for Frank. Take Mr. Brackett to his stash and bring back the merchandise. Here's a list." He handed a piece of paper to Death From Above.

That got through. So the bastard was going to clean him out, take more than just the *Ninth*. Something inside him still wanted to tell LeBarron to go to hell, but his flesh screamed at him to stay quiet. His body, at least, had learned Death's lessons.

When they'd finally let him piss this morning, there was more blood than urine in the weak stream that dribbled out. Something inside felt torn, a deep pain that didn't shout as loudly as the superficial burns and lacerations on his skin, but muttered of serious damage somewhere inside.

Death From Above jerked him out of the chair. "Be nice, sweetheart. Make this easy."

LeBarron had turned back to the window, once again staring down on the golden statue of Moroni atop the temple. His voice followed them from the room. "You're getting off easy. Remember that, Mr. Brackett. You could just as easily be a faceless body floating in the Jordan River."

Brackett's head cleared a bit in the ride down the elevator. Whatever drug Lela had injected into his system let him ride over the pain, let him move almost normally in spite of the grinding ache in his lower back.

At the car, Death patted Lela's butt. "Want me to drive? This machine might be too big for you to handle."

"Asshole," Lela muttered as she slid behind the wheel. She took the Lincoln smoothly through the streets, her hands firm on the wheel.

Brackett slumped into the butter-smooth leather. His head was light enough to float through the top of the car. He felt his heart flutter, its rhythm missing the beat, steadying, then taking off again into a wild fugue. He tried for Vivaldi, but nothing came. The sounds refused to form in his mind.

Death sat wedged in one corner of the deep leather back seat, alert, the ever-present grin stretching his lips. Brackett ignored him as much as possible. He gave directions to Lela, east on 4th, right onto 9th East, then south to Ramona, a quiet, tree-shaded street in the cleared zone, lined with modest brick houses surrounded by small yards planted with fuschia and lilacs. Halfway down the block, Brackett said, "Stop here."

Death shifted in his seat. "Park it, *puta*." In the rearview mirror, Brackett saw Lela's face go hard. "Watch who you're calling a whore. Rulon buys you the same as he buys me." She didn't bother pulling over, just braked and shut off the engine. No one was going to mess with a car with Priority One plates.

The curtain twitched in a side window as Brackett led them down the cement driveway to the rear entrance to his basement apartment. Brackett noticed but didn't expect any help from his landlord. The jackal's uniform guaranteed that Brackett had too much trouble coming down for anybody with half a brain to get involved. Like LeBarron, all Brackett wanted was to get this over with so he could work on finding an underground doctor who could fix whatever was wrong inside him. If it was fixable. That fear crept to the surface of his mind as he unlocked the double deadbolts on his door.

The basement was black-dark. Death pushed Brackett inside and snapped, "Light."

Brackett flipped the wall switch.

"Holy shit," Death said.

There was one room with a door leading to a tiny bathroom. A hotplate on the counter beside a rust-stained sink sufficed for the little cooking Brackett bothered with. A bright Mexican blanket covered an iron bedstead. The slit windows were stuffed with styrofoam slabs and hung with black cloth. A metal chair was shoved under the sink. Wooden crates served as cupboards for the few shirts and Levis Brackett owned. An industrial-sized humidifier hummed quietly in the middle of the room.

There wasn't room for much else. Tapes, CDs, old vinyl LPs, Technics DAT units, TEAC open reel decks, a Pyramid mixer, equalizers, pre-amps, a couple of Marantz duplicators, a jumble of Bang & Olufson components, even a few outdated Sony and Sansui and Pioneer stereos covered every centimeter of wall space and piled in the corners.

Death whistled softly. "You got enough stuff here to go to jail for a few million years." He prowled the length of the shelves, drawing one finger along the catalogued titles. "And would you just look at this. Dealer, I'm impressed. You got a stash here that'd make Rulon cream his pants."

"He ain't got no speakers," Lela said. "Why not?" Having them poke through his equipment and the music he'd painstakingly collected over the years felt like rape. Brackett nodded at the Sennheiser HD-250s hanging on a pegboard. "Headphones. They're quieter than speakers."

"He's the careful sort."

"Lot of good that did you," Lela said. "Too bad. What all you got here?" She peered at the titles under the neatly labelled heading *Rock*.

The drug-hazed pain was beginning to creep back at Brackett. "Take what you want and get out. Leave me alone."

The jackal quit grinning. "Afraid we can't do that, Dealer. Something Rulon didn't tell you." He reached up and tore the styrofoam from a window over the sink. Grabbing the chair, Death From Above used it to break out the glass. He dumped a metal wastebasket and set it in the sink. He reached into a pocket in the gray uniform and pulled out what looked like an orange sausage wrapped in 7 mil polyplastic. "You got proscribed, unAmerican material here, sweetheart. Rulon don't like that," he said, then ripped the plastic off the chub. Flicking open a Zippo, Death held the flame to the orange gel. It flared into white fire as he dropped it into the trash can.

Death handed Lela the paper LeBarron had given him. "See which ones of these he's got. Pull them out."

Lela read the list. "What about this other stuff? I sorta like some of them." She took a CD box from the shelf. "Pink Floyd. This is a good one."

Death grabbed her wrist, twisting. He caught the disk as it slipped from her grasp.

Lela's eyes slitted. "Bastard." She rubbed her wrist. He held the box over the flaming trashcan. "See, Dealer, Rulon thinks you're slime. You pervert everything a decent America stands for with this foreign rot." Smoke was beginning to rise from the bottom edge of the box when Death drew his hand back. "At least that's what Rulon thinks."

Brackett stilled the sudden throb of hope. "What do you think?"

Death From Above looked at Brackett with serious blue eyes. Then the grin curled around his face. "Me? I think you're a dumbass. You just haven't learned when to bend over. It's a new order, sweetheart. If you're too stupid to figure that out, then we better get you out of the gene pool. You made the number one stupid mistake, Dealer. You got involved with your product. Bad news, bad news." He tossed the CD into the trashcan. Dark smoke billowed up from the can and out through the broken window.

"You miserable slime," Lela said.

Brackett jumped him, swinging. Death stepped into Brackett's rush. Two short punches, one to the sternum and one in the pit of his belly put Brackett down, curled up, trying to suck air into his shocked lungs.

Death From Above used two fingers to pull out another CD, holding it like he had a rat by the tail. "Prokofiev." He shook his head. "Trash." It sailed into the fire.

Brackett watched, swearing weakly when he could breathe again, as Death went down the line. "Rachmaninoff, Moussorgsky, Tchaikovsky, more Russian garbage. As differentiated from French garbage." A handful of DAT cassettes went into the fire. "Or Italian garbage. Or Polish garbage. My, my, Dealer, you've been a busy little sucker. This looks like a lifetime's work."

Lela folded her arms around her purse, holding it to her breasts. "For Christ's sake, get on with it, you psychotic moron. Just do it. You don't have to enjoy it."

Death froze, a *La Bohéme* LP in his hand. His teeth snapped together. His voice hissed out flat and deadly. "Your turn is coming, whore. I hear Rulon's getting tired of you. Guess who's second in line."

Lela backed up a step.

Brackett watched as the jackal grabbed a handful of cassettes under *Rock* and waved them before Lela's white face. "This is the kind of crap you like, isn't it?" He slung them into the trashcan and took several more. Turning the slim plastic boxes, he read, "*Tommy, Rock Opera by The Who.* Bye-bye, *Tommy.*" He flipped it over his shoulder.

"Stop it," Lela said.

Death From Above went back to the trashcan. "How about this one. U2, *The Joshua Tree.*" He tossed it up and caught it just before it dropped into the flames. "You like this one? What'll you give me for it?"

"I won't give you shit."

She wanted it. From the sudden tension in her body, Brackett could tell she wanted it real bad. He spat to clear the blood out of his mouth. "Give him what he wants. Give him anything. Once that tape is gone, it's gone forever."

Lela looked down at Brackett. She looked at Death grinning, then she looked back at the shelf of music.

Brackett got to his knees, shutting out the pain that lanced through his back and darkened his vision. "He's going to burn them all. Gabriel, Police, Beatles, Collins, everything. Stop him and you can have them."

Brackett pitched his voice low, talking to her like a lover. "The only copies left. You can have them all."

Death laughed. "Right, slut. Stop me." He held the tape out to her. "Come and take it. It's yours."

Lela reached for the tape. Death From Above caught her wrist, pulling her close, wrapping both arms around her. "Of course, you've got to pay for it."

Lela jerked free of his embrace. "I'd rather screw a snake."

His face went cold. "That can be arranged. Might be fun to watch."

"In your dreams, asshole."

Death grabbed Lela, pinioning her arms. He covered her mouth with his, grinding a kiss onto her lips. Lela twisted her face away. He took her face in both hands and kissed her again. She bit him.

"Bitch!" Death slapped her, a hard openhanded slap that knocked her back onto Brackett's bed. "You like that kind of game? Fine with me. Let's play."

Lela's hand came out of her purse gripping a short-barreled .357. She leveled the gun at Death's chest and pulled the trigger. The heavy slug slammed the jackal back, crashing against the humidifier. Death folded over the humidifier then slumped to the floor. Blood ran from under his body to puddle on the worn, yellow linoleum.

Lela dropped the .357 on the bed. She looked at Death From Above's body and put both hands over her mouth.

Brackett's ears rang from the blast. His mind was empty. A couple of the orange chubs had spilled out of Death's pocket. He picked one up, rolling it between his palms.

Lela sagged off the bed onto the floor. "Oh, no." The room stank of blood and piss and cordite. The chub gave under Brackett's fingers, not liquid, not solid. He coughed to clear the rasp from his throat. "What is this stuff?"

Lela looked blankly at him. She closed her eyes, opened them, shrugged. "Plastic explosive. Death keeps a couple of boxes in the trunk. Kept a couple of boxes."

Brackett put the chub down very gently. Lela managed a laugh. "Don't worry. It's stable. Won't explode without a detonator." She stretched out one foot and prodded Death's flaccid body. "What am I going to do now?" Pinning Brackett with a dark gaze, she said, "For that matter, what are *you* going to do now, Dealer?"

The takeup reel in Brackett's brain started turning again. Death

From Above wasn't just going to rip off his stash, the son of a bitch was destroying it. Deciding what was good and what was bad according to LeBarron's list. Destroying everything that didn't fit within LeBarron's narrow range of approval. He looked at Death and was gut-deep sorry that he hadn't been the one who pulled the trigger.

There wasn't any music left in his head. Nothing to orchestrate the destruction of his life. His pulse fluttered, fast, slow, fast. His head pounded in time to the thump of pain growing in his body, shrieking that, beyond any doubt, the beatings had ripped something irreparable. Kidneys. Spleen. The diagnosis wasn't important. They said you always knew when you were dying.

And with the music gone, maybe it didn't matter. Or maybe it did.

Brackett got to his hands and knees and crawled to the jackal's body. Going through the pockets, he found several more chubs. "How do you detonate these?"

"Plain old blasting caps. There's some of them in the trunk, too. Be Prepared, that was Death's motto. Oh, Jesus, Dealer, we're dead."

"You're half right." Ignoring the wrench of abused muscles, Brackett turned Death over. He unbuckled the jackal's belt and began tugging at the gray uniform pants. "Help me."

"Why?"

"Because I want his pants."

"You gotta take his boots off first," Lela said. Her fingers fumbled at the metal buckles. "Why do I have the feeling you're going to do something real stupid?"

There was a little blood on the front waistband, but the black belt hid it. The shirt was soaked with Death's blood, useless. The boots were too big; laced tight, they would do. He set the maroon beret on his head.

Lela looked at him, the livid welts and yellow-green bruises that covered his torso. She shook her head. "His gray jacket is in the car. I'll get it."

While she was gone, Brackett rummaged through the pile of CDs she had pulled from the shelves. He found the *Ninth,* with the photo of von Karajan, face intent, both arms lifted, eyes looking beyond human limitation, raising the Berlin Symphony into a soaring act of inspired creation. The disk was still safely spindled inside the transparent plastic. Brackett took a small canvas bag, put the *Ninth* inside it, then added a tape and a Panasonic portable DAT deck with lightweight phones.

Lela returned just as he was scraping the last crumpled bills from their hiding place in the wall behind the huge, antique Akai open-reeler. He took the jacket and handed her the money. She took it, her eyes full of questions. "You want to get out of Salt Lake City?" Brackett asked.

"It would be a real good idea, Dealer. Rulon is gonna be real pissed."

Brackett nodded, feeling the tang of old blood in his throat. He stretched his shoulders carefully. It hurt. The ache in his kidneys felt like something chewing at his flesh from the inside. "Don't worry about LeBarron. Show me how to use the blasting caps. Help me pack what's left of my stash in the Lincoln. There's over ten thousand dollars here. That and the car should get you to Seattle. I've got a phone number for you. Memorize it. If you give the music to the guy who answers, he'll get you into Canada."

"Drive from here to Seattle with a car full of contraband music. Uh-uh. I'm not stupid. You're going to have to come up with a better idea than that."

Brackett rubbed one hand over his face, swearing as he touched the crushed cartilage in his nose. Eventually, when the reek of Death's decomposing body called the landlord to check out his room, all the music would be lost anyway. "All right, forget the rest of it. Just save the *Ninth.* You'll need it to get over the border."

Lela edged around Death From Above, stooped in the corner and came up with *The Joshua Tree.* "I want this one, too. I heard it when I was a kid." She moved back to Brackett and put one cool hand on his cheek. Her head tilted. She looked at him through long, black eyelashes. "You could come with me. No use dying for a pile of plastic."

He didn't try to explain that it was more than ribbons of plastic, electronic parts, metal fittings, digital storage and laser optics, copper wires, and shreds of solder. He shrugged the jackal's gray windbreaker over his shoulders. The decision made, he felt disconnected, his skin gone cold.

Bent over the trunk of the Lincoln, the car's plates and the jackal uniform making them invisible to the muted inhabitants of Ramona Avenue, Lela showed him the simplicity of attaching blasting caps to the chubs. When he understood, she brought a book of Alta Club matches from her purse. "Go out in a blaze of glory, you idiot."

Brackett settled into the front passenger seat of the Lincoln. The car's door shut with a solid clunk. Like maybe the door to hell. Lela started the engine, heavy-footed, revving it a couple of times. "You're sure about this?"

Brackett inserted the *Ninth* into the Blaupunkt CD/Cassette player. He leaned back into the soft headrest. His eyes closed. "Take the long way back. You have about 24 minutes to kill." He punched *play*. The last movement of Beethoven's *Ninth Symphony*, the *Ode to Joy*, swelled into the car, drowning out the rumble of the engine, drowning out thought; washing the ugly reality of Insulation America from his consciousness; leaving only the wonder of a rich baritone voice proclaiming *Freude, schöner Götterfunken!* Strangely enough, Brackett knew the joy. Maybe even the bright spark of divinity. He couldn't analyze his actions. Saving this piece of music would have to be enough.

Lela turned right onto 9th East and headed south. She raised her voice over the music. "You could change your mind, Dealer."

"Shut up," Brackett said.

Alle Menschen werden Brüder.

Her timing was good. The car rolled to a stop as the final notes faded into silence. She watched Brackett as he checked the plastique chubs stuffed into his pockets, more of them bulking inside his black Deadhead T-shirt until the jacket barely fastened. She leaned across the wide seat and brushed her lips across his battered cheek. "Good luck, Dealer."

Standing outside the car, Brackett dropped the Panasonic DAT portable into the pocket with the fused chubs and matches. He settled the headphones under the maroon beret and shoved the tape in. He passed into the Hotel Utah with Te Kanawa's crystalline soprano pouring Strauss' *Beim Schlafengehn* into his head. It gave him courage, for a bit, anyway. For long enough.

Heading north on I-15 towards Idaho, weaving the car through the sparse traffic, Lela saw the flash of the blast in her rearview mirror. The concussion shook the Lincoln two miles away as the explosion took out the southwestern corner of the building's top floor, blowing the peregrine falcons from their nest under the cornice. A flying chunk of granite sheared Moroni from his perch atop the temple. Dense black smoke roiled from the shattered stone and glass and twisted steel.

Lela lit a cigarette and inhaled deeply. "Here's to ya, Dealer." She shoved the U2 tape into the player and cranked the volume up.

PAGEANT WAGON

ORSON SCOTT CARD

eaver's horse took sick and died right under him. He was sitting on her back, writing down notes about how deep the erosion was eating back into the new grassland, when all of a sudden old Bette shuddered and coughed and broke to her knees. Deaver slid right off her, of course, and unsaddled her, but after that all he could do was pat her and talk to her and hold her head in his lap as she laid there dying.

If I was an outrider it wouldn't be like this, thought Deaver. Royal's Riders go two by two out there on the eastern prairie, never alone like us range riders here in the old southern Utah desert. Outriders got the best horses in Deseret, too, never an old nag like Bette having to work out her last breath riding the grass edge. And the outriders got guns, so they wouldn't have to sit and watch a horse die; they could say farewell with a hot sweet bullet like a last ball of sugar.

Didn't do no good thinking about the outriders, though. Deaver'd been four years on the waiting list, just for the right to apply. Most range riders were on that list, aching for a chance to do something important and dangerous—bringing refugees in from the prairie, fighting mobbers, disarming missiles. Royal's Riders were all heroes, it went with the job, whenever they come back from a mission they got their picture in the papers, a big write-up. Range riders just got lonely and shaggy and smelly. No wonder they all dreamed of riding with Royal Aal. With so many others on the list, Deaver figured he'd probably be too old and they'd take his name off before he ever got to the top. They wouldn't take applications from anybody over thirty, so he only had about a year and a half left. He'd end up doing what he was doing now, riding the edge of the grassland, checking out erosion patterns and bringing in stray cattle till he dropped out of the saddle and then it'd be his horse's turn to stand there and watch *him* die.

Bette twitched a leg and snorted. Her eye was darting every which way, panicky, and then it stopped moving at all. After a while a fly landed on it. Deaver eased himself out from under her. The fly stayed right there. Probably already laying eggs. This country didn't waste much time before it sucked every last hope of life out of anything that held still long enough.

Deaver figured to do everything by the book. Put Bette's anal scrapings in a plastic tube so they could check for disease, pick up his bedroll, his notebooks, and his canteen, and then hike into the first fringe town he could find and call in to Moab.

Deaver was all set to go, but he couldn't just walk off and leave the saddle. The rulebook said a rider's life is worth more than a saddle, but the guy who wrote that didn't have a five-dollar deposit on it. A week's wages. It wasn't like Deaver had to carry it far. He passed a road late yesterday. He'd go back and sit on the saddle and wait a couple days for some truck to come by.

Anyway he wanted it on his record—Deaver Teague come back saddle and all. Bad enough to lose the horse. So he hefted the saddle onto his back and shoulders. It was still warm and damp from Bette's body.

He didn't follow Bette's hoofprints back along the edge of the grassland—no need to risk his own footsteps causing more erosion. He struck out into the thicker, deeper grass of last year's planting. Pretty soon he lost sight of the grey desert sagebrush, it was too far off in the wet hazy air. Folks talked about how it was in the old days, when the air was so clear and dry you could see mountains you couldn't get to in two days' riding. Now the farthest he could see was to the redrock sentinels sticking up out of the grass, bright orange when he was close, dimmer and greyer a mile or two ahead or behind. Like soldiers keeping watch in the fog.

Deaver's eyes never got used to seeing those pillars of orange sandstone, tortured by the wind into precarious dream shapes, standing right out in the middle of wet-looking deep green grassland. They didn't belong together, those colors, that rigid stone and bending grass. Wasn't natural.

Five years from now, the fringe would move out into this new grassland, and there'd be farmers turning the plow to go around these rocks, never even looking up at these last survivors of the old desert. In his mind's eye, Deaver saw those rocks seething hot with anger as the cool sea of green swept on around them. People might tame the soil of the desert, but never these temperamental, twisted old soldiers. In fifty years or a hundred or two hundred maybe, when the Earth healed itself from the war and the weather changed back and the rains stopped coming, all this grass, all those crops, they'd turn brown and die, and the new orchard trees would stand naked and dry until they snapped off in a sandstorm and blew away into dust, and then the grey sagebrush would cover the ground again, and the stone soldiers would stand there, silent in their victory.

That's going to happen some day, all you fringe people with your rows of grain and vegetables and trees, your towns full of people who all know each other and go to the same church. You think you all belong where you are, you each got a spot you fill up snug as a cork in a bottle. When I come into town you look hard at me with your tight little eyes because you never seen my face before, I got no place with you, so I better do my business and get on out of town. But that's how the desert thinks about you and your plows and houses. You're just passing through, you got no place here, pretty soon you and all your planting will be gone.

Beads of sweat tickled his face and dropped down onto his eyes, but Deaver didn't let go of the saddle to wipe his forehead. He was afraid if once he set it down he wouldn't pick it up again. Saddles weren't meant to fit the back of a man, and he was sore from chafing and bumping into it. But he'd carried the saddle so far he'd feel like a plain fool to drop it now, so never mind the raw spots on his shoulders and how his fingers and wrists and the backs of his arms hurt from hanging onto it.

At nightfall he hadn't made the road. Even bundled up in his blanket and using the saddle as a windbreak, Deaver shivered half the night against the cold breeze poking here and there over the grass. He woke up stiff and tired with a runny nose. Wasn't till halfway to noon next day that he finally got to the road.

It was a thin ribbon of ancient grey oil and gravel, an old two-lane that was here back when it was all desert and nobody but geologists and tourists and the stubbornest damn cattle ranchers in the world ever drove on it. His arms and back and legs ached so bad he couldn't sit down and he couldn't stand up and he couldn't lie down. So he set down the saddle and bedroll and walked along the road a little to work the pain out. Felt like he was light as cottonwood fluff, now he didn't have the saddle on his back.

First he went south toward the desert till the saddle was almost out of sight in the haze. Then he walked back, past the saddle, toward the fringe. The grass got thicker and taller that direction. Range riders had a saying: "Grass to the stirrup, pancakes and syrup." It meant you were close to where the orchards and cropland started, which meant a town, and since most riders were Mormon, they could brother-and-sister their way into some pretty good cooking. Deaver got sandwiches or dry bread in towns too small to have a diner.

Deaver figured all those Mormons formed a big piece of cloth, all woven together through the whole state of Deseret, each person like a thread wound in among the others to make a fabric, tough and strong and complete right out to the edge—right out to the fringe. Those Mormon range riders, they might stray out into the empty grassland, but they were still part of the weave, still connected. Deaver, he was like a wrong-colored thread that looks like it's hanging from the fabric, but when you get up close, why, you can see it isn't attached anywhere, it just got mixed up in the wash, and if you pull it away it comes off easy, and the cloth won't be one whit weaker or less complete.

But that was fine with Deaver. If the price of a hot breakfast was being a Mormon and doing everything the bishop told you because he was inspired by God, then bread and water tasted pretty good. To Deaver the fringe towns were as much a desert as the desert itself. No way he could live there long, unless he was willing to turn into something other than himself.

He walked back and forth until it didn't hurt to sit down, and then he sat down until it didn't hurt to walk again. All day and no cars. Well, that was his kind of luck—government probably cut back the gas ration again and nobody was moving. Or they sealed off the road 'cause they didn't want folks driving through the grassland even on pavement. For all Deaver knew the road got washed through in the last rain. He might be standing here for nothing, and he only had a couple days' water in his canteen. Wouldn't that be dumb, to die of thirst because he rested a whole day on a road that nobody used.

Wasn't till the middle of the night when the rumble of an engine and the vibration of the road woke him up. It was a long way off still, but he could see the headlights. A truck, from the shaking and the noise it made. And not going fast, from how long it took those lights to get close. Still, it was night, wasn't it? And even going thirty, it was a good chance they wouldn't see him. Deaver's clothes were all dark, except his T-shirt. So, cold as it was at night, he stripped off his jacket and flannel shirt and stood in the middle of the road, letting his undershirt catch the headlights, his arms spread out and waving as the truck got closer.

He figured he looked like a duck trying to take off from a tar patch. And his T-shirt wasn't clean enough for anybody to call it exactly white. But they saw him and laid on the brakes. Deaver stepped out of the way when he saw the truck couldn't stop in time. The brakes squealed and howled and it took them must be a hundred yards past Deaver before they stopped.

They were nice folks—they even backed up to him instead of making him carry the saddle and all up to where they finally got it parked.

"Thank heaven you weren't a baby in the road," said a man from the back of the truck. "You wouldn't happen to have brake linings with you, young man?"

The man's voice was strange. Loud and big-sounding, with an accent like Deaver never heard before. Every single letter sounded clear, like the voice of God on Mount Sinai. It didn't occur to Deaver that the man might be making a joke, not in that voice. Instead he felt like it was a sin that he didn't have brake linings. "No, sir, I'm sorry."

The Voice of God chuckled. "There was an era, before you remember, when no American in his right mind would have stopped to pick up a dangerous-looking stranger like you. Who says America has not improved since the collapse?"

"I'd like a bag of nacho Doritos," said a woman. "That would be an improvement." Her voice was warm and friendly, but she had that same strange way of pronouncing every bit of every word. Jackrabbits could learn English hearing her talk.

"I speak of trust, and she speaks of carnal delights," said the Voice of God. "Is that a saddle?"

"Government property, registered in Moab." He said it right off, so there'd be no thought of maybe making that saddle disappear.

The man chuckled. "Range rider, then?"

"Yes sir."

"Well, range rider, it seems trust among strangers isn't perfect yet. No, we wouldn't steal your saddle, even to make brake linings."

Deaver was plain embarrassed. "I didn't mean to say —"

"You did right, lad," said the woman.

The truck was a flatbed with high fencing staked around—ancient, but so were most trucks. Detroit wasn't exactly churning them out anymore. Inside the fence panels, straining against them, was a crazy jumble of tarps, tents, and crates stacked up in a way that made no sense, not in the dark anyway. Somebody flung their arm over the top of one of the softer-looking bundles, and then a sleepy-looking, mussy-haired girl about maybe twelve years old stuck her head up and said, "What's going on?" It was a welcome sound, her voice—none of that too-crisp talking from her.

"Nothing, Janie," said the woman. She turned back to Deaver. "And as for you, young man, show some sense and get your shirt back on, it's cold out here."

So it was. He started to put it on. As soon as she saw he was doing what she wanted, she climbed back into the cab.

He could hear the man tossing his saddlebags onto the truck. Deaver put his foot on the saddle till he had his shirt on, so the man wouldn't come back and try to lift it. Not that he could tell for sure, but by the little light from a sliver of moon, he didn't look like a young man, exactly, and Deaver wouldn't have an old guy lift his saddle for him.

Somebody else came around the front of the truck. A young man, with an easy walk and a smile so full of teeth it caught the moonlight brighter than a car bumper. He stuck out his hand and said, "I'm his son. My name's Ollie."

Well, if Deaver thought the Voice of God was weird, his son was even weirder. Deaver'd picked up a lot of riders back in his salvage days, and he'd been picked up himself more times than he could remember. Only a couple of people ever gave or asked for a name, and that was only at the end of the ride, and only if you talked a lot and liked each other. Here was a guy expecting to shake hands, like he thought Deaver was famous—or thought *he* was famous. When Deaver took his hand, Ollie squeezed hard. Like there was real feeling in it. There in the dark, people talking and acting strange, Deaver still half asleep, he felt like he was inside a dream, one that hadn't decided yet whether to be a nightmare.

Ollie let go of Deaver's hand, bent over, and slid the saddle right out from under Deaver's foot. "Let me get this up onto the truck for you."

It was plain that Ollie had never hoisted many saddles in his life. He was strong enough, but awkward. Deaver took hold of one end.

"Do horses really wear these things?" asked Ollie.

"Yep," said Deaver. Deaver knew the question was a joke, but he didn't know why it was funny, or who was supposed to laugh. At least Ollie didn't talk like the older man and woman—he had a natural sound to his voice, an easy way of talking, like you'd already been friends for years. They got the saddle onto the truck. Then Ollie swung up onto the truck and slid the saddle back behind something covered with canvas.

"Heading for Moab, right?" asked Ollie.

"I guess," said Deaver.

"We're heading to Hatchville," Ollie said. "We'll spend no more than two days there, and then it happens we'll be passing through Moab next." Ollie glanced over at his father, who was just coming back around the truck. Ollie was grinning his face off, and he spoke real loud now, as if to make sure his father heard him. "Unless you have a faster ride, how about you travel with us the whole way to Moab?"

The Voice of God didn't say a word, and it was too dark to read much expression on his face. Still, as long as Deaver didn't hear him saying, "Yes, Ollie's right, come ride with us," the message was plain enough. The son might've shook his hand, but the father didn't hanker for his company past morning.

Truth was Deaver didn't mind a bit. Seemed to him these people didn't have all their axles greased, and he wasn't thinking about their truck, either. He wasn't about to turn down a ride with them tonight— who knew when the next vehicle would come through here?—but he wasn't eager to hang around with them for two days, listening to them talk funny. "Hatchville's all I need," said Deaver.

Only after Deaver had turned down the offer did the Voice of God speak again. "I assure you, it would have been no trouble to take you on to Moab."

That's right, thought Deaver. It would've been no trouble, but you still didn't want to do it and that's fine with me.

"Come on, get aboard," said Ollie. "You'll have to ride in the cab—all the beds are occupied."

As Deaver walked up to the cab, he saw two more people leaning over the railing of the truck to get a look at him—a really old man and woman, white-haired, almost ghost-like. How many people were there? Ollie and the Voice of God, these two really old ones, the lady who was probably Ollie's mother, and that young girl named Janie. Six at least. At least they were trying to fit in with the government's request for folks to carry the most possible riders per vehicle.

Ollie's father got up into the cab before Deaver, giving him the window. The woman was already in the middle, and when Ollie got into the driver's seat on the other side, it made for a tight fit all across. Deaver didn't mind, though. The cab was cold.

"It'll warm up again when we get going," said the woman. "The heater works, but the fan doesn't."

"Do you have a name, range rider?" asked the Voice of God.

Deaver couldn't understand this curiosity about names. I'm not renting a room with you people, I'm just taking a ride.

"Maybe he doesn't want to share his name, Father," said Ollie.

Deaver could feel Ollie's father stiffen beside him. Why was it such a big deal? "Name's Deaver Teague."

Now it was Ollie who seemed to tighten up. His smile got kind of set as he started the engine and put the truck in gear. Was this a bet? Whoever got Deaver to say his name won, and Ollie was mad because he had to pay off?

"Do you hail from anywhere in particular?" asked Ollie's father.

"I'm an immigrant," said Deaver.

"In the long run, so are we all. Immigrant from where?"

Am I applying for a job or something? "I don't remember."

The father and mother glanced at each other. Of course they assumed he was lying, and now they were probably thinking he was a criminal or something. So like it or not, Deaver had to explain. "Outriders picked me up when I was maybe four. All my people was killed by mobbers on the prairie."

Immediately the tension eased out of the parents. "Oh, I'm sorry," said the woman. Her voice was so thick with sympathy that Deaver had to look at her to make sure she wasn't making fun.

"Doesn't matter," Deaver said. He didn't even remember them, so it wasn't like he missed his folks.

"Listen to us," said the woman. "Prying at him, when we haven't so much as told him who we are."

So at least she noticed they were prying

"I told him *my* name," said Ollie. There was a trace of nastiness in the way he said it, and suddenly Deaver knew why he got mad a minute ago. When Ollie introduced himself outside the truck, Deaver didn't give back his own name, but then when Ollie's father asked, Deaver told his name easy enough. It was about the stupidest thing to get mad over that Deaver ever heard of, but he was used to that. Deaver was always doing that, giving offense without meaning to, because people were all so prickly. Or maybe he just wasn't smart about dealing with strangers. You'd think he'd be better at it, since strangers was all he ever had to deal with.

The Voice of God was talking like he didn't even know Ollie was mad. "We who travel in, on, and around this truck are minstrels of the open road. Madrigals and jesters, thespians and dramaturges, the second-rate sophoclean substitute for NBC, CBS, ABC, and, may the Lord forgive us, PBS."

The only answer Deaver could think of was a kind of smile, knowing he looked like an idiot, but what could he say that wouldn't let the man know that Deaver didn't understand a word he said?

Ollie grinned over at him. Deaver was glad to see he wasn't mad anymore, and so he smiled back. Ollie grinned even more. This is like a conversation between two people pretending not to be deaf, thought Deaver.

Finally Ollie translated what his father had said. "We're a pageant wagon."

"Oh," said Deaver. He was a fool for not guessing it already. Show gypsies. It explained so many people on one truck and the strange-shaped objects under the canvas and most of all it explained the weird way Ollie's father and mother talked. "A *pageant* wagon."

But apparently Deaver said it the wrong way or something, because Ollie's father winced and Ollie snapped off the inside light and the truck sped up, rattling more than ever. Maybe they were mad because they knew all the stories that got told about show gypsies, and they figured Deaver was being snide when he said *"pageant* wagon" like that. Fact was Deaver didn't much care whether pageant wagons left behind them a string of pregnant virgins and empty chicken coops. They weren't his daughters and they weren't his chickens.

Deaver moved around so much that a traveling show never came to any town he was in, at least that he knew about. In Zarahemla he knew they had an actual walk-in theater, but for that you had to dress nicer than any clothes Deaver owned. And the pageant wagons only traveled out in the hick towns, where Deaver never hung around long enough to know if there was a show going on or not. Only thing he knew about pageant wagons was what he found out tonight—they talked weird and got mad over nothing.

But he didn't want them thinking he had a low opinion of pageant wagons. "You doing a show in Hatchville?" asked Deaver. He tried to sound favorable to the idea.

"We have an appointment," said Ollie's father.

"Deaver Teague," said the woman, obviously changing the subject. "Do you know why your parents gave you two last names?"

Seemed like whenever these people ran out of stuff to talk about, they always got back to names. But it was better than having them mad. "The immigrants who found me, there was a guy named Deaver and a guy named Teague."

"How awful, to take away your given name!" she said.

What was Deaver supposed to say to that?

"Maybe he likes his name," said Ollie.

Immediately Ollie's mother got flustered. "Oh, I wasn't criticizing —"

Ollie's father jumped right in to smooth things over. "I think Deaver Teague is a very distinguished-sounding name. The name of a future governor."

Deaver smiled a little at that. Him, a governor. The chance of a non-Mormon governor in Deseret was about as likely as the fish electing a duck to be king of the pond. He may be in the water, but he sure ain't one of *us*.

"But our manners," said the woman. "We still haven't introduced ourselves. I'm Scarlett Aal."

"And I'm Marshall Aal," said the man. "Our driver is our second son, Laurence Olivier Aal."

"Ollie," said the driver. "For the love of Mike!"

What Deaver mostly heard was the last name. "Aal like A-A-L?"

"Yes," said Marshall. He looked off into the distance even though there was nothing to see in the dark.

"Any relation to Royal Aal?"

"Yes," said Marshall. He was very curt.

Deaver couldn't figure out why Marshall was annoyed. Royal's Riders were the biggest heroes in Deseret.

"My husband's brother," said Scarlett.

"They're very close," said Ollie. Then he gave a single sharp hoot of laughter.

Marshall just raised his chin a little, as if to say he was above such tomfoolery. So Marshall didn't like being related to Royal. But definitely they were brothers. Now that Deaver was looking for it, Marshall Aal even looked kind of like Royal's pictures in the paper. Not enough to mistake them for each other. Royal had that ragged, lean, hardjawed look of a man who doesn't much care where he sleeps; his brother, here in the cab of the pageant wagon, his face was softer.

No, not softer. Deaver couldn't call this sharp-featured man *soft*. Nor delicate. Elegant maybe. Your majesty.

Their names were backward. It was Marshall here who looked like a king, and Royal who looked like a soldier. Like they got switched in the cradle.

"Do you know my Uncle Roy?" asked Ollie. He sounded real interested.

It was plain that Marshall didn't want another word about his brother, but that didn't seem to bother Ollie. Deaver didn't know much about brothers, or about fathers and sons, not having been any such himself, but why would Ollie want to make his father mad on purpose?

"Just from the papers," said Deaver.

Nobody said anything. Just the sound of the engine rumbling on, the feel of the cab vibrating from the road underneath them.

Deaver had that sick feeling he always got when he knew he just didn't belong where he was. He'd already managed to offend everybody, and they'd offended him a few times, too. He just wished somebody else had picked him up. He twisted a little on the seat and leaned his head against the window. If he could go to sleep till they got to Hatchville, then he could get out and never have to face them again.

"Here we've been talking all this time," said Scarlett, "and the poor boy is so tired he can hardly stay awake." Deaver felt her hand pat his knee. Her words, her voice, her touch—they were just what he needed to hear. She was telling him he hadn't offended everybody after all. She was telling him he was still welcome.

He could feel himself unclench inside. He eased down into the seat, breathed a little slower. He didn't open his eyes, but he could still picture the woman's face the way she looked before, smiling at him, her face showing so much sympathy it was like she thought he was her own son.

But of course she could look like that whenever she wanted to—she was an actress. She could make her face and voice seem any old way she chose. Wasn't no particular reason Deaver should believe her. Smarter if he didn't.

What was her name again? Scarlett. He wondered if her hair had once been red.

The sky was just pinking up with dawn, clear and cold outside the heated cab, when they rattled over a rough patch in the road. Deaver wasn't awake and then he was awake. First words he said were from his dream even as it skittered away from him just out of reach. "It's your stuff," he said.

"Don't get mad at *me* about it," said the woman sitting next to him. It took him a moment to realize that it wasn't Scarlett's voice.

In the night sometime the pageant wagon people must have stopped and switched places. Now that he thought about it, Deaver had half-awake memories of Scarlett and other people talking soft and the seat bouncing. Marshall and Scarlett were gone, and so was Ollie. The man at the wheel wasn't one of the people Deaver saw last night. They had called Ollie their second son; this must be his older brother. The young girl he saw on the back of the truck last night—Janie—she was asleep leaning on the driver's shoulder. And next to Deaver was about the prettiest woman he could remember seeing in his life. Of course women got to looking nicer and nicer the more time you spent on the range, but it was sure she was the best-looking woman he ever woke up next to. Not that he'd ever say such a thing. He was plain embarrassed even to think it.

She was smiling at him.

"Sorry. I must have been—"

"Oh, it was some dream," she said.

I look at you and I think maybe I'm still dreaming. The words were so clear in his mind that he moved his lips without meaning to.

"What?" she asked.

She looked at him like she'd never look at another soul until he answered. Deaver was plain embarrassed. He blurted out something like what he was thinking. "I said if you're part of the dream I don't want to wake up."

The man at the wheel laughed. Pleasantly. Deaver liked his laugh. The woman didn't laugh, though. She just smiled and crinkled up her eyes, then looked down at her lap. It was the absolutely perfect thing for her to do. So perfect that Deaver felt like he was starting to float. "You've done it to this poor ranger man already, Katie," said the driver. "Pay no attention to her, my friend. She specializes in enchanting handsome strangers she discovers in the cab of her family's truck. If you kiss her she turns into a frog."

"You wake up very sweetly," said Katie. "And you turn a compliment so a woman can almost believe it's true."

Only now did Deaver really come awake and realize he was talking to strangers and had no business saying what came to mind, or trying to make his jokes. In the roadside inns where he used to stop while he was driving a scavenger truck, he always talked to the waitresses like that, giving them the most elegant compliments that he thought they might believe. At first he was flirting, teasing them, which was the only way he knew to talk to a woman—he couldn't bring himself to talk crude like the older drivers, so he talked pretty. Soon, though, he stopped making it a joke, because those women would always look at him sharp to see if he was mocking them, and if they saw he wasn't, why, it brightened them, like pulling the chain on a light inside their eyes.

But that was back when he was seventeen, eighteen years old, lots younger than the women he met. They liked him, treated him like a sweet-talking little brother. This woman, though, she was younger than him, and sitting tight up against him in a cab so small it caught all her breath so he could breathe it after, and the sky outside was dim and the light made soft pink shadows on her face. He was wide awake now, and shy.

You don't flirt with a woman in front of her brother.

"I'm Deaver Teague," he said. "I didn't see you last night."

"I didn't exist last night," she said. "You dreamed me up and here I am."

She laughed and it wasn't a giggle or a cackle, it was a low-pitched sound in her throat, warm and inviting.

"Deaver Teague," said the driver, "I urge you to remember that my sister Katie Hepburn Aal is the best actress in Deseret, and what you're seeing right now is Juliet."

"Titania," she said. In that one word she suddenly became elegant and dangerous, her voice even more precise than her mother's had been, like she was queen of the universe.

"Medea," her brother retorted nastily.

Deaver figured they were calling names, but didn't know what they meant.

"I'm Toolie," said the driver.

"Peter O'Toole Aal," said Katie. "After the great actor."

Toolie grinned. "Daddy wasn't subtle about wanting us to go into the family business. Nice to meet you, Deaver."

All this time Katie didn't take her eyes off Deaver. "Ollie said you know Uncle Royal."

"No," said Deaver. "I just know about him."

"I thought you range riders worked under him."

Was that why she was sitting next to him? Hoping he'd talk about their famous uncle? "He's over the outriders."

"You want to be an outrider?"

It wasn't something he talked about much to anybody. Most young men who signed on as rangers were hoping some day to get into Royal's Riders, but the ones who got in usually made it before they reached twenty-five, which meant they had five or six years on horseback before they applied to the outriders. Deaver was twenty-five when he joined up, and he hadn't had four years as a range rider yet. Except for a couple of older guys, most rangers would have a good laugh if they knew how much Deaver wanted to ride with Royal Aal.

"It's something that might happen," said Deaver.

"I hope you get your wish," she said.

This time it was his turn to search her face to see if she was making fun. But she wasn't. He could see that. She really hoped for something good to happen to him. He nodded, not knowing what else to say.

"Riding out there," she said, "helping people make it here to safety."

"Taking apart the missiles," said Toolie.

"Ain't too many missiles now," said Deaver.

Which pretty much ended the conversation. Deaver was used to that, having his words be the ones that hung in the air, nobody saying a thing afterward. A long time ago he tried to apologize or explain what he said, something to make that embarrassed silence go away. Last few years, though, he realized he probably hadn't said something wrong. Other people just had a hard time talking to him for long, that's all. Nothing against him. He just wasn't the kind of person you talk to.

Deaver wished he actually knew their uncle, so he could tell them about him. It was plain they were hungry for word about him. If their father'd been feuding with Royal for a long time, they might hardly know him. That'd be strange, for the kinfolk of the best-loved hero of Deseret not to know a bit more about him than any stranger just reading the paper.

They crested a hill. Toolie pointed. "There's Hatchville."

Deaver had no idea how long ago they left the grassland and came into the fringe, but from the size of Hatchville he figured this town was probably twelve, fifteen years old. Well back from the edge now, really not fringe at all anymore. Lots of people.

Toolie slowed enough to gear down the truck. Deaver listened with an ear long attuned to motors from his years nursing the scavenger trucks from one place to another. "Engine's pretty good for one this old," said Deaver.

"You think so?" said Toolie. He perked right up, talking about the engine. These folks made a living only as long as the motor kept going.

"Needs a tune-up."

Toolie made a wry face. "No doubt."

"Probably the mix in the carburetor's none too good."

Toolie laughed in embarrassment. "Do carburetors mix something? I always thought they just sat there and carbureted."

"Ollie takes care of the truck," Katie said.

The little girl between them woke up. "Are we there yet?"

They were passing the first houses on the outskirts of town. The sky was pretty light now. Almost sunrise.

"You remember where the pageant field is in Hatchville, Katie?" Toolie asked.

"I can't tell Hatchville from Heber," said Katie.

"Heber's the one with mountains all around like a bowl," said Janie.

"Then this is Hatchville," said Katie.

"I knew that," said Toolie.

They ended up at the town hall, where everybody stood around the truck in the cold morning air while Ollie and Katie went in looking for somebody to give them a permit for a place to set up for the pageant. Deaver figured that this time of morning the only one on duty'd be the night man who did the data linkups with Zarahemla—every town had one—so he didn't bother going in on his own business. As for them going in, well, it was their business, not his.

Sure enough, they came out empty-handed. "The night guy couldn't give us a permit," said Ollie, "but the pageant field's up on Second North and then out east to the first field that's got no fence."

"And he gave us such a *Christian* welcome," said Katie. Her smile was full of mischief. Ollie hooted. Deaver was having fun just watching them.

Toolie shook his head. "Small-town pinheads."

Katie launched into a thick hicktown accent, full of r's so hard Deaver thought she must have her tongue tickling the back of her throat. "And you better stay there till you come back in at nine and get a permit, cause we respect the law around here."

Deaver couldn't help but laugh along with the others, even though the accent she was making fun of, that was pretty much the way he talked.

Marshall, though, he wasn't laughing as he stood there combing his sleep-crazy hair with his fingers. "Ungrateful, suspicious, small-minded bigots, all of them. I wonder how they'd like to pass this autumn without a single visit from a pageant wagon. There's nothing to stop us from driving on through." This early in the morning he didn't talk so careful. Deaver heard a little naturalness in his speech, and even though it was only by accident, it kind of made Deaver feel better to know that the real person Marshall used to be wasn't hidden all that deep after all.

"Now Marsh," said Scarlett. "You know that our calling comes from the Prophet, not from these small-town people. If their minds are little and ugly and closed, isn't it our job to bring them a broader vision? Isn't that why we're here?"

Katie sighed pointedly. "Why does it always have to come back to the church, Mother? We're here to make a living."

She didn't speak harsh or nasty, but people acted like she'd slapped her mother. Scarlett immediately put her hands to her cheeks and turned away, tears filling her eyes. Marshall looked like he was about to tear into Katie with words so hot they could start a brushfire, and Ollie was grinning like this was the best thing he'd seen all year.

But right then Toolie took a step toward Deaver and said, "Well, Deaver Teague, you can see how it is with show people. We have to make a grand scene out of everything."

That reminded folks that there was a stranger among them, and all at once they changed. Scarlett smiled at Deaver. Katie laughed lightly like it was all a joke. Marshall started nodding wisely, and Deaver knew the next words he said would be as elegant as ever.

It was plainly time for Deaver to say thank you and get his saddle off the truck and go take a nap somewhere out of the wind till it got time to report in to Moab. Then the Aals could quarrel with each other all they liked. Parting would be fine with Deaver—he'd been a bit of painless charity to them, and they'd been a ride into town for him. Everybody got what they needed and good-bye.

What messed things up was that when Marshall got pretty much the same idea—that it was time for Deaver to go—he didn't trust Deaver to have sense enough to figure it out himself. So Marshall smiled and nodded and put his arm around Deaver's shoulder. "I suppose, Son, that you'll want to stay here and wait until the offices open up at eight o'clock."

Deaver didn't take offense at what he said—he was just hinting for Deaver to do what he already meant to do, so that was fine. Folks had a right to keep their family squabbles away from strangers. But giving him a hug and calling him "son" while telling him to go away, it made Deaver so mad he wanted to hit somebody.

All the time he was growing up Mormons kept doing that same thing to him. They always fostered him out to live in some Mormon family's house who'd always make him go to church every Sunday even though they knew he wasn't a Mormon and didn't want to be one. The other kids knew right off he wasn't one of them and didn't make any bones about it—they left him alone and didn't pretend they liked him or even cared whether he lived or died. But there was always some Relief Society president who patted his head and called him "sweetie" or "you dear thing," and whenever the bishop passed him, he'd put his arm around him and call him "son" just like Marshall, and pretend they were only joking when they said, "How long till you see the light and get baptized?"

That friendly and nice stuff always lasted until Deaver finally told them "never" loud enough and nasty enough that they believed him. From then on until he got fostered somewhere else, the bishop would never touch him or speak to him, just fix him with a cold stare as Deaver sat there in the congregation and the bishop sat up on the stand being holy. Sometimes Deaver wondered what would have happened if just once, some bishop had kept on being friendly even after Deaver told him he'd never get baptized. If maybe he might've felt different about

Mormons if ever their friendship turned out to be real. But it never happened.

So here was Marshall Aal doing just what those bishops always did, and Deaver plain couldn't help himself, he shrugged Marshall's arm off and stepped back so fast that Marshall's arm was still hanging there in the air for a second. His face and his fists must have shown how mad he was, too, because they all stared at him, looking surprised. All except Ollie, who stood there nodding his head.

Marshall looked around at the others. "Well, I don't know what I . . ." Then he gave up with a shrug.

Funny thing was, Deaver's anger was gone already, gone in a second. He never let rage hold onto him—that only gets you in trouble. Worst of all, now they all thought he was mad because they were sending him away. But he didn't know how to explain that it was OK, he was glad to go. It always ended up like this whenever he left a foster home, too. The family was sending him away because they were tired of him, which was fine cause he never much liked them either. He didn't mind leaving and they were glad to see him go, and yet nobody could just come out and say that.

Well, so what. They'd never see him again. "Let me get my saddle," Deaver said. He headed for the side of the truck.

"I'll help you," said Toolie.

"No such thing," said Scarlet. She caught ahold of Deaver's elbow and held it tight. "This young man has been out in the grassland for I don't know how many days, and we're *not* sending him away without breakfast."

Deaver knew she was just saying that for good manners, so he said no thanks as polite as he could. That might have been the end of it except right then Katie came to him and took his left hand—which was his only free hand, since Scarlett had tight hold on his right elbow. "Please stay," she said. "We're all strangers in this town, and I think we ought to stick together till we have to go our separate ways."

Her smile was so bright that Deaver had to blink. And her eyes looked at him so steady, it was like she was daring him to doubt that she meant it.

Toolie picked up on it and said, "We could use another hand setting up, so you'd be earning the meal."

Even Marshall added his bit. "I meant to ask you myself. I hope you *will* come with us and share our poor repast."

Deaver was hungry, all right, and he didn't mind looking at Katie's face though he wished she'd let go of his hand, and he particularly wished Scarlett would unclamp his elbow—but he knew he wasn't really wanted, and so he said no thanks again and got his arms back from the women and headed over to get his saddle off the truck. That was when Ollie laughed and said, "Come on, Teague, you're hungry and father feels like a jerk and Mother feels guilty and Katie's hot for you and Toolie wants you to do half his work. How can you just walk off and disappoint everybody?"

"Ollie," said Scarlett sternly.

But by now Katie and Toolie were laughing, too, and Deaver just couldn't help laughing himself.

"Come on, everybody into the truck," said Marshall. "Ollie, you know the way, you drive."

Marshall and Scarlett and Toolie and Ollie piled into the cab, so Deaver had to ride in back with Katie and Janie and a younger brother, Dusty. The two really old people he saw last night were way in the back of the truck. Katie kept Deaver right up front, behind the cab. Deaver couldn't figure out if she was flirting with him or what. And if she was, he sure didn't know why. He knew his clothes stank of dirt and sweat and the horse he'd been riding till it died, and he also knew he wasn't much to look at even when he shaved. Probably she was just being nice, and didn't know how to do that except by using that smile of hers and looking at him under heavy eyelids and touching his arm and his chest whenever she talked to him. It was annoying, except that it also felt pretty nice. Only that made it even more annoying because he knew that it wasn't going anywhere.

The town was finally coming awake as they drove to the pageant field. Deaver noticed they didn't go straight there. No, they drove that noisy truck up and down every road there was in town, most of them just dirt traces since nothing much got paved these days outside Zarahemla. The sound of the rattletrap truck brought people looking out their windows, and children spurted out the doors to lean on picket fences, jumping up and down.

"Is it Pageant Day?" they'd shout.

"Pageant Day!" answered Katie and Janie and Dusty. Maybe the old folks in back were shouting, too—Deaver couldn't hear. Pretty soon the news was ahead of the truck, and people were already lined up along the edge of the road, straining to see them. That was when the Aals started pulling the tarp off a couple of the big pieces. One of them looked like the top of a missile, and another one was a kind of tower—a tall steep pyramid like a picture Deaver saw in school, the Pyramid of the Sun in Mexico City. When the people saw the rocket, they started yelling, "Man on the moon!" and when they saw the pyramid, which they couldn't see till the truck passed, they'd scream and laugh and call out, "Noah! Noah! Noah!"

Deaver figured they must have seen the shows before. "How many different pageants do you do?" he asked.

"Three," said Katie. She waved at the crowd. "Pageant Day!" Then, still talking loud so he could hear her over the truck and the crowds and her little brother and sister yelling, she said, "We do our *Glory of America* pageant, which Grandfather wrote. And *America's Witness for Christ,* which is the old Book of Mormon pageant from the Hill Cumorah—everybody does that one—and at Christmas we do *The Glorious Night,* which Daddy wrote because he thought the regular Christmas pageants were terrible. That's our whole repertoire in towns like this. Pageant Day!"

"So it's all Mormon stuff," said Deaver.

She looked at him oddly. *"Glory of America* is American. *The Glorious Night* is from the Bible. Aren't you Mormon?"

Here it is, thought Deaver. Here comes the final freeze-out. Or the sudden interest in converting me, leading up to a freeze-out soon enough. He had forgotten, for just a while this morning, that he hadn't told them yet, that they still figured he was one of them, that he basically belonged. The way that these show gypsies were still part of Hatchville, because they were all Mormons. The way most of the other range riders liked being in town, among fellow Mormons. But now, finding out he wasn't one of them, they'd feel like he fooled them, like he stuck himself in where he didn't belong. Now he really regretted letting them talk him into coming along to breakfast like this. They never would've tried to talk him into it if they knew he wasn't one of them.

"Nope," said Deaver.

He couldn't believe it when she didn't even pause. Just went on like nothing got said. "We'd rather do other shows, you know, besides those three. When I was little we spent a year in Zarahemla. I played Tiny Tim in *A Christmas Carol.* Do you know what I've always wanted to play?"

He didn't have any idea.

"You have to guess," she said.

He wasn't sure he'd ever even heard the name of a play, let alone a person in one. So he seized on the only thing he could halfway remember. "Titanic?"

She looked at him like he was crazy.

"In the cab. You said you were—"

"Titania! The queen of the fairies from *A Midsummer Night's Dream*. No, no. I've always wanted to play—you won't tell anybody?"

He sort of shrugged and shook his head at the same time. Who would he tell? And if it was a real secret, why would she tell *him?*

"Eleanor of Aquitaine," she said.

Deaver had never heard that name in his life.

"It was a part Katherine Hepburn played. The actress I was named after. A movie called *A Lion in Winter.*" She almost whispered the title. "I saw a tape of it once, years ago. Actually I saw it about five times, in one single day, over and over again. We were staying with an old friend of Grandpa's in Cedar City. He had a VCR that still ran on his windmill generator. The movie's banned now, you know."

Movies didn't mean much to Deaver. Hardly anybody ever got to see them. Out here on the fringe nobody did. Electricity was too expensive to waste on televisions. Besides, a former salvage man like Deaver knew there just weren't enough working televisions in Deseret for more than a couple in each town. It wasn't like the old days, when everybody went home every night and watched TV till they fell asleep. Nowadays folks only had time for a show when a pageant wagon came to town.

They were past the houses now, pulling onto a bumpy field that had been planted in wheat, long since harvested.

Katie's voice suddenly went husky and trembled a little. "I'd hang you from the nipples, but you'd shock the children."

"What?"

"She was such a magnificent woman. She was the first to wear pants. The first *woman* to wear them. And she loved Spencer Tracy till he died, even though he was Catholic and wouldn't divorce his wife to marry her."

The truck pulled to a stop at the eastern edge of the field. Janie and Dusty jumped right off the truck, leaving them alone between the set pieces and the back of the cab.

"I rode bare-breasted halfway to Damascus," said Katie, in that husky, quavery voice again. "I damn near died of wind burn, but the troops were dazzled."

Deaver finally guessed that she was quoting from the movie. "They did a movie where a woman said *damn?*"

"Did I offend you? I thought since you weren't a Mormon, you wouldn't mind."

That sort of attitude made Deaver crazy. Just because he wasn't a Latter-day Saint, Mormons thought he'd want to hear their favorite dirty joke, or else they started swearing 'cause they thought it would make him more comfortable, or they just assumed that he slept with whores all the time and got drunk whenever he could. But he swallowed his anger without showing it. After all, she meant no harm. And he liked having her so close to him, especially since she hadn't moved any farther away when she found out he was a gentile.

"I just wish you could see the movie," said Katie. "Katherine Hepburn is—magnificent."

"Isn't she dead?"

Katie turned to him, her face a mask of sadness. "The world is poorer because of it."

He spoke the way he always did to a sad-looking woman who was too close to ignore. "I guess the world ain't too poor if you're in it."

Her face brightened at once. "Oh, if you keep saying things like that I'll *never* let you go." She took hold of his arm. His hand had just been hanging at his side, but now that she was pressed up against him, he realized his hand was being pressed into the soft curve of her belly just inside her hip bone. If he even twitched his hand he'd be touching her where a man had no right without being asked. Was she asking?

Toolie, standing on the ground beside the truck, pounded one fist on Deaver's boot and the other on Katie's shoe. "Come on, Katie, let go of Deaver so we can use him to help with the loading."

She squeezed his arm again. "I don't have to," she said.

"If she gets annoying, Deaver, break her arm. That's what *I* do."

"You only did it once," said Katie. "I never let you do it again." She let go of Deaver and jumped off the truck.

For a moment he stood there, not moving his hand or anything. She just talked to him, that's all. That's all it meant. And even if she meant more, he wasn't going to do anything about it. You don't answer folks' hospitality by diddling with their daughter. After a minute—no just a few seconds—he swung himself off the truck and joined the others.

Except for picking the exact spot to park and leveling the truck, the family didn't set to work right away. They gathered in the field and Parley Aal, the old man from the back of the truck, he said a prayer. He had a grand, rolling voice, but it wasn't so clear-sounding as Marshall's, and Parley said his r's real hard like the Mormons Katie made fun of back in town. The prayer wasn't long. Mostly all he did was dedicate the ground to the service of God, and ask the Lord's spirit to touch the hearts of the people who came to watch. He also asked God to help them all remember their lines and be safe. So far only Katie knew Deaver wasn't Mormon, and he said amen at the end just like the others.

Unloading the truck and setting up for the show was as hard as the hardest work Deaver'd ever done in his life. There was more stuff on that truck than he would ever have thought possible. The tower and the missile had doors in back, and they were packed tight with props and machinery and supplies. It took only an hour to pitch the tents they lived in—four of them, plus the kitchen awning—but that was the easy part. There was a generator to load off the truck on a ramp, then hook up to the truck's gas tank. It was so awkward to handle, so heavy and temperamental, that Deaver wondered how they did it when he wasn't there. It took all the strength he and Toolie and Ollie and Marshall had.

"Oh, Katie and Scarlett usually help," said Toolie.

So he was saving Katie work. Was that why she was treating him so nice? Well, that was all right with him. He was glad to help, and he didn't expect payment of any coin. What else was he going to do this morning? Call in to Moab and then sit around and wait for instructions, most likely. Might as well be doing this. Best not to remember the way her body pressed against his hand, the way she squeezed his arm.

They carried metal piping and thick heavy blocks of steel out about fifteen yards from the truck, one on each side of where the audience would be, and then assembled them into trees that held the lights. They kept tossing around words that Deaver never heard of— *fresnel, ellipsoidal*—but before long he was getting the hang of what each light was for. Ollie was the one in charge of all the electrical work. Deaver had a little bit of practice with that sort of thing, but he made it a point not to show off. He just did whatever Ollie ordered, fast and correct and without a word unless he had to ask a question. By the time the lights were wired, aimed, and focused, Ollie was talking to Deaver like they were friends since first grade. Making jokes, even teasing a little—"Do they make some special horse perfume for you range riders to spray on?"—but mostly teaching Deaver everything there was to know about stage lighting, why the different colored filters were used, what the specials did, how the light plot was set up, how to wire up the dimmer board. Deaver couldn't figure what good it was ever going to do him, knowing how to light a stage show, but Ollie knew what he was talking about, and Deaver didn't mind learning something new.

Even with the lights set up the work was hardly started. They had breakfast standing around the gas stove. "We're working you too hard," said Scarlett, but Deaver just grinned and stuffed another pancake in his mouth. Tasted like they actually had sugar in them. A gas stove, their own generator, pancakes that tasted like more than flour and water—they might live on a truck and sleep in tents, but these pageant wagon people had a few things that people in the fringe towns usually had to do without.

By noon, dripping with sweat and aching all over, Deaver stood away from the truck with Ollie and Toolie and Marshall as they surveyed the stage. The missile had been taken down and replaced with the mast of a ship; the side of the truck had been covered with panels that made it look like the hull of a boat; and the machinery was all set up to make a wave effect with blue cloth out in front of it. A black curtain hid the pyramid from sight. Dusty raised and dropped the curtain while the men watched. Deaver thought it looked pretty exciting to have the pyramid suddenly revealed when the curtain dropped, but Marshall clucked his tongue.

"Getting a little shabby," said Marshall.

The curtain *was* patched a lot, and there were some tears and holes that hadn't been patched yet

"It's shabby at noon, Daddy," said Toolie. "At night it's good enough." Toolie sounded a little impatient.

"We need a new one."

"While we're wishing, we need a new truck a lot more," said Ollie.

Toolie turned to him—looking a little angry, it seemed to Deaver, though he couldn't think why Toolie should be mad. "We don't need a new truck, we just need to take better care of this one. Deaver here says it isn't carbureting right."

All of a sudden the cheerfulness went right out of Ollie's face. He turned to Deaver with eyes like ice. "Oh, really?" said Ollie. "Are you a mechanic?"

"I used to drive a truck," said Deaver. He couldn't believe that all of a sudden he was in the middle of a family argument. "I'm probably wrong."

"Oh, you're right enough," said Ollie. "But see, I take all the huge amounts of money they give me to buy spare parts and use it all up in every saloon and whorehouse in the fringe, so the engine just never gets repaired."

Ollie looked too mad to be joking, but what he was saying couldn't possibly be true. There weren't any saloons or whorehouses in the fringe.

"I'm just saying we can't afford a new truck, or a new curtain either," said Toolie. He looked embarrassed, but then he deserved to—he *had* as much as accused Ollie of doing a lousy job with the truck.

"If that's what you were doing," said Ollie, "why'd you have to get Teague here on your side?"

Deaver wanted to grab him and shout straight into his face: I'm not on anybody's side. I'm not part of your family and I'm not part of this argument. I'm just a range rider who needed a lift into town and helped you unload eight tons of junk in exchange for breakfast.

Toolie was trying to calm things down, it looked like, only he wasn't very good at it. "I'm just trying to tell you and Father that we're broke, and talking about new curtains and new trucks is like talking about falling into a hole in the ground and it turns out to be a gold mine. It just isn't going to happen."

"I was just *talking,*" said Ollie.

"You were getting sarcastic and nasty, that's what you were doing," said Toolie.

Ollie just stood there for a second, like some really terrible words were hanging there in his mind, waiting to get flung out where they could really hurt somebody. But he didn't say a thing. Just turned around and walked away, around the back end of the truck.

"There he is, off in a huff again," said Toolie. He looked at his father with a bitter half-smile. "I don't know what I did, but I'm sure it's all my fault he's mad."

"What you did," said Marshall, "was humiliate him in front of his friend."

It took Deaver a moment to realize Marshall was referring to him. The idea of being Ollie's friend took Deaver by surprise. Was that why Ollie worked so close to him so much of the morning, teaching him how the electrical stuff was done—because they were friends? Somehow

Deaver'd got himself turned from a total stranger into a friend without anybody so much as asking him if he minded or if he thought it was a good idea.

"You need to learn to be sensitive to other people, Toolie," said Marshall. "Thank heaven you don't lead this company, the way you do what you like without a thought for your brother's feelings. You just run roughshod over people, Toolie."

Marshall never exactly raised his voice. But he was precise and cruel as he went on and on. Deaver was plain embarrassed to watch Toolie get chewed on. Toolie did kind of pick a fight with Ollie, but he didn't deserve this kind of tongue-lashing, and it sure didn't help matters much to have Deaver standing there watching. But Deaver couldn't figure how to get away without it looking like he disapproved. So he just stood there, kind of looking between Marshall and Toolie so he didn't meet anybody's eyes.

Over at the truck, Katie was sitting on the top of the pyramid, sewing. Dusty and Janie were setting up the fireworks for the end of the show. Ollie had the hood open, fiddling with something inside. Deaver figured he could probably hear every word Marshall said, chewing out Toolie. He could imagine Ollie smiling that mean little smile of his. He didn't like thinking about it, particularly knowing that Ollie thought of him as a friend. So he let his gaze wander to the pyramid, and he watched as Katie worked.

It seemed an odd thing, to sit so high, right in the sun, when there was plenty of shade to sit in. It occurred to Deaver that Katie might be on top of the pyramid just so he'd be sure to see her. But that was pure foolishness. What happened this morning didn't mean a thing—not her talking to him, not her pressing close to him, meant nothing. He must be a plain fool to imagine a smart, good looking woman like her was paying heed to him in the first place. She was on top of the pyramid cause she liked to look out over the town.

She raised her hand and waved to him.

Deaver didn't dare wave back—Marshall was still going strong, ragging on Toolie about things that went back years ago. Deaver looked away from Katie and saw how Toolie just took it, didn't even show anger in his face. Like he switched off all his emotions while his father talked to him.

Finally it ended. Marshall had finally wound down and now he stood there, waiting for Toolie to answer. And all Toolie said was, "Sorry, sir."

Not angry, not sarcastic, just simple and clean as can be. Sorry, sir. Marshall stalked off toward the truck.

As soon as his father was out of earshot, Toolie turned to Deaver. "I'm sorry you had to hear that."

Deaver shrugged. Had no idea what to say.

Toolie gave a bitter little laugh. "I get that all the time. Except that Father likes it better when there's somebody there to watch."

"I don't know about fathers," said Deaver.

Toolie grinned. "Daddy doesn't live by the standards of other men. Mere logic, simple fairness—those are the crutches of men with inferior understanding." Then Toolie's face grew sad. "No, Deaver, I love my father. This isn't about Ollie or how I treat him, jus' like what I said to Ollie wasn't about the truck. I'm too much like my dad and he knows it and that's what he hates about me." Toolie looked around him, as if to see what needed doing. "I guess I better head to town for the official permit, and you need to get in there and report to Moab, don't you?"

"Guess so."

Toolie stopped with his mother to see if she needed anything from town. Scarlett recited a list, mostly staples—flour, salt, honey. Things they could get without paying, cause it was their right to have it from the community storehouse. As they talked, Ollie came by and tossed a dirty air filter at Toolie's chest. "I need a new air filter just like that one only clean."

"Where are you going, Laurence?" asked Scarlett.

"To sleep," he said. "I was up all night driving, in case you forgot." Ollie started to walk away.

"What about brake linings?" asked Toolie.

"Yeah, see if they've got a mechanic who can do that." Ollie ducked into a tent. Anger was still thick in the air. Deaver noticed that Scarlett didn't even ask why.

She finished telling her list to Toolie, sometimes talking over what they would probably get donated by the audience in a place like Hatchville. Then Toolie set out, Deaver in tow. Deaver wanted to take his saddle with him, but Toolie talked him out of it. "If they tell you to get a ride today, your driver can come out and pick it up. And if you end up riding to Moab with us day after tomorrow, you might as well leave the saddle here." As if he was holding the saddle hostage to make sure Deaver came back.

Deaver wasn't sure why he didn't just say no thanks and then pick up the saddle and carry it with him anyway. He knew they hadn't wanted him in the first place, and it was just good manners or maybe guilt or embarrassment or something that made Toolie want to keep the saddle so Deaver had to come back at least one more time. Funny thing, though: Deaver didn't mind. It had been a long time since anybody went to any trouble to try to get him to stay with them. Them saying he was Ollie's friend. The way Katie treated him. That was part of it. A lot more of his feeling came out of just working alongside them, helping unload the truck and set up for the show. Deaver had enough sweat spilled in this field that he really wasn't hoping to leave for Moab today. He wanted to see what all the fuss was about. He wanted to see the show. That's all it was, nothing more.

Yet even as he reached that conclusion, he knew it was a lie. Sure, he wanted to see the show, but there was something more. An old hunger, one so deep and ancient, so long unsatisfied that Deaver mostly forgot he was even hungry. Like some part of his soul had already starved to death. Only something was happening here to wake up that old hunger, and he couldn't go away without seeing if somehow maybe it could be satisfied. Not Katie. Or not just Katie, anyway. Something more. Maybe by the time he left for Moab, he'd find out what it was he wanted so bad that it made his dream of joining Royal's Riders seem kind of faint and far away.

He and Toolie walked a direct route to the town hall, not winding through the whole village the way they had that morning. There were still children excited to see them, though. "Who are you!" they called. "Are you Noah? Are you Jesus? Are you Armstrong?"

Toolie waved at them, smiled, and usually told them, "No, my daddy plays that part."

"Are you Alma?"

"Yes, that's one of the parts I play."

"What's the show tonight?"

"*Glory of America.*"

All the way through town Deaver noticed how bright-eyed the children were, how daring they thought it was to talk right to somebody from the pageant wagon.

"Sounds like your show's the biggest thing they ever see," Deaver said.

"Kind of sad, isn't it?" said Toolie. "In the old days, a show like this—it would've been nothing."

Deaver went with Toolie into the mayor's office. The secretary had neat, close-cropped hair. Plainly he was the kind of man who never spent a week without a barber—or a day without a bath, probably. Deaver wasn't sure whether he despised or envied the man.

"I'm with the pageant wagon," said Toolie, "and I need to change our temporary permit to a regular one." Deaver saw how he put on an especially humble-but-cheerful tone, and he couldn't help but think that his own life would have been a lot easier if he'd only learned how to act like that toward his foster parents or the bishops of the wards he lived in. Of course, Toolie only had to act like that for a few minutes today, while Deaver would've had to keep it up for days and weeks and years on end. Like crossing your eyes—sure, you can do it, but keep it up too long and you get a headache.

And then he thought how when he was little, somebody told him that if you cross your eyes too often they'll stick that way. What if acting all humble and sweet worked that way? What if it got to be such a habit you forgot you were acting, the way Marshall's and Scarlett's fancy acting voices came out of their mouths even when they were picking up a range rider in the middle of the night. Do you become whatever you act like?

Deaver had plenty of time to think about all this, because the secretary didn't say a word for the longest time. He just sat there and eyed Toolie up and down, not showing any expression at all on his very clean and untanned face. Then he looked at Deaver. He didn't exactly ask a question, but Deaver knew what he was asking anyway.

"I'm a range rider," Deaver said. "They picked me up out on the road. I need to call Moab."

A range rider—town people pretty much despised them, but at least they knew what to do with them. "You can go right in there and call." The secretary indicated an empty office. "The sheriff's out on a call."

Deaver went on into the office and sat at the desk. An old salvage desk—might be one of the ones he found and brought in himself in the old days when he was a kid. Not ten years ago.

He couldn't get an operator—the line was tied up—and as he waited, he could hear what went on in the other room.

"Here's our family business license from Zarahemla," Toolie was saying. "If you just look us up in the business database—"

"Fill out the forms," said the secretary.

"We are licensed by the state of Deseret, sir," said Toolie. Still polite, still humble.

There was no answer. Deaver leaned over the desk and saw Toolie sitting down, filling out the forms. Deaver understood why Toolie was doing it, all right—giving in to get along. This was how the secretary proved he was in charge. This was how he made sure the show gypsies knew they didn't belong here, that they had no *rights* here. So Toolie would fill out the forms, and as soon as he was gone the secretary would call up the business database, verify their license, and throw out the forms. Or maybe he'd go through the forms line by line, looking for some contradiction, some mistake, so he could have grounds to throw the pageant wagon out of Hatchville. And it wasn't right. The Aal family had natural troubles all their own, they didn't need some short-haired overwashed flunky in the mayor's office adding to their trouble supply.

For a moment, pure rage flowed through Deaver, just like this morning when Marshall put his arm around him and called him *son*. His arms trembled, his toes pumped up and down, like he was getting ready to dance or wrestle—or punch some power-hungry bastard right in the face and break his nose and cover him with his own blood, mat it in his hair, all over his clothes, so even when he didn't hurt so bad, there'd be stains in his shirt to remind him that people can only be pushed so *far* and then one day they bust out and do something about it, show you what all your power's good for—

And then Deaver got it under control, calmed himself down. There was no shortage of volunteer self-trained sons-of-bitches in the world, and this secretary wasn't the worst of them, not close. Toolie was doing the right thing, bowing down and letting the man feel important. Letting him have the victory now, so that the family would have the greater victory later. 'Cause when they left this town, the Aals would still be themselves, still be a family, while this secretary, he wouldn't have a speck of power over them. That was freedom, the power to leave whenever you wanted to. Deaver understood that kind of power. It was the only kind he'd ever had or ever wanted.

He finally got an operator and told him who he was and who he needed to talk to and why. It took the operator forever to check the computer and verify that Deaver was indeed a range rider and that he was therefore authorized to make an unlimited number of calls to regional headquarters in Moab. At last he got through. It was Meech, the regular dispatcher.

"Got the scrapings?" asked Meech.

"Yeah."

"Fine, then. Come on in."

"Quick?"

"Not quick enough to pay money for. Just catch a ride. No hurry."

"Two, three days all right?"

"No rush. Except I got approval here for you to apply to Royal's Riders."

"Why the hell didn't you say so, dickhead!" cried Deaver into the phone. He'd been on that waiting list for three years.

"I didn't want you to wet your pants right off, that's why," said Meech. "Please note that this is just permission to apply."

How could Deaver tell him that he never expected to get permission even for that? He figured that was the way they'd freeze non-Mormons out, by keeping them from applying for the job in the first place.

"And I got about five guys, Teague, asking if you'll transfer your right to apply. They're pretty eager."

It was legal to sign over your spot to somebody farther down the list—it just wasn't legal to accept money for it. Still, the outrider waiting list was long, and there were bound to be some men on it who never meant to apply, who signed up just to make a little money selling their spot when it came along. Deaver knew that if he said yes and Meech gave him the names of those eager applicants, he'd start getting promises and favors. What he wouldn't get, though, was another chance to apply. "No thanks, Meech."

The secretary appeared in the doorway, glowering. "Just a second," Deaver said, and put his hand over the phone. "What is it?"

"Are you aware of the public decency laws?" asked the secretary.

It took a second for Deaver to figure out what he was talking about. Had the secretary heard Meech hint about selling the right to apply? No—it was the public decency laws the secretary was talking about. Deaver thought back over his phone conversation. He must have said *hell* too loud. And even though *dickhead* wasn't on the statutory list, it fit quite easily under "other crude or lascivious expressions or gestures."

"Sorry," he said.

"I hope you're *very* sorry."

"I am." He did his best to imitate the humble way Toolie'd been talking before. It was especially hard because he was suddenly in the mood to start laughing out loud—they were going to let him apply to the outriders!—and he figured the secretary wouldn't like it if Deaver suddenly laughed. "Very sorry, sir." He picked up that *sir* bit from Toolie, too.

"Because in Hatchville we don't wink at sin."

In Hatchville you probably don't piss, either, you just hold it all inside until you die. But Deaver didn't say it, just looked right at the secretary as calmly as he could until the man finally took his unbearable burden of righteousness back to his desk.

That's all Deaver needed, a misdemeanor arrest right when he was about to apply to be an outrider. "You still hanging on there, Meech?"

"By my fingernails."

"I'll be there in two days. I've got my saddle."

"Ain't you cool."

"Am too."

"Are not."

"See you, Meech."

"Give your erosion reports to the reporter there, OK?"

"Got it," said Deaver. He hung up.

The secretary grudgingly told him where the reporter's office was. Of course the reporter wasn't transmitting—that was done at night, over the same precious phone lines used for voice calls during the day. But he'd enter it into the computer today, and he didn't look thrilled at getting even Deaver's relatively slim notebook.

"All these coordinates," said the reporter.

"It's my job to write them down," said Deaver.

"You're very good at it," said the reporter. "Yesterday's desert, today's grass, tomorrow's farm." It was the slogan of the new lands. It meant the conversation was over.

When Deaver got back, Toolie wasn't in the secretary's office anymore. He was in the mayor's office, and because the door was partly open, Deaver could hear pretty well, especially since the mayor wasn't trying very hard to talk softly.

"I don't *have* to give you a permit, Mr. Aal, so don't start flashing your license from Zarahemla. And don't think I'm impressed because your name is Aal. There's no law says a hero's kinfolk got to be worth shit, do you understand me?"

Shit was definitely on the statutory list. Deaver looked at the secretary, but the secretary just moved more papers around. "Just don't wink," said Deaver quietly.

"What?" asked the secretary.

If he could hear Deaver's comment, he could sure hear the mayor. But Deaver decided not to make a big deal about it. "Nothing," he said. No reason for him to provoke the secretary any further. Since he came into town with the pageant wagon, anything he did to annoy people would put the Aal family in a bad light, and it sounded like they had trouble enough already.

"Young girls see you in those lights and costumes, they think you really are the prophet Joseph or Jesus Christ or Alma or Neil Armstrong, and so they're suckers for any unscrupulous bastard who doesn't care what he does to a girl."

Finally Toolie raised his voice, dropping the humility act just for a moment. Deaver was relieved to know Toolie had a breaking point. "If you have an accusation—"

"The Aal Pageant and Theatrical Association is implicated in a lot of these, do I make myself clear? No warrants, but we'll be watching. You tell everybody in your company, we're watching you."

Toolie's answer was too mild to hear.

"It will not happen in Hatchville. You will not ruin some girl and then disappear with your commission from the prophet."

So somebody *did* believe all those stories about show gypsies. Maybe Deaver used to believe them, too. But once you know people like the Aals, those stories sound pretty stupid. Except in Hatchville, of course, where they don't wink at sin.

Toolie was real quiet when he came out of the mayor's office, but he had the permit and the requisition form for the bishop's storehouse— both signed by the same man, of course, since the mayor *was* the bishop.

Deaver didn't talk about what he heard. Instead he told Toolie all about his getting permission to apply for a job change, which meant he at least had a shot at getting into the outriders.

"What do you want to do that for?" asked Toolie. "It's a terrible life. You travel thousands of miles on horseback, tired all the time, people looking to kill you if they get a chance, out in the bad weather every day, and for what?"

It was a crazy question. Every kid in Deseret knew why you wanted to be one of Royal's Riders. "Save people's lives. Bring them here."

"The outriders mostly deliver mail from one settled area to another. And make maps. It isn't that much more exciting than the work you're doing now."

So Toolie *had* looked into the work his uncle Royal was doing. How would Marshall feel about that?

"You ever think of joining?" asked Deaver.

"Not me," said Toolie.

"Come on," said Deaver.

"Never since I grew up enough to make intelligent choices." No sooner were the words out of his mouth than Toolie must have realized what he'd said. "I don't say it isn't an intelligent choice for you, Deaver. It's just—if one of us leaves, the family show is pretty well dead. Who'd do my parts? Dusty? Grandpa Parley? We'd have to hire somebody from outside the family—but how long would somebody like that work for nothing but food and shelter, like we do? If anybody leaves the show, then it's over for everybody. What would Dad and Mom do for a living? So how could I go off and join the outriders?"

There was something in Toolie's tone of voice, something in his manner that said, This is real. This is something I'm really afraid of—the family breaking up, the pageant wagon going out of business. And also: This is why I'm trapped. Why I can't have any dreams of my own, like you do. And because he was speaking true, like Deaver was somebody he trusted, Deaver answered the same way, saying stuff he never said out loud to anybody, or not lately, anyway.

"Being an outrider, it's got a name to it. A range rider—what do they call us? Rabbit stompers. Grass-herders."

"I've heard worse," said Toolie. "Something about getting personal with cows. You rangers have almost as low a name as we do."

"At least you're somebody every town you go into."

"Oh, yes, they roll out the red carpet for us."

"I mean you're Noah or Neil Armstrong or whatever."

"That's what we *play.* That's not who we are."

"That's who you are to *them.*"

"To the children," said Toolie. "To the grownups all a person is is what he does here in town. You're the bishop or the mayor—"

"The bishop *and* the mayor."

"Or the sheriff or the Sunday school teacher or a farmer or whatever. You're somebody regular. We come in and we don't fit."

"At least some of them are glad to see you."

"Sure," said Toolie. "I'm not saying we don't have it better than you, some ways. A gentile in a place like this."

"Oh. Katie told you." So it *had* mattered to her he wasn't Mormon, enough to tell her brother. Mormons *always* cared when somebody wasn't one of them. In a way, though, it made it so the way Toolie talked to him, like a friend—it meant even more, because he knew Deaver was a gentile all along.

And Toolie had the grace to act a little embarrassed about knowing something Deaver only told to Katie. "I wondered, so I asked her to find out."

Deaver tried to put him at ease about it. "I'm circumcised, though."

Toolie laughed. "Well, too bad it isn't Israel where you live. You'd fit right in."

Some trucker'd told him when he was about sixteen that Mormons were so damned righteous because they couldn't help it—after you get your dick cut all the way around, the sap can't flow anymore. Deaver knew the part about sap flowing wasn't true, but not till this moment did he realize that the trucker was also putting him on about circumcision being part of the Mormon religion. Once again Deaver had said something stupid and offensive without meaning to. "Sorry. I thought you Mormons—"

But Toolie was just laughing. "See? The ignorance is thick on every side." He clapped his hand onto Deaver's shoulder and left it there for a minute as they walked along the street of Hatchville. And this time it didn't make Deaver mad. This time it felt right to have Toolie's hand on him. They got to the storehouse and arranged for a cart to deliver their supplies that afternoon.

"Soldiers of the United States! We could march on Philadelphia and—we could march—"

"March under arms and grind Philadelphia beneath our boots."

"Soldiers of the United States! We could march under arms and boot Phila—"

"Grind Philadel—"

"Grind Philadelphia beneath our boots, and what then could—"

"What Congress then could—"

"What Congress then could deny our rightful claim upon the treasury of this blood which we created by—"

"Nation which we created—"

"I'll start over, I'm just confused a little, Janie, let me start over."

Old Parley had gone over George Washington's speech to his troops so many times that Deaver could have recited it word perfect, just from hearing it while he worked on bypassing a relay to the heater fan. With his head buried deep in the truck's engine, one leg holding him in place by hooking across the fender, the sound of Parley memorizing echoed loud. Sweat dripped off Deaver's forehead into his eyes and stung him a little. Nasty work, but as long as the fan kept blowing they'd remember him.

Got it. Now all he had to do was climb out, start up the truck, and try it to see if the fan motor actually worked.

"I've got it now, Janie," said Parley. "But are we now, for the sake of money, to deny the very principles of freedom for which we fought, and for which so many of our comrades fell? Help me here Janie, just a word."

"I."

"I what?"

"I say."

"Got it! I say thee, Nay!"

"I say that in America, soldiers are subject to the lawful government, even when that lawful government acts unjustly against them."

"Don't read me the whole speech!"

"I thought if you heard it once, Grandpa, you could—"

"You are my prompter, not my understudy!"

"I'm sorry, but we've been over it and—"

Deaver started the truck engine. It drowned out the sound of Parley Aal unfairly blaming Janie for his collapsing memory. The fan worked. Deaver turned off the motor.

"—suddenly starting up! I can't work on these lines under these circumstances, I'm not a miracle worker, nobody could hold these long speeches in their heads with—"

It wasn't Janie's voice that answered him now—it was Marshall's. "The motor's off now, so go ahead now."

Parley sounded more petulant. Weaker. "I say the words so often they don't mean anything to me anymore."

"They don't have to mean anything, you just have to say them."

"It's too long!"

"We've cut it down to the bare bones. Washington tells them they could seize Philadelphia and break Congress, but then all their fighting would be in vain, so be patient and let democracy work its sluggish will."

"Why can't I say *that?* It's shorter."

"It's also not at all what Washington would say. Dad, we can't have a *Glory of America* pageant without George Washington."

"Then you do it! I just can't do these things anymore! Nobody could remember all these long speeches!"

"You've done them a thousand times before!"

"I'm too old! Do I have to say it that plain, Marshall?" Then, more softly, almost pleading, "I want to go home."

"To Royal." The name was like acid sizzling on wood.

"To *home.*"

"Home is under water."

"*You* should be doing Washington's speech, and you know it. You've got the voice, and Toolie's ready to play Jefferson."

"Is he ready to play Noah?" Marshall spoke scornfully, as if the idea was crazy.

"*You* were his age when you started playing Noah, Marshall."

"Toolie isn't mature enough!"

"Yes he is, and you should be doing my parts, and Donna and I should be home. For the love of heaven, Marsh, I'm 72 and my world is gone and I want to have some peace before I die." Parley's speech ended with a ragged whisper. It was the perfect dramatic touch. Deaver sat in the cab, imagining the scene he couldn't see: Old Parley staring at his son for a long moment, then turning slowly and walking with weary dignity back to the tent. Every argument in this family is played out in set speeches.

The silence lasted long enough that Deaver felt free to open the door and leave the cab. He immediately looked back to where Janie and Parley had been practicing. Both gone. Marshall too.

Under the kitchen awning sat Donna, Parley's wife. She was old and frail, much older-seeming than Parley himself. Once they brought down her rocking chair early in the morning, she just sat there in the shade, sometimes sleeping, sometimes not. She wasn't senile, really; she fed herself, she talked. It was like she wanted to sit in her chair, close her eyes, and pretend she was somewhere else.

Now, though, she was here. As soon as she saw that Deaver was looking at her, she beckoned to him. He came over.

He figured she had in mind to tell him he ought to be more careful. "I'm sorry for starting the truck right then."

"Oh, no, the truck was nothing." She patted a stool sitting in the grass next to her. "Parley's just an old man who wants to quit his job."

"I know the feeling," said Deaver.

She smiled sadly, as if to say that there wasn't a chance in the world he knew that feeling. She looked at him, studying his face. He waited. After all, she had called him over. Finally she said what was on her mind. "Why are you here, Deaver Teague?"

He took it as a challenge. "Returning a favor."

"No, no. I mean why are you here?"

"I needed a ride."

She waited.

"I thought I ought to fix the heater fan."

Still she waited.

"I want to see the show."

She raised an eyebrow. "Katie had nothing to do with it?"

"Katie's a pretty girl."

She sighed. "And funny. And lonely. She thinks she wants to get away, but she doesn't. There is no Broadway anymore. The rats have taken over the theater buildings. They chewed up the NBC peacock and didn't leave a feather." She giggled at her own joke.

Then, as if she knew she'd lost the thread of her own conversation, she fell silent and stared off into space. Deaver wondered if maybe he ought to just go back to the truck or take a walk or something.

She startled him by turning her head and gazing at him again, her gaze sharper than ever before. "Are you one of the three Nephites?"

"What?"

"Appearing on the road like that. Just when we needed an angel most."

"Three Nephites?"

"The ones who chose to stay behind on Earth till Christ comes again. They go about doing good, and then they disappear. I don't know why I thought that, I know you're just an ordinary boy."

"I'm no angel."

"But the way the young ones turned to you. Ollie, Katie, Toolie. I thought you came to—"

"To what?"

"Give them what they want most. Well, why don't you anyway? You don't have to be an angel to work miracles, sometimes."

"I'm not even a Mormon."

"I'll tell you the truth," said the old lady. "Neither was Moses."

He laughed. So did she. Then she got that faraway look again. After he waited awhile, her eyelids got heavy, flickered, closed. He stood up, stretched, turned around.

Scarlett was standing not five feet away, looking at him.

He waited for her to say something. She didn't.

Voices off in the distance. Scarlett glanced toward them, breaking the silent connection between them. He also turned. Beyond the truck, the first group of townspeople were coming—looked like three families together, with benches and a couple of ancient folding chairs. He heard Katie call out to them, though he couldn't see her behind the truck. The families waved. The children ran forward. Now he could see Katie emerging, out in the open field. She was wearing the hoop skirts of Betsy Ross—Deaver knew the Betsy Ross scene because he'd had to learn the cue when to raise the flag, so that Janie could help Dusty with the costume change. The children overran her, turned her around; Katie squatted and hugged the two smallest both at once. She stood up then and led them toward the wagon. It was very theatrical; it was a scene played out for the children's parents, and it worked. They laughed, they nodded. They would enjoy the show. They would like the pageant family, because Katie greeted their children with affection. Theatrical—and yet utterly honest. Deaver didn't know how he knew that. He just knew that Katie really did love to meet the audience.

And then, thinking about that, he knew something else. Knew that he'd seen Katie play out some scenes today that she didn't mean, not the same way, not with that fervency that he saw when she greeted the children. This was real. Her flirting with Deaver, that was false. Calculated. Again, Deaver didn't know how he knew it. But he knew. Katie's smile, her touch, her attention, all that she'd given him today, all that she'd halfway promised, it was an act. She was like her father, not like Toolie. And it tasted nasty, just thinking about it. Not so much because she'd been faking it. Mostly because Deaver'd been taken in so completely.

"Who can find a capable wife?" asked Scarlett softly.

Deaver felt himself blush.

But it wasn't a real question. Scarlett was reciting. "Her worth is far beyond coral. Her husband's whole trust is in her, and children are not lacking."

He could see how the children clung to Katie. She must be telling them a story. Or just pretending to be Betsy Ross. The children laughed.

"She repays him with good, not evil all her life long. When she opens her mouth, it is to speak wisely, and loyalty is the theme of her teaching. She keeps her eye on the doings of her household and does not eat the bread of idleness. Her sons with one accord call her happy; her husband too, and he sings her praises: Many a woman shows how capable she is; but you excel them all."

It might be a recitation, but it had to have a point to it. Deaver turned to Scarlett, who was smiling merrily. "Are you proposing to me?" asked Deaver.

"Charm is a delusion and beauty fleeting; it is the God-fearing woman who is honored. Extol her for the fruit of all her toil, and let her own works praise her in the gates."

As best Deaver could figure it out, Scarlett was trying to get Deaver thinking about a wife when he looked at Katie. "You hardly know me, Mrs. Aal."

"I think I do. And call me Scarlett."

"I'm not a Mormon, either." He figured she'd probably been told already, but Deaver knew how much store Mormons set by getting married in the temple, and he also knew he never planned to set foot inside another Mormon temple in his life.

But Scarlett seemed to be ready for that objection. "That's not *Katie's* fault, now, is it, so why punish the poor girl?"

He couldn't very well say to her, Woman, if you think your daughter's really in love with me, then you're a plain fool. "I'm a stranger, Scarlett."

"You were this morning. But Mother Aal told us who you *really* are."

Now he understood that she was teasing him. "If I'm an angel, I got to say the pay isn't too good."

But she didn't really want to play. She wanted to talk seriously.

"There's something about you, Deaver Teague. You don't say much, and half what you say is wrong, and yet you caught Katie's eye, and Toolie said to me today, 'Too bad Teague has to leave,' and you made a friend of Ollie, who hasn't made a friend in years." She looked away, looked toward the truck, though nothing was happening there. "Do you know, Deaver, sometimes I think Ollie is his uncle Roy all over again."

Deaver almost laughed out loud. Royal? The hero of the outriders shouldn't be compared to Ollie, with his mocking smile, his petulant temper.

"I don't mean Royal the way he is now, and I especially don't mean his carefully constructed public image. You had to know him before, back before the collapse. A wild boy. He had to put his nose in everything. And more than his nose, if you understand me. It seemed as though anything his body craved, he couldn't rest until he got it. Terrible trouble. Stayed out of jail only by luck and praying, Mother Aal's praying, his luck."

As she spoke, Deaver noticed that her voice was losing that precision, that studied warmth. She sounded more like a normal person. Like as if just remembering the old days made her talk the way she used to, before she got to be an actress.

"He couldn't hold a job," she said. "He'd get mad at somebody, he couldn't take getting bossed around or chewed out, couldn't stand doing the same thing day after day. He got married when he was eighteen to a girl who was so pregnant the baby could have tossed the bouquet. He couldn't stay home, he couldn't stay faithful. Right before the Six Missile War, he up and joined the army. Never sent a dime home, and then the government fell apart and all that time, you know who took care of his wife and baby? Babies by then."

"You?"

"Well, I suppose. But not by *my* choice. *Marsh* took them in, they lived in our basement. I was so angry. There was barely enough for Marsh and me and our children, so every bite they ate, I felt like they were taking it out of the mouths of little Toolie and Katie and Ollie. I said so, too—not to them, but to Marsh. In private. I'm not a complete bitch."

Deaver blinked at hearing her use that word. "What did he say?"

"They're family, that's what he said. Like that was the whole answer. Family looks out for family, he said. He wouldn't even consider turning them out. Even when the university stopped classes and nobody had jobs, when we were eating dandelion greens and planting the whole yard for a garden just so the rain could come down and rip it all out—that terrible first year—rain tearing it out again and again—"

She stopped a moment to remember, to live in those days again. When she finally spoke again, she was brisk, getting on with the story.

"Then he came up with the idea of the pageant wagon. The *Aal Family* pageant was the very first, you know. Not a truck, not then—a trailer in those days, so it really was a kind of wagon, and we built the sets and Marsh wrote *The Glory of America* and adapted the old Hill Cumorah pageant so we'd have a Book of Mormon show and we went on the road. Oh, we were always a theatrical family. I met Marsh when his mother was directing plays at church."

She looked down at her mother-in-law, asleep in the chair.

"Whoever would have thought play-acting would keep us alive! It was Marsh took the Aal name and made it stand for something, one end of Deseret to the other. And somehow he made it—we made it pay enough to raise our own kids and Royal's too, kept bread on the table for all of us. His wife wasn't easy to live with, never pulled her weight, but we kept her the whole time, too. Until she ran off one day. And we still kept her kids, never put them in foster homes. They knew they could count on a place with us forever."

She couldn't possibly know how those words stung deep in Deaver's heart, reminding him of foster homes that always began with promises of "you're here for good" and ended with Deaver putting his ugly little brown cardboard box in the back of somebody else's car and riding off without ever even a letter or postcard from one of the old families. He didn't want to hear any more talk about places you could count on. So he turned the conversation back to Ollie. "I don't see how Ollie's like Royal. He hasn't left any children behind and run off."

She got a hard look in her eyes. "Hasn't he? It isn't for lack of trying."

Deaver thought of what the mayor said to Toolie this morning. The Aal family was implicated. Getting girls pregnant and running off, that was no joke, that could get a man in jail. And here Scarlett was as much as confessing that the accusation wasn't just small-town rumors, it was true and she knew it. And after what the mayor said, Deaver knew that if Ollie got caught, it would surely mean the loss of the family's license. They'd be dead broke—what value would their costumes and set pieces have to anybody else? They'd end up on some fringe farm somewhere. Deaver tried to imagine Marshall getting along with other farmers, fitting in. Tried to picture him covered with dirt and sweat, mud high up on his boots. That was what Ollie was flirting with, if Scarlett's accusation was true.

"I bet Ollie wouldn't do that," said Deaver.

"Ollie is Roy all over again. He can't control himself. He gets a desire, then he'll fulfil it and damn the consequences. We never stay in the same place long enough for him to get caught. He thinks he can go on like this forever."

"You ever explain it to Ollie like this?"

"You can't explain things to Ollie. Or at least *I* can't, and certainly Marsh and Toolie can't. He just blows up or walks away. But maybe you, Deaver. You're his friend."

Deaver shook his head. "That's the kind of thing you don't talk about to somebody you met this morning"

"I know. But in time—"

"I just got my chance to apply to the outriders."

Her face went grim. "So you'll be gone."

"I was going anyway. To Moab."

"Range riders come into town. They get mail. We might keep in touch."

"Same with outriders."

"Not for us," she said. Deaver knew it was true. They couldn't stay in touch with one of Royal's Riders. Not with Marshall feeling the way he did.

But still—if Ollie was really like Royal when he was younger, they could find some hope in that. "Royal came home, didn't he? Maybe Ollie'll grow out of it."

"Royal never came home."

"He's got his wife and kids now," said Ollie. "I've read about them. In the papers."

"That's how Royal came home—in the papers. We started reading stories about the outriders, and how the most daring one among them was a man named Royal Aal. In those days we were famous enough that they used to put in a little tag 'No relation to the theatrical Aal family.' Which meant they were asking him, and he was denying it. His kids were old enough to read, some of them. *We* never denied him. We'd tell the kids, 'Yes, that's your daddy. He's off doing such an important work— saving people's lives, destroying the missiles, fighting the mobbers.' We'd tell them how everybody sacrifices during hard times, and their sacrifice was doing without their daddy for a while. Marshall even wrote to Roy, and so did I, telling him about his children, how they were smart and strong and good. When Joseph, the oldest, fell from a tree and shattered his arm so badly the doctors wanted to take it off, we wrote to him about his son's courage, and how we made them save the arm no matter what—and he never answered."

It made Deaver sick to think of such a thing. He knew what it was like to grow up without a mother and father. But at least he knew that his parents were dead. He could believe that they *would* have come for him if they could. What would it be like to know your father was alive, that he was famous, and still have him never come, never write, never even send a message. "Maybe he didn't get the letters."

She laughed bitterly. "He got them, all right. One day—Joseph was twelve, he was just ordained a deacon a few weeks before—the sheriff shows up at our campsite in Panguitch, and he's got a court order. A court order, listing Royal and his wife as co-complainants—yes, they were back together now. Telling us to surrender the children of Royal Aal into the sheriff's custody or face kidnapping charges!"

Tears flowed down her face. They weren't beautiful, decorous actress tears; they were hot and bitter, and her face was twisted with emotion.

"He didn't come himself, he didn't write to ask us to send the children, he didn't even thank us for keeping them alive for ten years. Nor did that ungrateful bitch of a wife of his, and she ate at our table for five of those years."

"What did you do?"

"Marsh and I took his kids into the tent and told them that their father and mother had sent for them, that it was time for them to be together with their family again. You've never seen kids look happier. They'd been reading the papers, you see. That's who they thought Royal Aal was, the great hero. Like finding out that after years of being an orphan, your father the king had finally found you and you were going to be a prince and princesses. They were so happy, they hardly said goodbye to us. We don't blame them for that. They were children, going home. We don't even blame them for never writing to us since then— Royal probably forbade them to. Or maybe he told them lies about us, and now they hate us." Her left hand was in front of her face; her right hand clenched and unclenched on her lap, gathering folds of her dress in a sodden mass. "So don't tell me how Royal grew out of it."

This wasn't exactly the story folks usually told about Royal Aal.

"I read an article about him once," said Scarlett. "Several years ago. About him and his oldest son Joseph riding together out on the prairies, a second generation of hero. And they quoted Roy about how he had such a hard family life, that there were so many rules he always felt like he was in prison, but that he had rescued his boy Joseph from that prison."

Deaver had read that article, the way he read everything about Royal Aal. He thought he understood it when he read it; thought how he was in prison, too, and began to dream that maybe Royal Aal could rescue him, too. But now he'd spent a day with Royal's family. He could see how confining it was. Fights and squabbles. But also working together, everybody with a place that nobody else could fill. The kind of family he always wished for as a kid.

A thousand times over the years Deaver had imagined going to the outrider headquarters in Golden and going up to Royal Aal and shaking his hand, hearing Royal welcome him as one of his outriders. Only now if it really happened he'd be thinking of something else—like Marshall and Scarlett being served that court order. Like kids growing up without a word from their father. Like telling lies to make folks who'd done good to you look bad.

At the same time, Deaver could also see how it might look different to Royal, how as a kid he might have come to hate his brother Marshall—the man really was hard to take sometimes—and Deaver could guess that Parley wasn't the nicest, most understanding father in the world. This wasn't a family full of perfectly nice people. But that didn't mean they deserved dirt from him.

So how could Deaver become an outrider, knowing all this about Royal Aal? How could he follow such a man? Somehow he'd have to put all this out of his mind, forget that he knew it. Maybe some day he'd even get to know Royal well enough that he could sit down by him one night and say, What about your family? I met them once—what about them? And then he'd hear Royal's side of the story. That could change everything, knowing the other guy's side of the story.

Only he couldn't imagine any story Roy could tell that would justify what Scarlett went through—what she was still going through, just remembering. "I can see why you don't like to hear much about Royal now."

"We don't use our name much anymore," said Scarlett. "Do you know what that does to Marsh? Everybody thinks Roy's a hero, while every town we go into, they treat us like we're all thieves and vandals and fornicators. Someone once asked us if we stopped using the Aal name on our pageant wagon in order to protect Roy's reputation." She laughed—or sobbed. It wasn't too easy to tell. "It near eats Marsh alive. We still live from the charity of the church. Every bit of food from the bishop's storehouse. You don't know this, probably, Deaver Teague, but back in the old days, you only ate from the bishop's storehouse if you were down and out. A failure. It still feels that way to Marsh and me. Roy doesn't eat from the storehouse. Nor does his family these days. Roy doesn't move from town to town in the fringe."

Deaver knew something about how it felt when every bite you ate was somebody's charity, when you being alive at all was a favor other people did for you out of the goodness of their hearts. No wonder there was a touch of anger always under the surface in this family, ready to lash out whenever something went even a little bit wrong.

"And the thing that hurts worst about the way they treat us in these pitiful little towns is that we deserve it."

"I don't think so," said Deaver.

"Sometimes I wish Ollie would just run off like Roy—only do it now, *before* he has a wife and children for his brother Toolie to take care of."

That didn't seem fair to Deaver, and for once he felt bold enough to speak up about it. "Ollie works hard. I was with him all morning."

"Yes, yes," said Scarlet. "I know that. He isn't Roy. He tries to be good. But he always stands there with that little half-smile, as if he thinks we're all so terribly amusing. I saw that smile on Roy's face the whole time he was with us, before he ran of. That smile's like a sign that says, I may be with you, but I'm no part of you."

Deaver had noticed the smile, but he never thought that was what it meant. It seemed to Deaver that Ollie mostly smiled when he was embarrassed about the way his family was acting, or when he was trying to be friendly. It wasn't Ollie's fault that when he smiled, his face reminded people of Royal Aal.

"Ollie's old enough to be on his own," said Deaver. "When I was his age, I'd been driving a scavenger truck for a couple of years."

Scarlett looked at Deaver in disbelief. "Of course Ollie's *old* enough. But if he left, who'd do the lighting? Who'd keep the truck running? Marshall and Toolie and Katie and me—what do we know except the shows."

Didn't she see the contradiction in what she said? Ollie couldn't go because the family needed him—but all the time he was there, his own mother was wishing he'd run off so he wouldn't cause the harm his uncle caused. There was no sense in it at all. For all Deaver knew, Ollie was nothing at all like his uncle. But if his own mother saw him that way, then it was hard to see how Ollie could ever prove to her it wasn't true.

Deaver had seen a lot of families over the years. Even though he was never really a part of any one of them, he lived right with them, saw how the parents treated their children, saw how the children treated their parents. Better than most people, he understood how it was when something was wrong in a family. Everybody tries to hide it, to pretend everything's OK, but it always squeezes out somewhere. The Aals had all that pain from what Royal did and they couldn't get back at Royal, not a bit. But it so happened that they had a son who was a little bit like Royal. It was bound to squeeze out there, some of that pain. Deaver wondered how long Scarlett had thought of Ollie as being just little Roy. Wondered if Ollie had ever caught a scrap of a sentence about it. Or if one time when she was mad Scarlett had said it right out, "You're just like your uncle, you're exactly like him!"

That was the kind of thing a kid doesn't forget. One time a foster mother called Deaver a thief, and when it turned out her own kid had stolen the sugar and sold it, even though she made a big deal about apologizing to Deaver, he never forgot it. It was like a wall between them for the months before he was fostered somewhere else. You just can't unsay what's been said.

Thinking of that, of people saying cruel things they can't take back, Deaver remembered how Marshall gave a tongue-lashing to Toolie that morning. There was more going on in this family than Ollie reminding his mother of Roy Aal.

"I shouldn't have said any of this to you, Deaver Teague."

Deaver realized he must have been silent a long time, just standing there. "No, it's all right," said Deaver.

"But there's something about you. You're so sure of yourself."

People had said that to Deaver before. He long since figured out that it was because he didn't talk often, and when he did, he didn't say much. "I suppose," he said. "And when Mother Aal called you an angel . . . "

Deaver gave a little laugh.

"I thought—maybe the Lord led you to us. Or led us to you. At a time when we are in such great need of healing. Maybe you don't even realize it yourself, but maybe you're here to work a miracle."

Deaver shook his head.

"Maybe you can work a miracle without even knowing you're doing it." She took Deaver's hand—and now the theatricality was back. She was trying to make him feel a certain way, and so she was acting. Deaver was glad to know he could see the difference so clearly. It meant he could believe what she said when she wasn't acting "Oh, Deaver," she said. "I'm so scared about Ollie."

"Scared he'll run away? Or scared he won't?"

She whispered. "I don't know what I want. I just want things to be better."

"I wish I could help you. But about all I can do is work the flag in the Betsy Ross scene. And rewire the heater fan in the truck."

"Maybe that's enough, Deaver Teague. Maybe just by being who you are, maybe that'll do it. What if God sent you to us? Is that so impossible?"

Deaver had to laugh. "God never sent me anywhere."

"You're a good man."

"You don't know that."

"You only have to take one bite of the apple to know if it's ripe."

"I just happened to come along."

"Your horse happened to die that day and you happened to walk with your saddle so you arrived just when you did and we had brake trouble so we arrived when we did and you just happened to be the first person in years that Ollie's cared for and Katie just happened to take a liking to you. Pure chance."

"I wouldn't set much store on Katie taking a liking to me," said Deaver. "I don't think there's much in it."

Scarlett looked at him with deep-welling eyes and spoke with well-crafted fervor. "Save us. We don't have the strength to save ourselves."

Deaver didn't know what to say. Just shook his head and moved away, out into the gray, away from the truck, away from everybody. He could see them all—the crowd out front, the Aals working behind the truck, getting makeup on, setting up the props so they'd be ready to take onstage when they were needed. He walked a little farther away, and everybody got smaller.

If the crowd kept coming like this, there'd be hundreds of people by showtime. Everybody in town, probably. Pageant wagons didn't come through all that often.

The sun was still up, though, and people were still arriving, so Deaver figured he could take a minute to walk off by himself and think. Old Donna was crazy as a loon, calling him an angel. And Scarlett, asking him to somehow stop Ollie from wrecking them. And Katie, wanting whatever it was she wanted.

He only met these people last night. Not twenty-four hours ago. And yet he'd seen them so close and so clear that he felt like he knew them. Could they possibly also know him?

No, they were desperate, that's all it was. Wanting to change and using the first person who came along to help them do it. What Deaver couldn't understand was why they wanted to keep up their show-gypsy life in the first place. It wasn't much of a life, as far as Deaver could see. Working too hard, just to put on shows in towns that hated them.

Katie, what do you want?

She was probably part of this conspiracy of women—Scarlett, Donna, and Katie, all trying to get Deaver to stay in hopes he could make things better for them. The worst thing was he halfway wanted to stay. Even knowing Katie was faking it, he still was drawn to her, still couldn't keep his eyes off her without trying. What was it Meech said when a guy left the rangers to marry some woman? "Testosterone poisoning," that's what he called it. "Man gets sick with testosterone poisoning, that's the one disease takes you out of the rangers for good." Well, I got that disease, and if I wanted to I could plain forget everything else except Katie, at least for a while, long enough to wake up and find myself stuck here with a wife and babies and then I'd never go even if I wanted to, even if I found out Katie was play-acting all the time and never really wanted me at all—I'd never go because I'm no Royal Aal, I'm no foster father. If I ever got me a family I'd never leave my kids, never. They could count on me till I was dead.

Which is why I can't stay, I can't let myself believe any of this or even care about it. They're actors, and I'm not an actor, and I could no more be a part of them than I could be a part of Hatchville not being a Mormon. And as for Katie, I know better than to think a woman like that could ever love me. I'm a fool for even thinking about staying. They're all so unhappy, I'd just be guaranteeing myself as much misery as they've got. My life's work is out on the prairie with the outriders.

Even if Royal Aal is a gold-plated turd, even if I didn't fit in there, either, at least I'd be doing a work that made some difference in the world.

Deaver wound up in the apple orchard about a hundred yards south of the truck. Hatchville was enough years back from the fringe that the trees were big and solid enough to climb. He swung up into a branch. He watched the crowd still coming. It was getting late. The sun was about touching the mountains to the west. He could hear Katie's voice calling. "Ollie!"

Like hide and seek the neighborhood kids played when Deaver was little. Ollie ollie oxen free. Deaver was a champion hider. He heard that call more than once.

Then Toolie's voice. And Marshall's. "Ollie!"

Deaver imagined what would happen if Ollie just didn't come back. If he ran off like Royal did. What would the family do? They couldn't run the show without somebody running lights and firing off the electrical effects. Everybody else was on stage but Ollie.

Then Deaver got a sickening jolt in the pit of his stomach. There was one other person who knew something about the lighting and wasn't on stage. Can you help us, Deaver Teague? What would he say then? No, sorry, I got grass to tend, good luck and good-bye.

Hell, he couldn't say no and walk off like that, and Ollie knew it. Ollie sized him up right off, pegged him for the kind of guy who couldn't just go off and leave people in the lurch. That's why he made such a point of teaching Deaver how the lighting system worked. So Ollie could run off without destroying the family. And here everybody thought Ollie had chosen Deaver as a friend. No sir, Deaver Teague wasn't Ollie's friend, he was Ollie's patsy.

But he had to give Ollie some credit here. Scarlett was wrong about him—Ollie wasn't the kind just to run away like Royal did, and to hell with the family and the show. No, Ollie waited till he had a half-likely replacement before he took off. Too bad if Deaver didn't particularly want to run lights for the Aal family show—that wasn't Ollie's problem. What did he care about Deaver Teague? Deaver wasn't one of the family, he was an outsider, it was all right to screw around with his life because he didn't amount to anything anyway. After all, Deaver didn't have any family or any connections. What did *he* matter, as long as Ollie's family was all right?

Even though Deaver was burning, he couldn't help imagining Katie coming to him, frantic—no actress stuff now, she'd really be upset—saying, "What'll we do? We can't do the show without somebody running lights." And Deaver'd say, "I'll do it." She'd say, "But you don't know the changes, Deaver." And Deaver'd say, "Give me a script, write them down. I can do it. Whoever isn't on stage can help me." And then her lips on his, her body pressed up against him after the show, and then her sweet hot breath against his cheek as she murmured, "Oh, thank you, Deaver. You saved us."

"Don't *do* that." It was a girl's voice that snapped Deaver out of his imagination. Not Katie's voice. Behind him and to the north, deeper in the orchard.

"Don't *do* that." A man's voice, mocking. Deaver turned to look. In the reddish light of sunset, he could see Ollie and a girl from Hatchville. She was giggling. He was kissing her neck and had both hands on her buttocks, gripping so tight she was standing on tiptoes. Not very far away from Deaver at all. Deaver kept his mouth shut, but he was thinking, Ollie didn't run off after all. What he couldn't decide was whether he was glad of it or ticked off about it.

"You can't," said the girl. She tore away from him, ran a few steps, then stopped and turned away. Plainly she wanted him to follow her.

"You're right, I can't," said Ollie. "Time for the show. But when it's over, you'll be there, won't you?"

"Of course. I'm going to watch it all."

Suddenly Ollie got all serious-looking. "Nance," he said. "You don't know how much you mean to me."

"You just only met me a few minutes ago."

"I feel like I've known you so long I feel like—I feel like I've been lonely for you my whole life and didn't know it till now."

She liked that. She smiled and looked down, looked away. Deaver thought: Ollie's as much of an actor as anybody else in the Aal family. I ought to be taking notes on how to seduce a Mormon girl.

"I know it's right between us," said Ollie. "I know—you don't have to believe me, I can hardly believe it myself—but I know we were *meant* to find each other. Like this. Tonight."

Then Ollie reached out his hand. She tentatively put her hand in his. Slowly he raised her hand to his lips, kissed her fingers gently one by one. She put a finger of the other hand in her mouth, watching him intently.

Still holding her hand, he reached out and caressed her cheek with his other hand, just the backs of his fingers brushing her skin, her lips.

His hand drifted down her neck, then behind, under her hair. He drew her close; her body moved, leaning toward him; he took a single step and kissed her. It was like Ollie had every step planned. Every move, every word. He'd probably done it a hundred times before, thought Deaver. No wonder the Aals were implicated in a lot of ugly stories.

She clung to him. Melted against him. It made Deaver angry and wishful both at once, knowing what he was seeing wasn't right, that Ollie was fooling with a girl who believed all this stuff, that if he got caught he could cost his family their license to put on shows; yet at the same time wishing it was him, wishing to have such lips kissing him, such a sweet and fragile body clinging to him. It was enough to make a man crazy, watching that scene.

"Better go," Ollie said. "You first. Your folks would just get mad and not let you see me again if they saw us come out of the orchard together."

"I don't care, I'd see you anyway. I'd come to you at night, I'd climb right out my window and find you, right here in the orchard, I'd be waiting for you."

"Just go on ahead, Nance."

Far away: "Ollie!"

"Hurry up, Nance, they're calling me."

She backed away from him, slow, careful, like Ollie was holding her with invisible wires. Then she turned and ran, straight west, so she'd come up to the audience from the south.

Ollie watched her for a minute. Then he turned squarely toward Deaver and looked him in the eye. "Got a cute little ass on her, don't you think, Deaver?" he asked.

Deaver felt sick with fear. He just couldn't think what he was afraid of. Like playing hide-and-seek, when somebody you hadn't heard coming suddenly says, I see Deaver!

"I can feel you condemning me, Deaver Teague," said Ollie. "But you've got to admit I'm good at it. You could never do it like that. And that's what Katie needs. Smooth. Gentle. Trying the right thing. You'd just make a fool of yourself trying. You aren't fine enough for Katie."

Ollie said it so sad that Deaver couldn't help believing it, at least partly. Because Ollie *was* right. Katie could never really be happy with somebody like him. A scavenger, a range rider. For a moment Deaver felt anger flare inside him. But that was what Ollie wanted. If somebody lost his head here, it wouldn't be Deaver Teague.

"At least I know the difference between a woman and a cute little ass," said Deaver.

"I've read all the science books, Deaver, and I know the facts. Women are just bellies waiting to get filled up with babies, and they pump our handles whenever they get to feeling empty. All that other stuff about true love and devotion and commitment and fatherhood, that's all a bunch of lies we tell each other, so we don't have to admit that we're no different from dogs—except our bitches are in heat all the time."

Deaver was just angry enough to say the cruelest thing that came to mind. "That's just a story, too, Ollie. Fact is the only way you ever get to pretend you're a real man is by telling lies to little girls. A real woman would see right through you."

Ollie turned red. "I know what you're trying to do, Deaver Teague. You're trying to take my place in this family. I'll kill you first!"

Deaver couldn't help it—he busted out laughing.

"I could do it!"

"Oh, sure, I wasn't laughing at the idea of you killing me. I was laughing at the idea of me taking your place."

"You think I didn't notice how you tried to learn my whole job today? The way you had Katie hanging all over you? Well I belong in this family, and you don't!"

Ollie turned and started to walk away. Deaver dropped out of the tree and caught up to him in a few strides. He put his hand on Ollie's shoulder, just to stop him, but Ollie came around swinging. Deaver ducked inside the blow, so Ollie's arm caught him alongside the ear. It stung, but Deaver'd been in some good hard fights in his time, and he could take a half-assed blow like that without blinking. In a second he had Ollie pressed up against an apple tree, Deaver's right hand holding Ollie up by his shirt, his left hand clutching the crotch of Ollie's pants. The fear in Ollie's face was plain, but Deaver didn't plan to hurt him.

"Listen to me, fool," said Deaver. "I don't want to take your place. I got me a chance to apply to Royal's Riders, so what in hell makes you think I want to sit and run your damn fool dimmer switches? You were the one teaching me."

"Hell I was."

"Hell you *were*, Ollie, you're just too dumb to know what you're doing. Let me tell you something I'm not taking your place. I don't want your stupid place. I don't want to marry Katie, I don't want to run the lights, and I don't want to stay with your family one second after we reach Moab."

"Let me down."

Deaver ground his left hand upward into Ollie's crotch. Ollie's eyes got wide, but he was listening. "If you want to leave your family, that's fine by me, but don't do it by sneaking away and trying to stick me with your job. And don't do it by poking dumb little girls till their folks get your family's license pulled. However much you want to get away, you got no right to destroy your own people in order to do it. When you walk out, you walk out clean, you understand me?"

"You don't know me or anything about me, Deaver Teague!"

"Just remember, Ollie. For the next couple days till we get to Moab, I'm on you like flies on shit. Don't touch a girl, don't talk to a girl, don't even look at a girl here in Hatchville or I'll break more ribs on you than you thought you had, do you understand me?"

"What's it to you, Teague?"

"They're your family, you dumb little dickhead. Even dogs don't piss on their own family."

He let Ollie slide down the tree till he was standing on the ground, then let go of his pants and his shirt and stepped back a safe distance. Ollie didn't try anything though. Katie was still calling "Ollie! Ollie!" He just stood there, looking at Deaver, and then got his little half-smile, turned around, and walked out of the orchard, straight toward the pageant wagon. Deaver stood there and watched him go.

Deaver felt all jumpy and tingly, like all his muscles had to move but he couldn't think what he should do with them. That was the closest Deaver'd come to really tearing into somebody since he was in his teens. He'd always kept his anger under control, but it felt good to have Ollie pressed up against that tree, and he wanted so bad to hit him, again and again, to pound some sense into his stupid selfish head. Only that wasn't it, after all, because he was already ashamed of letting himself go so far. I was being a stupid kid, making threats, pushing Ollie around. He was right—what's it to me? It's none of my business.

But now I've made it my business. Without even meaning to, I've got myself caught up in this family's problems.

Deaver looked over toward the pageant wagon, silhouetted in the last light of dusk in the western sky. Just then the generator kicked on, and bank by bank the fresnels and ellipsoidals lit up, making a dazzling halo around the pageant wagon, so it looked almost magical. He could hear the audience clapping at the sight of the stage, now brightly lit.

The backstage worklights had also come on, and now in that dimmer light he could make out people moving around, and seeing them, grey shadows moving back and forth on business he didn't understand, he felt a sweet pain in his chest, a hot pressure behind his eyes. A longing for something long ago, something he used to have. So long lost that he could never name it; so deeply rooted that it would always grow in him. They had it, those men and women and children moving in silent business behind the truck, hooded lights glowing in the dusk. It was there in the taut lines that connected them together, a web that wound them together, binding them with every pass. Every blow they struck, every tender caress, every embrace, every backhanded shove as they ran from each other, and left still another fine invisible wire like a spider's thread, until the people could hardly be understood as individuals at all. There was no Katie, but Katie-with-Toolie and Katie-with-Scarlett; there was no Marshall, but Marshall-with-Scarlett and Marshall-with-Toolie and Marshall-with-Ollie and Marshall-with-Parley and above all Marshall-with-Roy. Roy who had hacked at those lines, cut them—he thought. Roy who went away never to return—he thought—but still the lines are there, still each move he makes causes tremors in his brother's life, and through him in all their lives, all the intersections of the web.

I've been caught in this net, too, and every tug and jiggle of their web vibrates in me.

A fanfare of music came over the loudspeakers. Deaver ducked under a branch and walked across the field toward the truck.

The music was loud, almost painful. An anthem—bugles, drums. Deaver came around the truck partway, well back from the lights, till he could see that Katie was onstage, sewing with big movements, so even the farthest audience member could see her hand move. What was she sewing? A flag.

The music suddenly became quieter. From his angle, Deaver couldn't see, but he knew the voice. Dusty, saying, "General Washington has to know—is the flag ready, Mrs. Ross?"

"Tell the general that my fingers are no faster than his soldiers," Katie said.

Dusty stepped forward, facing the audience; now Deaver could see him, right up to the front of the truck. "He must have the flag, Betsy Ross! So every man can see it waving high, so every man will know that his nation is not Pennsylvania, not Carolina, not New York or Massachusetts, but America!"

Suddenly Deaver realized that this speech was surely written for Washington—for Parley. It was only given to Dusty, as a young soldier, because of Parley's failing memory. A compromise; but did the audience know?

"A flag that will stand forever, and what we do in this dark war will decide what the flag means, and the acts of each new generation of Americans will add new stories to the flag, new honor and new glory. Betsy Ross, where is that?"

Katie rose to her feet in a smooth, swift motion, and in a single stride she stood at the front, the flag draped across her body in vivid red and white and blue. It was a thrilling movement, and for a moment Deaver was overcome with his feelings—not for Katie, but Betsy Ross, for Dusty's fervent young voice, for the situation, the words, and the bitter knowledge that America was, after all, gone.

Then he remembered that he was supposed to be backstage, ready to raise the flag when Katie was finished with the very speech she was beginning now. He was surely too late; he ran anyway. Janie was at the lever, not far away, Parley, in his full George Washington regalia, was standing behind the pyramid, ready to enter and deliver his speech to the soldiers. Onstage, Katie was saying her last few words: "If your men are brave enough, then this flag will ever wave—"

Deaver reached up and took the lever in his hand. Janie didn't even look at him; she immediately removed her hand, snatched up a script, and scrambled up the ladder to a position halfway up the back of the pyramid.

"O'er the land of the free!" cried Katie.

Deaver pulled the lever. It released the weight at the top of the flagpole; the weight plummeted, and the flag rose swiftly up the pole. Immediately Deaver grabbed the wire that was strung around the other side of the truck, invisibly attached to the outside top of the flag, by pulling and releasing the wire, he made the flag seem to wave. The music reached a climax, then fell away again. Deaver couldn't see the flag from where he was, but he remembered the cue and assumed the lights were dimmed on the flag by now. He stopped the waving.

Janie wasn't helping Dusty with a costume change at all, though that was the original reason why they asked Deaver to run the flag effect. Dusty had run straight back to the tent, and Janie was halfway up the pyramid, prompting Parley in Washington's speech to the troops. She did a good job. Parley's fumbling for his lines probably seemed to the audience to be nothing but Washington searching for just the right word to say. Yet Deaver knew that Parley botched the speech, leaving out a whole section despite Janie's prompting.

The speech ended. Parley came down in the darkness. Onstage Toolie was playing Joseph Smith and Scarlett was playing his mother. Marshall moved through the darkness wearing brilliant white that caught every scrap of light that reached him; he was going to appear as the angel Moroni. Parley came down the steps and turned, a few steps toward Deaver, into the darkest shadow. He bent over, resting his head and hands against the edge of the stage, the edge of the flatbed truck. Deaver watched him for a while, fascinated, knowing that Parley was crying, unable to bear knowing it. A man shouldn't have to wait until he wasn't any good before he retired. He should be able to quit while he still has some fresh accomplishment in him. But this—to have to stay on and on, lying again every night.

Deaver didn't dare speak to him; had he and Parley even spoken yet? He couldn't remember. What was Parley to him? An old man, a stranger. Deaver took a step toward him, another, reached out his hand, rested it on Parley's shoulder. Parley didn't move, not to move away, not to show a sign that he felt the hand and accepted it. After a while, Deaver took his hand away and went back around the truck to watch the show from the side, where he'd been before.

It took awhile to get back into the pageant, to follow what was happening. Dusty was onstage in blackface, to be the slave that Lincoln freed; Marshall made an imposing Lincoln, fine to look at. But Deaver also kept looking at the audience. He'd never watched a crowd like that before. The sun was long gone, the sky black, so all he could see was the people in front, where the light from the stage spilled back onto their faces. Mouths open, they watched the stage, unmoving, as if they were machines waiting for someone to switch them on. And now, onstage, Lincoln's hand reached out to the young slave and lifted him up out of bondage. "O happy day!" cried Dusty. The music picked up the refrain. O happy day. The Tabernacle Choir singing it.

Then Lincoln reached out both his arms to embrace the boy, and Dusty impulsively jumped up and hugged Lincoln around the neck. The audience roared with laughter. Deaver saw how, almost with one movement, their heads rocked back, then forward again; they stirred in their seats, then settled. The comic moment had released the tension of their stillness. They relaxed again. Then burst into applause at something they saw. Deaver didn't even bother looking at the stage to see what it was. The audience itself was a performance. Moving, shifting, laughing, clapping, all as one, as if they were all part of the same soul.

Toolie played Brigham Young as he led the Saints across the plains to Utah. Deaver vaguely remembered that the settlement of Utah was before the Civil War, but it didn't seem to matter—it worked fine this way in the show. To Deaver it seemed a little strange that a show called *Glory of America* should have an equal mix of Mormon and American history. But to these people, he realized, it was all the same story. George Washington, Betsy Ross, Joseph Smith, Abraham Lincoln, Brigham Young, all part of the same unfolding tale. Their own past.

After a while, though, he lost interest in the audience. They only did the same things—hold still, rapt; laugh; clap; gasp in awe at some spectacle. Only a limited sort of entertainment for someone watching them. Deaver turned back and watched the stage again.

It was time for the rocket. Even though it actually looked like a missile, and nothing at all like the Apollo launches, it was still something to watch Marshall put the helmet over his head and climb into the missile. All wrong—one man, not three, and riding in the rocket itself. Every school in Deseret taught better than that. But everyone understood. There was no way to put a fullsize Saturn rocket on the back of a pageant truck. What mattered was that it was a rocket with the letters NASA and USA on it, and the man getting in was supposed to be Neil Armstrong. A large puff of smoke represented the launch. Then the door opened again, Marshall came out; the music was soft, a high, thrilling violin. He opened the rigid American flag on its little stand and placed it on the ground in front of him. "A small step for a man," he said. "A giant leap for mankind."

The music reached a towering climax. Deaver's eyes filled with tears. This was the moment, America's climax, the supreme achievement, the highwater mark, and no one knew it at the time. Couldn't those people back in 1969 see the cracking, feel the crumbling all around them? Not thirty years later it was all gone. NASA, the USA itself, all gone, all broken up. Only the Indians to the south were making nations anymore, calling themselves Americans, saying that the white people of North America were Europeans, trespassers—and who could tell them no? America was over. It grew two hundred years, feeding and devouring the world, even reaching out to touch the moon, and now the name was up for grabs. Nothing left but scraps and fragments.

Yet we were there. That little flag was on the moon, the footprints unstirred by any wind.

Only gradually did Deaver realize that these things he was thinking were all being spoken; he heard the whispered words in the trembling voice of Scarlett Aal. "The footprints still are there, and if we go back, we will recognize them as our own."

Deaver glanced at the audience again. More than one hand was brushing a tear away. Just as Deaver's own hand went up to his cheek.

Now the collapse. Cacophonous music. Parley as the evil Soviet tyrant, Marshall as the bumbling fool of a president, together they mimed the blundering that led to war. Deaver couldn't believe at first that the Aals had chosen to show the end of the world as a comic dance. But it was irresistibly funny. The audience screamed with laughter as the Soviet tyrant kept stomping on the president's feet, and the president kept bowing and apologizing, picking up his own injured foot and hitting it himself, finally shaking hands with the Russian, as if making a formal agreement, and then stomping on his own foot. Every mimed cry of pain brought another roar of laughter from the crowd. This was their own destruction being acted out, and yet Deaver couldn't keep himself from laughing. Again he was wiping away tears, but this time so that he could see the stage at all through the blur of his own laughter.

The Russian knocked off the president's hat. When the president bent over to pick it up, the Russian kicked him hard in the behind and the president sprawled on the stage. Then Parley beckoned Dusty and Janie, dressed as Russian soldiers, to come over and finish him off.

Suddenly it wasn't funny anymore. They both held submachine guns, and jammed the butts again and again into the president's body. Even though Deaver knew that the blows were being faked, he still felt them like blows to his own body, terrible pain, brutal, unfair, and it went on and on, blow after blow after blow.

The crowd was silent now. Deaver felt what they all felt. It has to stop. Stop it now. I can't bear anymore.

At the moment when he was about to turn away, a drum roll began. Toolie entered, and to Deaver's astonishment he was dressed as Royal Aal. The plaid shirt, two pistols in his belt, the grizzly beard—there was no mistaking it. The audience recognized him at once, and immediately cheered. Cheered and leapt to their feet, clapping, waving their arms. "Royal! Royal! Royal!" they shouted.

Toolie strode down to where the Russian soldiers were still pounding the corpse of the President. With both hands he thrust them apart, knocking them down. Then he reached down to the president's body—to lift him up? No. To draw out of his costume the gold and green beehive flag of Deseret. The cheers grew louder. He carried it to the flagpole, fastened it where the American flag had been. This time the flag rose slowly, the anthem of Deseret began to play. Anyone who wasn't standing stood now, and the crowd sang along with the music, more and more voices, spontaneously becoming part of the show. As they sang, the flag of Deseret suddenly flowed outward, disappearing, as the American flag moved in behind it. Then the American flag flowed out and the flag of Deseret replaced it. Again and again, over and over, the flags changing. Even though Deaver had helped Katie set up the effect and knew exactly how it was done, he couldn't keep himself from being caught up in the emotion of the moment. He even sang with all the others as they reached the chorus. "Well sing and we'll shout with the armies of heaven! Hosanna! Hosanna to God and the King! Let glory to them in the highest be given, henceforth and forever, amen and amen!"

The lights went out on the stage; only a single spot remained on the flag, which had come to rest on the old American flag. It could have been the end of the show right there. But no. A single spotlight now on stage. Katie came out, dressed as Betsy Ross. "Does it still wave?" she asked, looking around.

"Yes!" cried the audience.

"Where does it wave!" she cried. "Where is it!"

Marshall, now dressed in a suit and tie, wearing a mask that mad ehim look pretty much like Governor Monson, strode into the light.

"O'er the land of the free!" he cried.

The audience cheered.

Toolie, dressed as Royal Aal, stepped into the light from the other side.

"And the home of the brave!"

The music immediately went into the "Star Spangled Banner" as the lights went out completely. The audience shouted and cheered. Deaver clapped until his palms stung and kept on beating his hands together until they finally ached and throbbed. His voice was lost in the crowd's shouting—no, rather the crowd's voice became his own, the loudest shout he had ever uttered in his life. It seemed to last forever, one great voice, one single cry of joy and pride, one soul, one great indivisible self.

Then the shouting faded, the clapping became more scattered. The faint audience lights came on. A few voices, talking, began among the crowd. The applause was over. The unity was broken. The audience was once again the thousand citizens of Hatchville. Little children were gathered up in their parents' arms. Families moved off together into the darkness, many of them lighting lanterns they had brought with them for the trek home in the night. Deaver saw one man he recognized, though he didn't think why; the man was smiling, gathered his young daughter into his arms, putting his arm around his wife, a little boy chattering words that Deaver couldn't hear—but all of them happy, smiling, *full.* Then he realized who the man was. The secretary from the mayor's office. Deaver hadn't recognized him at first because of that smile. It was like he was someone else. Like the show had changed him.

Suddenly Deaver realized something. During the show, when Deaver felt himself to be part of the audience, like their laughter was his laughter, their tears his tears—the secretary was part of that audience, too. For a while tonight they saw and heard and felt the same things. And now they'd carried away the same memories, which meant to some degree they were the same person. One.

The idea left Deaver breathless. It wasn't just him and the secretary, it was also the children, everybody there. All the same person, in some hidden corner of their memory.

Once again Deaver was alone on the boundary between the pageant wagon and the town, belonging to neither—yet now, because of the show, belonging a little bit to both.

Out in the crowd, Ollie stood up from behind the light and sound control panel. The girl from the orchard—Nance?—was standing by him. It made Deaver sad to see her, sad to think that she would translate all those powerful feelings of the pageant into a passion for Ollie. But there was nothing to worry about. The girl's father was right there with her, pulling her away. The town had been warned, and Ollie wasn't going to have his way tonight.

Deaver walked around behind the truck. He was still emotionally drained. Toolie had the door of the truck open and was peeling off his beard and putting it in its box by the light from the cab. "Like it?" he asked Deaver.

"Yeah," Deaver said. His voice was husky from yelling.

Toolie looked up, studied his face for a moment. "Hey," he said. "I'm glad."

"Where are the others?"

"In the tents, changing. I stay out here to make sure nothing walks away from the truck. Ollie watches out front."

Deaver didn't believe anyone would steal from the people who brought them such a show as this. But he didn't say so. "I can keep watch," he said. "Go in and change."

"Thanks," Toolie said. He immediately closed the box, shut the cab door, and jogged off to the tent.

Deaver walked out into the space between the tents and the truck. Because he was supposed to be keeping watch, he faced the truck, scanning across it. But his mind was on the people in the tents behind him. He could hear them talking, sometimes laughing. Did they know what they had done to him?

I was on both sides of this tonight, thought Deaver. I saw it, I was in the audience. But I also raised the flag the first time, made it wave. I was part of it. Part of every part. I'm one of you. For one hour tonight I'm one of you.

Katie came out of the girls' tent, looked around, walked over to Deaver. "Silly, wasn't it?"

It took a second before Deaver realized that she was talking about the show.

"Of course the history in it is pure nonsense," said Katie, "and there isn't a genuine character in the whole thing. It isn't like real acting. Watching that show, you wouldn't think any of us had any talent at all." She sounded angry, bitter. Hadn't she heard the crowd? Didn't she understand what the show had done to them? To *him?*

She was looking at him, and now she finally realized that his silence didn't mean he agreed with her at all. "Why, you liked it, didn't you," she said.

"Yes," he answered.

She took a little step backward. "I'm sorry. I forgot that you—I just guessed you haven't seen many shows."

"It wasn't silly."

"Well, it is, you know. When you've done it over and over again like we have. It's like saying the same word again and again until it doesn't mean anything anymore."

"It meant something."

"Not to me."

"Yes it did. There at the end. When you said—"

"When I said my *lines*. They were memorized speeches. Father wrote them, and I said them, but it wasn't me saying it. It was Betsy Ross. Deaver, I'm glad you liked the show, and I'm sorry I disillusioned you. I'm not used to having audience backstage." She turned away.

"No," Deaver said.

She stopped, waited for him to say more. But he didn't know what to say. Just that she was wrong. She turned around. "Well?"

He thought of how she was this morning, coming so close to him, holding on to him. How she went back and forth between real and fake, so smooth he could hardly tell the difference. But there *was* a difference. Talking about Katherine Hepburn, saying how she loved that movie, that was real. Flirting with him, that was fake. And tonight, talking about the show being silly, that was phony, that was just an attitude she was putting on. But her anger, that was real.

"Why are you mad at me?"

"I'm not."

"All I did was like the show," said Deaver. "What was so wrong about that?"

"Nothing."

He just stood there, not taking the lie for an answer. His silence was too demanding a question for her to ignore.

"I guess I was the one who was disillusioned," said Katie. "I thought you were too smart to be taken in by the show. I thought you'd see it for what it really is."

"I did."

"You saw Betsy Ross and George Washington and Neil Armstrong and—"

"Didn't you?"

"I saw a stage and actors and makeup and set pieces and costumes and special effects. I saw lines getting dropped and a flag that went up a little bit too late. And I heard speeches that no real human being would ever say, a bunch of high-flown words that mean nothing at all. In other words, Deaver, I saw the truth, and not the illusion."

"Bullshit."

The word stung her. Her face set hard, and she turned to go.

Deaver reached out and caught her arm, pulled her back. "I said bullshit, Katie, and you know it."

She tried to wrench her arm away.

"I saw all those things too, you know," said Deaver. "The screwed-up lines and the costumes and all that. I was backstage too. But I guess I saw something you didn't see."

"It's the first show you ever watched, Deaver, and you saw something I didn't?"

"I saw you take an audience and turn them into one person, with one soul."

"These tawnies are all alike anyway."

"Me too? I'm just like them? Is that what you're saying? Then why've you been trying so hard to make me fall in love with you? If you think I'm one of them and you think this show isn't worth doing, then why have you been trying so hard to get me to stay?"

Her eyes widened in surprise, and then a grin spread across her face. "Why, Deaver Teague, you're smarter than I thought. And dumber, too. I wasn't trying to get you to stay. I was trying to get you to take me with you when you left."

Partly he was angry because she was laughing at him. Partly he was angry because he didn't want it to be true that she was just using him, that she wasn't attracted to him at all. Partly he was angry because the show had moved him and she despised him for it. Mostly, though, he was so full of emotion that it had to spill out somehow, and anger would do.

"Then what?" he demanded. He talked low, so that the others wouldn't hear him in the tents. "Suppose I fell in love with you and took you with me, then what? Did you plan to marry me and be a range rider's wife and have my babies? Not you, Katie. No, you were going to get me hooked on you and then you were going to find some theater somewhere so you could play all those Shakespeare parts you wanted, and if that meant me giving up my dream of being an outrider, why, that was fine with you, wasn't it, because it doesn't matter to you what I sacrificed, as long as you got what you wanted."

"Shut up," she whispered.

"And what about your family? What kind of show can they do if you walk out? You think Janie can step in and do your parts? Is the old lady going to come back on stage so you can run away?"

To his surprise, she was crying. "What about me, then? Doing these stupid little backwater shows all my life—am I supposed to be trapped here forever just because they need me? Don't I get to need anything? Can't I ever do anything with my life that's worth doing?"

"But *this* show is worth doing"

"This show is worthless!"

"You know who goes to plays in Zarahemla? All the big shots, the people who work in clean shirts all day. Is that who you want to do plays for? What difference is your acting going to make in their lives? But these people here, what is their life except rain and mud and lousy little problems and jobs always needing to get done and not enough people to do them. And then they come here and see your show, and they think—hey, I'm part of something bigger than this place, bigger than Hatchville, bigger than the whole fringe. I know they're thinking that, because *I* was thinking that, do you understand me, Katie? Riding the range and checking the grass, all by myself out there, I thought I was worthless to everybody, but tonight it went through my head—just for a minute, it came to my mind that I was part of something, and that whatever it was I was part of, it was pretty fine. Now maybe that's worthless to you, maybe that's silly. But I think it's worth a hell of a lot more than going to Zarahemla and play-acting the part of *Titanic*."

"Titania," she whispered. "The Titanic was a boat that sank."

He was shaking, he was so angry and frustrated. This was why he gave up years ago trying to talk about anything important to people—they never listened, never understood a thing he said. "You don't know what's real and you don't know what matters."

"And you do?"

"Better than you."

She slapped his face. Good and sharp and hard, and it stung like hell. "That was real," she said.

He grabbed her shoulders, meaning to shake her, but instead his fingers got tangled up in her hair and he found himself holding onto her and pulling her close and then he did what he really wanted to do, what he'd been wanting to do ever since he woke up and found her sitting beside him in the cab of the truck. He kissed her, hard and long, holding her so close he could feel every part of her body pressed against his own. And then he was done kissing her. He relaxed his hold on her and she slipped down and away from him a little, so he could look down and see her face right there in front of him. *"That was real,"* he said.

"Everything always comes down to sex and violence," she murmured.

She was making a joke about it. It made him feel sick. He let go of her, took his hands off her completely. "It was real to me. It mattered to me. But you've been faking it all day, it didn't matter to you a bit, and I think that stinks. I think that makes you a liar. And you know what else? You don't deserve to be in this show. You aren't good enough."

He didn't want to hear her answer. He didn't want anything more to do with her. He felt ashamed of having showed her how he felt about her, about the show, about anything. So many years he'd kept to himself, never getting close to anybody, never talking about anything he really cared about, and now when he finally blurted out something that mattered to him, it was to *her.* He turned his back on her and walked away, heading around the truck. Now that he wasn't so close to her, paying so much attention, he realized that there were other people talking. Sound carried pretty good tonight in the dear dry air. Probably everybody in the tents heard their whole conversation. Probably they were all peeking out to watch. No humiliation was complete without witnesses.

Some of the talking, though, got louder as he rounded the back of the truck. It was Marshall and somebody else out by the light and sound control panel. Ollie? No, a stranger. Deaver walked on over, even though he didn't feel like talking to anybody, because he had a feeling that whatever was going on, it wasn't good.

"I can be back with a warrant in ten minutes and then I'll find out whether she's here or not," said the man, "but the judge won't like having to make one out this time of night, and he might not be so easy on you."

It was the sheriff. It didn't take Deaver long to guess that Ollie'd got himself caught doing something stupid. But no, that couldn't be, or the sheriff wouldn't need a warrant. A warrant meant searching for something. Or somebody. Whatever was happening, it meant Deaver hadn't stayed on Ollie tight enough. Hadn't the girl said something about meeting him after the show, even if she had to sneak out of her window to do it? He should have remembered before. He shouldn't have let his eyes off Ollie. It was all Deaver's fault.

"Who you looking for, sheriff?" Deaver asked.

"None of your problem, Deaver," said Marshall.

"This your son?" asked the sheriff.

"He's a range rider," said Marshall. "We gave him a ride and he's been helping out a little."

"You seen a girl around here?" asked the sheriff. "About this high, name of Nancy Pulley. She was seen talking to your light man after the show."

"I saw a girl talking to Ollie," said Deaver. "Right after the show, but it looked to me like her father pulled her away."

"Yeah, well, could be, but she isn't home right now and we're pretty sure she meant to come back here and meet somebody."

Marshall stepped in between Deaver and the sheriff. "All our people are here, and there aren't any outsiders."

"Then why don't you just let me go in and check, if you got nothing to hide?"

Of course Deaver knew why. Ollie must be missing. It was too late to go find him before trouble started.

"We have a right to be protected against unreasonable searches, sir," said Marshall. He would've gone on, no doubt, but Deaver cut him off by asking the sheriff a question.

"Sherlff, the show's only been over about fifteen minutes," said Deaver. "How do you know she isn't off with some girlfriend or something? Have you been checking their houses?"

"Look, smart boy," said the sheriff, "I don't need you telling me my business."

"Well, I guess not. I think you know your business real good," said Deaver. "In fact, I think you know your business so good that you *know* this girl wouldn't be off with a girlfriend. I bet this girl has caused you a lot of trouble before."

"That's none of your business, range rider."

"I'm just saying that—"

But now Marshall had caught the drift of what Deaver was doing, and he took over. "I am alarmed, sir, that there might be a chance that this girl from your town is corrupting one of my sons. My sons have little opportunity to associate with young people outside our family, and it may be that an *experienced* girl might lead one of them astray."

"Real smart," said the sheriff, glaring at Marshall and then at Deaver and then at Marshall again. "But it isn't going to work."

"I don't know what you mean," said Marshall. "I only know that you were aware that this girl was prone to illicit involvement with members of the opposite sex, and yet you made no effort to protect guests in your town from getting involved with her."

"You can just forget that as a line of defense in court," said the sheriff.

"And why is that?" asked Marshall.

"Because her father's the judge, Mr. Aal. You start talking like that, and you've lost your license in a hot second. You might get it back on appeal, but with Judge Pulley fighting you every step of the way, you aren't going to be working for months."

Deaver couldn't think of anything to say. To Deaver's surprise, neither could Marshall.

"So I'm coming back in ten minutes with a warrant, and you better have all your boys here in camp, and no girls with them, or your days of spreading corruption through the fringe are over."

The sheriff walked a few paces toward the road, then turned back and said, "I'm going to call the judge on my radio, and then I'll be sitting right here in my car watching your camp till the judge gets here with the warrant. I don't want to miss a thing."

"Of course not, you officious cretin," said Marshall. But he said it real quiet, and Deaver was the only one who heard him.

It was plain what the sheriff planned. He was hoping to catch Nancy Pulley running away from the camp, or Ollie sneaking back.

"Marshall," said Deaver, as quiet as he could, "I saw Ollie with that girl in the orchard before the show."

"I'm not surprised," said Marshall.

"I take it Ollie isn't in camp."

"I haven't checked," said Marshall.

"But you figure he's gone."

Marshall didn't say anything. Wasn't about to admit anything to an outsider, Deaver figured. Well, that was proper. When the family's in trouble, you got to be careful about trusting strangers.

"I'll do what I can," said Deaver.

"Thanks," said Marshall. It was more than Deaver expected him to say. Maybe Marshall understood that things were bigger than Marshall could handle just by telling people off. Deaver walked along after the sheriff, and came up to him just as he was setting down his radio mouthpiece. The sheriff looked up at him, already looking for a quarrel. "What is it, range rider?"

"My name's Deaver Teague, Sheriff, and I've only been with the Aals since this morning when they picked me up. But that was long enough to get to know them a little, and I got to tell you, I think they're pretty good people."

"They're all actors, son. That means they can seem to be anything they want."

"Yeah, they're pretty good actors, aren't they. That was some show, wasn't it?"

The sheriff smiled. "I never said they weren't good actors."

Deaver smiled back. "They *are* good. I helped them set up today. They work real hard to put on that show. Did you ever try to lift a generator? Or put up those lights? Getting from a loaded truck to a show tonight—they put in an honest day's work."

"Are you getting somewhere with this?" asked the sheriff.

"I'm just telling you, they may not do farm work like most folks here in town, but it's still real work. And it's a good kind of work, I think. Didn't you see the faces of those kids tonight, watching the show? You think they didn't go home proud?"

"Shoot, boy, I know they did. But these show people think they can come in here and screw around with the local girls and . . ." His voice trailed off. Deaver made sure not to interrupt him. "That man you talked to, sheriff, this isn't just his business, it's his family, too. He's got his wife and parents with him, and his sons and daughters. You got any children, sheriff?"

"Yes I do, but I don't let them go off any which way like some people do."

"But sometimes kids do things their parents taught them not to do. Sometimes kids do something really bad, and it breaks their parents' hearts. Not your kids, but maybe the Aals have a kid like that, and maybe Judge Pulley does too. And maybe when their kids are getting in trouble, people like the Aals and the Pulleys, they do anything they can to keep their kids out of trouble. Maybe they even pretend like anything their kid does, it was somebody else's fault."

The sheriff nodded. "I see what you're getting at, Mr. Teague. But that doesn't change my job."

"Well what is your job, sheriff? Is it putting good people out of work because they got a grown-up son they can't handle? Is it causing Judge Pulley's daughter to get her name dragged through the mud?"

The sheriff sighed. "I don't know why I started listening to you, Teague. I always heard you range riders never talked much."

"We save it all up for times like this."

"You got a plan, Teague? Cause I can't just drive off and forget about this."

"You just go on and do what you got to do, sheriff. But if it so happens that Nancy Pulley gets home safe and sound, then I hope you won't do anything to hurt either one of these good families."

"So why didn't that actor talk good sense like you instead of getting all hoity-toity with me?"

Deaver just grinned. No use saying what he was thinking—that Marshall wouldn't have gotten hoity-toity if the sheriff hadn't treated him like he was already guilty of a dozen filthy crimes. It was good enough that the sheriff was seeing them more like ordinary folks. So Deaver patted the door of the car and walked on up the road toward the orchard. Now all Deaver had to do was find Ollie.

It wasn't hard. It was like they wanted to be found. They were in tall grass on the far side of the orchard. She was laughing. They didn't hear Deaver coming, not till he was only about ten feet away. She was naked, lying on her dress spread out like a blanket under her. But Ollie still had his pants on, zipped tight. Deaver doubted the girl was a virgin, but at least it wasn't Ollie's fault. She was playing with his zipper when she happened to look up and see Deaver watching. She screeched and sat up, but she didn't even try to cover herself. Ollie, though, he picked up his shirt and tried to cover her.

"Your daddy's looking for you," Deaver said.

She made her mouth into a pout. To her it was a game, and it didn't matter that much to lose a round.

"Do you think we care?" said Ollie.

"Her daddy is the judge of this district, Ollie. Did she tell you that?" It was plain she hadn't.

"And I just got through talking to the sheriff. He's looking for *you*, Ollie. So I think it's time for Nancy to get her clothes back on."

Still pouting, she got up and started pulling her dress on over her head. "Better put on your underwear," said Deaver. He didn't want any evidence lying around.

"She didn't wear any," said Ollie. "I wasn't exactly corrupting the innocent."

She had her arms through the sleeves, and now she poked her head through the neck of her bunched-up dress and flashed a smile at Deaver. Her hips moved just a little, just enough to draw Deaver's eyes there. Then she shimmied her dress down to cover her.

"Like I told you," said Ollie. "We men are just pumps with handles on them."

Deaver ignored him. "Get on home, Nancy. You need your rest—you've got a long career ahead of you."

"Are you calling me a whore?" she demanded.

"Not while you're still giving it away free," said Deaver. "And if you have any idea about crying rape, remember that there's a witness who saw you taking down his zipper and laughing while you did it."

"As if Papa would believe you and not me!" But she turned and walked off into the trees. No doubt she knew all the paths home from this place.

Ollie was standing there, making no move to put on his shirt or his shoes. "This was none of your business, Deaver." It was light enough to see that Ollie was making fists. "You got no right to push me around."

"Come on, Ollie, let's get back to the camp before the judge gets there with a warrant."

"Maybe I don't want to."

Deaver didn't want to argue about it. "Let's go."

"Try and make me."

Deaver shook his head. Didn't Ollie realize his fighting words were straight out of third grade recess?

"Come on, Deaver," Ollie taunted. "You said you were going to protect the family from nasty little Ollie, so do it. Break all my ribs. Cut me up in little pieces and carry me home. Don't you carry a knife in your big old ranger boots? Isn't that how big tough strong guys like you get other people to do whatever you say?"

Deaver was fed up. "Act like a man, Ollie. Or don't you have enough of the family talent to fake decency?"

Ollie lost his cockiness and his swagger all at once. He charged at Deaver, waving both arms in blind rage. It was plain he meant to do a lot of damage. It was also plain he had no idea how to go about doing it. Deaver caught him by one arm and flung him aside. Ollie sprawled on the ground. Poor kid, thought Deaver. Traveling with this pageant wagon all his life, he never even learned how to land a punch.

But Ollie wasn't done. He got up and charged again, and this time a couple of his blows did connect. Nothing bad, but it hurt, and Deaver threw him down harder. Ollie landed wrong on his wrist and cried out with pain. But he was so angry he still got up again, this time striking out with only his right hand, and when he got in close he swung his head from side to side trying to butt Deaver in the face, and when Deaver got hold of his arms Ollie kicked him, tried to knee him in the groin, until finally Deaver had to let go of him and punch him hard in the stomach. Ollie collapsed to his knees and threw up.

The whole time, Deaver never got mad. He couldn't think why—rage had been close to the surface all day, and yet now, when he was really fighting somebody, there was nothing. Just a cold desire to get through with the fighting and get Ollie home.

Maybe it was because he'd already used up his anger on Katie. Maybe that was it.

Ollie was finished vomiting. He picked up his shirt and wiped off his mouth.

"Come on back to camp now," said Deaver.

"No," said Ollie.

"Ollie, I don't want to fight you anymore."

"Then go away and leave me alone."

Deaver bent over to help him to his feet. Ollie jabbed an elbow into Deaver's thigh. It hurt. Deaver was pretty sure Ollie meant to get him in the crotch. This boy didn't seem to know when he was beat.

"I'm not going *back!*" said Ollie. "And even if you knock me out and carry me back, I'll tell the sheriff all about the judge's daughter, I'll tell him I balled her brains out!"

That was about the stupidest, meanest thing Deaver ever heard. For a second he wanted to kick Ollie in the head, just to bounce things around a little inside. But he was sick of hurting Ollie, so he just stood there and asked, "Why?"

"Because you were right, Deaver, I thought about it and you were right, I *do* want to get away from my family. But I don't want you to take my place. I don't want anybody to take my place. I don't want anybody to *have* a place. I want the whole show closed down. I want father to be a dirt farmer instead of bossing people around all the time. I want perfect little Toolie up to his armpits in pigshit. You understand me, Deaver?"

Deaver looked at him kneeling there, a puddle of puke in front of him in the grass, holding his hurt wrist like a little boy, telling Deaver that he wanted to destroy his own family. "You're the kind of son who doesn't deserve to have parents."

Ollie was crying now, his face twisted up and his voice high-pitched and breaking, but that didn't stop him from answering. "That's right, Deaver, O great judge of the earth! I sure as hell don't deserve *these* parents. Mommy who keeps telling me I'm 'just like Royal' till I want to reach down her throat and tear her heart out. And Daddy who decided I didn't have enough talent so *I* was the one who had to do all the technical work for the show while Toolie got to learn all the parts so someday he'd take Daddy's place and run the company and tell *me* what to do every day of my life until I die! Well, the joke's on Toolie, isn't it? Cause Daddy's never going to give up his place in the company, he's never going to take over the old man part and let Grandpa retire, because then Toolie would be the leading actor and Toolie would run the company and poor Daddy wouldn't be boss of the universe anymore. So Toolie's going to keep on playing the juvenile parts until he's eighty and Daddy's a hundred and ten because Daddy won't ever step aside, he won't even die, he'll just keep on running everybody like puppets until finally somebody gets up the guts to kill him or quit. So don't give me any shit about what I deserve, Deaver."

A lot of things were suddenly making sense now. Why Marshall wouldn't let Parley retire. Why Marshall came down so hard on Toolie, kept telling him that he wasn't ready to make decisions. Because Ollie was right. Their places in the show set the order of the family. Whoever had the leading role was head of the company and therefore head of the family. Marshall couldn't give it up.

"I never realized how bad I wanted to get out of this family till you said what you said tonight, Deaver, but then I knew that getting out isn't enough. Because they'd just find somebody to take my place. Maybe you. Or maybe Dusty. Somebody, anyway, and the pageant wagon would go on and on and I want it to *stop*. Take away father's license, that's the only way to stop him. Or no, I've got a better way. I'll go shoot my Uncle Royal. I'll take a shotgun and blast his head off and *then* Daddy can retire. That's the only reason he can't let go of anything, because Royal's in charge of the outriders, Royal's the biggest hero in Deseret, so Daddy can't bear to let himself shrink even the teensiest bit, even if it wrecks everybody's life because my father is just as selfish and rotten as Uncle Royal ever was."

Deaver didn't know what to say. It all sounded true, and yet at the core of it, it wasn't true at all. "No he isn't," Deaver said.

"How would you know! You've never had to live with him. You don't know what it's like being a *nothing* in this family while he's always sitting in judgment on you and you can never measure up, you're never good enough."

"At least he didn't leave you," said Deaver.

"I wish he had!"

"No you don't," said Deaver.

"Yes I do!"

"I'm telling you, Ollie," Deaver said slowly. "I've seen how your father is and how your mother is and they look pretty good to me, compared."

"Compared to what," said Ollie scornfully.

"Compared to nothing."

The words hung there in the air, or so it felt to Deaver. Like he could see his own words, could hear them in his own ears as if somebody else said them. He wasn't talking to Ollie now, he was talking to himself. Ollie really did need to get free. His parents really were terrible for him, Ollie hated his place in the family and it wasn't right to force him to stay in it. But Deaver wasn't a son in this family. He never was, he never would be. So he could do Ollie's job and never feel the same kind of hurt at not being the chosen son. The bad things in the family would never touch him, not the way they touched Ollie—but the good things, Deaver could still have some of those. Being part of a company that needed him. Helping put on shows that changed people. Living with people that you knew would be there tomorrow and the next day, even if all the rest of the world changed around you.

What Deaver realized then was that he really did want Ollie to leave, not so Deaver could take Ollie's place, but so he could have a chance to make his own place among the Aals. Not so he could have Katie, he realized now, or at least not so he could have Katie in particular. He wanted to have them all. Father and mother, grandfather and grand-mother, brothers and sisters. Some day children. To be part of that vast web reaching back into the past farther than anybody could remember and down into the future farther than anybody could dream. Ollie had grown up in it, so all he wanted to do was get away—but he'd find out soon enough that he could never get away, not really. Just little Royal, he'd find that the web held firm, for good or ill. Even if you try to hurt

them, even if you cut them to the heart, your own people never stop
being your own people. They still care about you more than anyone else,
you still matter to them more, the web still holds you, so that Royal
might have a million people adoring him, but none of them knew him
as well, none of them cared about him as much as his brother Marshall,
his sister-in-law Scarlett, his old parents Parley and Donna.

Deaver knew what he had to do. It was so plain he wondered why
he never saw it before.

"Ollie, come back to camp tonight, and spend tomorrow teaching
me everything you can about your job. Then when we get to Moab, I'll
take you in and transfer my outrider application rights to you."

Ollie laughed. "I've never ridden a horse in my life."

"Maybe not," said Deaver. "But Royal Aal is your uncle, and he owes
the life of his wife and children to your father. Maybe there's too much
bad blood between them for them ever to talk to each other again, but
if Royal Aal is any kind of man at all, he'll feel a debt."

"I don't want anybody taking me on because they owe my father
something."

"Hell, Ollie, do you think somebody's going to take you on cause
you look so good? Try it out. See if you like being away from the pageant
wagon. If you want to come back, fine. If you want to go on somewhere
else, fine. I'm giving you a chance."

"Why?"

"Because you're giving me a chance."

"Do you think Father would ever let you be part of the company, if
you helped me sneak away?"

"I'm not talking about sneaking away. I'm talking about walking
away, standing up, no hard feelings. You doing no harm to the company
cause I'm there to do your jobs. Them doing no harm to you because
you're still family even if you aren't part of the show anymore. That's
what I think is wrong with all of you. You can't tell where the show
leaves off and the family begins.

Ollie stood up, slowly. "You'd do that for me?"

"Sure," said Deaver. "Beat you up, give you application rights,
whatever you want. Just come on back to camp, Ollie. We can talk it
over with your father tomorrow."

"No," said Ollie. "I want his answer tonight. Now."

Only now, with Ollie standing up, could Deaver see his eyes clearly
enough to realize that he wasn't looking at Deaver at all. He was looking

past him, looking at something behind him. Deaver turned. Marshall Aal was standing there, maybe fifteen yards back, mostly in the shadow of the trees. Now that Deaver had seen him, Marshall stepped out into the moonlight. His face was terrible, a mix of grief and rage and love that about tore Deaver's heart out with pity even though it also made him afraid.

"I knew you were there, Father," said Ollie. "I knew it the whole time. I wanted you to hear it all."

Well then what the hell was *I* doing here, thought Deaver. What difference did *I* make, if Ollie was really talking to his father all along? All I was good for was talking sense to the sheriff and punching Ollie in the belly so he'd puke his guts out. Well, glad to oblige.

They didn't pay any attention to him. They just stood there, looking at each other, till Deaver figured that it wasn't any of his business anymore. What was going on now wasn't about Deaver Teague, it was about Marshall and Ollie, and Deaver wasn't part of the family. Not yet, anyway.

Deaver walked on back into the orchard and kept walking till he got to the truck. The sheriff was standing there alone, leaning on the hood.

"Where you been, Teague?"

"Judge still coming?"

"He's come and gone. I've got the warrant."

"I'm sorry to hear that," said Deaver.

"The girl's home safe," said the sheriff. "But she's sure pissed off at you."

Deaver's heart sank. She told. Probably lies.

"She says she was just doing a little hugging and kissing, and along you come and make her go home."

Well, she lied, all right, but it was a decent kind of lie, one that wouldn't get anybody in trouble. "Yeah, that's it," said Deaver. "Ollie, though, he didn't appreciate my help. His father's out there now, talking him into coming home."

"Right," said the sheriff. "Well, the way it looks to me, there's no harm done, and the judge isn't calling for blood either, since he believes whatever his sweet little girl tells him. So I don't plan to use this warrant tonight. And if everybody behaves themselves tomorrow then these show gypsies can do their pageant and move on down the road."

"No bad report on them?" said Deaver.

"Nothing to report," said the sheriff. Then he sort of smiled. "Heck, you were right, Teague. They're just a family with the same kind of problems we got here in Hatchville. Sure talk funny, though, don't they?"

"Thanks, sheriff."

"Good night, range rider." The sheriff walked away.

Moments later, Scarlett and Katie and Toolie were out of their tents, standing beside Deaver, watching the sheriff get in his car and drive off.

"Thank you," whispered Scarlett.

"You were terrific," said Toolie.

"Yeah," said Deaver. "Where do I sleep?"

"It's a warm night," said Toolie. "I'm sleeping on the truck, if that's all right with you."

"Better than lying on the ground," said Deaver.

As he was getting ready for bed, Marshall and Ollie came back to the camp. Scarlett came out of her tent and made a big to-do about his hurt wrist, putting a sling on his arm and all. Deaver just sort of stayed back out of the way, not even watching, just laying out his bedroll and then standing there leaning on the audience side of the truck, listening to the scraps of conversation he could hear. Which actually was quite a lot, since Marshall and Scarlett hardly knew how to talk without making the sound carry across an open field. Nobody said much about how Ollie's wrist came to be hurt.

One thing, though, that maybe changed everything. It was when Marshall said, "I think I'd better play Washington the next time we do *Glory of America*. You know how to do Toolie's parts, don't you, Ollie? As long as Deaver's with us, he can run lights and you can fill a spot on stage. Let Papa go home and retire."

Deaver couldn't hear what Ollie said.

"There's no rush to decide these things," said Marshall. "But if you do decide to join the outriders, I don't think you need to use Deaver's right to apply. I think I could write a letter to Royal that would get you a fair chance."

Again, Ollie's answer was too quiet to hear.

"I just don't think it's right to take away one of Deaver's choices if we don't have to. It's about time I wrote to Royal anyway."

This time it was Scarlett who answered, so Deaver could hear just fine. "You can write to Royal all you like, Marsh, but the only way Parley and Donna can retire is if Ollie comes on stage, and the only way he can do that is if Deaver runs the lights and sound."

"Well, sometime before we get to Moab, I'll ask Deaver if he'd like to stay," said Marshall. "Since he can probably hear us talking right now, that'll give him plenty of time to decide on his answer."

Deaver smiled and shook his head. Of course they knew he was listening—these show people always know when there's an audience. Right at the moment Deaver figured he'd probably say yes. Sure, it'd be sticky for a while with Ollie, partly because of beating him up tonight, but mostly because Ollie had some bad habits with local girls and he wasn't going to cure them overnight. Ollie still might end up needing to get away and join the outriders. Deaver could teach him to ride, just in case. And if Ollie left, then Dusty'd have to move up to doing some more grown-up parts. It wouldn't be long till his voice changed, judging from the height he was getting.

Or things might not work out between Deaver and Katie, in which case it was a good thing the right to apply was good for a year. All kinds of things might change. But it'd all work out. The most important change was the one Marshall made tonight, to take some of the old-man parts and give the leads to Toolie. It meant real change in the way the company ran, and changes like that wouldn't be undone no matter what else happened. No way to guess the future, but it was a sure thing the past would never come back again.

After a while things quieted down and Deaver stripped down to his underwear and crawled inside his bedroll. He tried closing his eyes, but that didn't take him any closer to sleep, so he opened them again and looked at the stars. That was when he heard footsteps coming around the front of the truck. He could tell without looking that it was Katie. She came on over to where Deaver was lying, his bedroll spread out on the pyramid curtain.

"Are you all right, Deaver?" Katie asked.

"Softest bed I've slept on in a year," he said.

"I meant—Ollie was walking kind of doubled over, and it looked like he hurt his hand a little. I wondered if you were OK."

"He just fell a couple of times."

She looked at him steady for a while. "All right, I guess if you wanted to tell what really happened, you would."

"Guess so."

Still she stood there, not going away, not saying anything.

"What's the show tomorrow?" he asked.

"The Book of Mormon one," she said. "No decent parts for women. I spend half my time in drag." She laughed lightly, but Deaver thought she sounded tired. The moonlight was shining full on her face. She looked a little tired, too, eyes heavy-lidded, her hair straggling beside her face. Kind of soft-looking, that's how she was in the moonlight. He remembered being angry at her tonight. He remembered kissing her. Both memories were a little embarrassing now.

"Sorry I got so mad at you tonight," said Deaver.

"I should only have people mad at me for that reason—because they liked my show better than I did."

"I'm sorry, anyway."

"Maybe you're right. Maybe pageants really are important. Maybe I just get tired of doing them over and over again. I think it's time we took a vacation, did a real play. We could get town people somewhere to take parts in the play. Maybe they'd like us better if they were part of a show."

"Sure." Deaver was tired, and it all sounded fine to him.

"Are you staying with us, Deaver?" she asked.

"I haven't been asked."

"But if Daddy asks you."

"I think maybe."

"Will you miss it? Riding the range?"

He chuckled. "No ma'am." But he knew that if the question was a little different, if she'd asked, Will you miss your dream of riding out on the prairie with Royal Aal, then the answer would've been yes, I miss it already. But I've got a new dream now, or maybe just the return of an old dream, a dream I gave up on years ago, and the hope of joining the outriders, that was just a substitute, just a make-do. So let's just see, let's find out over the next few weeks and months and maybe years just how much room there is in this family for one more person. Because I'm not signing on for a pageant wagon. I'm not signing on to be a hireling. I'm signing on to be family, and if I find out there's no place for me after all, then I'll have to go searching for another dream altogether. He thought all that, but he didn't say anything about it. He'd already said too much tonight. No reason to risk getting in more trouble.

"Deaver," she whispered. "Are you asleep?"

"Nope."

"I really do like you, and it wasn't all an act." That was pretty much an apology, and he accepted it.

"Thanks, Katie. I believe you." He closed his eyes.

He heard a rustle of cloth, a slight movement of the truck as more of her weight leaned against it. She was going to kiss him, he knew it, and he waited for the brush of her lips against his. But it didn't come. Again the truck moved slightly and she was gone. He heard her feet moving across the dewy grass toward the tents.

The sky was clear and the night was cool. The moon was high now, as near to straight up as it was going to get. Tomorrow it might well rain—it had been four days since the last storm, and that was about as long as you got around here. So tomorrow there might be a storm, which meant tying little tents over all the lights, and if it got bad enough, putting off the show till the next night. Or canceling and moving on. It felt a little strange, thinking how he was now caught up in a new rhythm—tied to the weather, tied to the shows, and which towns had seen which ones within the last year, but above all tied to these people, their wishes and customs and habits and whims. It was kind of scary, too, that he'd be following along, not always doing things his own way.

But why should he be scared? There was going to be change anyway, no matter what. With Bette dead, even if he stayed with the range riders there'd be a new horse to get used to. And if he'd applied to the outriders, that'd all be new. So it wasn't as though his life wasn't going to get turned upside down anyway.

Sleep came sooner than he thought it would. He dreamed, a deep hard dream that seemed like the most important thing in his life. In his dream he remembered something he hadn't been able to think of in his whole life: what his real name was, the name his own parents gave him, back before the mobbers killed them. In his dream he saw his mother's face, and heard his father's voice. But as he woke in the morning, the dream fading, he tried to think of that voice, and all he could hear inside his head was an echo of his own voice; and the face of his mother faded into Katie's face. And when he shaped his true name with silent lips, he knew that it wasn't true anymore. It was the name of a little boy who got lost somewhere and was never found again. Instead he murmured the name he had spent his life earning. "Deaver Teague."

He smiled a little at the sound of it. It wasn't a bad name at all, and he kind of liked imagining what it could mean some day.

ABOUT THE CONTRIBUTORS

GLENN L. ANDERSON is author of two novels, *The Millennium File* and *The Doomsday Factor*, both published by Horizon Publishers (Bountiful, Utah). He has written a wide range of multi-image scripts and screen material, including *The Thanksgiving Promise* which aired as the Disney Sunday Movie in 1986. He holds a B.A. in communications from Brigham Young University and is assistant manager and supervisor of photography at BYU's Department of Instructional Graphics. He lives in Orem, Utah.

VIRGINIA ELLEN BAKER has published short fiction in *Isaac Asimov's Science Fiction Magazine* and elsewhere. Notable stories include "Pictures of Daniel," in *Tomorrow: Speculative Fiction* 1 (Jan. 1993), and "Rachel's Wedding," in *Writers of the Future* (5), for which she won first place in the 1989 Writers of the Future contest. Her poetry includes "Sinai," in *Sunstone* 14 (June 1990): 58. She holds a B.A. in Near Eastern studies and an M.A. in English, both from Brigham Young University. She has worked as a technical writer for Novell, Wicat, and *LAN Times*, and is currently the marketing communications manager for Folio Corporation. She lives in Provo, Utah.

M. SHAYNE BELL is author of the novel *Nicoji* (New York: Baen Books, 1991). His short fiction has appeared in *Tomorrow: Speculative Fiction*, *Amazing Stories*, and elsewhere. Notable are "Dry Niger" and "The Sound of the River," both in *Isaac Asimov's Science Fiction Magazine* 14 (Aug. 1990), 16 (Dec. 1992); and "With Rain, and a Dog Barking," in *The Magazine of Fantasy and Science Fiction* 84 (Apr. 1993). Bell's poetry includes "One Hundred Years of Russian Revolution: 7 November 1917 to 7 November 2017, Novaya Moskva, Mars," in *Amazing*

Stories 64 (Sept. 1989). He is poetry editor for *Sunstone* magazine. He has worked as a technical writer for M&T Books, *LAN Times, Utah Business Magazine,* and GTE Health Systems, and written guidebooks to Egypt for the Simpkins Splendors of Egypt series. He lives in Salt Lake City.

PAT BEZZANT makes her science fiction debut with "Finale," in this anthology. Her play based on this story received honorable mention in Brigham Young University's Meyhew contest. She has written for four Utah newspapers and Associated Press under the byline Pat Birkedahl. Bezzant chaired the 1989 BYU science fiction symposium, "Life, the Universe, and Everything." She holds a B.S. in economics from George Mason University where she received a Wall Street Journal Award for excellence in economics. She lives in Provo, Utah.

ELIZABETH H. BOYER has published ten novels through Dell Ray Books (New York): *The Sword and the Satchel; The Elves and the Otterskin; The Thrall and the Dragon's Heart; The Wizard and the Warlord; The Troll's Grindstone; The Curse of Slagfid; The Dragon's Carbuncle; Lord of Chaos; The Clan of the Warlord;* and *The Black Links.* Her short fiction includes: "The Stillborn Heritage," in *Four from the Witch World,* André Norton, ed. (New York: Tor, 1989); "Borrowing Trouble," in *Catfantastic,* and "The Last Gift," in *Catfantastic 2,* André Norton and Martin H. Greenberg, eds. (New York: DAW, 1989, 1991). Boyer holds a B.A. in English from Brigham Young University. She is currently writing a movie script of her novel *The Sword and the Satchel* and is under contract with Dell Ray Books for two more novels. She lives in Herriman, Utah.

ORSON SCOTT CARD is author of sixteen novels, eleven of which were published by Tor (New York): *Ender's Game; Speaker for the Dead; Xenocide; Seventh Son; Red Prophet; Prentice Alvin; The Memory of Earth; The Call of Earth; The Worthing Saga; Saints;* and *Lost Boys.* Other novels include *A Planet Called Treason* (New York: St. Martin's Press, 1979); *Wyrms* (New York: Arbor House, 1987); *Hart's Hope* (New York: Berkeley, 1983); *The Abyss* (New York: Pocket Books, 1989); and *Songmaster* (New York: Dial, 1980). He is the recipient of two Hugo awards and two Nebula awards. Card has published short fiction in

Omni; The Magazine of Fantasy and Science Fiction; Aboriginal Science Fiction; Amazing Stories; Analog; and elsewhere. Notable stories include "Salvage" and "America," both in *Isaac Asimov's Science Fiction Magazine* 10 (Feb. 1986), 11 (Jan. 1987); and "West," in *Free Lancers: Alien Stars 4,* Elizabeth Mitchell, ed. (New York: Baen Books, 1987). His short fiction has been collected in *Unaccompanied Sonata and Other Stories* (New York: Dial, 1981); *Maps in a Mirror: The Short Fiction of Orson Scott Card* (New York: Tor, 1990); *The Folk of the Fringe* (Bloomfield, MI: Phantasia Press, 1989); and *Cardography* (Eugene, OR: Hypatia Press, 1987). In 1987, his short story "Hatrack River," in *Isaac Asimov's Science Fiction Magazine* 10 (Aug. 1986), won the World Fantasy Award for best novella. He has edited three anthologies of short fiction: *Dragons of Light* (New York: Ace, 1980); *Dragons of Darkness* (New York: Ace, 1981); and *Future on Fire* (New York: Tor, 1991). Card has written two nonfiction works published by Writer's Digest Books (Cincinnati): *Character and Viewpoint* and *How to Write Science Fiction and Fantasy.* He writes a monthly review of books for *Fantasy and Science Fiction.* An important critical study of Card's fiction is Michael R. Collings, *In the Image of God: Theme, Characterization, and Landscape in the Fiction of Orson Scott Card* (Westport, CN: Greenwood Press, 1990). Card holds a B.A. in theater from Brigham Young University and an M.A. in English from University of Utah. He lives in Greensboro, North Carolina.

JAMES CUMMINGS was in a master's program in creative writing at University of Utah when he died in 1992. He had worked for some time on a fantasy novel which was left unfinished and had written a number of unpublished short stories. He held a B.A. in English from University of Utah.

KATHLEEN DALTON-WOODBURY authored "Cinders of the Great War," a finalist in the 1992 Writers of the Future contest, and which appears in volume nine of *Writers of the Future.* She is director of Science Fiction and Fantasy Workshop, a support network for new and aspiring writers. She holds a B.A. in math education and an M.S. in mechanical engineering, both from University of Utah. She teaches a creative writing class at East High Community School in Salt Lake City.

DAVID DOERING has published short fiction in *The Leading Edge*, including "Voyager" (Spring 1981) and "Next Year" (Fall 1981). He holds a degree in political science from University of Utah. Doering chaired the Brigham Young University science fiction symposium for four years. He has worked as a technical writer for Prentice-Hall, M&T Books, *LAN Times*, Novell, and Wicat, and is now a partner at Network Technical Services. He lives in Provo, Utah.

B. J. FOGG makes his first fiction sale with his story, "Outside the Tabernacle," in this anthology. He has published essays in *The University of New Mexico Review* and elsewhere. His poetry includes "Dad in the Kitchen," in *Inscape* (Fall 1992); "Welfare Farm Raisins," in *Wasatch Review International* 1 (1992); and "Summer Games," in *Sierra Nevada College Review* (Spring 1991). Fogg won the Brigham Young University annual McKay Essay Contest five out of six years in competition. In 1992 he received honorable mention in the Utah Arts Council's annual Original Writing Competition. He holds a B.A. and an M.A. in English, both from BYU. He is currently a Ph.D. student in communications at Stanford University.

MELVA GIFFORD has published over one hundred short stories in fanzines such as *Gambit, Magnificent Seven,* and *Abode of Strife.* Notable are "Take Out the Trash," in *The Leading Edge* 12 (Fall 1986); "Proximity," in *Dark Between the Stars* 4 (1991); and "The Meeting," in *Dark Lord* 1 (July 1982). Two of her stories are used in an interactive computer program in teaching English as a second language. She edits *Integrity* and has edited an issue of *The Monocle.* Her poetry has appeared in *Compadres, Rassilon's Star,* and elsewhere, and she has written about the art of writing for *Solar Winds.* Gifford currently works at Intel as a tech-support engineer. She lives in Provo, Utah.

CHARLENE C. HARMON has published poetry in *The Leading Edge, Zarahemla, The Poet's Pen,* and elsewhere. Notable poems include "Moonspider," in *Amazing Stories* 63 (July 1989); and "Evanescence," in *Midnight Zoo* 2 (3). Her contribution to this anthology, "Pueblo de Sión," is her first published short story, which she intends to expand into a novel. Harmon holds B.A. degrees in Spanish and English from Brigham Young University. She lives in Salt Lake City.

DIANA LOFGRAN HOFFMAN makes her science fiction debut with "Other Time," in this anthology, and is currently writing her first novel. She holds a B.A. in illustration from Brigham Young University. She lives in Cupertino, California.

BARBARA R. HUME is author of "A Hearth on Terra," serialized in *The Leading Edge*, 2-5 (Fall 1981-Spring 1983). Her short fiction includes "Tribute" and "Truth or Consequences," both published in *The Leading Edge*. Hume holds a B.A. in English education from Radford University, an M.A. in English literature from Virginia Polytechnic Institute and State University, and is completing a Ph.D. in English from BYU. She has worked as a technical writer for M&T Books, Novell, and *LAN Times*. In 1989 she founded her own company, Tristan Gareth, Inc., and is also a partner with Network Technical Services. She lives in Provo, Utah.

CAROLYN NICITA is currently writing her first novel. Her short fiction includes "Recycling," in *Tomorrow: Speculative Fiction* 1 (July 1993), and "Eye Hath Not Seen," in *The Leading Edge* 6 (Fall 1983). She has written a radio drama, "Saboteur," which was broadcast on KUER in Salt Lake City in 1993. Nicita composes songs and scores and writes multimedia fiction for the computer. She holds a B.A. in English from Brigham Young University. She lives in Provo, Utah.

MICHAELENE PENDLETON has published short fiction in such publications as *Amazing Stories*. Notable are "Professionals," in *Isaac Asimov's Science Fiction Magazine* 15 (mid-Dec. 1991); "Sardines," in *Omni* 11 (Apr. 1989); and "Rising Star," in *The Magazine of Fantasy and Science Fiction* 84 (June 1993). She co-authored a book on the Anasazi, *Canyon Country Prehistoric Indians: Their Culture, Ruins, Artifacts, and Rock Art* (Salt Lake City: Wasatch Publishers, 1979). Pendleton holds a B.A. in psychology. She lives in Moab, Utah, where for several years she operated a bed and breakfast and now writes full time.

D. WILLIAM SHUNN sold fiction to *2AM Magazine*, *Eldritch Tales*, and other publications. Notable are "From Our Point of View We Had Moved to the Left," in *The Magazine of Fantasy and Science Fiction* 84 (Feb.

1993); "In the Dark," in *Science Fiction Age* 1 (Sept. 1993); and "Cut without Hands," in *LDSF-2* (Ludlow, MA: Parables, 1985). In 1990 he received the University of Utah Madelyn S. Silver Scholarship for achievement in literature. He holds a B.S. in computer science from University of Utah and works as a software developer for WordPerfect Corporation. Shunn lives in Orem, Utah.

DIANN THORNLEY is author of the novel *Ganwold's Child* (Xenia, OH: Synapse Press, 1991). She has published short fiction in *The Leading Edge* and elsewhere. She holds a B.A. in political science from Brigham Young University, served as a captain in the U.S. Air Force, and now lives in Xenia, Ohio.

DAVE WOLVERTON has authored five novels: *On My Way to Paradise, Serpent Catch, Path of the Hero, Star Wars: The Courtship of Princess Leia,* and *The Golden Queen,* all published by Bantam (New York). His short fiction has appeared in such publications as *Tomorrow: Speculative Fiction.* Notable are "The Sky Is an Open Highway," in *Isaac Asimov's Science Fiction Magazine* 12 (July 1988); "Siren Song at Midnight," in *The Ultimate Dinosaur,* Robert Silverberg and Martin H. Greenberg, eds. (New York: Bantam, 1992); and "My Favorite Christmas," in *Christmas Forever,* David Hartwell, ed. (New York: St. Martin's Press, 1993). Wolverton is a full-time writer who occasionally teaches writing workshops. In addition, he is coordinating judge for the Writers of the Future Contest and edits the annual *Writers of the Future* anthology. He lives in Provo, Utah.

LYN WORTHEN has published fiction in *The New Era* and poetry in *The American Poetry Annual.* She holds B.A. degrees in communications and Spanish translation and has worked as a free-lance writer since 1989. She is married to M. W. Worthen, who also has a story in this anthology. They live in Provo, Utah.

M. W. WORTHEN publishes his first science fiction story, "You Can't Go Back," in this anthology. He holds a B.A. in Spanish translation and an M.A. in Hispanic linguistics and teaching English as a second language.